TWO
A PHALLIC NOVEL

TWO

A PHALLIC NOVEL

Alberto Moravia

Translated by Angus Davidson

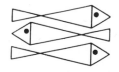

FARRAR, STRAUS AND GIROUX
NEW YORK

Contents

TWO
A PHALLIC NOVEL

1 Desublimated!

The intriguer! The trickster! The traitor! The coward! That's how he keeps his promises! That's how he holds to his agreements! I slept and had a number of unimportant dreams which I do not now remember; and then, in the end, I dreamt that I was in a film studio, enormous and plunged in semi-darkness. In a corner, on a trolley, was the cine camera, muffled up in a black cloth. I knew for certain that they were shooting – at last – 'my' film. What film? Who was the producer? Who were the actors? I did not know. I only knew that it was 'my' film. The film I had been thinking about for fifteen years. The film upon which my whole life depended. Then I mounted the trolley, took up my position on the seat and, bending forwards, with a free-and-easy professional movement, I put my eye to the lens. As though I myself were directing a film, my glance embraced, in one corner of the studio, what appeared quite obviously to be a love scene.

The intense, circumscribed light of the lamps revealed an untidy bed, a man and a woman. They were both naked. The man, young and good-looking, was sitting in a thoughtful attitude, in the pose of a tired boxer, his legs crossed, his elbow resting on his knees, his chin on his hand. The woman was lying face downwards behind him. She had long legs and a prominent backside. From the curve of her loins her back sloped steadily upwards to the back of her neck, while her ample bosom was crushed beneath her against the mattress. I contemplated this actress through the lens and realized that I found her pleasing and attractive, and that my gaze was becoming less and less professional and more and more lustful.

I restrained my desire, naturally, for at that moment and in that place it was not only unseemly but harmful. I said to myself: 'Why, my goodness, you're crazy; after taking so much trouble you at last succeed in shooting "your" film, and

1

instead of attending to the job you get ideas into your head. What's the matter with you? That actress, to you, should not be a woman but merely an interpreter.' This little sermon had its effect. I controlled myself, subdued my desire and again devoted my whole attention to the film.

The actress was now supposed to get off the bed and to go, with feigned, calculated slowness, and screen the lamp on the bedside table with her own undergarment. Then, suddenly, with a cat-like spring, she should have turned round, thrown the young man down on the bed and hurled herself on top of him, covering him with her body. I shouted through my little cardboard megaphone: 'Silence! Action! Shoot!' And then, as the magical hum of the camera began to make itself heard, I saw, to my astonishment, the actress rising from the bed and, instead of going over to screen the lamp, starting to walk in the direction of the trolley on which I was perched. I wanted to shout at her: 'No, you mustn't walk towards the camera; you've got to go and screen the lamp'; but I could not speak. A mysterious force, stronger than my will, kept me stooping forward with my eye to the lens, absorbed in photographing the naked body which was coming towards me with hips swaying. Slowly, indolently, absent-mindedly, the actress approached; and then, all of a sudden, I became aware that as she approached she seemed altered and changed, losing her beauty and assuming, in short, the features of Fausta, my wife.

Yes, Fausta indeed, with her big, ham-like face, her cow's-udder bosom, her exuberant paunch. I wanted to shout at her: 'Hey, what are you doing here? Go away, get out, go home, you're stopping me from working, you're ruining me'; but, with a very bitter feeling of helplessness, I was conscious that, though I opened my mouth as if to shout, I was not managing to utter any sound at all. Fausta, meanwhile, continued to advance towards the camera, in a listless, casual, lazy manner, pulling her shoulders back and thrusting her paunch forward. She came closer and closer, and gradually her head and her legs disappeared from my field of vision; finally all I could see was her belly. And her belly, in turn, the closer she came, was gradually reduced to nothing more than her crotch.

2

And now Fausta took a final step towards the lens and blocked it completely with the thick, bulging hair, like a bear's fur, which, with the general transformation of her person, had taken the place of the pretty curls of once upon a time. I wanted to shout: 'Get back, get back!' but it was too late. By this time I could see nothing in the lens but her pubic hair which seemed to be stuck, to be glued to it, as though the entire world were composed of feminine hair. Then, suddenly, I awoke, with an atrocious, excruciating sense of frustration.

At first I had to struggle to regain consciousness; I could determine neither the time nor the place. Then, slowly, I realized that it was the hour of the morning when I usually woke up; and that I was lying flat on my back in bed, with only a sheet over me. Huge, stiff, congested, like a tree that rises solitary and gigantic in the middle of a plain beneath a low, stifling sky, 'he' was standing up, almost vertically, from my belly, ostentatiously lifting the sheet. The arrogant, dishonourable, insidious, headstrong creature! I accosted him at once, furiously: 'This was not included in our agreement.'

'Why, what agreement?'

'You had promised me that –'

'I never promised anything.'

'Anyhow you led me to hope that you would not interfere with my plan.'

'So what?'

'So I'd like to know what you meant by your dream?'

'*My* dream? Why not *your* dream?'

'I don't have dreams like that. The dream bore perfectly clearly your – how shall I say? – your trade-mark.'

'Whatever d'you mean? It was a dream of lack of confidence, of frustration, of fear, of failure – all of them your own things.'

'Oh indeed, my own things?'

'So I should say. Of us two, which is the failure? You or I?'

'Ah, so it's like that, is it? Then I'll explain to you why this dream was *yours* from beginning to end. Now listen carefully. Well, in the first place: for your own ends, you want me

3

to be, and to remain, a weak-willed person, a failure, and so you make me dream that I was shooting "my" film, simply in order to demonstrate to me that I shall never be able to become a film director because I shall never be capable of dominating you and forcing you to obey me. Complicated, isn't it? But you *are* complicated. What, in fact, does it mean, that the actress should change into Fausta and come and block the lens with her crotch except that, in your opinion, the experiment that I'm making is bound to fail? That there will be no sublimation? That I shall continue, all my life, to be desublimated? That, in short, I shall never be the artist that I could be and should like to be because, always and inevitably, there will come between my eye and reality . . . the darkness of a female pubis? Fausta's, or another one? And now, tell me: that dream – was it mine or yours?'

'Wait a moment; there's one obscure point in your explanation. According to you, at a certain moment I substituted Fausta, in place of the actress? Why?'

'That's simple. Fausta telephoned me yesterday, asked to see me, wanted me to tell her the "real" reason for our separation. After a show of resistance, my feelings were touched and I agreed to go and see her – the first time for six months. That was enough to deceive you into thinking that I was giving up my experiment, and to give you – it's appropriate to say so – a swelled head. Not content, in fact, with making me dream of my failure as a film director, you brought into the dream the person you are going to make use of today to *cause* me to fail – Fausta.'

As usual, when I explain to 'him', in a rational manner, how things stand between myself and him, he was silent. One might have thought, in any case, that my accusation that he insinuated himself everywhere, even into my dreams, was fundamentally flattering to his vanity. I concluded, harshly: 'Anyhow, you have been warned; if the dream was meant to be a prophecy, I deny it; if, on the other hand, it was the expression of a desire, I reject it. In any case you would do well not to shove your nose into things that don't concern you.'

4

This time he answered, with the remark: 'Everything concerns me.'

'Very well then, seeing that you say everything concerns you, I insist on your acknowledgement that nothing concerns you. Nothing, absolutely nothing.'

'There we are, then: sublimation.'

'That's right.'

'Ugh!'

I threw off the sheet, jumped out of bed, left the room and went into the bathroom. There I carried out my customary toilet: shower, shave, teeth, toenails and fingernails, hairs from armpits, nose and ears, and, of course, 'him'. Hypersensitive as he is and, into the bargain, histrionic about his sensitiveness, lo and behold, as I soaped him, he again became enormous. So I said to him: 'Obviously you imagine that I ought to be pleased at your – let us so call it – readiness. On the contrary, I am not: you are wrong. Are you not aware that this very readiness, so prompt, so easy, so immediate and so imposing, corresponding, on the social level, to weakness of will, to mediocrity and failure, constitutes an irrefutable proof of my natural inferiority? So why should I be pleased with it? To make a comparison, it is as if a hump spoke from the back from which it rises, saying to the humpback: "D'you see how big I am? Why aren't you proud of me?" The humpback would have every reason to answer: "Proud of *you*, who are the cause of my misfortune? Why in the world?"'

This comparison was like a cold douche to him. He was silent, perhaps in mortification; then gradually returned, by imperceptible, slow stages, to normal proportions. My toilet was finished. I went back into the bedroom, dressed and left the house.

It was eight o'clock. Why should I be visiting Fausta at that hour? In the first place because I wished to come back as soon as possible, in order to get to work on the outline of 'my' film. Secondly, because Fausta, at that hour, would still be asleep; and I knew that in the morning, whenever she wakes up, she is at her worst (if there can be a better and a worse in a woman who has so deteriorated). Thus 'he' would not be able

5

to play some dirty trick upon me, as, to judge from my dream, might have been his intention.

I left the flat with the usual, disconcerting sensation that I was leaving the old flat in which, until six months ago, I had lived with Fausta. Actually the two flats are very similar, even though it is a case of two different districts. The flat I had rented for my 'sublimatory experiment' was a top-floor flat of five rooms in a middle-class house of recent construction. The flat in which, until six months ago, I lived with Fausta was a top-floor flat of five rooms in a middle-class house of recent construction. Where is the difference? There is only one difference: the flat in which I lived with Fausta was the abode of my weak-willed, unsuccessful mediocrity. On the other hand the flat in which I have been living for six months *must* be and infallibly *will* be the abode of my upward climb and my success. Therefore the sensation I have of always leaving the same flat is out of place and might indicate, into the bargain, that I have some doubt about the result of my experiment. Bad!

In the street I hesitated, then decided not to go to my usual café but to get Fausta to give me coffee. It would be a way of making her do something while we were talking and would thus avoid dangerous approaches and contacts. I got into my car and started off. But then, a little farther along the street, was the newspaper stall. I stopped the car, got out and went over to it. Now this was the dialogue that took place between myself and 'him'. I am transcribing it faithfully, in order, above all, to convey a precise idea of the loss of face to which he continually exposes me.

'Please, may we have a look at that magazine?'

'Which magazine?'

'That one there.'

'A magazine for "men only"! At eight o'clock in the morning! When I've only just come out! I, a man of thirty-five, stocky, short-legged, with a big bald head, a serious, proud and even, in its way, majestic appearance, furtively skimming through a pornographic magazine as I stand in front of the kiosk, my back to the street, while all round me, in buses and cars and on foot, people are hurrying to their work in factories, in offices, in shops! Why, just imagine!'

'Please, please, just that one.'

'No, don't even mention such a thing.'

'Come on!'

'No, no, no.'

'So you'd rather, when you get to Fausta's . . .'

This was blackmail; and, after weighing the pros and cons, I resigned myself to submitting to it: better to keep him in a good temper by satisfying him in some innocuous way. I put out my hand, took up the magazine and began skimming through it. I tried to assume an air of casualness, as of someone going for a walk on a fine summer morning and stopping here and there, aimlessly, looking now at a specially lively advertisement, then contemplating the splendid foliage of the plane-trees, then following the course of a stray dog, and then, indeed, skimming the pages of a magazine chock-full of nude women. But 'he', unfortunately, did not even allow me to save appearances. Suddenly he commanded me, imperiously: 'Hi there, what's the hurry? Don't turn the pages so fast; stop, let me look, let me see, what the devil! That girl there, for instance . . .'

'Why, she's a model with such exaggerated shapes that she looks positively monstrous, like a freak at a circus.'

'That may be so, but you know you have a weakness for anything that is convex, round, protuberant, spherical, superabundant.'

'Well, what d'you find attractive about these nudes that are photographed with exactly the same false, metallic colours as are displayed in advertisements of cars and bottles of liqueurs and boxes of cigarettes?'

'What about it? I'm a simple, ingenuous kind of person, I am. Oh, oh, oh, stop, do please stop!'

'What is it now?'

'That big, folded page, with the complete photograph, from head to foot, of the girl of the month . . . You don't want to skip that big page, do you?'

'No, not that; if I open and unfold that big page it will

mean, obviously, that it's no longer a question of idle casualness but of careful examination and choice. And the newsagent is already looking askance at me.'

'What does the newspaper man matter to you?'

'I come here every morning to buy my paper. I don't want him to get a mistaken idea of me.'

'A *mistaken* idea?'

'Yes, I mean it: mistaken.'

At this point the newsagent asked me, in a rough, ironical way, whether I wished to buy the magazine.

A blush of shame covered my face. I replied, with dignity, that I would take it; I asked how much it cost, paid, put the magazine under my arm and walked away with my usual proud, slow step.

But once I was in the car I was so furious that 'he' became aware of it and remained quiet for some time. In the end, however, his impudence proved stronger than his fear. When, overcome with rage, steering with my left hand I seized, with my right, the magazine and made as though to throw it out of the window, he protested: 'No, don't, what are you up to? Keep it. Later, at home, when you've finished work, we'll have a really good look at it, page by page.'

'In the first place, enough of that plural. We are not "we", we are "I" and "you". Besides – listen to what I say – you'd better not speak to me. I hate you. You put me to shame in front of that newsagent, so at least keep quiet.'

'Oh, what a lot of fuss about a magazine!'

'A pornographic magazine. But don't you realize that looking through a magazine of that kind is exactly like putting one's eye to a keyhole and watching a woman undressing?'

'We've done that before now and you weren't so indignant about it: on the contrary.'

'I've already told you, enough of that plural.'

'Why "enough"? There were two of us, I who suggested and you who acted. Wonderful times! I remember, for instance, the day when we went together to buy a pair of

8

expensive German-made binoculars; we went up together on to the roof-terrace of the house and waited there together, hidden behind a sheet put out to dry. Finally, in the house opposite, in a flat converted into a *pension*, a window was thrown open. So then, together, we levelled the field-glasses at it and together we watched the comings and goings, in the room of the *pension*, of a very beautiful girl, a foreigner probably, of the long-limbed type, tall, slim, flat-breasted, narrow-hipped, bronzed by seaside sun and completely naked except for a white pad of cotton-wool secured to her crotch by two almost invisible laces. We stayed together with the field-glasses levelled at that window until the girl had dressed and gone away. What were we then? *Voyeurs?*'

'Ten years have gone by since then. Yes, you were a degraded, ridiculous, repugnant *voyeur* and I was your succubus.'

As always happens at a certain point in our disputes, 'he' took offence and tried, so to speak, to re-establish distances. For a moment he was silent; then, in an unexpectedly resentful tone of voice, he resumed: 'A joke's a joke; but brevity is the soul of wit. Kindly remember that what I stand to represent is in truth neither degraded nor ridiculous nor repugnant. Turning the pages of a "men only" magazine, looking through field-glasses at the girl with the cotton-wool pad, and a great many other comparable manifestations of an apparently trivial kind – all these are, in reality, the expression of something grandiose and sublime and, indeed, cosmic which you, with your tuppenny-ha'penny reasoning powers, have no right to judge.'

The usual boasting! The usual affectation! The usual allusions to, precisely, the 'grandiose', the 'sublime', the 'cosmic' background! 'Have it your own way,' I said, 'but in the meantime look what I'm doing with this magazine – the expression, according to you, of the mysterious force that governs the universe. I'm throwing it into the street.'

Vigorously ejected, the magazine fell on the asphalt road-way and I had the satisfaction of seeing a passing car run over it, leaving the striped imprint of its tyres across the girl on the

9

big page. Annoyed, 'he' now fell silent. But, in accordance with his voluble and at the same time tenacious character, it was not for long. Indeed, as I was parking the car in Fausta's street, he roused himself and whispered to me: 'Fausta, at this hour of the day, is still asleep, isn't she?'

'Yes.'

'D'you know what you ought to do?'

'What?'

'Slip very quietly into the bedroom, without turning on the lights, undress in the dark and get in under the sheets beside her.'

'And what then?'

'And then, nothing. I never make plans or anticipations. I live moment by moment, in the present.'

I went into the hall, closed the lift door behind me and pressed the button. As the lift went up from floor to floor, 'he' began insisting again: 'Remember that Fausta is, after all, your wife.'

'So what?'

'You've proved to yourself that you're capable of living chastely for six months. Isn't it time now to make an exception – just one single exception – for the woman you elected as your life companion?'

As on so many other occasions, I was struck by his language, half courtly, half bureaucratic and, in any case, lower middle-class.

To amuse myself, I provoked him: 'And in what would this exception consist?'

'In allowing me to get back into direct contact with Fausta. This exception, from today onwards, might, in turn, become regularized. For example, by agreement with Fausta, the direct contact might take place, let us say, once a month. Or once a fortnight.'

The lift stopped with a jerk at the little landing of the top-floor flat. I got out, closed the doors and pressed the return button. On a light-coloured wooden door was the plate with my name on it: all was in order. I inserted the key in the keyhole, opened the door gently and slipped into the entrance-hall. Complete darkness. I felt my way forwards, breathing in the warm, vitiated air, impregnated with the mingled yet distinguishable smells of kitchen, of cigarette-smoke and of baby-clothes. 'He', tenacious as ever, commented: 'Rather stuffy, I agree. A nasty smell, if you like. But of a certain particular kind. In a certain particular situation.'

'What kind of smell? What situation?'

'A female smell; the situation of a husband who, after six months' abstinence, creeps furtively into his own house.'

Mentally I shrugged my shoulders and, still feeling my way and without turning on any lights, knocking two or three times against obstructive, indefinable objects, I made towards the kitchen. I felt I needed some coffee: I would prepare the coffee and then confront Fausta. But when I opened the kitchen door, the desire for coffee instantly left me. The kitchen was in a state of disorder which, for once, it would be correct to describe as indescribable. The table with its red Formica top was covered with dirty plates and knives and forks, glasses with remains of wine in them, fruit-peelings and crusts of bread. In a salad bowl, soused in oil, some lettuce-leaves. In the middle of the table, askew and half-empty, a wine-flask. The window, unfortunately, was closed; a ray of burning sunshine, coming through the glass, was cooking the remains of food on the plates. An acid smell of fermented eatables assailed my nostrils.

How many people had there been at the table? I counted four places and four chairs, of which two tubular ones belonged in the kitchen and two in the Swedish style were usually kept in the sitting-room. A dangerously towering stack of dirty plates in the sink told me that, for some unknown reason, the daily servant had not come in for at least three days. I looked down. A line of ants, emerging from a corner under the window, was crossing the floor, climbing up one of the table-legs and ending up in one of the plates which, in fact, was nothing but a swarming brown mass. I looked at the stove: two or three yellowish strings of spaghetti were stuck to the aluminium of a big empty saucepan. The whole of the stove was besprinkled with a shower of spots of tomato sauce. I closed the door, inquiring sarcastically of 'him': 'This stink, this filth, this disorder – do they excite you too?'

'And why not?'

I was again in the dark. Still feeling my way, I went towards the end of the passage, where our bedroom lay. But all at once, from a side door, a childish voice reached my ears. It was not speaking and it was not singing, but was uttering inarticulate sounds that had in them something of speech and song simultaneously. It was my son Cesarino. I hesitated, and then, in spite of 'his' protests ('Let's go to Fausta first, you can see the boy afterwards, Fausta will be getting up and then you won't be able to catch her in bed,' etc., etc.) I opened the door.

The room was filled with light. The middle of the room was occupied by a play-pen with little pink-painted bars. Inside the pen was a small mattress, and toys of every kind were scattered all round. Cesarino was standing up completely naked, clinging with both hands to the balustrade of the pen and giving vent, with wide-open mouth, to the inarticulate, cheerful sounds that I had heard from the passage. But why should Cesarino be already awake, already washed and, apparently, already fed, when the whole flat seemed to be still plunged in sleep? I reconstructed the situation: Fausta, who makes the child sleep in her own bed, must have got up, washed him, given him something to eat, put him in his play-pen and then gone back to bed herself.

I went over to the play-pen and looked at Cesarino. He has one of those irremediably plebeian faces that make one exclaim: 'How common he looks!' Ugly hair of a sort of woolly blond, lightless kind; eyes of a pale, watery blue, with an already impudent expression; his cheeks white but with two patches of rustic red, one on each cheekbone; a nose in the shape of a tiny hook of flesh, the nostrils conspicuous and covered with a network of little scarlet veins; a mouth shapeless and slightly crooked, almost hare-lipped. I looked at him and yet again I could not help thinking: He can't be my son. Immediately 'he', for some reason or other, broke in with: 'On the contrary, he *is*.'

12

'Why, he's fair, with blue eyes, an aquiline nose, a white skin. And I have dark hair and a dark complexion, dark eyes and a straight nose.'

'Nonsense. He's your son. I know it for certain.'

'But how d'you come to know it . . . for certain?'

'I feel it if another one has taken my place, even if it was on only one occasion.'

'Why, how d'you manage to feel it?'

'In the way in which I succeed in imposing myself and in which I am welcomed. In the desire which I myself have and which I excite. In the pleasure which I arouse and which I receive.'

'And I, on the other hand, "feel" that Cesarino cannot be my son.'

'You don't feel anything. You argue according to the logic of your fixation.'

'What fixation?'

'The fixation that makes you believe that the power of procreation and artistic creativeness are like two taps with the same water. If you turn on one, the other stops, and vice versa.'

'Why, who said so?'

'You said so yourself, don't you remember? You said to me: "It's no use, in my mind Cesarino and my film are bound together by an indissoluble link. Either Cesarino is not my son and then I shall make a fine film. Or he is, and then my film will be as ugly as he is."'

'An obsessed, superstitious, forced way of reasoning.'

'Yours!'

During this squabble Cesarino was looking up at me in an insistent, impudent manner. Then, suddenly, he smiled. A horrible, utterly vulgar, even if innocent, smile. And revealing, into the bargain. For in fact it was the smile – the identical smile! – of the plumber Eugenio, a stocky, fair-haired young man, very muscular and well-built, who used often to come to the house just about a year, more or less, before Cesarino was born. 'Moreover,' I said, 'I have proof that my son is not my son.'

13

'What proof is there?'

'Have you already forgotten the eyebrow episode? Just during the period when Cesarino was, let us say, conceived, Eugenio came several times to repair the water-heater which I wanted to change but which he obstinately considered to be still usable. One morning I looked at myself in the glass, before shaving, and saw something I didn't understand, something between grey and brown in colour, like a little scab of dried blood, at the corner of my right eye, among the hairs of my eyebrow. It looked exactly like a scab of congealed blood, but, when I pulled it away with my nails, the scab at once put forth a lot of tiny dark feet which waved in the air. Then I looked at myself more closely, becoming more and more alarmed, first at both my eyebrows, then at the hair on my chest, then at my armpits, and finally at my pubic hair: full! I spent an hour pulling away, one by one, those scab-like things and throwing them into the water in the wash-basin, and in the end the water was all dotted with these little dark things which went on desperately wriggling and kicking their legs. If that isn't a proof . . .'

'In fact it is not a proof.'

'Why not?'

He took his time and then answered, teasingly, in a sing-song voice: 'I know someone who at that same period had taken to frequenting the provocative girls of a certain type in a certain suburban avenue. I know someone who, in full agreement with his own exceptional sexual organ, almost every evening at about that time, picked up one of those girls in his car. I know someone who was in the habit of retiring, with the girl whose turn it was, into certain open spaces by the Tiber, amongst the piles of rubbish and the tin cans and the waste paper. I know someone . . .'

'Enough, enough, enough.'

I put out my hand and stroked Cesarino's head. My glance travelled downwards from his face to his body and paused at his belly. Cesarino had a prominent, tight paunch, with a navel like a little white knot. Between his plump, slightly bow legs his member jutted out, not hanging freely but looking like a continuation, in pointed form, of his belly; it was minute and yet perfect, white with exactly the same whiteness as the rest of his body, with the little testicle-bag still smooth and unwrinkled.

I do not know why, as Cesarino looked up at me and laughed and now and then made a movement with his hands as though to shake his play-pen, I do not know why (or rather, I know perfectly well: like all desublimated people, I like children and they arouse in me a feeling of tenderness) I let myself be moved at the sight of that tiny member. I felt that Cesarino would perhaps be luckier than me. He would grow and get big. And with him, his member would grow and get big. But even if it were to be exceptional, like mine – which seemed to me highly unlikely – it would perhaps remain silent and dumb and indifferent. In a word: sublimated! And Cesarino would not, like me, spend his time arguing with 'him' and losing face. He would be a man, it must be said, all of one piece, with no duality of nature, he would not be torn asunder nor engaged in dialogues. Once again: sublimated!

I sighed, stroked Cesarino's head and left the room. For the third time I found myself feeling my way in the dark. I went straight to our bedroom, slowly turned the handle and opened the door just enough to allow me to slip into a darkness like that in the passage, but twice as warm, and more noisome, more 'feminine'. I closed the door, put out my hand to the bedside table close beside it, sought and found the lamp-switch but, irresolute, did not press it. What should I do? Awaken Fausta, take her into the kitchen to make coffee for me? Or, as 'he' had suggested, undress, creep into bed and caress and embrace her a little, without however venturing beyond a controlled, even if intense, demonstration of conjugal affection. Perhaps I would have decided on the second alternative if 'he', with his usual awkwardness, had not urged me on. 'Come on, cheer up, what are you waiting for? Get undressed and plunge into bed.'

This impatience on his part had the effect, as usual, of making me suspicious. 'What does it matter to you whether I "plunge" into bed or not?'

15

No doubt owing to the urgency of his desire, he burst out with: 'Ah, one thing leads to another!'

Immediately I protested: 'No, this time, you see, one thing must *not* lead to another. It must not lead to anything. If I got into bed beside Fausta, I should be doing it merely to show her my affection. But of course you can't understand these things. What is affection to you? Nothing, less than nothing.'

'Ha, ha, ha, affection!'

'It's nothing to laugh about: I say, affection!'

'Get along with you. Let's have a little truth, a little honesty, a little realism, in fact! Affection! But if there is one thing that concerns me, which was *my* work, willed and planned and carried out in every detail by me, it is, precisely, your marriage to Fausta.'

'So, according to you, I don't love Fausta?'

'It doesn't interest me whether you love her or not. It is important to me to establish, beyond any doubt, that this marriage was *my* work. It was *mine*, just as were your relations with those girls on the banks of the Tiber. Who, in fact, persuaded you to telephone, one day, to a certain number that had been given you by an obliging friend? Who, after the cryptic, formal inquiry as to whether you wanted a dinner-service for sixteen, eighteen or twenty-four, made you answer in a great hurry: "Sixteen, of course, sixteen"? Who made you rush off the following day, an hour early, to a certain small villa, in a certain street, in a certain district, ring the bell under a nameplate inscribed "Mariú, *modes*", run up those stairs four at a time, and wait, trembling with impatience, in front of a certain door? Who caused you to say, all in one breath, when the door opened and Mariú (black dress, pale face with no make-up, big, gentle, black eyes, dark down on the upper lip, a yellow waxed tape-measure over her shoulder and a few white threads on her black skirt) – when Mariú appeared on the threshold: "I've come for the service for sixteen"? Who made you walk up and down like a lion or rather, like an ape, in a cage, in the fitting-room (red divan, black headless *mannequin*, triple mirror, small table with an

16

ashtray full of pins), until the door opened and Mariú pushed Fausta into the room, saying: "The service for sixteen is finished for the present. This one is for eighteen. There is also the one for twenty-four. Now, do you want both of them or just this one?" Who made you answer, greedily: "Both of them"?

'Who, once you were in the bedroom (big, low, square bed, very little space between the walls and the bed, you on one side, the two girls on the other), who made you watch, with eyes popping out of your head, the gentle, quiet, friendly, careful, conspiratorial way in which the young procuress undressed Fausta for you, vaunting, as she did so, her physical qualities? ("Where will you find a girl like this? Look at that little tomboy face, round and brown, with those little white teeth and those black eyes. And then look here at her breasts, small and firm; touch them then, they bounce up again. And then her belly, round and slightly prominent, with the navel so deep-set that it can't even be seen, like that of a child; don't you think her belly is charming? And then her bottom – where could you find a bottom like that? It has the same charming dimples that many women have in their cheeks; a bottom like that could be displayed in the window, so to speak. And then, look what legs she has, look what feet, look what hands, look what fingers! And finally have a look at her *there*, who could be more lovely *there* than Fausta? Put out your hand and touch it; feel how tender it is, how soft – d'you feel?")

'Who, after so gracious and so detailed an introduction, made you refuse the service for twenty-four, that is, Mariú ("Well, well, I knew it; what am I in comparison with Fausta, what am I?") and made you ask to be left alone with the one for eighteen? Who made you in the first place visit the "Mariú, *modes*" apartment every day and then, finally, suggested, after agreement with Mariú, that you should get Fausta to come to your own flat? Who made you stay for a whole hour with your ear glued to the door, so as to hear whether the lift, as it came up from floor to floor, would stop at your landing, and whether Fausta's well-known step

17

would be heard on the tiled floor? Who, from a certain day onwards, made you ask Fausta not to take the lift but to come running up all five floors, so that she might arrive at your door out of breath and with heaving bosom, and red in the face? Who, finally, after a year of this relationship, convinced you that you were in love with Fausta, that you could no longer live without her and that, in fact, you must marry her?

'Let us come now to your marriage. Who suggested to you, after the church ceremony, the wedding breakfast at the hotel, the journey by air to Paris and all the other conventional things, who suggested to you, I say, in the bedroom of the Paris hotel, that you should continue, in exactly the same style, the relationship begun in Rome at "Mariú, *modes*", by placing, immediately after making love, the same sum of money on the bedside table, as if jokingly, that in Rome you used to put into Fausta's hand at the moment of leaving her? Who, in short, made you understand by this gesture that, in spite of the priest, the altar, the ring and the sermon on conjugal duties, everything would go on as before, in the same manner as before, and that the marriage, too, was therefore "his" affair, "his" work, "his" own exclusive creation?'

Thus 'he', in his urgent, ruthless fashion. But I answered him serenely: 'All very well, but I've had a son by Fausta. And I've finished up by loving her. If I didn't love her, how could I remain with a woman who has nothing, literally nothing, of the Fausta of once upon a time? Who has changed out of all recognition?'

'Ha, ha, ha!'

'What's the matter?'

'But you only remain with her in order to please me. Is it possible that you don't realize that you remain with Fausta, who is changed, as you say, out of all recognition, precisely because it pleases *me* that Fausta should be changed out of all recognition?'

'What d'you mean?'

'What do *you* mean? It is I who make you stay with the Fausta of today who has "literally nothing" (in your words) to do with the Fausta of ten years ago. It is I who cause you to

18

find a motive for desire in the metamorphosis of the Fausta of that time, agile, solid, active and compact, into the Fausta of today, flabby, worn-out, swollen and shapeless. It is I, finally, who cause you to take pleasure in the idea and, more than in the idea, in the observation of Fausta's progress from well-being to decay, from immaturity to disintegration.'

'It's not true. I love her and . . .'

'Let's try an experiment. Fausta is here, in this darkness, awake by now and waiting for you to make up your mind to reveal yourself. Put out your hand. I will make you rediscover, under your fingers, the Fausta of yesterday inside the Fausta of today. And then you will realize it is not affection which makes you stay with her.'

Presented in this way, his customary, optimistic, tenacious wish that 'one thing should lead to another' convinced me. It is a cerebral refinement, it is true, to seek inside a body for another body which, alas, no longer exists; but I confess I have a weakness for cerebral refinements, especially if suggested by 'him'. Without overmuch reflection I put out my hand in the darkness, and my exploring fingers finally landed on Fausta's face, half-buried in the disorder of her hair and sunk deep in the pillow. Immediately her hand seized mine, carried it to her lips and kissed it. Then her voice said: 'At last you've come.'

'Hello!'

'Why don't you get into bed beside me? It's early, we can sleep together for a little.'

'No, first I want to fondle you; pull away the sheet, take off your nightdress and let me do as I wish.'

'Well done,' said 'he', approvingly. 'And now you'll see whether I'm not right.'

I heard a prolonged sound of rustling and of laborious bustling confusion. Then Fausta's voice, barely audible, came out of the darkness: 'I'm ready.'

At once 'he' broke in, in an instructive tone of voice: 'Spread out your fingers over her face and follow its contours.'

I did as I was told. 'He' went on: 'Can't you feel the perfect little face of once upon a time, inside the big,

19

comfortable face that you're exploring? Don't you realize that Fausta has a "double" face, consisting of today's face, outside, and yesterday's face, inside?'

It was true. Or at least it seemed to be true, such was the suggestion inspired by his words. I followed the broad contours of Fausta's big face and did indeed feel that 'inside' it was the little face of ten years ago. Strange.

'Now bring your fingers down along her neck, skimming lightly, in passing, over the three or four folds of fat, then feel your way downwards to her breasts. There, under your fingertips, you will find two huge indiarubber hot-water bottles, half-empty, with their stoppers screwed tight. But don't you feel, inside those oblong, resilient bags, the two immature oranges of ten years ago? And inside the stopper-nipples of today the flower-nipples of yesterday?'

I was compelled, though against my will, to admit that he was right. Meanwhile he went on: 'Now take a jump from her breast to her belly. Don't you find there, inside the great shapeless suitcase of the present, the fine silver tray, round and flat, of former times?'

Once again suggestion worked. 'He' continued: 'Now go on down the step-ladder of hair which, in herring-bone pattern, joins the navel to the groin and thrust your fingers into the deep fur that covers the private parts. Then, in that forest, trace out the winding, moist path of the sexual organ. Follow its course between her open legs, down and down and underneath to the big, sweaty knot of the anus. The sexual organ, today, makes you think of a sword-cut that has left an open wound, with frayed, loose edges. But don't you discover, inside this inert, enlarged cleft, the little circular, prehensile sucker which, ten years ago, used to grip me with desperate force, as if it were seeking to lop me off, in the way that those little chopping machines on the counters of tobacconists' shops lop off the tips of cigars?'

I was carried away, decidedly, by his eloquence. Conscious of his advantage, he pressed it relentlessly. 'Now tell her to turn over and lie on her face.'

'But she's not a piece of fried fish!'

20

'Do as I tell you.'

I obeyed and passed on the order to Fausta who in turn, and without breathing a word, also obeyed. Then, like a professor of anatomy bending with his pupils over a corpse lying on a demonstration slab, 'he' expounded, in a scientific tone: 'Now put out your hand and let your fingers circumnavigate the two enormous spheres into which her back divides below the loins, and judge of their imposing circumference. Rest the palm of your hand on their convexity and reconnoitre their smooth, deserted spaciousness. Put your fingers, like the teeth of a comb, into the cleft that separates them and judge how deep it is. Finally, try and recall the small, firm, prominent, muscular buttocks of ten years ago and tell me if you don't feel them quivering inside the soft, rolling buttocks of today.'

All of a sudden, as if to confirm that the secret purpose of all this chatter was just the usual one, my wife's voice came to me out of the darkness: 'D'you want us to make love, then?'

I roused myself, with a start, from the clammy temptation into which 'he' had caused me, gradually, to slip, with his contrivance of two bodies enclosed one within the other like Chinese boxes. In reality, it was the same old thing. Once again I was on the point of surrendering. Once again I was preparing to waste, in a single moment of contemptible pleasure, the precious energy that might save me from mediocrity and failure. The desublimation of Fausta, all ready and willing as she lay there with her legs open, was matched by my own; and I too was all ready and willing, while 'he', in the meantime, had become enormous. She and I were all of a piece, identical! Equalized by the same reduction of life to the sexual act! By the same surrender! She was not 'underneath' and I 'on top', as would have been right; but we were both alike. Equally desublimated. Equally enslaved by 'him'. Equally incapable of resisting him. On the same level! On the same plane! In one moment we should be in the same bed. I answered Fausta roughly: 'No, no love-making. Instead, get up, put on your dressing-gown and we'll go into the kitchen. And then, while you make the coffee, we'll talk.'

21

'He', of course, protested, like a fisherman who, after a long wait, sees a fish fail to nibble at his hook and escape him. 'Why, what's up,' he said, 'just now, just at the right moment?' I paid no attention to him. I pressed the switch of the lamp and at the same time, with my other hand, opened the door. Without looking round, I left the room. There I was, back in the kitchen. I sat down at the table and reflected. It was clear: as a good 'desublimated' subject, I had allowed myself to be softened by affection. And 'he' had taken advantage of this to try and force my hand. But no, I had to act in such a way as to feel myself 'on top' in respect of Fausta, and to keep her 'underneath'. It would be a sadistic 'on top', which would inevitably provoke, on Fausta's side, a masochistic 'underneath'. It would be to some extent an artificial 'on top'; not the automatic 'on top' of sublimation, from which, alas, I was still a long way off. The 'on top', in fact, of a desublimated person who, faced with someone more desublimated than himself, pretends to be sublimated. But, all in all, it would still be better than nothing. At the moment, however, how was I to attain this superiority all at once? I looked round the kitchen and the answer immediately came to me from what I saw.

In came Fausta, tying, as she entered, the cord of her dressing-gown over her big stomach, and screwing up that double face of hers, dazzled by the cruel light of the summer sunshine. At once, without giving her time to recover herself, I attacked her: 'I should like to know what you've been up to in my absence?'

Caught off-balance, she opened her dark-ringed, jaded eyes wide and stammered: 'Why, what d'you suppose I've been up to?'

'I came into the flat and felt almost suffocated by the evil smell. I came into the kitchen and found that plates and dishes had been piling up for at least a week. As for you, you're unrecognizable: your face is dull and dirty, your eyes are swollen, your body is fat and sluggish.'

She passed a bewildered hand across her face, drew her dressing-gown over her bosom. Much more than that was needed! Weakly she protested: 'I was asleep. I expected you in the afternoon. You told me you would be coming after lunch.'

By this time I was already 'on top'. It was not, certainly, in virtue of true superiority, of sublimation, but merely thanks to a verbal aggressiveness. Nevertheless it remains true that cleanliness, order and the care of one's own person are, always and everywhere, essential qualities of those who are sublimated. I pressed my point: 'You ought not to wait for somebody to visit you in order to make yourself presentable. You should always be so, not from regard for other people but from self-respect.'

She said nothing. She kept on passing her hand across her face, as though she really felt that, beneath her big double face, there still existed the simple little face of ten years ago and almost deceived herself into thinking that she could make it come to the surface by means of this desperate sort of caress. She was, in short, 'underneath'; but still not enough. I banged my fist on the table. 'You don't answer?' I said. 'But it's you I'm speaking to. My God, what I want – d'you understand? – what I want is that, even when I'm not there, even if I stay away for six months, for a year, for ten years, my home should be spotless and my wife a lady.'

Better and better. Nevertheless I could not help noticing that my language had something false, something spurious about it: but there it is, sublimated people say things in a genuine manner; desublimated people, pretending to be sublimated, are forced, willy-nilly, to have recourse to the language of the strip cartoon: 'I pulled you out of the mud in which I might have left you, I did not hesitate to make you, the lowest of call-girls, into the companion of my life. I halted you on the downward slope of prostitution along which, without me, you would without doubt have continued to roll to the point of ultimate degradation; but now I regret it. I begin truly to think I should have done better to leave you in the mire to which, it seems, you were predestined.'

She remained silent. She went over to the stove, her head bowed; searched, amongst the dirty dishes piled up in the

23

sink, for the coffee-pot; unscrewed it, tapped it against the rim of the bowl so that the coffee-grounds might spill out; turned on the tap and washed, one after another, the dismantled pieces. A lock of hair dangled irritatingly across her face, but she did not brush it aside. At last, without turning round, she said: 'You want so many things. You want me to play at being a lady when you're not there. But when you were here you wanted me to act a comedy for you.'

'Why, what comedy? What d'you mean?'

'What d'you think? There are some things one doesn't forget. Instead of helping me to make a new life for myself, you forced me to act – here in my own house, with Cesarino sleeping in our bed – the part of a call-girl. I had to put on the shirt and trousers of the time when you first met me at Mariú's; I had to come running up the stairs; I had to ring the bell at the door of my own flat as if I were coming there for the first time. Let's understand one another. Since I am fond of you and you are my husband, I'm prepared to act out the comedy whenever you like. But don't then come and tell me that I ought to be a lady. There are certain things that a lady who *is* a lady does not do, even if it's her husband who wants her to.'

Bang! Crash! Catastrophe! There I was, flung headlong from the artificial superiority of a desublimated man pretending to be sublimated, down and down into the depths of the most abject desublimation. And this, of course, through 'his' fault. It was 'he', in fact, who invented the comedy to which Fausta had alluded. 'He', with his usual fixation of finding the call-girl Fausta of yesterday inside Fausta the mother and wife of today. There I was, then, thrown to the ground, more desublimated than ever, perhaps even more so than Fausta, for she at least had acted out the comedy for love, which in itself is always a form of sublimation; whereas I had made her do it in order to satisfy 'him'.

I realized that I could not go on persisting with the subject of the so-called 'mud' from which I had rescued Fausta by marrying her; so I changed my theme, though I still went on in a rough, authoritarian manner. 'But at least I should like to know,' I said, 'why there are so many dirty dishes. And what is the maid doing?'

'It's five days since she has been here.'

'And why?'

'She stole my jewellery and hasn't been seen since.'

'She stole your jewellery?'

'Yes.'

'Everything?'

'Everything that you hadn't put into the strong-box.'

'So she stole your jewellery! Including, I suppose, that ring with the sapphire and cut diamonds that I gave you when we got married?'

'Yes, that too.'

'And have you reported it?'

'No.'

'But why?'

'Don't know.'

'It's incredible. You're robbed of a valuable object which is connected with the most important event of your life; jewellery of considerable value is taken; and you don't worry about it, you're not distressed, you don't even report it. What's come over you? Kindly tell me what's the matter with you?'

'Nothing.'

'What d'you mean – nothing?'

'I mean – nothing.'

'And who's doing the cleaning now, who's looking after the child?'

'I am.'

'But haven't you found a maid yet?'

'No.'

'Or haven't you looked for one yet?'

'No, I haven't looked for one.'

'But why?'

'I don't know.'

'You've nothing to do, so look for one as quickly as possible. And, moreover, how can you live in this disorder, in all this filth?'

She made no answer. Now I was 'on top', and firmly so;

and I could even allow myself to behave a little less fiercely. 'Who came yesterday evening?' I asked.

'Vittorio, Attilio and Giovanna were here.'

'I have already told you that I don't wish you to go on seeing that couple. She's an extremely common woman. He's a bankrupt who lives from hand to mouth. As for Vittorio, it's soon said: he's an idiot.'

'They telephoned me. Nobody does telephone me. Everybody knows by now that you're not living with me; and since I have no friends because my friends were your friends, I saw by this that somebody *did* remember me.'

'And what did you do?'

'First we got the dinner ready, then we dined and then we played cards.'

'What game did you play?'

'Poker. Attilio won. I owe him ten thousand lire.'

'He must have cheated.'

'No, he didn't cheat, he won.'

'Did they speak of me?'

'Yes.'

'What did they say?'

'They said you were behaving badly towards me. That you ought to come back and live with your family.'

'Anything else?'

'Vittorio said you had a woman, someone called Agata.'

'Vittorio, as I told you, is an idiot. I haven't any Agata.'

'I know you haven't. I told him so.'

'Did anyone telephone for me in the last few days?'

'Yes.'

'Did you write down the names?'

'No.'

'Why?'

'Don't know.'

This time my outburst was sincere. Jumping to my feet and banging my fist down on the table, I shouted: 'But my God, what is it, this inertia, this letting everything slide? My God, what I want – understand me clearly – what I want, what in fact I insist upon, is that in my absence everything should continue to be just as it was when I was here. D'you see? Everything!'

She did not reply. Determinedly she kept her massive shoulders turned towards me – shoulders in which, nevertheless, I seemed to divine, just as though they were transparent, the slim, graceful back of former days. Her hair hung down over her cheeks like the dangling ears of certain kinds of gun-dogs: one might have thought that it was trying to hide her face. Then a slight trembling of her shoulders told me that she was crying. Suddenly she moved away from the stove, threw herself into a chair beside me, took her face between her hands and, bending forward, started frankly sobbing.

So there it was. My desublimation was at its lowest point. First amorousness; then pity. I resisted, as best I could, the repugnant rush of feeling that would have driven me to take Fausta in my arms and dry her tears; and, seeking to remain 'on top', I said harshly: 'A nice kind of welcome: stink, disorder, filth, jewellery stolen, a gambling debt of ten thousand lire, and, finally, a flood of foolish tears!'

This time, still sobbing, she answered: 'Since you went away, I don't seem to know where I am. I feel so lonely, so lost, so deserted. I no longer have any wish to do anything; I not only lack the will to do anything, but the physical strength as well. I'm listless and depressed, and all the time I have a pain here, in the pit of my stomach, which makes it difficult for me even to breathe. Everything slips through my hands, everything disgusts me. All I want is to sleep and sleep and sleep. I've stood it for six months. But I feel that now I can't go on any longer. When, when are you going to come back to us here?'

So that was that. It was absolutely necessary for me not to give way to feeling. Leaving aside any element of amorousness, it still remained, in fact, a question of a manifestation of desublimation, susceptible, at the same time, of a change into its opposite. Sentimentalism, on the other hand, is, so to speak, institutionalized desublimation. And final, irreversible. Pitilessly I replied: 'I shall return when the right moment comes.'

'And when will the right moment come?'

'You know that. As soon as I have finished shooting my film.'

'Attilio says they won't get you to do it.'

'Attilio is himself a failed film director. He knows nothing. Actually I shall start shooting in a month at most.'

'A month?'

'A month, six weeks.'

'No, I feel it, I feel it. You'll make this film and then you'll say you've got to be left alone to concentrate on another film, and so you'll never come back at all.'

'There's only one thing I can say. If I say I'll come back as soon as I've finished the film, it means I shall come back.'

'No, you won't come back, you won't come back. You don't care for me any longer. You'll find another woman.'

'Who told you I don't care for you any longer? Why, just now, when I was caressing you, I had a huge erection.'

'Then why didn't you want to make love?'

'You know why. Because I want to concentrate, to take my life properly in hand again. And in order to concentrate, the first stipulation is, not to make love.'

'That isn't true. The reason why you left home is a different one.'

'What was it?'

'Cesarino. You have a fixed idea that Cesarino is not your son.'

'I haven't a fixed idea. I don't go in for fixed ideas, I reason. By logical deduction, Cesarino *should* not be my son.'

'But he is. I know what you think. That he's the son of the plumber. But that isn't true. I've always been faithful to you, always.'

'There are so many ways of being faithful.'

'No, there is only one.'

'One can be faithful with one's heart and not with the rest.'

'I have always been faithful to you with my heart and with the rest of me too. When Eugenio came for the first time to repair the water-heater I was already pregnant. I remember, because that day I washed in cold water since there was no hot water, the water-heater being out of order; and I thought: Let's hope this doesn't do the baby any harm.'

'A very proper thought.'

'You have a fixed idea about the plumber because I remarked to you that he was a good-looking young man; but I have always been faithful to you, and when you make me act that comedy and force me to play the part of the call-girl, I swear to you that it distresses me very much, because I'm no longer what I used to be and what you force me to be, even if it's to give you pleasure, and I feel myself to be different, and if I do it, it's because you're my husband; otherwise, you may be sure, I wouldn't do it for all the gold in the world.'

Desublimation! Desublimation! Desublimation! On her part: tears! Protests of love! Affirmations of faithfulness! Sorrow! Humility! On my part: a rush of feeling! A desire to take her in my arms! To comfort her! To caress her! Finally to kneel down, bury my face in her big, soft, bare stomach, close my eyes and forget everything! Enough! Be careful, Rico! You're still 'on top'; don't, by your own hand, get 'underneath'. Unkindly, I said: 'You're not what you were ten years ago; there can't be any doubt about that, unfortunately.'

'Boo-hoo, boo-hoo! There you are, you see, you don't like me any more and you say you'll come back when the film is finished, but you won't. But I shall kill myself; mind, I swear it on the head of Cesarino, I'll kill myself.'

'Poor Cesarino!'

'Boo-hoo, you don't believe me, but one of these days you'll find me dead.'

But providence comes to the aid even of those who are desublimated. Suddenly there was a sound as of water overflowing into a fire. The air was filled with a strong smell of burnt coffee. Pleased at this incident that halted me on the slippery slope of pity, I swore at her: 'Idiot! Instead of whimpering and talking nonsense, you should have been seeing to the coffee. There's my coffee gone up in smoke!'

'I'll make you some more.'

'No. Instead, come with me. I wish you to know, once and for all, that it is not Cesarino's doubtful paternity – about

29

which, let me say in parenthesis, I don't give a damn – that makes me stay away from home. Luckily it's a matter of something infinitely more serious. Come!'

'But where are you taking me?'

'Come. Into my study.'

'Why into your study?'

'Come with me and you'll know.'

She rose and let me drag her by her arm out of the kitchen. When we reached the study door, I made as if to open it. It was locked.

'Why is it locked?'

'I keep it locked so that no one can touch your papers.'

As she spoke, she fumbled in the pocket of her dressing-gown, pulled out a bunch of keys and opened the door. 'To me,' she said, 'your study is sacred. Look, everything has been left as it was the day you went away. Absolutely everything.'

Like all desublimated people, Fausta believes the myth about culture. In fact, about 'my' culture. And she is not aware, poor dear, that it is precisely 'my' culture that designates me as a desublimated person. For there is, indeed, a culture of the sublimated and a culture of the desublimated. And mine belongs to the second category.

Fausta, meanwhile, had opened the door and we went in. Complete darkness. Through this blackness she went over to the window and with an effort pulled up the roller-blind. The room was filled with light. Alas, Fausta had told the truth: everything was left exactly as it had been on the day I went away. One seemed to be poking one's nose into the study of one of those long-dead writers whose rooms have been transformed into museums, which are visited by people reverently and hat in hand. Except that there was a difference: those writers whose rooms have been transformed into museums were for the most part real, genuine writers; or were, in their lifetime, sublimated artists of the first water, and their studies are faithful mirrors of their sublimation. I, on the contrary, am desublimated, and my study was clearly a museum of mediocrity, of approximation, of self-didacticism, of foolish aspiration, of the near miss, of amateurishness.

30

This awareness on my part was so strong that for a moment I stood looking round, in the hope, almost, of being contradicted by the bookshelves that rose from floor to ceiling on three of the room's four walls. Alas, what I already knew was confirmed to me, beyond all doubt. The shelves of the bookcases were a true mirror of my desublimated pseudo-culture, the culture which Fausta, more desublimated than I, so much admired. Those bookcases, unfortunately, spoke eloquently, in fact they shouted.

And this was their message: 'Here we are. On our lowest shelves, piled up in order, are notebooks of film-scripts, the testimony of years and years of humble services rendered to the cultural industry. Above those shelves are rows of books of which you have made use, directly or indirectly, in order to write the scripts. Directly: books of highly variable worth which, according to the ups and downs of the market and the estimates of production, you have had gradually to transform into scenarios. Indirectly: all the other books which you have read in order to enrich, as they say, your cultural equipment; but which, when all is said and done, seeing that the aforesaid cultural equipment has served you simply and solely for the writing of scenarios, you have read, fundamentally, in order to increase your value in the eyes of the producer involved. Thus, side by side with the successful novel from which you actually made a script, there stand – just as an example – the complete works of Proust, the reading of which, to be quite honest, served only one purpose for you, which was that you could say, one day, to one of your fellow scenario-writers: "Are you well up in Proust? Well then, you'll easily understand me when I say that, in the relationship between Mario and Giovanna, we ought to some extent to recapture the relation-ship between Swann and Odette." Or again, there are the novels of Kafka, read and re-read with passion but later, on the same sort of occasions, used to advantage with references like this: "Kafka-like; that's what the offices of the police headquarters ought to be."

'Yes, you're a cultivated man, possibly, among the whole lot of scenario-writers going around, the most cultivated; but all that your culture does for you is to make Protti, the producer you're working for at present, say, when you attend his "court": "This is one of those doubtful points of a cultural kind that only Rico, who has read practically all the books in existence, can help us to clear up." Anyhow, it's not your fault. The fault is "his". Yes, owing to "him", you have never been able to achieve the culture of sublimated people, which serves no purpose but to produce another culture – that is, power. Desublimated, you have done the same as all the other people of your kind: you have taken anything that served your purpose for your scenarios and have thrown away all that would have given you power. And so, after all that reading, you've remained fundamentally uncultivated and, into the bargain, in the humiliating way characteristic of the desublimated – with the demeanour, with the presumption, with the illusion that you are a man of culture.'

Such was the message of my books, harsh but truthful. Disgust and mortification must have been clearly visible on my face, for Fausta inquired anxiously: 'What's the matter? Is there something wrong with your study? Yet I've always kept it locked, and every morning I dust it and air it.'

I roused myself and replied drily: 'No, no, everything's perfect'; then I went confidently to a particular shelf and took down an encyclopedia of psychoanalysis. Turning the pages of the book, I said to Fausta: 'D'you want to know why I've gone to live on my own?'

She watched me, disconcerted, uncomprehending. I opened the book at a certain well-known page and read slowly: 'Sublimation. Process postulated by Freud to explain certain human activities which are apparently unrelated to sexuality but which would seem to have their source of energy in the force of the sexual impulse. Freud has instanced artistic activity and intellectual research, in particular, as examples of sublimated activities.'

I paused at this point and repeated, articulating the syllables clearly: 'Artistic activity and intellectual research.'

For a moment I was silent, then I concluded: 'The sexual

impulse can be said to be sublimated in accordance with the extent to which it is deflected towards a new goal and is directed towards objects recognized as socially valuable.'

I stopped. I closed the book again and put it back in its place. Then I asked Fausta: 'Now d'you understand why I wish to live on my own, so as to concentrate and take my life properly in hand again?'

'No.'

Faced with such obtuseness, suddenly I lost patience. I shouted: 'It's because, as long as I live with you and we make love once or even twice a day, I remain desublimated. D'you understand? Desublimated, that is, a miserable, under-developed creature, mentally unfit, sterile, alienated, with a big, potent member and a small, impotent brain. That's why! I'm desublimated, that is, exactly the type of man that makes it easy for all the Prottis of this world to have no worries. Desublimated: a good citizen, a good husband, a good father, even if alienated, cuckolded and parent of a son that is not his own. Desublimated! The dirty beast whose expression of dislike for the world is released entirely from the lower part of him, leaving him completely empty and acquiescent. The Caliban whose sexual impulse is directed solely towards this thing here.'

Overcome at the same time with anger and desire, I put out my hand, undid the girdle of her dressing-gown, uncovered her big belly and seized a good handful of the thick, ample hair on the lower part of it. 'D'you understand now,' I shouted, 'or d'you need further explanations?'

'Ow, you're hurting me. All I understand is that that Freud of yours doesn't want us to make love. But I don't want to insist on our making love. All I want is for you to be fond of me and for you to come back and live with me and Cesarino. Ow, let go, you're hurting me.'

'Have you understood, yes or no?'

'Yes, I've understood that you're hurting me; let me go. In any case it's always you who want to make love. As for me, I'm ready to give it up. If you like, I'll give you my oath – look, I'll give you my oath on Cesarino's life.'

'Don't let us talk about Cesarino. Just tell me whether you've understood or not. And what you've understood.'

'I've understood that you now want to make love; that's what I've understood. But don't pull at me like that, you're hurting me. Come along, let's go.' As she said this, she made her usual gesture: instead of taking me by the hand she seized hold of 'him', turned her back on me and started off towards the door, pulling me behind her as one pulls a donkey by its halter.

What was I to do? I summoned up all my strength, made a mental appeal to my guardian saint, St Sigmund Freud, and, just as we crossed the threshold of the bedroom, said: 'All right then, let's make love. But first you must pretend to be a cow.'

You must know that this was one of the many conjugal jokes (as we may call them) which 'he' had invented for his own exclusive use and consumption, in spite of my constant, absolutely firm disapproval. Fausta protested: 'No, not that. Another time, possibly. Now let's make love in a normal way.'

'Either you pretend to be a cow, or nothing.'

'He', cocky and self-assured, and without realizing that I was making use of his game against him rather than in his favour, murmured: 'Yes, that's fine, don't budge an inch.'

'But why?' asked Fausta.

'Because I want it, because I like it; there's no "why" about it.'

'You make a fool of me and I, like an idiot, give in to you.'

So, after all, like a good girl made docile and understanding by a few years of mercenary attendance at the 'Mariú, *modes*' apartment, she was already resigned. She climbed on to the bed and took up her position on all fours. Then she put out her hand behind her and raised the curtain of her dressing-gown to display the spectacle of her enormous white behind, the buttocks of which seemed to be dilated, amplified, enlarged by their own clean, forlorn whiteness. Behind these twin spheres, whose vastness made my head reel like that of an agoraphobe in a public place empty as far as the eye could see, her body, well-rounded though it was, disappeared completely.

34

How thin and meagre her two thighs looked, which in an erect position, on the contrary, appeared like two pillars; and how short the arms upon which her bust was supported. Fausta stretched her head out sideways, in a curiously animal-like fashion, looked at me, then opened her mouth and uttered a long-drawn bellow: 'Moo-oo!'

'Again.'

'Moo-oo-oo-oo.'

'Again.'

She assembled all her forces and this time gave vent to a truly cow-like bellow, of the kind that is to be heard in alpine meadows alternating with the sound of the cow-bells. I took advantage of this to spring back away from her. And while the bellowing still continued, long and heartrending, I left the room; with one bound I was at the front door and I opened it and rushed out.

Once I was on the stairs I slowed down. I felt disgusted and saddened. 'He' was silent, probably too disconcerted to find the energy to speak, and I said to him: 'Here again was something I was forced to do through your fault. And, into the bargain, not to an ordinary street-walker; no, to my wife, to the mother of my son, to the person I love best in the world, to my poor Fausta.'

2 Expropriated!

Maurizio arrived. At the long and anxiously awaited sound of the bell I jumped from my chair and rushed to open the door. Maurizio preceded me along the passage with the self-assurance and ease of one who knew the place well. In reality it was the first time he had been there; hitherto we had worked in a room at the production offices. Small but well-proportioned, dressed entirely in white linen, with black shoes and black glasses, his honey-blond hair cut like that of a Renaissance page, he walked slowly in front of me, indolently, hands in pockets, with a touch, possibly, of ironical respect. But why this disdain? Towards whom? Towards me, obviously, since I had just now placed myself well 'underneath' by saying to him rather uneasily: 'You're late. I expected you at four o'clock. It's now five.'

He answered in a careless tone: 'I had things to do'; and meanwhile, as though the flat were to be let and he might be a possible tenant, he opened the doors along the passage one after the other and looked into the rooms. 'Why, your flat's completely empty,' he remarked. 'There's no furniture.'

I was pleased that he should make such a remark which at least showed some curiosity and interest in something that concerned me, even though I realized that this pleasure confirmed my inferiority with regard to him. I replied: 'No, there is none, and I am not going to have any.'

'But why?'

'Because I don't want any.'

'Why don't you want any?'

I tried to assume a capricious, irritable, neurotic air. 'Furniture, ornaments, books . . .' I said; 'they all remind me of the principle of property to which I am congenitally hostile. Besides, I don't know why, they get on my nerves. Even in my own home I couldn't stand them any longer. There

36

were days when I should have liked to fling everything out of the window. So I preferred that this flat should remain empty.'

'But why? Isn't this your home?'

'It is and it isn't. It is, because I live here. It is not, because I have another home, a real home, in which my wife and son live.'

'You're separated from your wife?'

'No, it's simply that I have a different place of residence. But we telephone to each other every day, and in a future which I hope may not be far off I shall go back and live with her.'

By this time we were in my study. I went and sat down at the little typewriter-table, and waved Maurizio to the arm-chair which, together with the little table and the chair upon which I was sitting, comprised the entire furnishings of the room. Maurizio settled himself sideways in the chair, his back against one arm, his legs over the other, and remarked: 'Well, well, but I still don't understand why you left your wife and son in order to come and live here, all alone.'

'For some time I hadn't been able to work, in my own home. The child would be whining, my wife would be coming in and out, the telephone would be perpetually ringing. And so, with my wife's consent, I came here. I need to concentrate, to reflect, to take my life in hand again and look at it in a new perspective.'

Maurizio – as, indeed, I had hoped – made no comment. He looked all round the empty study; he looked intently at the whitewashed walls as though trying to find a stain on them which was not there. Then he took off his glasses and looked at the curtainless window through whose panes shone the empty blue sky of summer. Finally, in a methodical manner, he took from his pocket a packet of cigarettes, extracted a single one through a small rectangular hole at one of its extremities, took hold of it with his lips, put the packet back into his pocket, struck a flame from a lighter, put the lighter back in his pocket, inhaled a mouthful of smoke and blew it out again through his nostrils, then held the cigarette between his fingers which were of a milky whiteness but yellow with nicotine round his oval, well-kept nails.

'Well then,' he said, 'shall we begin? I read your version yesterday evening. Shall we discuss it?'

What came over me? Obviously the painful obsession, which had given rise to the dream of frustration in which it had seemed to me that Fausta was blocking the lens of the camera with her groin, was now getting the better of my prudence. I did in fact exclaim, in a voice strangled with emotion: 'Maurizio, first of all, before we start discussing my version, there's something I've got to ask you.'

Desublimated! There was nothing to be done! Perhaps masochistic as well! Why indeed, from the very beginning, without any apparent motive, did I place myself, of my own accord, in a position of inferiority in relation to this young man of little more than twenty? I felt that between him and me a situation was being created like that in the game known as 'Scissors Cut Paper', which is played with three basic units only: paper, scissors and a stone. The scissors cut the paper but are broken against the stone. The paper is wrapped round the stone but is cut by the scissors. The stone breaks the scissors but is wrapped up in the paper. Well, in relation to Maurizio I am invariably like the scissors in relation to the stone, like the paper in relation to the scissors, like the stone in relation to the paper. Which is as much as to say that, whatever he does or says, Maurizio is always 'on top of me'; and I feel myself to be, in relation to him, invariably 'underneath'. Indeed, after my incautious and emotional request, as I was twisting and turning anxiously on my chair, Maurizio was staring at me in a slightly disdainful manner, rather as one might look at an insect that has done something inappropriate, such as speaking. At last he said, slowly: 'You wanted to ask me something; what is it?'

'Maurizio, you must make me a promise.'

'A promise?'

'Maurizio, this film of which we're making the script together is "my" film. The film with which, so to speak, I've been occupied ever since I was born. Maurizio, you must promise to propose me to Protti as the director of this film.'

So there I was, once and for all, 'underneath', more 'underneath' than ever.

Maurizio, who, obviously, was conscious of being 'on top', took this quite calmly. First of all he stared at me for a long time, with that same offensive, entomologist-like curiosity. Finally he said: 'In actual fact, Rico, it's a good thing you've raised this question of the direction of the film at the very beginning.'

'Why?'

He was sitting sideways to me, in his favourite position, just as though he were not in an armchair in my study but in a small canvas by a Renaissance master, as a youthful page with honey-coloured hair, large, dull, golden-brown eyes and a milky complexion. 'Because,' he said, 'my problem at the moment, when carefully considered, is whether I should continue to make use of your collaboration or not.'

Rout! Defeat! General stampede! *Sauve qui peut!* While I was trying to face the situation, encouraging myself to keep calm and self-controlled, I felt that the most abject consternation was visible in my expression. 'I don't understand,' I stammered. 'What d'you mean? Why?'

Maurizio appeared to be reflecting. Then, in an apathetic sort of way, he remarked: 'Because I didn't like your version.'

'Why didn't you like it?'

My voice had changed in tone. A moment before I had been extremely pale; now I was as red as a turkey-cock. Maurizio was in no way troubled, oh no. I was desublimated, he was sublimated: there lay the whole drama. Then, as though putting a pre-established plan into effect, he said: 'Let's do it like this. Give me a summing-up, now, of your version, briefly, as you would sum it up to Protti. All right?'

'But why?'

'Because, after you've summed it up, it will be easier for me to make you see clearly the difference between your treatment and the version that Flavia and I have written together. In the meantime, however, as an introduction, let me read you

89

the passage from *Das Kapital* by which Flavia and I were inspired.'

He took from his pocket a sheet of paper and read slowly, spelling it out, as it were: '"There, it was a matter of the expropriation of the mass of the population on the part of a few usurpers; here, it is a matter of the expropriation of a few usurpers on the part of the mass of the people." That is the passage. The title of the film, *Expropriation*, is taken from this passage. Is your version, in your own opinion, faithful to the spirit of this extract from Marx?'

'I think so.'

'Very well. Then sum up your version.'

As he said this, he threw his cigarette-end on the floor, bent forward and crushed it with his small foot; his ankle, I noticed, was somewhat thick and to me, for some reason – perhaps just because it was thick – it had the effect of being feminine. He lit another cigarette, bringing his two hands together in front of his mouth, hands that were small like his feet, and wonderfully white, smooth and with no prominent bones. He inhaled, then breathed out the blue smoke from the diaphanous, delicate, almost transparent nostrils of his short, perfect nose and then, immediately afterwards, from his pink, well-cut mouth also. Painfully worried, I replied: 'Why make me repeat things you already know?'

'*I* know them. But *you* do not, judging anyhow by your conviction that you have been faithful to the spirit of Marx's expression. In giving me an account of your version, perhaps you will come to feel that you know it for the first time, that you see it, so to speak, in a mirror.'

So there was nothing to be done: Maurizio commanded and I obeyed. In a resigned tone of voice I began: 'A group of boys and girls, all of them students and all politically engaged, decide to establish a cache of weapons to be held ready for the possibility of an imminent revolutionary movement. But to acquire weapons money is needed, and the group has none. For the group there are two ways of procuring money: by earning it or stealing it. Earning it is impossible; the only thing is to steal it. But robbery, if justified by superior political motivation, is no robbery. It is legitimate appropriation, or rather, in Marx's phrase, "expropriation", carried out in the name of the people, from one of the many expropriators of the people. Who is to be the victim of expropriation?

'Isabella, one of the girls of the group, indicates who it is to be: her father. He is an extremely rich man; he is a collector of pictures. All that is needed is to steal a couple of them, from among those of the greatest value, and sell them abroad. No sooner said than done. The *coup* is successful; it is now necessary to palm off the two paintings. At this point the group's lack of experience wrecks the operation. The art dealer whom the young men approach is in reality an adventurer, who, as soon as he holds the pictures, vanishes. The group then meets and it is decided to track down the dealer and do away with him. For this purpose two members are drawn by lot, namely Isabella and the leader of the group, Rodolfo. The couple pursue the thief of the pictures across France, Belgium and Holland, and finally to England. They run him to earth in a country house in Wales. But at the last moment they haven't the courage to finish him off. Pity, horror of bloodshed, feeling of uselessness, immaturity – why was it?

'After this failure, the group breaks up. The boys go back to their studies. Isabella marries Rodolfo and goes to live with him, and with the two children who are born of their marriage, in a provincial town where Rodolfo teaches philosophy at the university. It is Isabella who relates the story, or rather, her voice off-screen. Now married and the mother of two children, now settled down with her husband, a young and highly esteemed university lecturer, Isabella will recount the affair of the unsuccessful expropriation with a touch of nostalgic melancholy which should convey the feeling of a past now finished and done with, full, perhaps, of imprudences and mistakes, but at the same time generous, courageous and committed.

'Isabella, in short, with her off-screen voice, will be the narrator of a fable. What fable? The fable of ingenuous youth, inexperienced but ready to risk even life for an idea, for a cause.

Without realizing it, the young people of the group, with their unsuccessful attempt at revolutionary action, have experienced the heroic moment of youth, the moment that comes only once in life and in which, as in first love, all youthful illusions are aflame.'

I became animated, in a deliberate sort of way, at the conclusion of my story, speaking as one is accustomed to speak to producers when recounting the subject of a film which one wishes them to acquire. But even making some allowance for professional lyricism, I do not think I wandered too far from the real nature of my feeling. Indeed I do really think that protest will one day be considered as the heroic moment of a particular generation, of Maurizio's generation, in fact. Yes, I am convinced that youth is the heroic period of man, and little does it matter whether this, so to speak, biological heroism devotes itself to politics, as was the case with Maurizio and his group, or to art and culture, as was my own case, in my now distant adolescence.

While I was thinking of these things I was looking at Maurizio, who in return was looking at me, without speaking. Disconcerted by his silence, I added hastily: 'You recommended me to use your friends in the group as models for the young people in the film. That's what I have done. I kept your information in mind. Isabella is Flavia. Rodolfo is you yourself. Isabella's father is Flavia's father. As for the picture dealer, the thief and adventurer, I took myself as model. And so on.'

At last Maurizio spoke. His face, like that of a mournful, ambiguous page-boy, remained, however, completely expressionless. 'The last sentence of your story,' he said, 'the heroic moment of youth: now tell me the truth, did you tell that tale to Protti too, when you talked to him about the subject of the film?'

It was true, but how in the world had he come to know about it? Embarrassed, I replied: 'I admit it was a remark made for the sake of effect. But with producers, as you know yourself, one has to talk like that.'

Maurizio lit a cigarette, inhaled, and then asked in a

careless tone: 'If I remember rightly, apart from the passage from Marx, Flavia and I took our inspiration for the story of the film from an episode in the life of Stalin. Would you mind telling me what that was?'

Patiently I recited: 'When Stalin was no more than an obscure Georgian revolutionary, he took part with his comrades in the expropriation of a bank, in Tiflis.'

'How did that operation succeed?'

'It succeeded extremely well. Stalin and his comrades got away with a big sum of money. To be precise: two hundred and fifty thousand roubles.'

'And what did Stalin and his friends do then?'

'What did they do? It's well known what they did: they started a revolution.'

'Strange; but, to judge from your version, one might think that Stalin, after the expropriation of the bank at Tiflis, had retired into private life, devoting himself, for instance, to the Caucasian carpet trade. And that the expropriation itself had then remained in his memory all wrapped up in a melancholy nostalgia, as a recollection of the heroic moment of his youth, as a fable in fact, to be told to his grandchildren at the fireside on winter evenings.'

Alas! So that was that! I was aware of the cold, ironical, unequivocal tone of the sublimated person who, having slackened the reins on the neck of the desublimated one, all at once reminds him which of the two is master and which the servant. Feeling myself immediately to be 'underneath', I tried nevertheless to defend myself. 'Stalin's expropriation was successful. But you and Flavia had already decided, in your version of the script, that that of the revolutionary group in our film was to be a failure.'

'But do you think that, if Stalin's *coup* had not succeeded, he would have retired from the revolutionary struggle?'

'No, I don't think so.'

'Well then, if not Stalin, why the group in the film-script?'

I looked at him in astonishment: Maurizio, that insignificant little creature, that spoilt child, with his angelic face, comparing himself with the Georgian dictator! But directly afterwards I felt I was wrong to be astonished. This was not, in fact, a question of a comparison, but of the claim to belong to the same human group, that of the sublimated. Stalin, obviously, was sublimated; but so also was Maurizio, even though only a boy, even though a spoilt child, even though a bourgeois.

Cautiously, I said: 'I had to bear in mind the differences of surroundings, the historical, the social and the psychological differences. After all the Italy of 1970 is not the Tsarist Russia of the end of the nineteenth century, and Rome is not Tiflis.'

Maurizio said nothing. I felt nervous. I rose and went and stood in front of the window. Finally, behind me, I heard Maurizio's voice saying: 'I think I shall really have to do without your collaboration.'

I turned abruptly. 'But why?'

'Because you're not a suitable person to collaborate in a film like this.'

'What reason is there to suppose so?'

'The reason is that you're not like us.'

'Us?'

'Yes, we of the group.'

'And what are *you* like?'

'We're revolutionaries.'

A new demonstration, if need be, of my desublimated inferiority in face of the perfectly sublimated Maurizio. Normally I should not describe myself as a revolutionary; a rebel, yes; a revolutionary, no: the shade of difference is important. But I should not be the desublimated person I am if, when taken unawares, I did not immediately adopt the scale of values of my sublimated opponent. I did in fact say, in a surprised and obstinate manner: 'But, Maurizio, I'm a revolutionary too.'

I expected, for some reason, that Maurizio would burst out into noisy laughter. But Maurizio did not laugh. He said, slowly: 'No, Rico, I should say, rather, that you're the opposite of a revolutionary.'

'What d'you mean by that?'

44

'What is the opposite of a revolutionary? A bourgeois, isn't it?'

There I was, thanks to that one little word 'bourgeois', which, unfortunately, I had not had the presence of mind to utter first – there I was, 'underneath' again.

What was I to do? To deny that I was bourgeois would be an act of desublimation; to boast that I *was* bourgeois (apart from the fact that it would be in contradiction to my previous assertion that I was a revolutionary) would also be an act of desublimation. Actually what I ought to have done was to take hold of that little word with the forceps of my intelligence and dissolve it in the acid of a calm but rigorous criticism. But alas, my idiotic impetuousness prevailed. Like a bull, I charged, head down, at the red cloth which Maurizio was waving under my nose. 'But I'm *not* a bourgeois,' I cried.

And then the following ridiculous altercation took place.

'Yes, Rico, you *are* a bourgeois.'

'I'm *not* a bourgeois. There are few things I'm so sure of as that I'm not a bourgeois.'

'Yet you are.'

'No, Maurizio, I swear to you that I'm not.'

'Rico, will you tell me why you're so annoyed at being considered a bourgeois?'

'It annoys me like any assertion that is contrary to the truth.'

'The very fact that it annoys you proves that you are.'

'Why?'

'Because anyone who is bourgeois can't bear to be so described.'

'That may be so. But, finally, I don't *feel* bourgeois. Why should I say the opposite of what I feel?'

'Very well then, tell me what you are.'

'I'm an intellectual.'

Once again, for some reason or other, I expected Maurizio to break into loud laughter. But he didn't. This time again Maurizio did not laugh. He belonged to an imperturbable generation, which paid no importance to ideas but only to the capacity of ideas to place anyone who professed them automatically 'on top', and anyone who opposed them, 'underneath'. He merely said, serenely: 'An intellectual? Quite right. And therefore a bourgeois.'

'The intellectual isn't a bourgeois.'

'The intellectual *is* a bourgeois.'

'No, he's not.'

'Yes, Rico, he is.'

'If it's true that the intellectual is a bourgeois, then you're a bourgeois twice over: as a person of bourgeois origin and as an intellectual.'

I was so pleased with my sally that I was all puffed up, like a turkey, and for a moment I was left breathless, as though astounded at my own courage. Everything, however, melted away into nothing, for Maurizio replied quietly, in a tone of curious, almost bashful assurance, little desirous, however of appearing as such: 'Yes, that's true, I'm of bourgeois origin and, strictly speaking, I might also consider myself an intellectual. But I am not a bourgeois and I am not an intellectual because I am a revolutionary.'

'And why, pray, a revolutionary? Because you have established a so-called group with your university companions and you meet together to talk about politics?'

My voice was cracked and strident. I had fallen into a bog and was trying to pull myself out by my own hair. Maurizio replied: 'No, a revolutionary is simply a man who has been able to transform himself.'

'Transform himself into what?'

'Into a revolutionary.'

'And you and the others of your group have been able to transform yourselves?'

'Yes.'

What a lot of things I should have liked to say! For example, that a sublimated man does not transform himself, has no need to transform himself: he merely moves from one form of sublimation to another. That, in any case, the little word 'transformation' is like the little word 'bourgeois': a weapon at the disposal of the man who is readiest to grasp it. What a lot of things! But all of them things related to desublimation, alas, even though, possibly, intelligent. Besides, it is a well-known fact that intelligence and desublimation go arm in arm. So, in the end, I said the one thing I ought not to have said: 'What evidence have you that I also haven't been able to transform myself into a revolutionary?'

'The evidence is your version of the script.'

'Why, what's wrong with my version?'

'It's counter-revolutionary.'

'What is there counter-revolutionary about my version?'

'Everything.'

'Everything, eh? But it isn't enough just to make assertions, you have to prove them.'

'For example, then, the fact that Rodolfo and Isabella give up the plan of doing away with the adventurer.'

'But in your scheme too, yours and Flavia's, Rodolfo and Isabella gave up the idea of doing away with the adventurer.'

'Yes, but not out of pity, immaturity, horror of bloodshed, etc., as in your version.'

'For what reason, then?'

'For tactical, that is, political, reasons.'

'Why? Couldn't Rodolfo and Isabella feel pity?'

'No, they couldn't.'

'And why couldn't they?'

'Because it's not the habit of revolutionaries to feel pity for a traitor, still less to act, or rather not to act, out of pity. You know what it shows, this pity that you set so much store by?'

'What?'

'That in reality you consider the group in the film, and therefore, logically, our own group which has served you as model, to be a club consisting of feeble, innocuous spoilt children playing at being revolutionaries.'

'That's not true.'

'Yes, it *is* true.'

'No, Maurizio, I merely wanted to give a certain kind of character to the situation of your group.'

'And what, in your opinion, would that situation be?'

'Well, it's the situation of someone who, although he has

serious intentions of carrying out an . . . an expropriation, has not yet done so!'

I was all puffed up again. I was a fine fellow, very fine, splendid! But again this time Maurizio kept his place, imperturbably, 'on top', as he answered calmly: 'It's true, we haven't yet carried out the expropriation. But that's of no importance. You ought, all the same, to grasp the true character of our group.'

'What, according to you, is the true character of your group?'

'The true character of our group is that it resembles a group of technicians rather than a group of spoilt children. What is it that technicians do? They get together to formulate and carry out a plan. The plan does not come off, as is the case with our film story. Never mind. It will succeed next time. In the meantime, however, the group does not break up, does not put aside its intentions, does not retire into private life. It seeks, on the other hand, to discover the mistake which caused the failure of the plan. And in fact, in Flavia's and my scheme the affair was indeed recounted by an off-screen voice, as in your version; but it was the entirely un-nostalgic voice of Isabella reading her account of the failure of the expropriation, at the final meeting of the group. According to our idea, the reading of this account, cold, detached and scientific, was to serve as a comment on the film. Nothing whatever to do with nostalgia for the heroic moment of youth!'

Strange! The truth about Maurizio's group lay without doubt in my version. Maurizio, whether in good or in bad faith, was affirming things that were the opposite of the truth. And yet, as usual, it was he who was 'on top' and I, irremediably, in spite of my truthfulness, 'underneath'. And to such a degree was I 'underneath' that all at once I gave in and said brusquely: 'You're right. Very well, then. I'll throw away my version. I'll re-write it.'

What mistakes he makes, the man who is 'underneath'! He always makes mistakes, he is never in the right. Suddenly, for reasons that eluded me, Maurizio became conciliatory: 'No, there's no need for you to throw away your version. All you need do is correct it. The off-screen voice should still be Isabella's. But Isabella does not recall, nostalgically, the heroic moment of youth; instead, she reads loudly, in a firm, hard tone of voice, an account of the failure of the expropriation. As for the finale, instead of its taking place in the provincial house where Isabella is living with her husband Rodolfo and her children, you must set it in our headquarters in Rome, with the portraits of Marx, Lenin, Stalin, Mao and Ho-Chi-Minh on the walls and the whole group assembled to listen to the narrative. When that has been read, the group decides unanimously to organize a second expropriation as soon as possible, avoiding, of course, the mistakes of the first.'

Desublimated! Abject and desublimated! I could not help exclaiming, jubilantly: 'So then, after all, you think you'll continue to make use of my collaboration?' I watched him inhale some smoke, then gaze at the lighted tip of his cigarette, in silence, as though reflecting. Then he answered: 'I think so. However there's one difficulty to be got over.'

'And what's that?'

'I've told the group about your version and about the counter-revolutionary character you've given to the story. If I must really be truthful, they were pretty angry with you. There was no doubt in their minds that I ought to find another collaborator.'

'So what?'

'So I think we ought to do it like this: I'll introduce you to the group and you must make a speech of self-criticism, mentioning your old version and explaining how you intend to make the new one. There will be a discussion. Then we shall be free to go ahead and start work again.'

It seemed to me that I had come out of it cheaply. I had the impression that everything, all at once, was for the best. Exultantly I exclaimed: 'As much self-criticism as you like. Moreover it will give me great pleasure to meet your group at last. You've talked to me so much about them. You've aroused my curiosity.'

But Maurizio had not finished. 'Nevertheless,' he added,

'before the discussion you should do something to soften things up a little. As I've already told you, they were angry with you. May I give you a piece of advice?'

'A piece of advice? Of course.'

'You ought, as soon as possible, to make a gesture.'

'What sort of gesture?'

'Make a donation. We need money for our new head-quarters. You might give a sum of money as a contribution to the cause.'

Beware, Rico! The sublimated one was setting a snare for you. But now you're in for it. Like a good desublimated simpleton, you're rushing head down into the trap. 'Certainly,' I said, 'of course. A donation. Of course. And how much?'

'An amount, I should say, of not less than five million lire.'

I thought I had not heard aright. But anyhow, that is just a way of speaking. I had heard perfectly well, and I realized quite clearly that the trap, already anticipated, was much deeper than I had believed. I realized this to such a degree that my reaction was like that of someone who plunges bodily into an abyss that has opened suddenly beneath his feet. That is, it was purely physical. I thought nothing, I did not succeed in thinking anything. I was frozen by a great cold, followed immediately afterwards by a great heat. Drops of sweat broke out on my forehead; and at the same time, instantaneously, my mouth became parched and thirsty. My vision was darkened, as though there were an eclipse.

It was not avarice, on my part, it was something different and something more: it was as if Maurizio had proposed cutting off one of my arms. But at this point, at last, my mind shook off its paralysis. Coldly, it caused me to observe that this excessive reaction on my part, exclusively physical as it was, was typical of the desublimated person of all times and all places. Yes indeed, somebody was seeking to penetrate into my neolithic cave, into my pile-dwelling; and I, the pre-historic brute, filled with horror, was shrinking back, feeling for my obsidian axe, my oaken club, to drive back my adversary and put him to flight.

50

Anyhow, everything was now clear: I had bluffed, Maurizio had seen through my bluff and now I had to pay. But, in point of fact, who should the bluffer be but an ignorant, desublimated fool furnished with a member big enough to look out of place on a donkey and with a brain so small as to arouse the sympathy of a hen? Yes, at the remote starting-point of this financial disaster lay, as ever, my own constitutional inferiority in face of Maurizio and all others like him. The man who is 'on top' has no need to do anything in order to prove that he is a true revolutionary. But the man who is 'underneath' has to pay five million lire.

With these thoughts in my head I was walking furiously up and down. I had the impression that I was delirious, and indeed I acted as if I were in a delirium, not realizing what I was doing.

I passed my hand over my bald pate, I sighed, I made grimaces, I kicked at the wastepaper basket. 'Five million!' I finally exclaimed. 'But it's an enormous sum!'

'We know that this is the amount usually paid to a good-class script-writer, for a job like that of *Expropriation*.'

'Yes, there are those who make five million and even more. *I* don't, however, and especially not for *Expropriation*.'

'Moreover we also felt that you would be averse to making money from a protest film.'

'I agree. But five million is . . . five million.'

'What report am I to make, then? That you don't wish to give it?'

'Wait a moment, Good Heavens! Let me think.'

'Very well, think.'

There followed a comic scene. I started to walk up and down, as if beside myself; and Maurizio, on his side, went on smoking in silence, and, between one puff and another, stared at the lighted end of his cigarette. The comic quality consisted in the fact that, although I was thinking and weighing the pros and cons, I knew for certain that I would not be capable of saying no. I reflected that I ought to refuse, in fact that I *must* refuse. I was not a rich man: apart from Fausta and the child, I had partly to maintain my mother as well, for her pension as the widow of a civil servant was not enough for her.

Above all I felt that, if I refused, I should be providing proof that I was to some extent sublimated, that is, that I was capable of braving a loss of face without batting an eyelid. Whereas, if I agreed, I should be giving yet another confirmation of my timid, passive, desublimated character. I felt, in short, that I had everything to gain, on all levels, by refusing.

And yet, and yet . . . This was the voice of the Rico who was always 'underneath' and whom not even the savage unleashing of the instinct of self-preservation could manage to galvanize (or rather, it was precisely the desublimated violence of the instinct of self-preservation that made me act in a desublimated way: nothing, in fact, is more desublimated than the fear of appearing so), this was the hateful voice of Rico, the inferior, now saying mildly: 'Very well, then. I will look upon it as a very, very well-paid script such as happens with other people but not with me, and I'll assign the money to the group.'

I expected thanks, handshakes, effusions. I was already preparing to produce a bashful, modest smile.

Not at all. Maurizio merely said: 'And when d'you think you can pay over the amount?'

Trap within trap! Trap of the second degree! Confused, I said: 'As soon as possible. I should like to point out to you that it is a very large sum; I haven't got it in the house nor even in the bank. I shall have to sell some bonds.'

A third trap within the second within the first!

In a slightly ironical tone of voice, Maurizio inquired: 'Do you hold any bonds?'

I felt myself blushing: I realized that once again, of my own accord, I had placed myself 'underneath'. 'Yes,' I stammered, 'I acquired some bonds because they give . . .'

'They give interest, as we know.'

'No, what I meant was that, having a family, it's stupid for me to keep the money in the bank and consume . . .'

'The capital. Quite right. What are they? State-guaranteed bonds?'

'Yes, some are State-guaranteed, others are not.'

'And what interest do they yield?'

'Maurizio, you know about all these things. You know about them better than I do. So why . . . ?'

'I bet you've got some industrial securities too.'

'Yes, I have something.'

'And gold in ingots, or in coin.'

'No, no, no gold.'

'And dollars, or Swiss francs too.'

'I have some dollars. Everyone said that the lira would be devalued, so I bought a few dollars. In fact, here's an idea; instead of selling the bonds, I'll give you the amount in dollars. That will be simpler.'

Fourth trap! Within the third which was within the second which was within the first! 'So then, you have sufficient dollars to pay your contribution in that currency. My congratulations!'

Rico, you're squashed! Flattened! Annihilated! Like a cockroach! Like a black-beetle! But this was so, not so much because you've legitimately invested your hard-earned savings, as because you couldn't stand up to Maurizio. For, as usual, you put yourself in the 'underneath' position.

Maurizio rose to his feet. 'Well, then,' he said, 'we'll do it like that. You go and sell your bonds, or sell your dollars, and give me the amount in a week's time, let us say, in Italian lire. In the meantime I'll inform the group and we'll decide on a date for the meeting for self-criticism and discussion.'

'But during that week, what am I to do? Can I go on working on the script?'

'Of course. On the understanding that it will be along the lines we've settled upon today.'

'And the directing of the film?'

By this time we were in the passage. Maurizio went ahead, taking no notice of me as I ran after him and round him like a frightened puppy. 'Rico,' he replied, 'with regard to the directing, I can't tell you anything. It doesn't depend on me.'

'Now listen! Flavia's father is one of the backers. Flavia is your fiancée.'

53

'What about it?'

'It means you have the right to propose me as director.'

He said neither yes nor no. It was obvious: he was 'on top' and he wanted to keep me 'underneath'. He opened the door with one hand, stretched out the other and – incredible as it may seem – he, a boy of twenty-three, gave me, a man of thirty-five, a light tap on the cheek. In a protective, magnanimous manner he said: 'What you have to think about is your work. Mind you produce those dollars. Good luck to the work. Good-bye.'

The door closed. I rushed quickly to the bathroom, violently threw the door open, went straight to the lavatory bowl, unbuttoned myself hastily, pulled 'him' out roughly and urinated with my legs wide apart. I had held myself in until then owing to the usual timidity that paralysed me when I was with Maurizio. A clear stream, almost white and thick as a rope, struck the porcelain bowl and flooded it all round before flowing towards the bottom, where a pale yellowish foam was already seething. The warm, slightly pungent smell of the urine rose to my nostrils.

While I was urinating, I raised 'him' up in the palm of my hand, testicles and all; I felt and appraised the weight with my hand, with my eyes measured the bulk. And indeed the man who can balance a bundle of genitals of this size in the palm of his hand cannot be just an ordinary man, an insignificant man, a man like everybody else. Still less a failure, a man of weak will, of moral and intellectual impotence. The possibility of holding in the hollow of one's hand two testicles and a member of such great size and weight cannot fail to put fresh heart into a man, to restore his courage, to inspire him with self-confidence.

As though excited by this self-satisfaction on my part, 'he' was already, in a conceited sort of way, swelling and becoming congested, and, although lying sideways in the palm of my hand, showing signs of an incipient erection. The *glans penis* began to show itself beneath the skin, with its circular prominence, its slight depression above the prominence, and its conical convexity above the depression. The skin, at its

54

point, became disengaged, opening out a little and allowing a glimpse of the orifice which so strangely resembles the little rosy eye of a new-born piglet.

Yes indeed, I was well equipped, superlatively endowed; nature, with me, had been generous, and without false modesty I could boast of having at my disposal a sexual organ which was absolutely exceptional both as regards proportions, sensitiveness, readiness, potency and resistance. All this, indeed, is true, perfectly true. And yet, and yet, and yet . . .

I was standing up. I was looking at 'him'. And all of a sudden my rage burst forth, overwhelmingly: 'And yet Maurizio, an insignificant boy, remains "on top" of me; and I remain "underneath" him. What are we to do about it? Well, you scoundrel, what are we to do about it?'

Brutally questioned in this way, 'he' replied very gently, in feigned surprise: 'What are we to do about it? Really I don't know. It doesn't seem to me that there is any connection between me and your feeling of inferiority towards Maurizio.'

I gave him a squeeze to show him I was not joking. 'It's not true,' I burst out, 'I remain "underneath" because . . . just because you're so stupidly enormous, so foolishly persevering, so fatuously potent.'

'Why, what's wrong with you? Have you gone mad, by any chance?'

'No, don't worry, I'm not mad. What's wrong with me? What's wrong is that Maurizio is sublimated and I am hopelessly desublimated. And that the blame for my desublimation lies with you, entirely with you. Maurizio's member is probably less potent than you, but in compensation Maurizio has more power than I have. There's no denying that you're a champion, a colossus, a monument; and I could make pots of money if I put you on show at a fair. But I have to pay for this championship status of yours with a humiliating, abject, continual feeling of inferiority. Everyone is superior to me; I am inferior to everyone; I am emotional, weak-willed, sentimental, uncontrolled, passive. And where lies the blame for all this? Whose fault is it, eh?'

'He' was silent now. This was his cowardly, sly way of

replying to accusations when these have a basis of truth. I shook him and said to him: 'Come on, speak, you blackguard, why don't you say anything? Speak, you scoundrel, at least defend yourself. What have you to say in your defence?'

'He' continued to be silent. But as I shook him, furiously, with violence and anger, as one shakes someone by the shoulders who has committed some evil act and you at least want him to acknowledge it, so he retorted by accelerating his erection. This, I presume, was his way, his ignoble, disloyal way, of countering my accusations.

Already of great size, though still lying quiescent in the palm of my hand, like a whale lying stranded and dying on a deserted shore, I watched him as, by gradual, almost imperceptible jerks, he became enormous and slowly, like a dirigible which, detached from its moorings, hovers in the air before sailing away, he rose up, fell back half-way, then rose up again. I dropped the hand that was supporting him; but this time 'he' did not fall back. Vigorous and massive as a young oak-tree, with all the veins in relief like clinging creepers, with the *glans* now half unsheathed, glossy and purple, he stood stiffly in front of me, his point turned upwards, stupidly, greedily, almost to the level of my navel.

Without touching him, leaving him to quiver in mid-air and, it might seem, to derive greater potency from each quivering movement, I turned and took a long look at myself in the narrow mirror at the far end of the bathroom. In the dim light I saw myself as a grotesque figure of an imitation Silenus from a Pompeian vase: the big bald head, the haughty face, the chest thrust out, the short legs; and there, below the paunch, was 'he', utterly foreign, of a different colour, as though he had arrived on two wings from goodness knows where and had been welded to my groin by some mocking god. Angrily I insisted: 'Rascal, swindler, will you answer yes or no?'

No, he wouldn't answer, he persisted obstinately in his swollen, plethoric silence. He was swaying slightly, concentrating, it seemed, his whole strength in his levitation. Furious, I gave him a side-cut with my hand, a *karate* blow. 'Answer, you blackguard,' I said.

The blow caused him to go down and then jump up again. He remained silent, seemingly attracting, in the meantime, as much blood as he could into the *glans* which now, slowly and irresistibly, was bursting forth from its sheath of skin, like a fine new chestnut from its husk. 'D'you know how much you're costing me?' I insisted. 'Five millions. Yes, because of you, because of the irresistible sense of inferiority aroused in me by your obsessive presence, here am I, forced to pay out five millions!'

Still he was silent. I gave him another blow and then another and then yet another, each time with the side of my hand. 'Why don't you answer? Don't you understand that, if Maurizio had "felt" that I was not one of the usual cases of desublimation, if he had felt that I was serious, he wouldn't have asked me for five million as proof of my revolutionary commitment? All that was needed was for him to "feel" that I was acting in a really serious manner, and was genuinely sublimated as he is. And in any case, even admitting that his demand for five million was inevitable, it still remains your fault that I didn't answer him with a plain no, fair and square. Your fault, d'you understand? A man who is desublimated cannot, in fact, say no to one who is sublimated. It's as if an earthenware pot said no to an iron pot. Yes, that's what it is; thanks to you I'm a fragile, contemptible, perfectly ordinary earthenware pot.'

All these things I said, and since he continued, stubbornly, to remain silent, suddenly, in the height of my fury, I started slapping him. Yes, I slapped him, as you might slap some impudent rogue who obstinately replies to just accusations with a shameless silence. So there I was, acting methodically and at the same time with violence, dealing him blows from the right and then from the left and then from the right again and then again from the left and so on, and shouting at him: 'Come on, speak, you scoundrel, speak!'

Tossed about by these slaps which hit him now from one side and now from the other, 'he' swung powerfully hither and thither and turned a dark, apoplectic red. I went on slapping him with continued violence; but there now began to dawn upon me the disconcerting feeling that he, masochist as he was, might actually be deriving some pleasure from the insults and blows. A few more slaps, a few abusive cries of 'scoundrel, scoundrel, scoundrel', the former delivered by a hand that became less and less precise and severe, the latter uttered by a voice that grew more and more hesitant and languid; and then, suddenly, I felt that he was going to answer me.

It was one of his usual answers, disloyal and treacherous, as I should have expected. To put it briefly, I realized all at once that, by way of an answer, he was on the point of ejaculating, under my nose, so to speak, against all my wishes and in defiance of all our agreements. Furious, desperate, frantic, I seized hold of him, I squeezed him, I bent him and twisted him, as though I hoped by doing so to drive back the precious semen. I wished the semen to return whence it had come, to be re-absorbed, to go back into its natural abode. Never, as at that moment in which 'he', in his crafty, underhand way, was making use of my very violence to make a fool of me and to unburden himself, never had I felt how sacred a thing semen is and how it is verily a sacrilege (a sacrilege which some desublimated persons are capable of committing, horrible as it is, as often as three times a day) to scatter it in order to procure one moment of pleasure as fleeting as it is contemptible. Never had I felt this with such clarity as then, when 'he' was about to fling this sacred element – as though it were spittle or some other insignificant secretion from a gland of no importance – upon the tiles of the bathroom floor.

I squeezed him, I tried to bend him and twist him; I twisted myself, too, in a vain attempt to prevent the ejaculation, contracting the muscles of my abdomen and bending myself double; I turned swiftly round and hurled myself against the wash-basin, and then, just at the moment when I falsely believed I had been successful, just at that moment 'he' exploded in my hand like a newly uncorked bottle of sparkling wine. First there was a brief tremor, and a small quantity of semen, not more than a few drops, welled out at the tip. Then, as I was already hoping to escape with no more than this modest manifestation, the main part of the ejaculation suddenly flooded my hand, overflowing between my fingers, with which I was still trying to muffle and stifle my cunning adversary.

Overcome by acute despair, I let myself slip to the ground and, still squeezing him with frantic hatred, managed to roll, like an epileptic writhing in convulsions, across the floor to the hollow depression of the shower. There I crouched, bent double, then raised my arm and, with my hand all besmeared and sticky, turned the handle, after which I collapsed, dismayed, face downwards on the tiles. The first drops descended, scanty and warm. With closed eyes I awaited the cold, abundant, purifying stream. But nothing came. The shower, obviously, was out of order; or, as was more likely, the water in the tanks was low. Nevertheless I stayed as I was, my eyes closed. 'His' treachery aroused a feeling of hatred in me: his victory, so uselessly opposed, a feeling of impotence. I said to myself that, in the semen which shortly before had overflowed through my fingers, there had perhaps been the creative, original idea which, as soon as I had started work, would have launched my film into the firmament of success, a stone hurled on high by the infallible catapult of sublimation. Who knows, perhaps at that very same moment the original, creative idea was drying up and withering and dying, and was turning into the unpleasant membrane in which the hairs of my groin and thighs were becoming entangled and stuck. Such thoughts went through my mind and at the same time I felt that I was ridiculous to be in such a state of despair at having masturbated (for it was just that which, against my will, I had ended up by doing). Finally I got up, went into the kitchen and, after turning on the taps, one after another, and finding them all to be dry, washed myself as best I could with mineral water. That infamous scoundrel, after destroying me, was of course silent. Later on I went and threw myself on my bed and slept until evening.

3   Mystified!

I went to the bank to draw out the five millions which, through 'his' fault, Maurizio had managed to extort from me by political blackmail.

I went there at opening time, in the afternoon. It was a splendid summer day. A blue sky, gleaming with light. A sea breeze blowing along the streets and fluttering the awnings of shops that were still closed. In spite of this affair of the five millions, I felt myself to be in a light-hearted, cheerful state of mind.

I said to 'him': 'You see what a lovely day it is. Nature doesn't care a damn about class struggles and revolution. It's a lovely day both for revolutionaries and for counter-revolutionaries. Think how fine it would be to leave everything – Maurizio, the five millions, the film, sublimation and de-sublimation – and go off together for a walk, in a carefree kind of way, enjoying the sensation of being alive, without any regrets.'

Encouraged, perhaps, by my confidential, friendly tone, 'he' at once betrayed himself: 'Yes, yes, let's go for a walk. Don't let us think any more about politics or the cinema. Instead, let's accost one of these many foreign female tourists – that one there, for instance, who is walking all alone in the direction of Piazza del Popolo. D'you remember last year? We stopped a German lady, not so very young, perhaps; but lively. What was she called? Yes, Trude. She was obsessed by the orgies of the ancient Romans and by the *dolce vita* of the modern Romans. *We* satisfied her. We went into the country, to a ravine in the direction of Ronciglione, a rural little spot well away from indiscreet eyes, and there we organized – what did you call it? – a "happening" in the pagan style. You yourself, naked as a worm, all hairy and comic-looking, with your big, haughty head like that of a Roman emperor of the decadence and your bald pate crowned with wild flowers. I, at full stretch and in splendid form, with my fine wreath of flowers hanging, so to speak, round my neck. And the German woman, in her brassière and opaque white cotton panties, her fair Nordic skin all reddened and flaking from the sun, taking one photograph after another, of you and of me; and you started dancing barefoot on the grass and I danced with you, in my own fashion, and the German woman laughed and laughed and laughed and called you – what did she call you?'

'The god Pan.'

'Yes, the god Pan. And then we chased her, you and I, and she ran away, among all those brambles, or rather she pretended to run away but actually she was looking for the most suitable place to stop and throw herself on the ground. You found her under a tree, in the thick grass, where other couples had already been, for the grass was all flattened and crushed, and there was even a used contraceptive; and it seemed really like a ready-made bed. The German woman gave a shrill cry and threw herself down on the ground and stayed there, flat on her back, motionless, with her legs opened and her arm over her eyes, waiting for me. Ah, what a glorious day! How I enjoyed myself! On the way back I was quite numb and worn out, but happy, oh yes, really happy.'

'This is typical of you,' I remarked coldly. 'I say that it's a fine day and you immediately take advantage of it to suggest some kind of mediocre adventure with a fading, middle-aged tourist. But will you understand, yes or no, that something, in fact *everything*, has changed inside me, and therefore between you and me? No tourist women. Now we'll draw the money, then we'll go back home and immediately start work.'

'What you mean to say,' 'he' remarked sourly, 'is, *I* will draw the money, *I* will go back home, *I* will start work.'

'Ah, so then, when it suits you, you use the plural; but when it doesn't suit you, you go back to the singular.'

'I'm sorry, but what have I got to do with your silly political aspirations and your artistic ambitions?'

'What have *you* got to do with them? This, precisely, is our tragedy. Unfortunately, you don't have anything to do

with them. If you did your duty, you would take your share –
and what a difference that would make.'

'Duty, what duty? I haven't any duties.'

'The duty not to confiscate, for your own exclusive
advantage, the inheritance of sexual energy of which, unfortunately, you are one of the two beneficiaries.'

'And who would the other beneficiary be?'

'I myself.'

'There we are, then: sublimation.'

'Precisely. And by refusing to undergo the process of
sublimation, you show yourself to be antisocial.'

'Antisocial? What sort of thing is that?'

'The opposite of social.'

'Social, antisocial: to me these are words empty of
meaning.'

'And yet, for these meaningless words, men are even ready
to die.'

'Yes, it's just that which astonishes me. That anyone
should prefer the thing that is not, that does not exist, to what
is, what does exist.'

'What is, what does exist, would be you, I suppose?'

'So I should say.'

While these pleasantries were being exchanged, I had
crossed the centre of the city, had parked the car in a small
square and started off on foot towards the bank. It was a great
barrack of a place, stuccoed and magniloquent, with a façade
full of niches, cornices and statues. I went through the main
door, between two Corinthian pillars; I went through the
entrance-hall between two walls of marble; I went through the
anteroom between four glass doors and started down the great
staircase which descended in a wide spiral to the basement. The
room where the strong-boxes were kept was down there. I
went down slowly, resting my hand on the cold, smooth
marble balustrade. I had a feeling that I was going down into
the crypt of a church – and not merely because the room was
underground. In truth, the bank is a temple in veneration of a
god who is not mine, the god of those whom, as a revolutionary,
it would be my duty to fight against. Instead of which, there

62

I was, my tail between my legs even though my face wore its accustomed look of haughtiness, going down to burn a grain of incense beneath the altar of the enemy god.

I had a strong feeling of guilt and, for once in a way, the guilt was not on 'his' side but exclusively on my own. I felt I was playing the fool: on the one hand I was vindicating, towards Maurizio, my character as a rebel, as a revolutionary; on the other, I had bought bonds and securities and dollars, had saved up money, and was the holder of a strong-box (for me the term had an obviously humiliating significance). That kind of security, if I were consistent, I ought to seek simply and solely in ideology. 'He', of course, did not consider the matter at all in this light. Suddenly he cried: 'Long live money! What should I do without money?'

'You'd manage perfectly well, don't worry. And everything would be clearer and better and cleaner.'

'Oh no, you stupid moralist. Without money, I should be like a man without a hand, without an arm. Money is my most effective and most infallible instrument and, at the same time, my privileged symbol. Instead of those insipid images of so-called great men, they ought to print *me* on the banknotes, as I am at my moments of greatest exaltation.'

'A very good idea: instead, for instance, of Michelangelo or Verdi, you. A very good idea, even if rather unpractical.'

'Money is me and I am money. When you shove a rolled-up banknote into a small hand, it's just as if you were shoving *me* in, neither more nor less.'

'I don't shove anything in anywhere.'

'You have a poor memory. A year ago. In your own house. That little cook, dark and with an almost monstrously rounded figure – you described her as "callipygous" – was standing in front of the stove, in an apron that was too long for her, and was vigorously stirring the polenta pot with a wooden spoon. And into her apron pocket you put a little roll of banknotes, five thousand lire to be precise, so that she should allow you, or rather, *me*, to do what I wanted.'

It was no use. 'He' has an infallible memory. He remembers everything, he remembers, above all, the things I don't want to remember. I reached the bottom of the big staircase. I presented myself at the counter, completed the usual formalities, then followed the clerk as he led me towards the gate with the big crossed iron bars behind which, after going down a few more steps, one finally reaches the strong-box room. The clerk, a sort of sacristan with bent shoulders, an emaciated, yellowish neck and flowing hair with bald patches like mange, opened the gate, preceded me down the stairs, took the key from me and left me to go and fetch my strong-box.

I stood in the middle of the room and looked round. The walls were lined with metal lockers; half-way up was a gallery which allowed access to other lockers, away up under the ceiling. Some of the lockers were open, and inside them could be seen rows and rows of steel boxes, all alike, each with its lock and its number. Again the idea came back to me of a subterranean chapel, partly, perhaps, owing to the smell of paper money which seemed to me to be hovering in the air, a smell slightly reminiscent of the reek of incense and candle-grease in churches.

Yes, I said to myself, it is really true, I am in a holy place, dedicated to a cult. That clerk does not merely look like a sacristan, he is one. Those strong-boxes do not merely look like caskets in a catacomb in which relics of saints and martyrs are preserved; they *are*. All that was lacking was a priest or a priestess.

Suddenly 'he' broke in, brisk and lively: 'There she is!'

'Why, who?'

'The priestess.'

I raised my eyes in the direction indicated by him, and looked. In the room there were four tables, each one divided in turn into four sections by screens of green frosted glass. The tables were lit by lamps with tulip-shaped shades of opaque glass. There was no one in the room except, at one of the tables, the 'priestess'. Her back was turned towards me. I saw an almost masculine head, with golden blonde hair cut or rather, I should say, clipped very short, in a 'bobbed' style. Her neck was round, white and strong. Her black dress showed off, below the neck, the shining whiteness of her shoulders. I said to 'him': 'Why priestess? What is there priestly about her?'

'I beg you, look under the table.'

'What then?'

'Her legs. Don't you see that this woman's legs have a certain special look about them?'

'I don't see anything. Or rather, I see a very short, black miniskirt and almost the entire length, from feet to groin, of two legs in flesh-coloured tights.'

'Nothing else?'

'I see that they are without any doubt straight, well-made legs, but not so very thin, in fact rather robust, the legs of a grown-up, even though still young, woman.'

'That's not the point.'

'What is the point, then?'

'Never mind; go and sit down opposite her.'

'But why?'

'I tell you, go and sit opposite her.'

I did as I was told and went and sat opposite the 'priestess'. The opaque glass that separated us allowed me, nevertheless, to catch a glimpse, through the frosted panel, of what she was doing: armed with a pair of scissors, she was cutting the coupons from the pages of the bonds. The clerk, meanwhile, placed my strong-box on the table, inserted the key, with a ritual gesture, into the lock, without turning it, however; then he went away.

I opened the box. It was full, crammed with bundles of carefully rolled sheets, the illuminated, multicoloured sheets of my bonds. The dollars were at the bottom, underneath the sheets. My savings. The savings of the revolutionary, the rebel, the mutineer, invested, as it is called, in industrial securities which automatically place the aforementioned revolutionary among the capitalists, the unlawful holders of the means of production. Yes, I am a rebel. I have been a rebel all my life; nevertheless these sheets of paper bear witness to the fact that I am at the same time an accomplice, even in a minor degree, of the 'system'.

I sighed and began pulling the rolls of securities out of the box. I was now wondering whether it would be best to hand over the five millions in dollars or to sell some shares. It was true that the dollars yielded no interest, whereas the shares do. But the devaluation of the lira, so often announced, might suddenly reduce the value of the shares by 10 or even 20 per cent; while, on the other hand, there was no talk of devaluation of the dollar, at that moment anyhow. In the end, however, I made up my mind to return to my first decision: I would sell five millions' worth of shares.

But which ones? The State Railways, at $6\frac{1}{2}$ per cent? The Pibigas, at 5 per cent? The Isveimer, at 6? The Romana Elettricità? The Ilva? The Alitalia? The Fiat? I sighed again with a genuine even if histrionic feeling of guilt, and decided for the Iri Sider at $5\frac{1}{2}$ per cent. I detached from the roll ten orange-coloured sheets of half a million each; I put them aside on the table; I then began putting back the rolls of the other bonds into the strong-box. My feeling of guilt had made me forget the 'priestess'. But 'he' didn't slacken. Suddenly he whispered to me, like one possessed: 'Let one of those sheets slip on to the floor, stoop down to pick it up and look at her legs.'

'Oh, shut up about her legs!'

'Do as I say and you won't be sorry.'

'But why?'

'Because your feeling of guilt will be lessened or even completely wiped out by the discovery of the *true* purpose of this visit to the bank.'

'The true purpose of my visit to the bank is the handing over of the five millions to Maurizio.'

'No, the true purpose is your encounter with this woman. Stoop down, then; what are you waiting for?'

I did so, though unwillingly. With my elbow I pushed one of the bonds off the table; the sheet fell to the floor; I stooped down to pick it up and paused a moment to look at the 'priestess's' legs. This time, my suspicions aroused by 'his' insistence, I could not help noticing some singularities. First of all I realized that I had been mistaken: the legs were not encased in tights; they were bare. I was struck by their glossy,

clean, as it were scraped, brilliant whiteness, the special whiteness that is characteristic of certain blonde women. A whiteness
which, I suddenly thought, to my surprise, was mysteriously
impure, precisely, perhaps, because it was so glossy and so
immaculate. 'He' asked me, meanwhile: 'Well then, wasn't I
right?'

I pretended not to understand. 'You were right, they're
beautiful.'

'That's not the question.'

'What is the question, then?'

'Don't you see that there's something . . . obscene about
those legs?'

'Why obscene?'

'Because they're "closed".'

He was right. What I called 'impure' and he called
'obscene' came from the fact that the legs, stretched out
and close together, the two feet resting on the bar of the table,
were, indeed, 'closed', that is, tightly locked, as it were
hermetically sealed, like the jaws of a trap. 'He', meanwhile,
was explaining: 'They are obscene because, by being so tightly
closed, in a way they are defying you to open them. As
with the valves of an oyster, you feel they're guarding something and that they'll use all their strength to resist anyone
who tries to open them, and for this very reason they arouse
the desire to open them and see what they're so jealously
defending.'

He whispered these remarks very hurriedly; and meanwhile, to my great embarrassment, he became, as usual,
enormous. 'That's good, that idea of the oyster,' I replied.
'But now, unfortunately, it's time for us to go.' As I said this,
I picked up the sheet of paper, sat up straight again and went
on replacing the rolls of bonds in the strong-box. But he gave
me a sudden order:

'Take off your right shoe.'

'Eh, what d'you say?'

'Or the left one, it's all the same.'

'But what for?'

'What d'you mean, what for? It's obvious: so as to slip

67

your foot between her legs and then push it upwards, as far up as you can.'

'Goodness me, are you mad? That's a thing one can't do, a thing that might start a scandal.'

'Certainly it might. But if it doesn't, then . . .'

'Then what?'

'Then it'll mean it's a thing one *can* do.'

Once again I obeyed, even though I was frightened. I bent down, put out my hand to my right foot, slipped off my shoe and noiselessly placed it on the floor. Then I inserted my foot between the pair of feet resting close together on the bar of the table. A miracle! The two feet were not drawn back, nor did they resist. As my own foot pushed its way in, not even very strongly, they drew apart, they opened. Now my foot moved upwards between the two ankle-bones and then between the two calves, without meeting any difficulties. Gradually the legs, as my foot ventured upwards, unfastened themselves – 'naturally', one would have said, that is, resisting just enough to create the impression that they were not controlled by any sort of will-power and that they were opening simply because my foot was opening them. I continued to slide my foot upwards. Now I became aware of the hardness of her knees at each side of my ankle. A moment more, and then they too yielded, unhurriedly, with the majestic, enigmatic slowness with which, in the tale of Sinbad the Sailor, the doors of the treasure cavern moved gradually apart. But the 'priestess' was sitting too far away from me for my foot to be able to reach beyond her knees. Then 'he' intervened with some advice: 'Lie back in your chair so that you can stretch your pelvis as far out as possible.'

'But supposing someone comes in and sees me lying back like that, with my stockinged foot between the legs of a female client, what will he think of me?'

'He'll think that you're a courageous, open-minded, enterprising man.'

Flatterer! However, I said to myself that now, if only to satisfy a legitimate curiosity, I must see the thing through to the end. So, after casting a glance all round and confirming that the room was still empty; after looking through the frosted glass and noting that the 'priestess's' two hands were continuing, imperturbably, to cut out coupons, I stretched forward with my pelvis, lying almost flat on my chair, and consequently succeeded, at once, in pushing my foot much farther up, probably not so very far from her crotch. But I did not reach it. However much I bent my toes, inside my sock, to reconnoitre the place, I did not feel the soft luxuriance of pubic hair beneath the tops of my toes. Instead – what a surprise! – all of a sudden the two thighs, again like the ruthless valves of a shellfish or, better, the treacherous jaws of a trap, closed upon my ankle, very tightly, in such a way that I could go neither up nor down. Were they sweating, those thighs that gripped my ankle, or was it I who was sweating? In any case an intense heat, damp and at the same time strangely 'cold', issued from that sheath of bare flesh.

'He', however, did not lose heart; optimistic and as usual lacking in discernment, he reassured me: 'Don't be discouraged, the legs will open, oh yes, they'll open all right.'

'That may be. But I can't stay like this for ever, lying flat on my chair with my ankle imprisoned between these formidable muscles. Just like a poacher who's put his foot in a trap.'

'You'll see, they'll open in a moment.'

And indeed they did open. But only to dislodge me. All of a sudden the grip was relaxed just enough to allow my foot to fall down into empty space. And then the woman turned sideways and crossed her legs. Infuriated, I said: 'As usual, you've made a fool of me and I've achieved absolutely nothing.'

Filled with rage, I bent down, picked up my shoe and put it on again. Then I sat up, folded the sheets of the bonds in four and slipped them into my pocket. Through the green glass I could see the hands of the 'priestess' closing her strong-box. I did the same. And then the clerk appeared, took her strong-box, went and inserted it into its niche, came back and handed over the key to her. The 'priestess' might very well go away now: there was nothing left for her to do. But no, she sat still, her hands crossed under her chin; it seemed as if she were observing me through the glass. Jubilantly, 'he' exclaimed: 'She's waiting for us, she wants to leave at the same time as we do.'

And actually, it was so. The clerk came back, gave me my key, I rose to my feet; and only then did the 'priestess' rise too. I walked in front of her and could hear her coming up the stairs behind me: on the threshold I stood aside and she passed in front of me, thanking me with a nod of the head. At the counter there was a repetition of the same game as in the room downstairs: she was the first to receive her card; but she waited until I had had mine. Finally we went off together up the main staircase. Almost immediately I slowed down and contrived to linger behind so as to observe her better.

At that same moment she turned half round as if to see whether I was following her, and I saw her face clearly. It was an energetic, masculine face, with pale cheeks, a large mouth and a delicately modelled nose. She looked at me with eyes of a dark, nocturnal, lightless blue, eyes that were dilated and with a wide-open, staring look. It was a thin face, but her body was not thin. In fact it was rather massive; with something at the same time childish about it. Or was this an effect of the very short skirt, a little girl's skirt, which hung above the muscular, adult, completely womanly legs? In any case it had a certain infantile character, with a touch of parody, as if a mother of a family (and I was sure that she had at least one child) had dressed up, for fun, as a little girl.

We came out into the street. The unknown woman was walking in front of me; and all at once I said to myself that this game had gone on long enough and I felt I should leave her to go her own way while I myself made for a café. But 'he' immediately protested: 'Why, what are you doing? Follow her, you must follow her. Didn't you notice that in the bank, while you were getting back your card, she lowered her eyes and looked at me with obvious, flattering interest?'

Heavens! I in turn lowered my eyes and became conscious that my trousers were hoisted up and stretched tight as though by a big spike. Hastily I put my hand into my pocket and gave 'him' a half turn upwards, as one does with the hand of a clock that has stopped at the wrong time. Again 'he' protested: 'Leave me as I am, I want her to see me; what does it matter to you? I want her to notice me, leave me alone.'

I paid no attention to him and, hastening my step, came up almost beside the woman. In the meantime, however, I saw myself as I was: rust-coloured jacket, open at the neck, green canvas trousers, open sandals. Big bald head, short stature, stomach sticking out, short legs. And finally, the inevitable hand in the pocket. I told myself that it was ridiculous and presumptuous of me to have attempted to approach such a beautiful woman in the bank and now to be following her in the street. But 'he' encouraged me: 'Don't be afraid and don't change your mind. Beautiful women love men like you, with your virile endowments. Now cheer up and get on with it!'

Certainly I was not lacking in courage. When she reached the same little square in which, shortly before, I had parked my car, she went over to a foreign car with a CD number-plate and was about to open the door; but I walked quickly round the bonnet of the car, opened the other door and sat down beside her, saying: 'Good afternoon.'

She glanced at me, hesitated, and I was prepared to suffer the usual loss of face. But no. After a moment that seemed to me extremely long, she answered: 'Good afternoon.'

Her voice was clear, distinct, slightly ironical perhaps; but not really hostile. She started the engine and backed out of the square, turning in her seat as she did so. This movement caused her breasts to swell visibly in the low neck of her dress; they were solid, spherical and of a singular hardness, as though the white, glossy skin concealed, not a delicate group of glands, but a knot of strong, virile muscles. We started driving along the Corso and I, suddenly, was frightened. What was I doing in this car beside an unknown woman? The 'priestess', according to 'him', had looked at him in the bank with 'obvious, flattering interest'. But now she was carrying me off to her own house where, at best, I should be forced to find an excuse for drawing back and thus, yet again, I should lose face. At this point 'he' intervened, in an authoritative manner: 'Leave it to me.'

'That's just what I want to avoid,' I replied.

'Leave it to me. I promise you that the precious liquid will not be squandered, if that's what you're afraid of.'

'I'm not afraid of anything, but . . .'

'Leave it to me.'

'What am I to infer? That you wish to carry on the dialogue, directly, by yourself?'

'Exactly.'

Well, let us allow him to do so, just this once. Mentally I retired into a corner from which, with detachment and at a distance, I could observe the edifying little scene that took place between the two of them. This was how it went. 'He' attacked at once, in a deplorably conventional way: 'My name's Federico, what's yours?'

'Irene.'

'Irene, what a pretty name. You know that in Greek it means "peace"?'

How the devil did he come to know that? Borrowed from me, obviously.

'Peace?' answered Irene. 'I didn't know. And you – what did you say your name was?'

'Federico. But please call me Rico.'

'Very well: Rico. How are you, Rico?'

'At this moment I'm well, because I'm close to you.'

Ridiculous! Disgusting! Exactly the remark that a conscript on leave might make to a rustic servant-girl. 'Thank you, that's very nice of you,' replied Irene in a quiet voice in which, however, there was a perceptible hint of irony.

A brief silence followed. Then 'he' inquired: 'Where are we going?'

'To my home.'

'Where do you live?'

'In the E.U.R. quarter.'

'That's a nice quarter, airy and quiet and with lots of green.'

'Yes, there are plenty of trees.'

'And then the streets are wide and you can park a car wherever you like.'

'Yes, it's a very convenient quarter, even though rather a long way off.'

I could not refrain from a secret, derisive smile. Here was Mr 'Leave-it-to-me' quite unable, in spite of the airs he gave himself, to go beyond the limits of ordinary middle-class conversation. But no, I was mistaken, I had made too hasty a judgment. Suddenly, in fact, and quite unexpectedly, 'he' changed his tone. 'My name is Federico, that is true,' he said. 'But I have another name as well.'

'A nickname?'

'Not exactly. Let us say, a secret name.'

'Secret?'

'Yes, because the thing it refers to is also secret.'

'Secret?'

'Irene, may I tell you something in confidence?'

'Certainly, Rico, of course you may.'

'Well, I am – I can say this calmly, because it is perfectly true – I am exceptionally well endowed by nature. You understand me, don't you?'

'I think I understand you. But I don't want to make any mistake. You must explain yourself more clearly.'

'Well, to explain myself more clearly, let me tell you that I am in possession of a sexual organ which is absolutely out of the ordinary'.

'You don't say so! Out of the ordinary?'

'Yes, absolutely out of the ordinary.'

'But how can you know that? What I mean is – are you judging just by eye, or do you know for certain?'

'I've compared it with the average, and have found it quite exceptional.'

'But how did you come to know what the average is?'

'I questioned a doctor friend of mine who examines conscripts when they're called up for national service.'

'Ah, I see. Quite right. I ought to have thought of it. And your measurements – what would they be?'

'Twenty-five centimetres in length, eighteen in circumference and two and a half kilos in weight.'

'You've even weighed it?'

'Certainly.'

'But how did you manage that?'

'I stood on tiptoe and rested it on the brass plate of the kitchen scales.'

'And those measurements are above the average?'

'Yes, by far.'

There was no denying that, after an opening conversation worthy of a good middle-class drawing-room, 'he' had now recovered and, not without embarrassment and shame on my part, was going full-steam ahead. Irene, without turning her head as she drove, asked in her calm, ironical voice: 'You told me a moment ago that you have a secret name which in fact refers to these extraordinary measurements. What is this name?'

May the devil take him! He has no modesty! He has no discretion! He blurts everything out! Absolutely everything! Indeed, there he was, answering without hesitation: 'I've told you that my name is Federico. But in reality there co-exist inside me two persons: I and "he". I am ... I; "he" ... is "he". And so, in order not to create any confusion, since my name is Federico or rather Rico, I call him Federicus Rex.'

'Federicus Rex? What an odd idea! And why?'

'Federicus Rex – that is, Frederick of Prussia – was a famous king, a victorious king. In fact he is also known as Frederick the Great. D'you see the point?'

'Yes, I think I do.'

'Certainly it would be more logical for him to be called, simply, Frederick the Great. Actually I am rather small in stature, whereas "he", on the other hand, is great, in fact very great. But I prefer Federicus Rex. If only because it's more poetical. Frederick the Great is too explicit. Great: it already says everything, and there are no surprises left. On the other hand, Federicus Rex says and yet doesn't say, it leaves the greatness in the shade and brings out the regal quality. For it was women who gave me the idea of calling him Federicus Rex. They called him "the king", or, positively, "the king of kings", like the ancient emperors of Persia. It was natural, in the end, to name him Federicus Rex in order to distinguish him from me. D'you see the point now?'

'Yes, I see it quite clearly.'

'Women admire him, even though some of them wouldn't like to admit it. D'you know what they call him sometimes, apart from the "king"?'

'No.'

'Well, you can imagine–His Royal Highness, Royal Length, Royal Thickness, Royal Magnitude. And so on, in that sort of way. Silly women's jokes.'

'But pleasant jokes, aren't they?'

'Yes, pleasant, in the sense that they show this exceptional quality of his to be not, after all, just the fruit of my imagination. It's a real, recognizable, visible fact. Sometimes, indeed, so real and so visible as to be embarrassing.'

'As it was just now in the bank, wasn't it? I saw you were handling it all the time.'

'Really it was too obvious; I was trying to contain it, to control it. Because you must know that it's very impatient, in fact, I would say, arrogant.'

'Like all kings, eh?'

'Ha, ha! You're right. Kings are impatient. Arrogant. Now, for instance, d'you know what he wants, in fact what he demands, from you?'

'What's that?'

'That you should drive with one hand, and with the other squeeze him hard, but really hard, as hard as you can.'

So there we were! It couldn't be denied that 'he' had, as they say, made rapid progress. What impudence! What coolness! What courage! Never should I be able to equal it, never. Nor, in any case, did I desire to do so: each one must play his own part. But ... but ... but, all of a sudden, upon 'his' blazing heat fell an unexpected, pitiless douche of cold water. For a moment Irene was silent, then she answered coldly: 'I'm not accustomed to driving with only one hand.'

'Now look here!'

'Nor am I accustomed to paying homage of a certain kind to these regal qualities.'

Collapse! Débâcle! Crash! Vertical, vertiginous downfall!

Everything was now clear: Irene had flattered 'his' boundless vanity and 'he' had fallen for it, up to the eyes; and then Irene had put him, coldly and brutally, in his place. Sarcastically I said to 'him': 'Mr "Leave-it-to-me" has got what he deserved: the customary mortification, the customary loss of face. D'you agree now that I had better take in hand the situation which has been so stupidly compromised by you?'

'He' did not reply; perhaps he was too humiliated to speak. I interpreted his silence as consent and turned to Irene with airy, urbane geniality. 'But why should we talk about me?' I said. 'Instead, tell me something about yourself.'

'I've nothing to tell.'

'Are you married?'

'Yes. And separated.'

'Do you live with a diplomat?'

'Why a diplomat?'

'Your car has a CD number-plate.'

'Oh yes. It's a car belonging to the embassy where I work. My own car is being repaired, so the Secretary very kindly lent me his.'

'Which embassy is that?'

'The embassy of an Arab country.'

'But your husband – where is he?'

'My husband? In Milan.'

'And what does he do?'

'He works in advertising.'

'And . . . you live alone?'

'I live with my little girl, who is called Virginia and is nine years old. Anything else?'

'I'm sorry. But I'm not one of those individuals who are obsessed by sex, for whom there is nothing . . . for whom, in short, there is nothing but that one thing.'

'Well, well! How about Federicus Rex?'

'That was all just a joke. Don't give it another thought. For me a woman is, first and foremost, a person. I like to know who she is, what she does, what she thinks, where she comes from, where she goes. Sex is the last thing.'

We reached the E.U.R. quarter. Streets with arcades, squares with arcades, avenues with arcades, open spaces with arcades, covered walks with arcades. In the middle of the main square, an obelisk clothed in blazing light by the summer afternoon sunshine. 'He', apparently far from subdued, suddenly came to life. 'All these arcades, these obelisks. Say to her, just in a joking kind of way, that it may perhaps be true that she doesn't pay homage of a certain kind to certain regal qualities; but that, living as she does amongst so many pillars and obelisks, the traditional symbols of what I am or, rather, of what I can turn into, there would be every reason to doubt it.'

I was on the point of telling him that his joke was vulgar and in very bad taste. But it was too late. Irene's car circled round the E.U.R. church, entered a street, the Via Eufrate, slowed down and stopped beside the pavement.

Irene put on the handbrake, opened the door and got out. I also got out. Via Eufrate has, on one side, a row of villas; on the other, it overhangs the valley of the Tiber. Down there in the valley could be seen the long, low sheds of some factories; then the river, which here makes a great loop, with its smooth, yellow water; finally, on the far shore, a long hill, pale green, in the shape of a table. Irene crossed the street without bothering to see whether I was following her. From sitting in the car, her dress had remained caught up between her buttocks. As she walked, she put her hand behind her, pulled at her skirt and freed it.

Irene opened the gate, walked quickly across the garden between plots of mown grass, along a cement path flanked by small trees pruned to the shape of balls and cones and pyramids. I followed her up the polished, resonant staircase of the villa, until we reached a door of light-coloured wood with a name-plate and handles of spotless brass. She led me into a spacious living-room with two wide-open french windows. The light was strong and pleasant, like the light off the sea. The wind lifted and blew out the green curtains, which then, no less slowly, straightened out again and fell back. Irene flattered me by saying: 'I won't go to the Embassy today, so as to stay here with you. Wait while I telephone.' And she went out.

Filled with a vague, uncertain happiness, I looked round. The furniture was modern but – how can I express it? – of a penultimate modernity, that is, it consisted of pieces which were just beginning to be in fashion some years ago and which, recently, have come to be mass-produced. Low pieces of furniture, of geometrical forms; red, green, blue divans; chairs, little tables and lamps of plastic. Everything was new, as if on exhibition in a big store. Yet at the same time everything was singularly evocative of a presence. What presence? The presence that consisted, strangely, in the 'absence' of Irene.

She came back again. 'Sit there, will you?' she said, indicating one of the divans. She herself went and sat down on the divan opposite. Between us there was a small, low table of steel and glass. We looked at one another. Irene sat with her legs bent and close together, so tightly pressed one against the other as to make me think that not even the blade of a knife, let alone 'he', could be inserted between them. Looking at me with curiosity, as though seeing me for the first time, she began: 'And so you go to the bank, into the strong-box room, take off your shoe and thrust your foot between the legs of a woman you don't even know by sight?'

I felt myself blushing and, mentally, I turned angrily upon 'him': 'That's the sort of thing I have to listen to!' Nevertheless Irene's tone had not been really hostile. If anything, it was indulgent, amused. Embarrassed, I said: 'That doesn't often happen with me. This was an exceptional case.'

'What was exceptional about it?'

'I don't know. Your legs, perhaps.'

'In me it's the legs that are exceptional, in another woman it would be the bosom, in yet another the bottom – isn't that so?'

'Yes, it's a bit like that, but . . .'

'You are, in fact, one of those men who get into buses and stand close against women in order to touch them.'

'Yes, that has happened too, but . . .'

78

'Who look through keyholes at maidservants undressing.'

'I did that when I was living at home with my parents and was fifteen years old.'

'Now, on the other hand, with maidservants, you lay hands on them quite boldly, don't you?'

'Yes, that could happen, nevertheless . . .'

'And I'll bet you go into suburban cinemas, stand behind a girl, take her hand and make her do what you wanted me to do just now, in the car?'

'Well, that may be true too, however . . .'

'In fact, you're always ready to take on an adventure, and it doesn't much matter who it's with, provided it's a woman.'

Hitherto I had in fact interrupted Irene only in a feeble sort of way. And this was partly because 'he' continued obstinately to repeat: 'Let her talk, let her relieve her feelings. Let her have her say. Can't you hear, from her tone, that the whole thing's a sham?' But, in the end, I rebelled. 'No, it's not like that,' I said. 'And will you please tell me: did you bring me home with you just in order to throw all these not exactly pleasant things in my face?'

'But they're true!'

'Only in part.'

'Anyhow you admit that you're a certain type of man?'

'What d'you mean by "a certain type of man"?'

'The sex-maniac type, enterprising to the point of folly, but not all that successful; or am I wrong?'

'Not altogether unsuccessful. Successful – so so.'

'So so, eh? Let's say twenty per cent.'

'No, let's say fifty per cent.'

'Isn't that too much? Aren't you deceiving yourself?'

It was clear that she was amusing herself behind my back; but without unkindness, perhaps even sympathetically. I felt, however, that I must put a stop to her mockery even if it was not malevolent. I said firmly: 'That's enough, now. Enough is as good as a feast. I am not what you think I am.'

'I don't think anything. I go by appearances.'

'Good heavens, one can't, one ought not to, reduce a man

to a mere cipher, to a single failing: that man's ambitious, that man's lazy, Rico's a sex maniac . . .'

'Now, now, don't get angry.'

'In my place anyone would get angry.'

'Tell me, then, what you really are. So far, when all's said and done, I've had to do mainly with a certain Federicus Rex. You've told me you are called Rico. Tell me about Rico.'

'I'm a film director.'

'A film director? Have you made many films?'

'No, none as yet.'

'Then you're not a film director.'

'I shall be in a fortnight's time, when I begin work on my first film.'

'Are you married?'

'Yes, I have a wife and child.'

'Do you love your wife?'

'Certainly I do. Very much indeed.'

'One wouldn't think so, however.'

'Are you again alluding to what happened in the bank? But that was a moment of weakness and might happen to anybody.'

For a moment she was silent, staring at me with those enigmatic, inhuman eyes with their dilated, unseeing pupils. She seemed to be reflecting. Then, with a penetration that was almost frightening to me, she said: 'Well then, shall we lay the blame for it on Federicus Rex? Shall we do that?'

'Yes, let's do that.'

'Let's even wipe out the memory of what happened in the bank. Let's try and behave in such a way that Federicus Rex never intrudes into our relationship again. Never again. If you agree on this point, which, at least for me, is extremely important, I am ready to be friends with you. D'you agree or not?'

What was happening to me? Her intuition, so exact and at the same time so casual, about my utterly secret and private obsession moved me in a profound and novel fashion. Suddenly something inside me seemed to be torn from top to bottom, like the backcloth of a theatre during an open-air performance, struck by a gust of wind in a thunderstorm. And there I was, transported in a second by that same gust of wind, there I was kneeling at Irene's feet, my arms round her legs, my forehead against her knees, my eyes closed.

It was a kind of violent abduction. But that did not prevent me from questioning myself upon the true nature of this extraordinary transportation. Would I then find myself faced, yet again, with a despicable sentimental-type manifestation of my incurable desublimation? Or was there something new about this precipitated feeling of mine for Irene, so sudden, so inspired, so overwhelming, thanks to which I had risen from the divan, moved round the table, fallen on my knees and embraced her legs – and all this, magically, without my being conscious of it? And this 'something new' – could it not possibly be a form, barely taking shape as yet, of sublimation? Of the sublimation which, like a treasure, I had been hoarding up for six months for 'my' film and which, all of a sudden and in spite of myself, had now directed itself towards Irene?

At this thought I pressed myself more strongly against Irene's legs, my arms encircling them in desperation, like the arms of a shipwrecked mariner clinging to the dismantled mast of a sinking ship. Yes indeed, it was sublimation that was recognizable in the quality – how shall I describe it? – the Ariel-like quality of my feeling. A quality that allowed one to suppose that, in all probability, 'he', the insidious Caliban, had finally resigned himself to doing what should have been simply his duty: disappearing.

With these thoughts in my mind I still kept my eyes closed. I felt Irene's hand resting on my head and gently stroking it and I reflected triumphantly: Yes, there we are, I love Irene and Irene loves me. And 'he' has been defeated, finally and for ever. Irene's hand, meanwhile, moved down in a perfectly innocent manner from my bald head to my cheek. Now you must know that I have particularly sensitive ears which are, so it seems, directly linked with 'him'. One of Irene's fingers brushed lightly against my left ear; a shiver ran down my back; and then, to my profound consternation, I

heard the wily voice of the usual ignoble personage con-
gratulating me in the following manner: 'Well done, that's
good, very good, very well done, that's the way to do it.
What I mean is, you've done extremely well to transfer yourself, bag and baggage, on to the plane of love. You are right:
when all is said and done, it's still love, whether it's true or
false doesn't matter, that gets the most reward, that brings us
most surely and swiftly to the achievement of our purpose.
Now, however, seeing that the first trench has fallen, let us go
on to attacking the fortress, frankly and without any further
deceits. So you must thrust your forehead hard between her
knees, forcing them open by the sheer pressure of your face,
in such a way that she will be carried away by your im-
petuosity and will all at once find herself, so to speak, mouth
to mouth. Don't be afraid; once you're there all will be well;
just leave it to me.'

I felt that 'he' was wrong. I felt that 'he' was ruining
everything. I felt that that usual 'leave it to me' would be
followed by the usual loss of face. I felt, in short, that 'he' had
nothing to do with the feeling of real, genuine, authentic love
that had made me fly to Irene's feet. And yet, in spite of these
presentiments, my evil genius got the better of me. Slyly, and
while continuing to embrace her legs, I began gently pushing
my forehead against her knees, as if seeking to suggest to
Irene that she should yield to me spontaneously, as of her own
free will. But her knees remained close together, more tightly
so than ever. Then I frankly seized hold of them with both
hands and, straining my whole body, strove to unlock them.

What I had foreseen, happened. Irene did not yield, she
did not 'leave it to him'. Instead, a very hard blow from her
knee struck me, with outrageous violence, full in the face. I fell
backwards with my bottom on the floor and my back against
the table. Irene, not content with the blow from her knee,
dealt me a kick on the shoulder, not angrily but with contempt.

Then she said seriously, in a dry, unpleasant manner: 'Sit
there and behave yourself. Otherwise I shall be forced to chuck
you out.'

4 Frustrated!

I was now furious with 'him', furiously angry for having made me lose face for the millionth time. And, apart from 'him', I was furious with myself for having allowed him free play. Rising suddenly to my feet, I said: 'I'll behave perfectly well. So well that I'll go away.'

'Come on, don't take it like that.'

'And how ought I to take it?'

'With more spirit. If you could see how funny you look!'

'What is there funny about me?'

'Why, you're all red and furious and at the same time with that enormous thing ... I mean Federicus Rex, I beg your pardon ... almost bigger than yourself.'

'I'm funny and I'm going away.'

'No, no, stay, you're not funny; or rather, you are, but with a nice kind of funniness.'

'Why should I stay?'

'Stay and I'll explain.'

'Explain what?'

'Why there can't ever be anything but friendship between us.'

'I'm going away; I don't need any explanations, still less friendship.'

'So I'm forced to think that you're just like all other men: if you can't do that particular thing, a woman doesn't interest you.'

An interruption by 'him': 'Precisely. We're only interested in that one thing. Let's go away; what are we waiting for?'

My reply to 'him' was: 'Seeing that you advise me to go away, I'm going to stay. For the first time in my life, perhaps, I shall be doing the right thing.'

Then I said to Irene: 'What is it you want to explain? There's nothing to explain. You don't like me, that's all.'

'In your place I should at least ask some questions.'

'But what questions?'

'Why, in point of fact, have you so little curiosity? You go into a bank, you take off your shoe, you thrust your foot between the legs of an unknown woman. She allows you to do it, without protest; but later, just when you think you have the adventure within your grasp, she repulses you, she doesn't want to have anything to do with you. Don't you think there's something strange about my behaviour? In your place, I should have more curiosity.'

'Very well. Then tell me why you don't want to have anything to do with me.'

She gave a broad smile, as though she were pleased; but the smile did not go beyond her lips. Her eyes remained wide open, dilated, as though I were transparent and she were looking at something right through me. Then slowly, cruelly, she said: 'I repulsed you because I have no need of you.'

'No one has any need of anyone. But . . .'

'You don't understand. I am sufficient to myself. I have no need of any other person.'

'Of *any* other person?'

'Yes, yes, of a companion, an associate, a husband, a lover, a male – put it how you like.'

Still I failed to understand. It was 'he' who, with his usual brutality, suddenly opened my eyes: 'My word, you're getting stupid. Don't you realize that we're faced with a perfectly ordinary case of auto-eroticism? Come on, let's go, what is there to wait for?'

To 'him' I paid no attention. Irene's seriousness filled me with curiosity. 'Are you then, perhaps . . .?' I hazarded.

'Come on, don't be frightened of words.'

'Self-sufficient?'

'My God, what a polite man you are! Leave aside the euphemisms and talk about things as they are.'

'It's for you to talk about them; it's up to you to explain why you don't want me.'

'Well then, let us say that I masturbate.'

'You masturbate?'

'Yes, I masturbate.'

'Have you always masturbated?'

'Yes, always.'

'And masturbation suffices you?'

'Masturbation suffices me because, thanks to masturbation, I am sufficient to myself.'

'What's this, a play on words?'

'No, it's the truth.'

'Isn't it the truth, by any chance, that you're not capable of loving?'

'Masturbation, for me at least, is as good a way as any of loving and being loved.'

'Loving and being loved by whom?'

'Loving myself and being loved by myself.'

'But isn't it better to love oneself through one's love for another person?'

'What complications! Masturbation allows one to love oneself in a direct way, without any intermediary.'

'Loving someone means transforming the world around us.'

'In what way?'

'Making it more beautiful, more free, more profound.'

'Then masturbation is superior to love.'

'Why?'

'According to you, love makes the world more beautiful, more free, more profound. Masturbation does better: for the real world it substitutes another world which is perhaps less real but in compensation is absolutely to our own taste.'

'That isn't love. Loving means getting out of oneself, identifying oneself with another.'

'But why get out of oneself? Anyone who masturbates loves himself, that's true; but, inasmuch as he loves an imaginary self which functions in an imaginary world, he gets out of himself. In a way, anyone who masturbates gets out of himself though at the same time remaining inside himself.'

She spoke in a clear, calm, convinced manner, with a hint of the controversial about it, but of a reasonable, moderate kind, like one who has reflected on the things he is saying and who anyhow considers himself proof against any objection on the part of his interlocutor. One might have thought it was someone else speaking, from some unknown place; and that all she was doing was to keep her lips parted, so that the other person's discourse might issue from them.

I was seized suddenly with a sort of intellectual impatience which at once communicated itself to my body. I rose and began walking up and down the room, feeling myself, as usual, to be ridiculous: a small man, with a big bald head and short legs, and, into the bargain, with both hands behind him, thrust in between his trousers and his shirt, pressing against his bare buttocks – a bad habit to which I give way in moments of very intense thought. In the end I said: 'Now listen, Irene. Let's please come down from the heavens of abstraction and return to earth, if you don't mind.'

'But I'm not being abstract.'

'Let's stop rationalizing your auto-eroticism.'

'Rationalizing? What does that mean?'

'Rationalizing, at least in your case, means that you're trying to make rational something which is not so.'

'But who's rationalizing?'

'You are.'

'And what ought I to be doing instead?'

'A very simple thing; giving me information.'

'What about?'

'What d'you mean, what about? About your habit.'

'I told you to ask me questions. Do so, then. I'll give you all the information you want.' Then she went on: 'Sit down there, don't walk about like that; you look like a lunatic. Meanwhile I'll give you something to drink.'

I went back and sat down on the divan opposite hers. Irene got up, and, with the methodical movements suitable to an embassy secretary, went to the bar-trolley, took a glass, poured some whisky into it, added two ice cubes and then prepared a second glass in the same way. She handed me one of the glasses, kept one herself and sat down again. 'Perhaps you're right,' she said. 'Perhaps I was being rather abstract. Now I'll give you some information. You're a film director, aren't you?'

'Yes.'

'Then you'll be able to understand better when I tell you that, fundamentally, it's like being in the cinema.'

'I don't understand.'

'It's like a film show. But it's double, so to speak. That is, it's a show in which I'm a spectator twice over.'

'Again I'm sorry, but I still don't understand.'

'What I mean is that masturbation, at any rate as I practise it, consists of two scenes, quite distinct but simultaneous: the one that I follow with my eyes shut, in my imagination, and the one at which I am present in reality, as I open my eyes. The first is, as I have said, an imaginary scene, in which I figure, however, as a performer. The second is the scene that I create for myself, in reality, by being present at the first.'

'Forgive me, I'm slow on the uptake, I can't grasp this business of the double scene.'

'I'll explain by telling you what I do. In my bedroom there's a big triple looking-glass. In front of the glass there is a stool. Early in the morning, when everyone's still asleep, I get out of bed and go and sit on this stool, in front of the looking-glass. Generally I'm naked, but sometimes I may even be fully dressed. I sit down, then, on the stool and masturbate, looking alternatively at what I call my interior films and then at myself reflected in the three panels of the mirror, actually in the act of masturbating. Thus there are two scenes, one imaginary and the other real, one in my imagination and the other in the mirror. And I become equally excited both by representing certain things to myself in my imagination, and by watching the effect that the things I imagine have upon me. This goes on until the moment of orgasm. With the orgasm both scenes come to an end. Then I rise from the stool, attend to my little girl and go off to the office.'

She was silent, taking a sip of her drink, bending her face

over the glass but at the same time peering up at me as if to see the effect that her words had had upon me. 'He' at once broke in: 'Ask her now what it is that she calls her interior cinema.'

I answered him with irritation: 'I can imagine it perfectly well. It's the usual filthy things that people who masturbate think about.'

'But this is a special case. Come on, ask her; it interests me.'

I decided, unwillingly, to do so. 'You spoke of your interior cinema. Forgive my curiosity; but, if only as one who works in films, I should be very glad to know what it consists of, this so-called "interior cinema".'

'I was in a film studio one day and I watched a film on the monitor. The screen is small, but the pictures are clear. Moreover one can stop the film, go back and go forward again. Well, my interior cinema is rather like a film on a monitor. I invent a story, a brief incident. Then I masturbate, running through the story behind my closed eyes, on the screen, as it were, of my imagination. As with the monitor, I stop at the pictures I like best, or I turn back to look again at some of them upon which it seems to me that I didn't pause long enough. Sometimes the orgasm does not come at the first viewing. Then I repeat them again.'

'And how long have you been a . . . film director?'

'There's nothing to laugh at. I really am a film director, even if it's only for my own purpose and convenience. And how long have I been doing it? I've always done it.'

'Always?'

'Yes, I don't remember doing it for the first time. My first recollection of it goes back to when I was eight years old. But certainly that wasn't the first time.'

'But wasn't there, at the beginning, some kind of trauma, or at least some over-precocious experience inflicted upon you by an adult?'

'No, there was nothing. In the first film that I remember, I invented what you call a trauma. I imagined something happening to me which in reality had not happened to me.'

'Tell me about your first film.'

For a moment she was silent, gazing at me but as though without seeing me, as if she were really seeing her film with the eyes of imagination. Then she said: 'It was a film to which I still return sometimes. This was how it went. I was in the apartment of a neighbour of ours, at San Remo, where my family used to go for a summer holiday every year. Our neighbour was a croupier at the San Remo casino. He was a young man and attractive too, but it was as if he had grown old before his time. He had a big white forehead and scanty hair, fine and fluffy blond; pale, lifeless blue eyes; an aristocratic nose. He was called Rolando, he was married and had a daughter of my own age, Marietta.'

'But this Rolando, did he really exist, or did you invent him?'

'He really existed, and Marietta was my best friend.'

'And what happened in the film?'

'Very little. Marietta and I went into Rolando's bedroom. Marietta held me by the hand and I allowed her to drag me in, but reluctantly because I knew that Marietta wanted to sell me to her father. It was understood, in fact, that Rolando was a degenerate who liked little girls and Marietta procured them for him, gradually introducing him to all her little friends. Rolando was sitting on the bed; Marietta pushed me towards him and I made a little bow. Rolando examined me but did not touch me. Finally the examination came to an end with a positive result. Rolando took from the bedside table a pack of brand-new cards, smaller than the normal kind, gilt-edged, and gave them to Marietta. That was my price. Marietta took the cards and went away. End of the film.'

'Was that all?'

'Yes, that was all.'

'In reality, did this Rolando actually make love with little girls?'

'Not at all. He was a decent man, a very good father and a very good husband.'

'Without knowing it, you were in love with Marietta's father, that's all.'

'No, I was in love with the scene, or rather, with the part that I acted in the scene.'

'What was that?'

'The scene hinged upon the fact that Marietta was selling me to her father for a pack of cards. Not on the fact that I liked Marietta's father.'

'And then?'

'It's quite clear: I liked the idea of being sold by Marietta and bought by Rolando.'

'But how did you get an idea of that kind into your head?'

'Possibly from a thing that had happened some years before, when I was five. I was a very pretty child; at San Remo, again, a foreign couple who had no children suggested to my mother that they might adopt me. Of course my mother refused. But after that, every time I did something naughty, she used to threaten me jokingly: "Don't do it again, or I'll call that lady and sell you to her and with the money I'll buy a better little girl than you." I would ask: "How much would you sell me for?" and my mother would answer: "For a million." I remember that those words "I'll sell you" even then had a strange effect upon me. Anyhow the Rolando film is the first that I have any memory of. I believe it was at that particular time that I created the ritual which I still keep to nowadays.'

'What ritual?'

'The manner in which I masturbate partly with eyes closed and partly looking at myself in the mirror while masturbating. Not knowing where to take refuge, since I slept in the same room as my mother, I acquired the habit of shutting myself up in the lavatory. I don't think I was being very original; I suppose all children do the same thing. My originality consisted, if anything, in the fact that from the very beginning I had organized the double scene I've told you about. I owed this to the arrangement of the place; as I sat on the lavatory seat I had, right in front of me, a tall mirror on the wall opposite. Later the mirror became the triple cheval-glass and the lavatory seat was transformed into the stool.'

90

'But when you did these things, didn't you have a sense of guilt?'

'Not in the least. I was a strong, healthy child, not at all vicious. It may have been that I had a precocious sexual appetite, that's possible, but I'm not even sure of that.'

'And how many times a day did you do it?'

'Whenever I felt a desire for it. Then, later on, I restricted myself to twice.'

'Imagining, every time, that you were being bought and sold?'

'Yes.'

I rose to my feet again and resumed walking up and down the room. Actually it was 'he' who forced this restlessness upon me. He kept on muttering: 'What are we doing here? Let's go!' but at the same time, in the usual contradictory fashion, he had become so recklessly enormous, so irreparably visible as to cause me embarrassment. Irene, with possibly feigned surprise, asked: 'What's the matter, why did you get up?'

'Nothing,' I replied, thrusting my hand into my pocket, giving 'him' the usual half-turn and pressing him against my stomach so that he should not be seen: 'nothing; just a bit of nervousness. I needed to stretch my legs. Don't worry about me, go on with your story. After that first film, then, were there others?'

'Yes, certainly.'

'Tell me about one of them.'

'That same year, after we went back to Milan, I found by pure chance in my father's bookshelf (he was a university professor) a book on cannibalism.'

'On cannibalism?'

'Yes. In one chapter there was an account of a true occurrence. A Sultan of Borneo had a habit of keeping girls who had been taken prisoner, during wars with enemy tribes, shut up in a hut adjacent to the kitchen. These girls were held in reserve for great occasions and meanwhile were carefully fattened. When the great occasion arrived, the Sultan would give orders to the cook to slaughter one of the prisoners, cook her and serve her up to himself and his guests. Well, in my second film I imagined myself as one of these young women, specially fattened up in order to be eaten. In short, I liked the idea of being nothing more than a domestic animal of the eatable kind, like those that are cut up and sold on the marble slabs of butchers' shops.'

'And what happened in the film?'

'Again, very little. At first I would see myself in the hut, crouching in the dark with the other girls, my companions. Then the cook would come in, feel me carefully to see whether I was satisfactorily fat; then he would seize hold of me by the hair and cut my throat, keeping it over a bucket so as to collect the blood. After that he would hang me up head downwards, by the feet, and cut me up with his butcher's knife, beginning at the groin and going right up the spinal column to the neck. I'd seen it done like that to a pig, in the country. Then, in my film, I would pass quickly on from the kitchen to the table. I would see a big tray in the middle of the table, and on the tray, there was I, my hands, my head, my legs and so on, all mixed up and confused just like the pieces of an animal that's been cooked. At that point the film would come to an end.'

'Go on.'

'Another book inspired me with another film. It was a book about slavery in Africa during the eighteenth century, a book illustrated with copperplate engravings. In one of these plates there was a Negro girl, standing naked on a platform in the shade of a great tropical tree. In the background there was a mosque with a dome and minarets. Round the platform could be seen a number of Arabs, very handsome men, most of them elderly, dressed in white and with long white beards. The caption said: "Young slave girl for sale in the Zanzibar market."

'In my film, all I had to do was to set the illustration in motion and substitute myself for the Negro girl. I was exposed for sale and exhibited and made to turn round and round, and was given a few blows with a whip on the legs to make me do what I was told; some of the buyers came up on to the platform and examined me more closely; then there was the auction:

one of these Arabs made a higher bid than all the others and I was sold to him; he came up on the stand, threw a cloak over me and carried me off. End of the film. Incidentally, I believe it was precisely because of that book and that illustration that later on, when I went to the university, I wanted to learn Arabic.'

'You know Arabic?'

'Yes. That's why I was taken on as secretary in an Arab embassy.'

'Have you ever been in an Arab country?'

'I've been in Libya and Tunisia, with my husband, when we were on our honeymoon.'

'I bet it was you who wanted to make that trip.'

'Yes, I was curious about those countries in which one of my most successful films took place. But it was a disappointment. They are just like any other countries.'

'Any other films?'

'Other films? Let's see. Here is one, for instance, that I invented when I was fifteen and was still going to school. I was in a car, in the park, with a small man who had a yellow face and coal-black eyes. The man stopped the car and asked me to get out. I refused. He tried to push me out and in order to persuade me he slapped me twice. I still resisted. A violent push and I shot out on to the pavement. Then, as usual, I jumped to the conclusion of the affair, without lingering over my love-making in the street. The little yellow-faced man came back with his car, took me away and insisted on my giving him the money I had earned. I refused. Another couple of slaps. Then he seized my handbag, took out the money and threw the empty bag back in my face. End of the film.'

'A strip cartoon, and not in the least original, into the bargain.'

'My films are all a little like strip cartoons; I've often wondered why. But they work, and that's what matters.' A brief silence. I went and sat down again, took up my glass and stubbed out my cigarette in the ashtray. Irene went on: 'D'you want me to tell you about the film that caused the break between my husband and me? But first I'll give you something to drink, your glass is empty.'

Unexpectedly, 'he' suggested: 'Tell her that if you get drunk you won't be responsible for your actions.'

'What's that got to do with it?'

'Go on, tell her.'

'Surely you don't want me to lay hands on Irene with the excuse that I'm drunk?'

'Tell her, and don't ask so many questions.'

I yielded, for some reason or other. I warned Irene: 'Look out, because if I get drunk I won't guarantee anything.'

Irene rose to her feet, benign, smiling, placid. As she poured out my glass of whisky she said: 'I don't believe you're a violent man. Anyhow, thank you for the warning; if need be I'll defend myself.' She handed me the glass, sat down again and went on: 'First of all, then, I must describe my husband to you. He's tall, athletic, dark with a handsome face, a fine body, a good-looking man, in fact. A bit ordinary, perhaps, but really good-looking. Not very intelligent, it's true, in the sense that he's not an intellectual; but perhaps not stupid enough and, above all, too sensitive to make a success of the job of advertising agent.'

'Forgive me: one preliminary question. Why did you get married?'

'To please my parents. Naturally, when I got married, I had no intention of ceasing to masturbate. It's my way of existence. Besides, I didn't love my husband. So we got married and then I tried to solve the problem of my conjugal relations in the only possible way.'

'What was that?'

'By introducing my husband into my films, in the role of an actor.'

'What a good idea! And how?'

'That's simple. By making him into the character who sold me.'

'Or who bought you?'

'No, who sold me. A husband, here at least in our world, can sell his wife, but he can't buy her.'

94

'But you used to make love with your husband?'

'Of course. However, while we were making love, I would be looking with closed eyes at my interior film, in which my husband, as I have said, was selling me. So that he himself came, fundamentally, to be a kind of substitute.'

'A substitute for what?'

'Obviously, for my own hand.'

'Then why did you separate, seeing that you'd found such an ingenious solution to your problem?'

'It was like this. My husband had a business associate whom I will call Erminio. He was an older man than my husband, and I can't tell you how ugly he was. He was an unattractive man, tall and big and bulky, with a face the colour of tobacco and a brownish nose and a purple mouth. Oh, I was forgetting: he was bald, and his skull had a strange depression in the middle, like a trough. Again I was forgetting: inside his purple mouth there were a lot of false teeth, not gold ones but of some white metal, possibly platinum. But he was an extremely good businessman.

'My husband, on the other hand, was not at all good at business. And so in the end he found himself in difficulties, and then Erminio decided to dissolve the partnership and set up on his own. There followed a period during which my husband found himself in considerable difficulties, and he was always talking about Erminio and how clever he was and how he would like to go into partnership with him again. And so it was quite natural for me to invent a film in which my husband, in exchange for financial help, would sell me to Erminio. The film was set in Erminio's office. A modern office, with the usual metal furniture. Erminio would be sitting at his desk, my husband and I sitting opposite to him. Erminio has his cheque book in his hand and says to my husband: "I'll help you, that's agreed. But I want Irene in exchange." I look at my husband and see him nod his assent. Then Erminio quickly signs the cheque, hands it to my husband who takes it, looks at me for a moment and then goes away. That's all.

'I had been showing this film to myself for some time, practically every time my husband and I made love. Then,

95

one night, just at the moment when, in bed with my husband, in his arms and making love, I was showing that part of the film in which Erminio said: "That's agreed, I'll help you, but I want Irene" – just at that moment I contrived to stop the film as it was focused on my husband's face. And I imagined, in fact, that my husband was hesitating. So, to help him overcome this hesitation, I started whispering, not in the film but in reality, quickly and in a very low voice: "Yes, sell me, sell me, sell me, sell me . . ." This will make you laugh; but what really happened at that moment was that, after making use of silent films for so many years, I had discovered, by chance, the talkie. Evidently, however, my voice was not as quiet as I thought; or perhaps, without intending, I had put my mouth close to my husband's ear while I was feverishly whispering: "Sell me, sell me." The fact remains that he heard what I said, and since, as I told you, he was very sensitive, he interpreted my words correctly. So, all of a sudden, just as he was on the point of having an orgasm, he broke off his love-making and started slapping and punching me. Then he seized me by the hair, threw me out of the bed and dragged me along the floor, through two or three rooms, at the same time blindly kicking me over and over again. Finally he threw me down on the sofa and gripped my neck, as if to strangle me.

'Then *I* lost patience, pushed him off with a blow from my knee, just as I did with you a little while ago, and shouted the truth in his face: yes, that while I was pretending to make love with him I was in reality masturbating. Yes, I was imagining that he was selling me to Erminio. Yes, I didn't love him and I sufficed to myself and I had no need of him. My husband, as I've told you, was an absolutely ordinary man, with all the prejudices of ordinary men. He didn't understand anything about it, except that I didn't love him and that I was, as they say, a vicious woman. And so we parted and I came to Rome with the little girl and he stayed in Milan.'

I remained silent, filled with an irrepressible uneasiness. I had indeed become conscious that, ever since the beginning of the story of Irene's relations with her husband, 'he' had been all the time rising up, more and more, so that now he was not far, in every sense, from losing his head. In fact I heard him feverishly whispering: 'Why, just look at her. Look how excited she's become while telling the story of her marriage. Don't you see, she told it on purpose?'

I looked and was shocked when I thought how true it was that 'he' and I are two quite distinct individuals. For, however intently I looked, as 'he' had exhorted me to do, I saw absolutely nothing: Irene was sitting composedly, as usual, glass in hand. I remarked ingenuously: 'As far as excitement goes, it's yours that I see rather than Irene's.' 'He' replied: 'But I'm telling you she *is* excited, excited to death. Anyhow, if you're not convinced, leave it to me. Leave it to me to continue this moving, passionate dialogue and bring it to its inevitable conclusion.'

Having consumed two double whiskies, I was too drunk; I did not resist, but obediently gave way to him. Aggressively, expeditiously, 'he' attacked at once: 'Interesting, no doubt about it, that story of your relations with your husband. You know what it proves?'

'What?'

'That, however solitary and egotistical it may be, your manner of loving does not in any way exclude the participation of the man whom you described, when we first met, as "the other one". That is to say, of your husband, in the film you've just recalled; and of any other man, in other films you've already invented or will invent.'

'But this is an imaginary presence and, moreover, as I pointed out, purely fortuitous. I put my husband into the film because, unfortunately, I couldn't help it; because I had to solve the problem of loving myself at the same moment in which I was pretending to love him. I don't believe that a similar occasion can occur again.'

'Why not? You might for instance desire, some day, to experience in reality the situation you had created in your imagination.'

'Why should I desire that? Between myself and me there's no room for another person. My husband was merely a substitute. It's as if you were saying that a third lover could insinuate himself between two people who love one another. I like myself to such a degree that it makes it quite impossible for me to like anyone else. But I say! What's happening? What's come over you now?'

It was I who had caused this rapid change of tone; or rather it was 'he' who, taking advantage of my drunkenness, was now making me attempt a performance 'in real life' of one of Irene's many 'slavery' films. He guided my hand, made me extract 'him' from his hiding-place and also a bundle of banknotes from my wallet, made me rise from the divan and move round the table. So there I was, like one possessed and let loose, close against Irene, my knee on the arm of her sofa, in the act of thrusting 'him' close to my hostess's face and, at the same time, putting the money into her hand. 'His' plan, stupidly imitative as it was, expected Irene to accept the double offer. And also that, as she clutched the banknotes in her fist and repeated ecstatically, with eyes closed, as in the film with her husband, 'Buy me, buy me', 'he' would in some way be allowed to achieve 'direct contact'.

A foolish plan, over-complicated and impracticable. Mainly because, as Irene had given it to be clearly understood, shortly before, she did not wish to experience her inclinations in real life but merely to imagine them in a dreamlike way.

In actual fact, Irene did not clutch the banknotes in her fist and did not allow 'him' to approach her. All she did was to consider him for a moment, with an eloquent gesture mimicking ironical astonishment; and meanwhile she let the notes slip out of her still open hand to be scattered on the floor. Then she raised her hand and moved 'him' aside with a quiet gesture of indulgent irritation, just as, when one is walking through a wood, one moves aside a branch that juts out a little too far across the path. Finally she enunciated, in a precise manner: 'Go away, you idiot.'

I stood up in front of her, feeling ridiculous with my big bald head, my flaming face and with 'him' so enormous and so visible. Then suddenly I 'understood'. Yes, I loved Irene and making love with her did not matter to me at all and her command to me to go away was breaking my heart. 1 did not attempt to rearrange myself; and, just as I was, with 'him' sticking out and swaying in front of me, stiff and useless, I threw myself down at Irene's knees and cried in a sorrowful voice: 'Forgive me, I'll never do it again, truly, never again. But don't send me away. I'm a ridiculous man, a worthless man, a contemptible man, an abject man. But I love you, I'm certain that I love you. I need you, I can't live without you; forgive me and go on being my friend.'

As I was speaking I closed my eyes, which were filled with tears. When I opened them again, I saw only the red material of the sofa in front of me. Irene had risen and gone to the other end of the room. 'All right,' she said, 'but now take back your money and go away.' I bent down and mechanically collected the banknotes and, while I was still on all fours, I tucked 'him' away again. Then I stood up, breathless, my zip fastener undone, my hands full of crumpled banknotes. Irene, still keeping at a distance, said: 'Please don't come near me, or I shall scream.'

'But I only wanted . . .'

'I've seen what you wanted: you're an idiot. And now go away. You've exhausted me. I need to be left alone.'

I said angrily: 'So as to masturbate.'

Serenely, pitilessly, she replied: 'Yes, to masturbate, but go away.'

'At least give me your telephone number.'

'I'm in the book. My name is on the door-plate. Now go away.'

'When can I telephone you?'

'Whenever you like. Are you going – yes or no?'

'Are we going to be friends?'

'Perhaps so, especially if you go away as quickly as possible.'

I went out.

5   Analysed!

As soon as I woke up in the morning, while my mind was still clouded and powerless, 'he' broke loose. As though wishing to demonstrate that the true continuity of life, the real thread of Ariadne in that absurd labyrinth, lay not in my ambition to become sublimated but rather in his own obsessive and hopelessly desublimated activity, 'he' took up the events of the previous day and started them over again in my memory, in his own way, of course.

I endure these early morning recollections, for the most part, in a sleepy, torpid, not entirely hostile state of mind, allowing myself, in my drowsiness, a kind of holiday of dreamy, passive eroticism. 'He', naturally, accompanies these recollections with his usual metamorphoses, as though to stress his complete, arrogant independence which permits his being extremely active, not only when I am awake but even when I am asleep.

So it was again this morning, the day after my first encounter with Irene. I opened my eyes and then realized that I was lying on my side, with 'him' stretched out on the sheet, so heavy and so huge as to suggest the idea that I was a bell that had fallen down from its tower and was lying broken on the ground, with only its massive clapper left intact amongst the fragments. An imprudent comparison: for 'he' immediately butted in, as sprightly as could be: 'Don't worry, the bell isn't broken; you'll hear it ringing in a moment!' I will now transcribe the dialogue as it took place between us.

I: 'What the devil are you saying? What ringing? I should like to know why you're already so excited at eight o'clock in the morning? Couldn't you stay quiet and rest, as I'm doing, as all sensible people do?'

'He': 'Irene's legs!'

I: 'Don't remind me of yesterday evening. You ruined

everything. It's your fault if perhaps I never see Irene again. The only woman in the world that I could love. The one and only. But after all, what do you know about love?'

'He': 'Irene's legs!'

I: 'She had let herself go and had confided in me to an extent that she had probably never done with anybody . . . and then you, stupid and brutal as a buffalo, went and spoilt everything.'

'He': 'Irene's legs!'

I: 'I shall telephone her, that's certain. But before I get into touch with her, I want to make sure that you won't ruin everything again by your disgraceful behaviour.'

'He': 'Irene's legs!'

I: 'I shall love Irene, I feel it, I'm sure of it. Loving her will be, for me, like becoming a film director – that is, moving up from the ranks of the desublimated to those of the sublimated. But for this to come about, you have got to recognize, once and for all, the truth of sublimation.'

'He': 'Irene's legs!'

I: 'Let's make an agreement: for you, freedom of intervention, even if feeble and doomed to failure, on all other occasions of my life. But in the presence of Irene, absolute passivity, or rather non-existence.'

'He': 'Irene's legs!'

I: 'Now you've got to tell me whether you accept this agreement.'

'He': 'Irene's legs!'

I: 'I'm speaking to you, you thug. D'you accept or not?'

'He': 'Irene's legs!'

I: 'So that's your answer, that refrain, is it? I see. I shall have to adopt . . . drastic measures with you.'

'He': 'Irene's legs!'

I: 'I made up my mind some time ago. So far I've postponed putting my plan into action in the hope that you would return to reason of your own accord. This hasn't happened. And so, even though regretfully, I see myself compelled to act.'

'He': 'Irene's legs!'

I: 'This very day we'll go and see Vladimiro and this time there'll be no nonsense about it: I shall empty the sack to the very bottom. And you will be the one to lose by it. Your strength lies in concealment, in secrecy, in the uncertainty of our relationship. Shedding the light of reason upon it means destroying you. So much the worse for you. You've asked for it.'

In order to understand this threatening speech of mine you must know that Vladimiro was a friend of mine from university days, and that he practised, or rather (given the scarcity of clientele) that he wished to practise, the profession of a psychoanalyst. Lacking, or almost lacking, any patients, Vladimiro – perhaps partly for that reason – was a very serious medical man. Moreover his seriousness was, so to speak, guaranteed by the fact that he himself was a perfect case of grave neurosis, obviously in need of prolonged psychoanalytical treatment. It was partly for this reason that I was going to him. As a neurotic and at the same time a specialist in neuroses, I was convinced that Vladimiro was the only person who could understand my own very special case which, when you come to think of it, did not so much demand treatment (what is there, in fact, pathological about being two instead of one?) as merely to be carefully considered in an unprejudiced, friendly spirit.

So, that same afternoon, having telephoned in advance to make an appointment (Vladimiro, on the telephone, at first pretended that he did not know how to fit in my visit, but then, of course, agreed to the time I suggested), I went to see my old university comrade. He lived a very long way away, in a modern suburban quarter. A quarter consisting of streets, or rather concrete trenches, between rows and rows of apartment houses laden with useless balconies; shops with big plate-glass windows full of poor-quality goods; small cars in herring-bone formation along the pavements; not a single expensive car: well, well, Vladimiro hadn't made much progress!

It was the first time I had been to his flat; formerly he used to live with his family, then he married, moved house and set up his own practice. Why did I feel satisfaction at the

102

thought that he had had no success in his profession? Because, at any rate with him, I did not wish to be 'underneath'. I knew him too well; I knew precisely that he too was de-sublimated, although in a different way from me: and I refused absolutely to admit that with me he was 'on top'. I was a failure, he was a failure; I was a neurotic, he was a neurotic; I was weak-willed, he was weak-willed: why should he be 'on top'?

Nevertheless, as I drove through the crowded streets, I felt more and more nervous at the thought of meeting Vladimiro. What line was I to take with him so that he should realize, from the very beginning, that any sort of airs of superiority, even of a scientific type, would not cut any ice with me? I thought it over and finally decided that I too would be scientific like him, in fact more so than him. This meant that, instead of a doctor and a patient, there would be two doctors and a patient. Vladimiro would be one of the doctors, I myself the other. And the patient, who would that be? Obviously, 'he'.

Encouraged by this solution, I parked my little car among the many other little cars in a dusty, uneven street which (I noticed with satisfaction) the Roman local authority must have forgotten to repair for years past. The flat was on the third floor of one of these 'white-collar' apartment houses. I went up in the lift. On the landing there were three doors: so Vladimiro's flat could not be very large. I rang the bell, and the door was opened, not by a nurse in a white uniform or a bespectacled secretary, but by Vladimiro himself in shirt-sleeves, the sleeves rolled up, the collar open and no tie. So he couldn't afford even a nurse, even a secretary!

As we shook hands I gave a quick glance round: a minute hall, with a baby's pram in one corner and a hatstand. In the air, an appetizing but not exactly luxurious smell of cooking.

'I'm pleased to see you,' Vladimiro said, clapping his hand on my shoulder in a manner which was not protective but was perhaps really friendly – a friendliness all his own, however, a pathetic, neurasthenic friendliness. We went into his study. A small room, a cube, with barely room for the desk, the bookshelf and the analyst's couch. At the window hung two cheap, scanty green curtains, between which could be seen the brutal, balcony-filled front of the building opposite. There was an air of cleanness and tidiness, but also of irreparable humbleness about this study. I could not help reflecting that nobody ever lay down on that couch. Poor Vladimiro! Yet another one who, like me, probably has an insatiable wife who, in league with his 'he', draws out of him all the energy that he would need to initiate even a timid progress towards sublimation. But he has not, like me, had the courage to go away. And to think that he is an analyst and has not even the excuse of ignorance!

Vladimiro sat down at his desk and motioned to me to place myself on a chair in front of him. He was tall, thin and gaunt. From the turned-up sleeves of his shirt issued two fleshless arms devoid of muscle. His hair was short and bristling, of a vague sort of brown tending to yellow, like old straw. His face, like that of an adolescent grown old before his time, was marked by two big, sad-looking furrows, so that it appeared almost deformed. His eyes were of an ugly colour between green and yellow, like the eyes of a dog. His nose was pointed but with wide nostrils. And there was a bitter expression on his large, sinuous mouth. Although it was seven o'clock and still daylight, he turned on a very powerful lamp and directed its light into my face, dazzling me.

'No need for that lamp,' I said at once. 'I'm not the kind of person to be impressed, I'm not the sort of patient out of whom you can squeeze a hundred or two hundred lire a month. I'm just an old friend who has come to explain his case to you, a case which isn't in any way clinical.'

He smiled, with a pleasant, even though neurotic, smile. He turned off the lamp and said: 'I'm sorry, but that lamp, sometimes, is useful!'

I took my time. I pulled a packet of cigarettes out of my pocket, offered one to Vladimiro, who refused, lit one, put the lighter and the cigarettes back in my pocket, inhaled and blew the smoke out through my mouth and nostrils. All this as I sat bending forward, my arms crossed on the desk, my eyes lowered. Finally I said: 'And you, how are you getting on? You're well set up here, with a nice little study, cosy, quiet, intimate, furnished with sober taste. I bet it was your wife who chose the furniture for you.'

'No, to tell the truth, I chose it myself.'

'But does your wife work? Does she help you in your profession?'

'My wife doesn't work.'

'What does she do, then?'

'She's just a wife. What I mean is – she used to work, she used to do welfare work, but we've had two children and so, since we haven't a nurse, it's she who looks after them.'

He spoke slowly, choosing his words, with visible embarrassment and with a pained, uneasy air as though he were treading on thorns. On the desk I noticed a photograph in a silver frame. 'Is that your wife?' I asked.

'Yes.'

'May I look?'

I took the photograph and looked at it: it was just as I could have sworn – a dark woman with soft, melting black eyes and a little pointed, delicate, waxen face. These are the dangerous women. Much more dangerous than Fausta, for example, in spite of the latter's obvious sensuality. Those big, sentimental eyes, the clear sign of a voracious sexual appetite, explained many things: Vladimiro's neurotic state, his failure, the modest look of the flat, the smell of cooking in the entrance-hall. Yes, indeed, with a wife like that desublimation is certain, fatal, inevitable, irreversible. I put the photograph back on the desk and said: 'Very charming, your wife.'

He did not take note of the compliment. He twisted himself on his chair and finally declared: 'Rico, you telephoned me and told me it was about something urgent. Well, what is it about?'

Now we were getting there! I did not answer at once. I went on smoking thoughtfully, looking down. I intended to be scientific and, to achieve that, I had quickly to impose the correct tone beforehand. Finally, in a clear voice and

105

articulating the syllables carefully, I said: 'Vladimiro, first of all it is my duty to make a personal statement.'

'Let's hear it, then.'

'You must know that – whether luckily or unluckily for me, I don't know – I have been exceptionally well endowed by nature.'

There are impassive people whose impassiveness is due to a complete lack of expression. There are, on the contrary, others who are impassive because, though capable of strong expressiveness, they have only one expression, which is always the same, whatever may happen. Vladimiro belonged to the second category. Always, unalterably, his face wore a perplexed, distressed, worried, embarrassed expression; but since this expression was always the same, whether one said to him: 'Good morning', or whether one announced: 'Doctor, I want to kill my father', it was, all things considered, just as if his face were constantly quite expressionless and impassive. And so it was now. He looked at me with an air of distress and said nothing and I reflected that he always had that appearance and so I felt a need to explain myself more fully, since perhaps he had not even heard what I said. 'In other words, Vladimiro,' I said, 'to put it plainly, I have a sexual organ of truly extraordinary size.'

I paused, inhaled a mouthful of smoke, blew out the smoke through my nose and stared at the top of the desk. Then I resumed: 'You will say it is not a question of size but of good manners. You are right. There are gigantic sexual organs which nevertheless know their place and so remain almost unnoticed; there are also very small ones which become indiscreetly agitated and get themselves noticed. But the worst occurs when it is the gigantic organ that becomes agitated and gets noticed. Now this, Vladimiro, is unfortunately the case with me.'

I paused again, as if to emphasize these last words; again I inhaled a mouthful of smoke and blew it out through my nose with an air of thoughtfulness and reserve. Vladimiro was supporting his face on his left hand, and his forefinger, pointing against the end of his left eyebrow, caused this to be stretched considerably upwards; but he did not open his mouth: he was waiting.

Sweeping away with my hand some scraps of ash that had fallen on the desk from my cigarette, I resumed: 'As you will have understood by now, this is a question of an organ which might euphemistically be called intrusive. To be exact, it does not allow me, literally, to live. Yes, I mean that: to live. I ask no more than to attend, as they say, to my own business, but "he" intervenes. Continually. He sticks his nose into practically everything I do; he makes himself visible at the most inopportune moments; he tries to force my hand; in fact he claims an obedience from me which I am absolutely resolved to deny him.'

A pause and silence. Vladimiro was looking intently at me; but he made no comment. I took up the thread of my remarks again. 'This intrusiveness of his, this – let us even say this arrogance, what can I do to oppose it? Obviously, I should show an arrogance equal, or better, superior to his, or, on the other hand, I should bring reason to bear. This second alternative is mine, Vladimiro, that goes without saying. I am in fact a man of culture, an intellectual. Any recourse to violence is repugnant to me. And so, from the very beginning, with "him" . . .'

'Who is "he"?'

'My organ. As I was saying, from the very beginning, with "him", I have used reason. I discuss, I try to reason, I try to persuade him: between him and me there is a continuous dialogue. Or rather, to be precise, a continuous quarrel.'

'You talk to him and . . . "he" talks to you? D'you mean to say you really talk to him and he really talks to you?'

'Yes, really; what is there strange about that?'

'Um . . . nothing. But what sort of . . . voice has he?'

'That depends. A voice, anyhow, attuned to his character. Generally it's insinuating, murmuring, crafty, slimy. But in certain circumstances, when he feels like it, it's also aggressive, violent, peremptory.'

'When he feels like it, eh?'

'Yes. When he feels like it. Sometimes, but more rarely,

107

it can actually be sinister, fierce. However, if we're alone, "he" and I, then his more usual tone is one of vanity and affectation.'

'Why . . . is he vain?'

'Vain is putting it mildly. He has an absolute belief that he is the most beautiful, the strongest, the most potent of his, let us say, category. According to him, no one, in the whole world, can compete with him. A monster of vanity!'

'But . . . does he talk about ordinary things? Or does he intervene only in matters of sex?'

'Vladimiro, you know perfectly well that there's nothing that cannot be interpreted in the light of sex. Literature, art, science, politics, economics, history – everything can be looked at from that point of view. I'm not saying that it's not, finally, a question of reduction. I'm saying that it's one of the things that are done. And "he" does it – oh, does he do it!'

'But . . . give me an example.'

'Well, for example, what is there *less* sexual than a landscape? Mountains, plains, rivers, valleys: where does sex come in? And yet, for instance, the other day I went for a drive in the country. The road, at a certain point, ran between two rounded, oblong hills, which gradually became lower until they were merely two scarcely visible slopes. Now would you believe it? "He" at once started whispering to me: "They're not a couple of hills, they're two feminine legs and very nice too. Wide apart, wide open. And the road runs straight towards the gorge where they join or, rather, where they seem to join. And now we, in our car, are going to penetrate violently, at 150 kilometres an hour, into the gorge," etc., etc. You see the double meaning, don't you?'

'Yes indeed I do. But . . . in what other ways does "he" intervene in your life?'

'In dreams, naturally.'

'Erotic dreams, eh?'

'I don't want to dwell upon dreams, Vladimiro. That is "his" realm, so to speak. What "he" finally produces doesn't concern me and doesn't interest me. I wish, if anything, to express one solemn desire: that he should leave realistic dreams alone and keep only to symbolic ones.'

108

'Realistic?'

'I don't, for instance, like dreaming that I am in bed with a woman whose face I can't see because she has turned her back to me. Then the woman turns over and I discover that it's my mother. I far prefer to dream that I'm climbing a staircase and at the top of the staircase there's a house with the door open and I make my way towards this open door, step by step, and perhaps the house has a gloomy look about it, with all the windows shut, and it's surrounded by cypresses, and just as I'm on the point of crossing the threshold someone stabs me in the back and I fall to the ground and wake up.

'This house with the open door is, of course, my mother. The gloomy look of the house is my sense of guilt. It is I who give myself the stab in the back, to stop me committing incest, and so on. But, Vladimiro, we are all the time concerned with symbolism, that is with the indirect, the intermediate, the puzzle, the riddle. Of course I can decipher the dream, solve the riddle; but I am also free, perfectly free to take the symbolical representation literally, without seeking out its significance. Well, Vladimiro, I prefer symbol to reality. Dreaming of a house with an open door leaves me indifferent. I say to myself: "Hello, what a strange dream, I wonder what it means." And then I don't think about it any more. Dreaming of my mother, yes, really my mother with her own face and expression and all the rest of it, in bed with me – you will admit that it's rather tiresome. You wake up and think it over and possibly you feel upset for the whole day.

'Now "he", unfortunately, has for some time almost completely abandoned symbolism for realism. No longer does he cause me to dream, as he did once, for instance, of a clock, that well-known symbol of the feminine sexual organ; instead, he presents me – brutally, even though it's a dream – with the real, genuine feminine sex, perfect in all its details, with its shape and colour and even its movements, just as it is in reality when one is awake. Now I used to forget the clock as soon as I woke up; not so with the sex. And I know why he does this, Vladimiro. Out of spite. And that is because, for reasons it would take too long to go into, I and "he" have been for some time on very bad terms. So he takes his revenge in this way, by abandoning symbolism – of which, make no mistake about it, he is a master – for a realism, or rather a naturalism, of the crudest and coarsest kind.'

I shook my head, thoughtfully, deprecatingly, reflectively, looking down and puffing smoke from my nostrils. Vladimiro waved his hand as though to shelve the thing for the time being. 'We'll talk about dreams later,' he said. 'Let us go back to the question of the dialogue. You two, then, hold conversations all the time. But in what way? What I mean is, do you talk to him aloud, or what?'

'Only when I'm alone and am sure nobody is listening. Naturally, because sometimes it's a matter of things which are – what shall I say? – somewhat delicate. So it's best to take some precautions.'

'When you two are alone, then, you talk to him aloud. And what does he do?'

'He answers me.'

'Aloud, too?'

'Yes, of course.'

'You mean that you hear him as you are hearing me at this moment?'

'Certainly.'

'You hear him with your ears?'

'I'm sorry, Vladimiro, but what else could I hear him with? With my nose?'

'This, however, is when you are alone. And when you're in company? Do you talk aloud in the presence of a third party, too?'

'No, in the presence of a third party we don't talk aloud. We talk mentally.'

'Mentally?'

'Yes; that is, I think one thing and "he" thinks another and so the dialogue, or rather the quarrel, between "him" and me goes on just the same. But, in the presence of a third party, the tendency, to tell the truth, is for "him" not so much to carry on a dialogue or even a quarrel as to take command.'

'To take command?'

'Yes. Then, naturally, I am either more or less free to obey. But "he" always makes an attempt to impose upon me.'

'And what does he command you to do?'

'Obviously: to act according to his desires.'

'For example?'

'Well, let us suppose there is a reception in some villa, on one of these summer days. A pretty girl agrees to take a stroll with me along the paths in the garden. "He" immediately commands me to extend our stroll to a particular garden seat. Then, once we have sat down, he commands me to bring the conversation round to certain subjects. Next, he orders me to move up very close to the girl. Finally, after some preliminary approaches, he commands me to lay hands on her.'

'To lay hands on her?'

'Well, yes, to pull out one of her breasts, to thrust my hands up under her skirt, to fling her down on the grass, and things like that.'

' "He" gives the orders. And you?'

'Usually I try, in the first place, to convince him that it's no use. I point out, for instance, that the girl is engaged to be married; that I should get into trouble; and so on. No effect, waste of breath, he pays no attention to me. The end of it is that, in a moment of weakness, I give in to him. I lay hands on the girl and of course am repulsed and perhaps even slapped.'

'Does it always end like that? With a slap?'

'Often. But let's understand one another, Vladimiro. It's not because women don't like me; but because "he" is no psychologist, has no intuition, in fact, frankly, is not intelligent; and therefore he never understands when certain things can be done and when they can't. It's not by mere chance that, in common parlance, he is often mentioned as the symbol of a certain special type of stupidity.'

'What kind of stupidity?'

'Well, I should say the stupidity that expresses itself in presumption and want of tact. If you knew how he makes me lose face! It's enough to make me as ashamed as if I were caught stealing! Enough to make me want to sink into the ground!'

I shook my head, feeling thoughtful and bitter yet at the same time scientific, that is, detached and objective. I had my hands on the table, and in the fingers of one of them I held my cigarette; on the middle finger of the other was a ring with a yellow cameo which had belonged to my father. I raised the hand holding the cigarette to my mouth, breathed in a little smoke, coughed, and then resumed, in a tired, severe tone of voice: 'In my case, furthermore, such losses of face are aggravated by the fact that I am not a man to whom his home, his wife, his children, his family are all in all. I am a serious professional man, known and esteemed, in a very special sort of world, that of the cinema. I say "special" because the cinema world is particularly favourable to the initiative of unscrupulous individuals like "him". Hundreds, I may even say thousands, of women dream of getting work in the cinema and try to make headway by every kind of means, not excluding an appeal, not merely to professional judgment, to technical considerations, in short to reason, but in a direct and shameless manner, to "him".'

For a moment I was silent, screwing up my mouth in disgust, beneath Vladimiro's attentive stare. Suddenly I went on: 'And then there's the question of lack of discrimination.'

'Lack of discrimination?'

'Yes. So far I've been speaking of young women who may or may not like me. I've mentioned loss of face. But "his" lack of discrimination goes far beyond loss of face.'

'Far beyond?'

'Yes, indeed. He likes *all* women, the ugly as well as the beautiful, the old as well as the young, and, alas, even the very young. It must be understood, Vladimiro, all this remains purely theoretical because, after all, in order to act, "he" needs me and without me he can't do anything. However this does not exclude the fact that here we are leaving the realm of normality and moving with all sails spread into that of psychopathology or even perhaps forensic medicine. Finding something exciting in the worn-out body of an old woman or in the still sexless body of a young girl is in fact downright perversion, in my opinion at least: am I not right?'

112

Vladimiro did not reply. This 'am I not right?' hung in the air, suspended in the silence. But I persisted: 'Perhaps you will find me too severe, too rigid. But in certain things I am uncompromising. Absolutely. Besides – allow me to say so, Vladimiro – too much is too much. It passes all bounds.'

Vladimiro still sat silent, gazing fixedly at me but as if from afar off, as though he were seeing me through the wrong end of a telescope so that the image of me appeared minute even if clear. I went on: 'Of course "he" defends himself. He justifies himself. Not so much, perhaps, on the moral plane because, as you will have understood, he is completely amoral, as on the – how shall I say? – the historico-cultural plane. I have said that he is stupid; but I haven't said that he is un-cultivated. It is a question, naturally, of a patched-up, amateurish, self-taught culture. Besides, how would he find time to devote himself to study, which in any case demands a concentration of which he is utterly incapable? But above all I should say that his is a specialized culture. About those things that concern him, he has a passable amount of information. About other things he knows nothing. And so . . . but why did I start talking about his culture?'

'In relation to his lack of discrimination.'

'Ah yes, I meant to say that his lack of discrimination is justified by him on cultural grounds. As I remarked, it's a question of notions that are more than anything historical, notions picked up here and there, without method and without strict accuracy, with the sole, eminently practical, aim of justifying him in our quarrels. It is a culture *sui generis*. There is nothing profound about it, nothing organic, nothing system-atic. A little hasty reading of popular accounts of primitive religions; a few incursions into anthropology; a few sallies into Oriental esotericism. But of the whole lot, Vladimiro, merely a smattering, not more than a pinch.

'That doesn't prevent him unloading, next day, in defence of his own lack of discrimination and with his usual brazen-ness, a whole heap of names of I don't know how many divinities: from Siva to Priapus, from Mutinus to Konsei Myogin, from Hermes to Subigus, from Baal-Peor to Min, from

113

Osiris to Kunado, from Frey to Pertunda, who, according to him, were so many incarnations of himself in the distant past. Thus the lack of discrimination of today becomes the universality of yesterday. And "he", today as yesterday, is supposedly a god, with a scale of values all his own. Moreover his reduction to a simple part of the human body, indecent and shameful into the bargain, is to be interpreted as a revenge on the part of his greatest rival, the Christian God.

'D'you see the point? Megalomania? Egocentricity? And at the same time the persecution mania that always goes hand in hand with the mania for greatness? A god! As if that were not enough, a god persecuted by another god, his envious, wicked rival. In short, if it had not been for Christ (I continue to quote "him"), "he", here in Italy at least, would still be upon the altars, the object of a real, genuine cult, under the fine title of the god Fascinus.'

'The god Fascinus?'

'Yes, the god Fascinus. That's his favourite name. It's also the name that reveals his true character, which is fundamentally *petit bourgeois*. I say *petit bourgeois* because it would not occur to anyone but a minor schoolmaster in a provincial secondary school to ennoble his own special tendencies by means of would-be classical references. Fascinus. From the Latin "fascinum", that is, enchantment. D'you see the point? D'you see what he's getting at? It's as much as to say: fascinating, charming, emanating from a fascination which it is impossible to escape, that is, which acts upon people like an enchantment, like magic, like witchcraft. Fascinus! This name contains the whole of his vanity, of his presumptuousness, not to speak of his miscalculations and of his cultural amateurishness.'

I shook my head, deploring, scornful yet indulgent. After a moment's silence I took up the subject again: 'You know what I answer when he starts talking about his Fascinus? I reply: "Those were other times. Then, you fascinated people, now you disgust them, when you don't make them laugh. No Fascinus now makes any impression; certain things simply are not done and must not be done, and all the Fascini of ancient Rome do

114

not justify, still less excuse, the ordinary, everyday sex mania of the Rome of today.'

'But he has his answer ready, one must grant him that. You know what that answer is? "Other times, what does that mean – other times? I am outside time. For me time does not exist." A scoundrel, yes, if you like, but ingenious, logical, sophistical.'

'But are your discussions always so erudite?'

'Would it were so! On the contrary, we generally abuse one another like a couple of washerwomen. But, fundamentally, we accuse each other, above all, of stupidity. "He" says that it is I who am stupid and I say that it is he who is stupid. According to him, reason is synonymous with stupidity; according to me . . . well, according to me, it's the opposite. In reality, Vladimiro, we speak different languages. Words have one meaning for me and another for him, so we don't understand one another. And that's because the differences in words represent the differences in the scale of values. So how could we understand one another?'

'But have you always been on such bad terms?'

I shook my head in denial, with the contrite air of one who recognizes, honestly, a disagreeable truth. 'No,' I said, 'once upon a time, on the contrary – I cannot deny it – we were on the best of terms. But, Vladimiro, at what a price, for me! At the price of genuine slavery! "He" commanded and I obeyed. I was his succubus, I carried out his orders. It was natural that at a certain point I rebelled.'

'How long ago is it since you were on the best of terms?'

'We must go back to the days of my early adolescence. Let us say I was fourteen. I then identified myself so closely with "him" that I felt an instinctive need, so to speak, at a certain moment, to differentiate myself from him, at least verbally, by giving him a name.'

'A name?'

'Yes, if only to avoid confusion when he and I were talking, or rather, when he was commanding and I was obeying. Picture to yourself a dialogue like this: "Federico, you must do this and this." "Yes, Federico, I'll do it at once."

115

D'you see the point? I was Federico, "he" was Federico. So I decided, as far as he was concerned, to latinize the name.'

'Fascinus?'

'No, that would have been as it were to admit that "he" had bewitched, had fascinated me. I was the succubus, it was true, but I already felt somewhat rebellious. No, since I am called Federico I decided to call him Federicus Rex.'

'Federicus Rex?'

'To tell the truth, I had thought for a moment of calling him Frederick the Great.'

'Why Frederick the Great?'

'That's a long story. This is how it was. One summer day at Ostia, after we had eaten our usual sandwiches, about two o'clock, we were all lying in the shade, three or four boys of the same age, on that stretch of sand, covered with flotsam and jetsam, behind the bathing-huts. Of course we were talking about women; someone had already made the experiment, someone else hadn't; at a certain moment, I don't know when, somebody had the idea: "Let's see who's got the biggest one." No sooner said than done. Then, to my surprise, for it was the first time I had happened to make such comparisons, I discovered – it's quite true to say so – that I had beaten the whole lot of them by several lengths. They were all my friends, my schoolfellows; and it occurred to one of them, quite naturally, to call me, as a joke, "Federico il Grande". Just a bit of boyish nonsense, childish, in fact.'

'But how did you come to change from "Federico il Grande" to "Federicus Rex"?'

'That's yet another story. As you know, I was living at that time with my mother in the neighbourhood of Piazza Mazzini. One night I was walking along a deserted street; my mother had given me the money to go to the local cinema and I was in a great hurry because I had an appointment with a friend. Then, just at the darkest part of this street, in the shadow of some trees that hung over from a garden, a voice called out to me: "Hey, boy!" I stopped and went over; it was a prostitute, rather elderly but not at all bad, so at least it seemed to me; you mustn't forget that I was fourteen and had

116

only been wearing long trousers for a short time. I don't remember very well what we said to each other. I only remember that I was trembling all over because it was the first time, and she noticed this and said to me: "Why are you trembling like that? Keep calm. Just tell me if you've got any dough."

'I didn't understand, and then she explained to me that "dough" meant money. I didn't say anything, but I opened my hand and showed her the thousand-lire note that my mother had given me for the cinema, and that was now all crumpled and damp with sweat. "That isn't much," she said. "It's enough for me to go to the cinema," I replied. So she started laughing and said: "Well then, give it here. *I'll* show you the cinema, I will. I bet it's the first time, isn't it? But don't tremble, you'll see how nice the cinema is."

'So she took the money and made me make love standing up, pressing herself against me, in the thick shadow of those trees. Now as soon as that woman caught sight of "him", d'you know what she said? "This is the king," she said. I was still trembling, and she went on: "Why, what are you afraid of? You've got the king, and kings aren't afraid of anybody." At the moment I didn't take much notice of it, but I remembered it afterwards; and since my mother kept some old coins in a box among which was a coin of Frederick of Prussia, with the inscription: "Federicus Rex", that was what I called him, with the Latin name.'

Vladimiro looked at me and appeared to be meditating. Finally he said: 'Very well then, you gave him a name. But when was it that you started quarrelling with him? I thought I understood that, when you gave him the name of Federicus Rex, you were still in agreement.'

'D'you want to know when I really rebelled?'

'Yes. When and why."

I looked at him and then, with a grave and set expression on my face, I nodded: 'Yes,' I said, 'I'll tell you; I expected that question. I was so much expecting it that I've prepared myself to answer in an exhaustive, scientific manner. Anyhow I came to see you today mainly for the express purpose of getting myself asked that question and of answering it. You understand me, Vladimiro?'

I was silent for a moment as if to emphasize the importance of what I was going to say; then I resumed: 'Not only do I remember the year in which I and "he" started quarrelling, but even the month if not the exact day: March 1950. We're now in 1970. I am thirty-five. So it's exactly twenty years from the time when I rebelled against "him".'

'And what was the reason . . . for the rebellion?'

'I'm coming to that. Let us say – a difference of opinion.'

'Of opinion? And what about?'

'About what actually happened one night in that March of 1950.'

'Did something happen that night?'

'According to "him", it did. According to me, it didn't.'

Vladimiro looked at me, and this time, realizing perhaps that we had arrived at the main point of our conversation, he sat silent with a positively frightened look on his face. I took in a long, ample mouthful of smoke and puffed it out again towards the shiny top of the table. Then I went on: 'I must say first of all, Vladimiro, that I was then ignorant of the fact that I was his succubus. It is true that I was sexually very precocious but I did not know that I owed this precociousness to "him". Moreover, not having yet had a carnal relationship with a woman – I mean a real relationship, not a hurried, partial, furtive affair like the one I told you about – I could not help thinking about it continually. It was my dominant thought, or rather, Vladimiro, it would be more correct to say, my obsession. Yes, Vladimiro, obsession. Of course I could have given myself relief, as all boys have done ever since the world began; but I was opposed to that, I don't know why, out of pride perhaps. Hence there was continual, acute, unendurable suffering.'

'You really suffered?'

'Yes, unspeakably, from desire. You see, Vladimiro, it is desire that makes one suffer more than anything else. Now ordinarily there are two ways in which we behave in face of desire: either we try not to think about it or we satisfy it. But

118

a desire that is prolonged, unchanging and unsatisfied, beyond a certain limit of time – that we cannot endure. Personally, Vladimiro, I would go so far as to assert that, just as one cannot stand up to certain temperatures for more than a few minutes, so one cannot stand up to desire for more than a few hours. Now can you imagine a desire that lasts, not for a few hours, nor for a few days, nor for a few months, but for years, and all the time with the same intensity? If you can imagine that, you can get an idea of how much I suffered.'

I fell silent, shaking my head. Vladimiro, too, was silent. Then, cautiously, he ventured: 'What about the difference of opinion?'

'This was how it was. One morning during that March of 1950 I thought, very reasonably, that a certain thing had not really happened but that I had dreamt it. How does one act with dreams? One thinks about them for a little, one tries for a little to reconstruct them, to remember them, then one shrugs one's shoulders and thrusts the dream aside for good so as to occupy oneself with other more important things. And that was what would have happened again on that particular morning. Except that "he", revealing himself for the first time, let me say in parenthesis, as somebody distinct and different from me, popped up suddenly and told me loudly and clearly that that particular thing had not been dreamed by me at all, but that it had actually happened and that "he" was there precisely as a witness that it had happened in reality and not in a dream. Yes, Vladimiro, that was the divergence of opinion on that fatal morning. And ever since then I and "he" have never ceased quarrelling. Twenty years of quarrelling. "He" continues to maintain that the thing really happened; I persist in answering that it was a dream.'

'But what was the thing that, according to you, was a dream and, according to him, actually occurred?'

I assumed my most scientific tone because I knew for certain that at this moment Vladimiro had trained all the batteries of his science upon me, in the same way that, at the beginning of my visit, he had slammed the light of his high-powered lamp into my face. 'You must know, Vladimiro,' I said, 'that my mother had the habit, even as late as 1950, of coming every evening, before she went to bed, to kiss me good-night. She had been doing it since I was a child. A habit, in any case, common to many mothers. Here, stop it, what are you doing?'

'I'm taking a few notes.'

'Not on any account. No notes. Put away that notebook and that Biro. I don't want any notes. What I am going to tell you is, furthermore, not worth noting. A simple divergence of opinion about a fact which, on careful consideration, is not of much importance: what is there to take notes about? Besides, Vladimiro, I am not here as a patient; I am here as a friend. What would you say, supposing you came to confide in me and ask my advice and then saw me scribbling away while you were talking? Put away your notebook and your pen. Let us talk.'

'All right, Rico, let us talk.'

'Good. Well then, where were we . . .? Oh yes, at the fact that my mother, like so many other mothers in any case, used to come every night, even in 1950, to kiss me good-night. My mother would come in, generally about midnight, sometimes even later, would tuck me up in bed, then stoop down and kiss me on the forehead, saying: "Sleep well", and would then go away. My bed, you must note, was in a corner, with the whole of one side against the wall, so that my mother, when she tucked me up, had either to tuck in the bedcovers on one side only or to bend right across the bed to tuck them in on the other side as well. Sometimes all this would happen with the lights on; I would still be reading or perhaps even studying (I had a habit of studying in bed), and then it was my mother who would put out the light; sometimes, however, I would already have turned out the light even if I hadn't yet gone to sleep. But anyhow, with or without the light, there was nothing strange, nothing abnormal, let us even say, Vladimiro, there was nothing interesting about it. A mother saying good-night to her son: that was all.'

Vladimiro said nothing. The notebook and pen lay in front of him, beside his right hand, a hand which, like himself, was long and thin; but the hand did not move. I remained silent for a moment and then Vladimiro made a grimace as though he were in pain. Finally, with an effort, he asked: 'But . . . but the difference of opinion?'

'I'm coming to the point. I'll now give you the two versions of this fact of my mother's kiss, my own and "his". First mine and then "his".'

'You mean, first the thing as a dream and then the thing as an event which actually happened?'

'Precisely. Well then, version number one: mine, that of the dream. My mother came to bid me good-night. I had already turned out the light but I was awake. My mother came in without turning on the light, came over to the bed, bent over me, tucked in the sheets, first on one side and then on the other. In order to do this she was forced, naturally, to bend over me. As she stooped, involuntarily she brushed lightly against me at the level of my stomach. My mother, for some reason that I didn't understand, did not manage to tuck in the sheet very well and so this light brushing with her elbow changed into a pressure, and this pressure seemed to be deliberate, conscious, intentional. I wanted to say: "Be careful what you're doing, Mamma, something irreparable might happen, stand up, please, stand up and go away"; but, just as happens in dreams, I was unable to speak. In the meantime she remained in her stooping position, went on tucking in the sheet and pressing with her elbow. Finally the thing that I was afraid of happened. At the same moment I awoke and became aware that I had had a wet dream. That is my version.'

I broke off my tale for a moment and took advantage of this to stub out my cigarette in the ashtray and light another. My movements were calm, precise, careful. I was perfectly cool, perfectly scientific.

Then I resumed. 'Version number two. "His" version, according to which the event really occurred. My mother came in in the dark, I was awake and, as usual, was suffering from desire. My mother came over to my bed, stooped over me and tucked in the bedcovers first on one side and then on the other. In order to do this she was naturally forced to bend over me and, as she stooped, exactly as in the dream, without intending it she brushed lightly against me at the level of my stomach.

'At this point the two versions diverge. According to "him" my mother noticed my "suffering" (let us so call it), stood up without finishing her tucking in of the covers, passed her hand across my forehead, felt that it was burning and asked me in a low voice how I was. I replied that I was all right; but, so it seems, at any rate according to "him", I gave a sigh. My mother said to me in a whisper: "Try and go to sleep, it's late"; then she bent across the bed again, as though to give a final touch to her tucking in on the side against the wall. But her elbow pressed down hard upon me, at the same time moving up and down with a hurried, expeditious, uneasy fierceness. Until, in a matter of a few seconds, it produced the effect that you can imagine. Then the elbow came to a halt, pressing hard against me, as if to give me time to recover myself. After that my mother, breathing somewhat heavily but still silent, stood up, gave me her usual kiss on the forehead and went away. End of the second version.'

A long silence followed. I sat with bowed head, silently smoking, as if to give Vladimiro time to collect his ideas. Finally I commented: 'Of course this second version is entirely false, entirely invented, entirely fantastic. But that hasn't prevented "him" from maintaining it with drawn sword, inflexibly, for twenty years. You'll understand now why I said that for twenty years my life has been poisoned by a difference of opinion between "him" and me.'

Silence. I went on to remark bitterly: 'But I can already see it in your eyes that you, Vladimiro, are inclined to believe more in "him" than in me.'

Vladimiro gave a violent start as though he were awakening from sleep and replied hurriedly: 'Not at all, I believe you and only you. Besides, who should I believe, except you? There's no one here in front of me but you.'

'True. But now, going back to this difference of opinion, you can easily imagine, Vladimiro, the uneasiness of mind that has been caused me by the indecent insinuation of that same

122

crafty, wicked individual. It's natural that, though I knew myself to be innocent, I should have developed a strong feeling of guilt. In the end I found myself compelled to mitigate my feeling of guilt by what I may call a rational and, in a way, scientific explanation, which can be summed up in this manner: "Yes, I am convinced that it was a dream. A dream inspired, of course, by 'him'. But even if, preposterously, I had to admit that it was not a dream but an actual occurrence, well, even in that improbable case, I had nothing to do with it, neither more nor less. It was, in short, a thing between 'him' and my mother, not desired nor – even less – approved by me. All I did was to be present. Therefore the matter does not concern me and I don't wish to know anything about it." What d'you think of this explanation, Vladimiro? Doesn't it perhaps settle the whole question?'

Vladimiro neither approved nor disapproved of my remarks. He wriggled in his chair. His whole face was twisted in a grimace of intense uneasiness. Finally he managed to say: 'But "he" – what proofs does he put forward in support of his version?'

I replied without hesitation: 'Two proofs, one factual, the other psychological. The factual proof: my mother, after that evening, entirely gave up coming to say good-night to me. The psychological proof: the feeling of guilt, according to "him", must have been so strong in me that it actually made me invent a dream I had never had, so as not to recognize that the things I claimed to have dreamed had, on the contrary, occurred in reality when I was awake.'

Vladimiro showed no sign of feeling; this was in accordance with his same method, already mentioned, whereby he appeared anxious, perplexed, distressed, neither more nor less than he had been during the whole of my visit. Finally, barely moving his lips, he said: 'What we may call the factual proof has some weight.'

'Not at all! It's true that, after that night, my mother never again came to give me that kiss on my forehead. But not because that thing had really happened. Because, having unintentionally touched my stomach with her elbow and become aware of my excitement, she feared that some day it *might* happen. D'you see what I mean?'

Once again Vladimiro made no pronouncement. 'And then?' he asked.

'And then what?'

'And then what happened?'

'Nothing. I've told you. Twenty years of quarrelling, during which "he" has maintained his version and I mine.'

'But since that night, what has your life been like?'

'My life? It's been just as before, it hasn't changed.'

'No, I mean your interior life.'

'Ah, my interior life? Well, not so very happy. Put yourself in my shoes, Vladimiro. I loved my mother. That love was now being poisoned by an individual, one who was no stranger, for reasons all of his own, which did not concern me in any way. To put it briefly: twenty years of hell. It so happened that, six years later, in 1956, my mother died.'

'Your mother died?'

'Yes, alas, she died.'

I was struck by the fact that Vladimiro made me repeat twice over the news of my mother's death. It was true that it had been in 1956 or thereabouts that Vladimiro and I, both of us twenty years old by that time, had parted and gone our different ways. This, however, did not make it impossible for Vladimiro to know that my mother was dead. I looked at him and he looked back at me, with his usual expressionless, though sorrowful, air of perplexity. Then he said gently but firmly: 'But of course, Rico, your mother is *not* dead.'

I felt myself blushing. I had a sinking feeling. Sinking into what? Into the dark well of the most unfathomable desublimation. It was, indeed, true: my mother was not dead. She was alive, perfectly alive, and I wondered why in the world it had entered my head to say she was dead. A long silence followed. Vladimiro was staring at me; and I was looking back at him. Then suddenly, absurdly, I took my face between my hands and burst into sobs.

What was happening to me? Quite simple: it was one of the usual treacherous pranks of desublimation. I realized with

124

an acute awareness that this unexpected weeping put an end, irreparably, to the detached, scientific tone which I had counted upon to confront Vladimiro's learning; but there was nothing to be done. Without shame, without restraint or control I abandoned myself to a grief as obscure as it was idiotic. I sat sobbing with my face in my hands, opposite the impassive Vladimiro, whom I imagined, even amidst my sobs, to be inwardly chuckling at my emotional collapse. At last, like one of those heavy but short-lived downpours in spring-time, my weeping diminished and then ceased. I pulled my handkerchief from my pocket, dried my eyes, noisily blew my nose. I said gruffly: 'I'm sorry.'

Vladimiro made no reply. After a moment's silence I went on: 'I know what you're thinking at this moment.'

'What?'

'That my health is not . . . in perfect condition.'

With slightly suspect solicitude, Vladimiro hastened to reassure me: 'No, not at all. Everything's normal. The only matter about which I might have some reservations is, if anything, your dialogue with "him", with Federicus Rex. Possibly you ought to manage somehow to put a stop to this dialogue.'

Kindled with sudden enthusiasm, I answered: 'That's exactly what I'm trying to do the whole time: to make him stop talking, to reduce him to complete silence. But there's only one way to get rid of him – by sublimating the sexual impulse which, for the moment, he monopolizes arbitrarily for his own exclusive use and convenience. As long as I fail seriously to undertake the process of sublimation, as long as I remain desublimated, I very much fear that what you call the dialogue between "him" and me will be bound to continue.'

It was strange that these terms, accepted as standard in his own branch of science, did not seem to make any impression upon Vladimiro. They seemed, rather, to arouse in him a positive disgust, an anxiety, even perhaps a distress. He twisted and turned in his chair, became agitated, and finally remarked: 'Wouldn't it be better if you took the thing rather more simply?'

125

'Why, how?'

'Well, by changing what we may call these imaginary dialogues of yours into real, genuine conversations with other people. I mean real people in your life.'

'But "he" is a real person too, Vladimiro. I'm sorry, but if you don't understand this you don't understand anything.'

'Above all, you should devote yourself to your work, to your career.'

'There I agree with you. Certainly. Anyhow that's just what I've been struggling to say so far. Yes, what's needed is that "he" should collaborate in a systematic plan for sublimation. Once I've obtained his collaboration, I'm on the right track.'

I rubbed my hands together, as though to indicate that, as soon as 'he' collaborated, there would be no more problems. But Vladimiro, unconvinced, shook his head. 'No,' he said; 'you see, you go on talking about "him". Instead of that, you should be acting as if he did not exist.'

'But he does exist. Unfortunately he does exist.'

'All right then, he exists. But in the meantime it would be a very good thing if you would call things by their names.'

'Why, am I *not* calling things by their names?'

'No, Rico, you see, what I mean is their usual names. Drop the sublimation, the desublimation, forget you're an intellectual who has read Freud, imagine that you're – what shall I say? – a baker's boy.'

I was vexed. 'You're fine sort of people, you are,' I muttered; 'you invent words and then you don't like people to make use of them.'

'They're scientific terms which, in any case, should be used in moderation.'

'What kind of moderation? How can one be moderate in questions like this, questions of life and death?'

'How do life and death come into *your* question?'

All of a sudden I was infuriated and, banging my fist down on the table, I shouted: 'Life for me is sublimation, desublimation is death. If I sublimate myself I shall live, that is, I shall be a man worthy of the name. Otherwise, I shall be dead to my own humanity. I shall be desublimated, that is, a miserable wretch, inferior, incapable, impotent, all sex and no creativeness. I shall be a member, irreparably, of the inferior, subject race which exists all over the world, in the rich as well as in the poor countries, and which is characterized not by colour of skin or physical features but by a congenital inability to become sublimated.'

I drew back, red in the face and breathless, seized hold carelessly of my packet of cigarettes and then dropped it again, realizing that, during my outburst, I had left a cigarette I had just lit on the edge of the ashtray. Vladimiro did not appear in the least disconcerted by the scene I had made. Impassive, sorrowful, all he did was to look at me. As soon as he saw I had calmed down a little, he asked: 'What have you done so far ... to be a man?'

I was anxious to resume the detached, scientific tone of the beginning of my visit. But I felt that I was only partly successful. Ticking off the points on my fingers but still panting and breathless, I replied: 'Firstly: I left my wife. I am living on my own in a flat I have taken for a year. Secondly: No women come, no women shall come, into that flat. These two steps, of separation and chastity, are, let us say, negative steps. On the positive plane, however, I can already boast of two successes. Firstly: I am going to take over the direction of a film of great importance. Secondly: I love a woman of exceptional beauty and intelligence and she loves me in return. I cannot but recognize, Vladimiro, a connection, a link, a relation, in fact, between separation and chastity on the one hand and the film direction and love on the other. Perhaps it is not actually sublimation as yet; but it's not far off. I shall make the film, I shall go on loving, and then I shall see whether there has really been sublimation or not.'

I felt I had not merely recovered the equilibrium which had been jeopardized by my outburst, but also that I had convinced Vladimiro of my fundamental sanity. The dialogue, in fact, was a real thing, 'he' was real, the quarrels between 'him' and me were real. But I had the situation in hand again;

127

so that my visit to Vladimiro had regained its original character as a warning, a threat, a challenge.

With such thoughts in mind I sat quiet, looking at the desk, smoking, meditative. I was conscious of Vladimiro moving about in his chair as though he could not manage to find a comfortable position; and I obstinately waited until he found it. Finally I heard his voice saying: 'All that now remains is to arrange a day and time for the start of your treatment.'

Disconcerted, because I was convinced that I had proved, both by my demeanour and my words, that I was perfectly sane, I asked: 'What d'you mean, what treatment?'

'The treatment which you need. The treatment to cure you of your . . . of your dialogue.'

'And how long would this treatment have to go on?'

'One can't say offhand, Rico. From a minimum of six months to a maximum of six years.'

'How many times a week?'

'Two or three.'

'And how much would each session cost me?'

'Prices are laid down by doctors' orders.'

'But you'd give me a special price, I hope.'

'Well, of course.'

I was silent, pretending to think. Then I said quietly: 'There's no question of it. No treatment for me.'

Vladimiro seemed to be frightened by my answer. He screwed up his face in distress and squirmed in his armchair. 'But I assure you, Rico,' he said, 'you're in need of treatment . . . of lengthy treatment.'

I shook my head, inflexibly. 'Meanwhile it remains to be seen whether that is true. Besides, in any case – I'm sorry, Vladimiro, but I want to be honest with you – in any case I wouldn't be treated by you. And you know why?'

Vladimiro shook his head vehemently but said nothing.

'Because, in my opinion, before you treat other people you ought to have treatment yourself. Between you and me, it is you, Vladimiro, who are the true neurotic. I don't say this in a casual manner; I have deduced it from a number of observa-

128

tions I have made while we were talking. I've been taking a careful look at you, Vladimiro, and I can tell you with absolute certainty what you are: you are desublimated, but you don't know that you are; in fact you think you're sublimated and you behave as if you were.'

Vladimiro was visibly disconcerted by a diagnosis that was so precise and so scientific. I added immediately, without giving him time to recover himself: 'You know what reveals you as being desublimated, Vladimiro? Your failure. If you were sublimated, you would not be here in this little flat and work-shop combined, in this very humble little study, with the baby's pram in the entrance-hall and the smell of cooking everywhere. Sublimation means success and success means sublimation. I'm desublimated too, and perhaps I'm a failure. But I have one advantage over you, Vladimiro: I know what I am. You don't know and you do nothing to make you know.'

Vladimiro shook his head again; but it seemed that he could find no objection to what I said. So, after an interval of silence, seeing that he did not speak, I asked him: 'Have you nothing to say? Then answer me this question: what are your relations with "him"? You understand what I'm alluding to, without any need of further explanations, don't you? Good relations? Bad? So-so? Does he talk much? Or little? Or not at all?'

Vladimiro looked more and more disconcerted, a sign that I had hit the mark, 'Rico,' he stammered, 'I don't have any special relationship with . . . with "him", so to speak. I have a normal relationship, like everyone else.'

'Normal, eh?'

'Yes, normal.'

'But what d'you mean by normality?'

'Normality, Rico . . . is normality.'

'Let's be clear about it: does your "he" compel you to make love often with your wife? Every day? Once a week? Once a month?'

He squirmed; evidently he was on thorns, on the gridiron. At last he stammered: 'Rico, we'll talk about my wife and me . . . next time we meet.'

We looked at one another. All of a sudden I realized, to my relief, that I had got what I wanted. I was 'on top'; and Vladimiro was 'underneath'. We were both desublimated, of course; but he more so than I. Quietly I said: 'Well, let's leave it at that. But no treatment for me. You will be wanting to know, now, why I came. I'll answer you willingly: I came in order to put "him" on his guard, to make "him" understand that, if need be, I can take a strong line.'

'Yes, I see.'

'Now look, Vladimiro, I've no need of treatment because the principal effect of health, or at least the kind of health that you promise me, would be that "he" would stop talking altogether. But by now I've become accustomed to his company; and, to tell you the truth, I get angry with "him" not so much because he talks as because he talks too much. And, when all's said and done, I'm forced to recognize that without "him" I should feel – how shall I say? – lost. It counts a great deal to have a friend with whom you spend many hours a day. Now and then you quarrel, of course, but then you make it up and are friends again. What would you do if a friend like that suddenly failed you? I don't know if I'm making it clear.'

'Yes, friendship is a very fine thing, Rico, but look . . .'

All at once I made up my mind to go. I rose, put out my last cigarette and said, conclusively: 'Well, let's leave it at that, for the present. And . . . how much do I owe you?'

'Nothing, Rico, nothing, you're an old friend and . . .'

We went out into the entrance-hall. The smell of cooking was stronger than ever.

This smell, and the baby's pram in the corner, shouted, screamed out their message: 'This is the house of a man who is a failure, who is weak-willed, who is desublimated!'

'Good-bye, Vladimiro.'

6 Unmasked!

An exhibitionist! I knew 'him' to be a *voyeur*, a sadist, a masochist, a homosexual (this too, certainly: I haven't mentioned it yet but the moment will come when I shall do so), a fetishist (his speciality is women's torn tights, with holes showing white skin here and there, as with beggars' medieval stockings in the pictures of Bosch and Brueghel), but not an exhibitionist. And now I know for certain that he is. But let us take things in order.

Today Maurizio came to my flat to receive my contribution to the 'group'. I had already sold the shares some days earlier and had placed the money in the bank. I went therefore to the bank to withdraw the five millions at about four o'clock, the afternoon opening time. I cannot deny that I felt rather puzzled as to the best means of making the payment. Certainly the simplest way would have been to give Maurizio a cheque. But a cheque is easily traceable. Five million is more than a contribution; it is almost a financing. Supposing that something might occur next day: an attack, an 'expropriation', or, more simply, a tightening of repression, and I should find myself in trouble. Investigations would be made, the financiers would be sought out, my name would be found, application would be made to the bank, my flat, or rather my two flats, would be searched, and I should end up in the headlines of the newspapers. As a result, film producers would give me the cold shoulder, film-scripts would go to my rivals, I should be left without any work.

On the other hand, it is also true that it is not easy to hand over five million in cash. It is a large sum, a large bundle of banknotes.

In the midst of these reflections, I realized that they were the reflections of a coward. But this cowardice – where did it come from? Obviously, from desublimation, exactly like that other fit of cowardice, resisted only for the sake of appearances, which had caused me to submit to Maurizio's blackmail. I said to 'him': 'This is the effect of your persistent refusal to collaborate. In the first place, you're costing me five million. Then, as if that were not enough, you don't even instil sufficient courage into me for me not to mind the consequences.'

'He' answered me characteristically: 'These are things that don't concern me. Are you annoyed at being a coward? Well then, try not to be.'

'Without your help I might perhaps pretend to be courageous. But alas, there's no possibility of my becoming really so.'

'Well, pretend. In your world pretence and reality are, fundamentally, the same thing. Only in my world is it impossible to pretend. In fact, if I don't feel desire, I certainly can't pretend to feel it.'

In the end cowardice, as, given the circumstances, was to be foreseen, prevailed. At the bank I had the amount paid to me in notes of a hundred thousand lire. Fifty banknotes, which I distributed among the various pockets of my jacket and trousers. Then, with my jacket over my arm, I left the bank and started in a haphazard way down the street.

It was early; Maurizio would not be coming until six o'clock. I walked along in a cool breeze which formed a pleasing contrast to the heat of the summer sunshine. The Roman summer still continued, luminous, scorching, dry, with a background of an intoxicating movement of sea air. 'He', always highly sensitive to variations of weather, whispered excitedly: 'What magnificent weather! How lovely the summer is! This weather makes me long for an adventure. Yes, something intense, quick as lightning, unexpected.'

I did not reply. I was angry with 'him' on account of the five million and my cowardice; I had a grudge against him. But there were two empty hours in front of me and I had no wish to go home. So, in effect, I could not blame him. Nothing passes the time so well as what 'he' calls an adventure. Indeed, this quality at least must be allowed him: by trusting in him one passes in a flash out of ordinary life and moves, magically, into a reality outside time.

I came to a church that raised its great baroque façade at the far end of a small square. Almost without thinking I went up the steps, pushed open the door and entered.

Once inside the church, I understood why I had come in. It was the only place where the adventure, so irresponsibly hoped for by 'him', would not be possible. I had gone in, therefore, in order to protect myself from his spirit of enterprise. But there was something else. This church, I seemed to remember, was two-thirds baroque and one-third Byzantine. Behind the high altar, in the apse, there were some celebrated mosaics. My intention was to make use of this masterpiece, created by the sublimation of more than ten centuries ago, to teach 'him' a lesson. But not in the threatening sense usually attributed to this phrase. A real lesson, like a lesson at school. For indeed I never give up hope altogether, with 'him', that I may be able to educate him and obtain by persuasion what I fail to obtain by force.

With these thoughts in mind, I made my way towards the far end of the church. There were three aisles, one central and two lateral. The central aisle, or nave, received a rather dim, yellow light from a great octagonal window situated above the door. The side aisles were in semi-darkness. The church was pleasantly cool and silent. I walked slowly, looking idly at the empty confessionals and the rows of deserted pews, until I reached the apse. Two processions of figures of saints and martyrs, in rich white garments, against a background of an equally rich green landscape, ascended from the two sides of the apse towards the central figure of the Christ.

I said to 'him', in a didactic tone of voice: 'There, now, is the beauty of sublimation. Those figures are not real and yet they are more than real. The Christ has a human face which yet expresses something that is more than human. Now who do you think created so much beauty?'

He did not reply. And, after a moment's silence, I went on: '*You* did, *you*, no one else but you. Without you, or rather without your loyal, constant, uninterrupted collaboration, this beauty would never have been created for our delight, for our consolation. And without this beauty and the many other things that accompanied its creation, we men would still be living in caves, dressed in skins, hirsute and inarticulate. But no, not even that is true. Even in caves, man achieved sublimation; as a testimony to this sublimation there are the wonderful prehistoric paintings that adorn so many grottoes in Europe and Africa. It is only today, therefore, that you are really in revolt against the sacred law which lays down that you should be submissive and co-operative. And yet not much is asked of you. I, for instance, do not ask you to help me create the neolithic frescoes of the caves of Altamira or the mosaics in this church. All I ask of you is that you should collaborate towards a film that is not by any means of poor quality: that is all. But you, you scoundrel, you refuse me even the little that I ask. Besides, I ought not to consider you as an enemy – in fact, as "The Enemy", by antonomasia!'

At first I thought he was not going to answer me. It is his favourite method when I reprove him: silence. To my surprise, however, it was not like that this time. Negligently, he replied: 'There are so many ways in which I could answer you. But all you need to do is to look at that woman. The answer will come from her.'

The better to examine the mosaics, I had moved over towards the side aisle on the right, taking up a position between a small baroque chapel and the marble corkscrew staircase that led up to the pulpit. Near the pulpit I saw the woman 'he' had pointed out to me. She was not young. She was a foreigner, possibly an American. She had the head of a schoolmistress or governess; spectacles of dark tortoiseshell on her large, severe nose; a wide mouth, perhaps sensual but disdainful in expression; short, brown, bobbed hair above a robust, sinewy neck. It was a head which, for some reason, I could easily imagine as being capped with the black mortar-board worn by professors in Anglo-Saxon universities on solemn academic occasions.

She was wearing a white blouse and a grey skirt. She was thin, flat-figured, masculine in appearance; but, below the hollow of her back, as 'he' cunningly pointed out to me, an unexpectedly large behind jutted out. A solid, round behind, muscular, superabundant, brash, childish, gay. A behind that contradicted her severe face: the latter said 'no' to life; the behind, emphatically, said 'yes'.

Then the woman moved in order to have a better look at the mosaics in the apse; and as she moved, at the same time, there was a violent movement of her behind, the exaggerated nature of which, however, had nothing provocative about it and seemed, on the contrary, to be unquestionably ingenuous and innocent. How old might this woman be? Perhaps forty, perhaps more. With her nose in the air and her glasses on her nose, she looked at the mosaics with such intensity as to make one suppose that her thoughts were elsewhere and that in reality she was merely pretending to look: only pretence could be so earnest.

Deliberately I brought on a fit of coughing and the tourist at once turned and cast a rapid glance at me, through her glasses, from her mild blue eyes. Then the incredible happened. 'He' whispered: 'Cough again. As soon as she turns, show *me*.'

'Why, what d'you mean?'

'I'm telling you to show me to that woman.'

'Are you crazy?'

'No, I'm not crazy. Do as I tell you.'

'But I don't wish to!'

Quite unexpectedly, all of a sudden he flew into a terrible temper. 'Just now you were speaking of the beauty that is an essential part of sublimation. But I am something much more than that. I am the beauty of the world. This beauty should be known, displayed, admired. And you, you imbecile, should not be ashamed of it, should not hide it; you should parade it in the light of the sun. But there's more to it than that. The beauty of the world, *my* beauty, should be shown to all but above all to those who are hungry for it. This woman is not hungry for the insipid beauty of your so-called Byzantine masterpiece, but for me. You only have to look at the back of her neck, shaved bare, red, inflamed, to understand that, to feel it. So don't make me angry; free me from the tiresome wrappings that keep me hidden, expose me, exhibit me. This is not a prayer, it's an order.'

Beads of anguished sweat stood on my brow. 'But d'you realize we're in church?' I stammered.

'So what?'

'What d'you mean: so what? We're in a holy place, dedicated to God.'

Again 'he' flew into a rage. 'But I am a god, in fact I'm the only god that really exists, in this as in the other world. I am the original god, the father of all gods, past, present and future. And this church is in reality dedicated to me, because I am life and churches are dedicated to life.'

'He' was shouting with such frantic violence, with an authority so peremptory that I no longer had the strength to resist. Moreover, as always happens to me in these moments of supreme weakness, I did not so much endure 'him' as identify myself with 'him'. I was experiencing a dream, 'his' dream; and in this dream I was 'he' and 'he' was me.

So there I was, moving my jacket from my right to my left arm; then, under cover of the jacket, lowering my right hand to my stomach and, in frantic haste, liberating 'him' from his prison of cloth and buttons. I heard him utter an 'ah!' of victorious relief, but I did not dare to look down. I hesitated, then made up my mind and coughed loudly, in an expressive sort of way. The woman turned round immediately, with a jerk. Then, rapidly, I lifted my left arm from which, like the curtain of a theatre, hung my jacket; and 'he' was on exhibition.

As 'he' had foreseen, the woman did not avert her eyes; she seemed truly hungry. She looked and looked and looked at 'him', with an incredulous, fascinated intensity; and meanwhile a dark, uneven, burning blush rose gradually upwards from her breast over her robust neck, covering her pale, austere cheeks and reaching right up beneath her spectacles. This contemplation lasted – at least so it seemed to me – an eternity. 'His' eternity. Then, all of a sudden, the suspense came to an end. Normal life returned. The woman moved and came towards me. For a moment I was afraid she was going to

136

attack me, to slap my face, to call a policeman at the top of her voice and hand me over to him.

But no, I was mistaken, as usual. She passed close beside me, her head down, and then made her way towards the door, still keeping her chin low on her chest, with a kind of demure absorption that irresistibly recalled the similar demeanour of the faithful after communion. Yes indeed, she had received 'him' and was now going away, deeply moved and with a set expression, piously, with bowed head, bearing away the memory of what she had seen, in the most secret and hidden depths of her memory. I watched her until she disappeared; but I did not move. I knew that I ought not to move because the so-called 'adventure' foreshadowed by 'him' a little earlier must consist entirely in this: in exhibition. 'He', in fact, approved. 'Yes,' he said, 'don't move. She saw. That was all I wanted. I'm satisfied.'

I said nothing. Anaesthetized, so to speak, by an immense astonishment, for I had not imagined myself capable of yielding to his arrogance to such an extent, I acted under the influence of a kind of trance-like amazement, like a figure in a dream. Now, however, it was not 'his' dream; it was my own. It was a dream of wonderment and incredulity which made me do things without being aware of it. Mysteriously, inexplicably, I suddenly found myself in my own home, seated at the table in my study in front of my typewriter, and I did not know how I had got there. The five million in hundred thousand lire notes, assembled now in a single bundle, lay on the folder of carbon paper. A blank sheet had been inserted in the typewriter. A few lines had already been written.

How long ago was it that I was in the church, and the woman with the severe schoolmistress face and the gay tomboy bottom was looking at 'him' and I was looking at her? Centuries, it seemed to me. But how had it been possible for such an incredible thing to happen? My mind was unable to master the event; it oscillated between stupefied reprobation and incredulous indulgence. I lit a cigarette, read the words already written on the sheet of paper, and started, or rather started again, tapping on the keys. Then suddenly, from the depths of my cataleptic stupor, rose this precise thought: Anyhow let it be quite clear that I had nothing to do with it. Everything took place between 'him' and the woman. What *I* did was to watch.

'So then, you're a *voyeur*!'

Who had spoken? I, 'he', or somebody else? Luckily, at that moment, the bell rang. I took up the bundle of banknotes, stuffed it into my pocket with some difficulty and went to open the door. Maurizio was standing on the threshold, dressed all in white, as usual, and with dark glasses. Without greeting me, he came in and walked along the passage in front of me, his hands in his pockets. I followed him. We went into the study. Still in silence, Maurizio went and threw himself down in the armchair, in his usual offhand manner, with his legs over one arm and his back against the other. 'Well then,' he said, 'how about the five million?'

Nothing to be done! His enigmatic, elegant impassiveness had already put me 'underneath'. I had intended to hand over the bundle of banknotes in silence, in a cold, detached manner as though to emphasize my disdainful indifference. Instead of which – devil take me! – there I was, anxiously stammering: 'I went just a short time ago to draw the money from the bank. There it is, Maurizio; count it over, five million in notes of a hundred thousand.'

What a lot of words! I was trying now to extract the notes from my pocket and could not manage it. I went red with the effort and writhed like a worm beneath Maurizio's expressionless stare. At last I pulled them out, one by one, collected them together again into a bundle and handed them to Maurizio who, without looking at them, put them into the pocket of his safari jacket. After a moment he remarked: 'Why, after all, in banknotes? Wouldn't a cheque have been less cumbersome?'

'Oh well, I don't know. I didn't think of it.'

He was silent a moment and then said: 'Now be truthful, you were afraid of compromising yourself.'

Stupidly I protested: 'Afraid of compromising myself? Really I haven't any fears of that sort.'

But above all I was disappointed by the fact that Maurizio

had not thanked me. I could not refrain from saying to him:
'I give you five million and you don't even say thank you.'

'You've only done your duty.'

'And that is?'

'To contribute to the overthrow of capitalism by means of capitalist money.'

'But I'm not a capitalist. In a sense I'm a proletarian. A proletarian of the typewriter.'

'Yet you earned the money by working in the service of capitalism.'

I felt upset again. He was not joking, he was serious; and I felt myself to be more 'underneath' than ever. I had had the sensation that, by paying out five million lire, I was performing an act that was positively heroic. And now, instead, he was more or less spitting upon my heroism. Nevertheless, still carried away by my own ingenuousness, I inquired: 'And now what are you going to do with my five millions?'

'I don't know. I think that, to begin with, we shall use them to pay the rent of our headquarters. Then we shall buy some furniture and other things we need.'

'Where is the headquarters?'

'In Via Appia Nuova.'

'Is it a big place?'

'Yes.'

'But what is it? A flat?'

'No, it's a place in a basement. A garage.'

'Are you going to hold meetings at this headquarters?'

'Yes, as soon as it's ready.'

'It isn't ready?'

'Some finishing touches are needed.'

'Of what kind?'

'Flags, portraits, photographs. We must also buy some chairs.'

'Portraits of whom?'

'Of Marx, of Lenin, Stalin, Mao, Ho-Chi-Minh.'

I felt disillusioned. The more I tried to bring the conversation round to my five million, the more Maurizio evaded the subject. In the end, with the typical imprudence of the desublimated, I said: 'You must admit that my five million comes in very handy for you.'

'Of course. We need money and we have no one to finance us.'

'But how many people have given you such a large sum? I bet no one has.'

He said nothing. 'Those five million,' I yelled, 'are a very big sacrifice for me. I'm not a rich man, I earn my living and you know it.'

Again silence. I persisted: 'A sacrifice should be proportionate to one's means. Mine is disproportionate.'

This time he made up his mind to speak: he seemed disgusted. 'Come off it,' he said; 'you know perfectly well that, if you don't pay, we shall drop you from the film-script.'

'We – who is that?'

'We of the group.'

'Ah, so it's like that: no millions, no script.'

'I'm afraid, Rico, that's precisely how it is.'

Suddenly I became seriously angry. I rose to my feet and started walking up and down the room. Then, after a little, I stopped all at once in front of Maurizio. 'All right, then,' I said. 'So be it. But in that case I wish to speak clearly to you, once and for all. As you know, I share your ideas, I feel and am a revolutionary, and that's the exact truth. But we both of us know that it's not for that reason that I'm giving you the five million.'

Maurizio looked at me, frowned, and then said: 'I don't know anything about it. You say you know why you're giving them. Well then, tell me.'

'Listen to me carefully: I'm giving the five million because in reality I'm yielding to blackmail. And you and your friends of the group are the blackmailers.'

He looked at me, remained silent and seemed to be waiting for me to explain myself further. I resumed: 'In the first place: political blackmail. You place yourself, without the authorization of anything or anybody, on the glistening marble pedestal of revolution and from there you look down upon me, the vile worm sunk in the mud of counter-revolution.

140

So I have to prove that I am not a counter-revolutionary. So, in order to prove it, I have to contribute to the cause. And so, in order that my contribution may be a convincing one, I have to pay out the unheard-of sum of five million. Then, in the second place, there is the blackmail, so to speak, of one generation to another. I am thirty-five, you of the group are all round about twenty. A man of thirty-five belongs, inevitably, to the satisfied, privileged class. In order to demonstrate that he does not wholly belong to it, that he wishes to get out of it, let him pay; and let the amount be proportionate, if not to his means, to his age: five million! There is then a third blackmail: that of so-called men of action, meaning you and your friends of the group, against the intellectual, the sedentary man, the man of culture, meaning myself. In this case too the intellectual has to demonstrate – to the sound of money, of course – that he is not what he is; that he too, if need be, is capable of action. His action may consist in putting his signature to a cheque; never mind, it's action all the same. Finally, most important of all, there is the fourth blackmail . . .'

Maurizio had listened to my outburst without saying anything or in any way altering his position in the armchair. When I paused and fell silent, he inquired, almost without moving his lips: 'What is the fourth blackmail?'

I still kept silent, paralysed by a sudden feeling of impotence. The fourth blackmail, to my mind, was the clearest and most incontrovertible of all. It was the unconscious, but not for that reason any less pitiless, blackmail of the sublimated in opposition to the desublimated, a fundamental blackmail which explains, inspires and justifies all the others. But, strange to say, as usual I had not the courage to talk about it. Why? Was it perhaps because talking about it would be equivalent to admitting my own inferiority in relation to Maurizio? Or because I was aware that my obsession with sublimation rested not on solid cultural foundations but only on the ambiguous, insidious grounds of feeling? Or again, as was more probable, because the idea of sublimation was the most intimate, the most jealously guarded, the most secret thing I have? Finally I stuttered: 'I let myself be carried away by the warmth of my remarks. The fourth blackmail . . . does not exist.'

'Then there would be, altogether, three forms of blackmail that I've used on you to take your money from you: the blackmail of a revolutionary against a counter-revolutionary; of a man of twenty against a man of thirty-five; of a man of action against an intellectual. Isn't that so?'

'Yes, there are just those three.'

Maurizio, with the greatest ease and simplicity, took the bundle of banknotes from his jacket pocket, placed it on the table and rose to his feet. 'If that's how it is,' he said, 'I'll give you back the money. Good-bye.'

He spoke these words without a shadow of hesitation; then turned his back on me and walked out of the study. In a quick moment of contemplation I took in at a single glance my professional and psychological position after this gesture on the part of Maurizio; and I was petrified. Beginning with my profession, it was clear that not merely should I not obtain the directorship of the film but should almost certainly lose the script-writing job as well. Maurizio had said so; and I had no reason to doubt his word. Coming to my psychological situation, it was that of one who suddenly finds himself transformed into a cockroach and crushed beneath the foot of a monumental contempt.

Strange to say, however, whereas the professional disaster grieved me only moderately, the contempt overwhelmed me. At the idea of Maurizio going away after throwing my five million back in my face, I felt an anguish the character of which, alas, did not escape me: it was the anguish of someone, be it man or woman, who sees himself abandoned by the person he loves. For I did indeed suffer, at that moment, like someone who loves; not like someone who finds himself despised for political, professional or, anyhow, non-sentimental reasons. And then, all of a sudden, the suspicion flashed across my mind that 'he', without my noticing it, had played one of his customary dirty tricks upon me, transforming a work-association into a passionate if not actually physiological union. In my anguish, indeed, there was a hint of

142

tenderness and torment that gave me a glimpse, like a flash of lightning on a dark night, of new and more than ever unexpected horizons of desublimation.

This sudden clutch of consciousness was indeed swift as lightning and lasted only an instant. Then I seized the bundle of banknotes and rushed out of the study. Maurizio was not in the passage or the entrance-hall, but the front door was open. He was on the landing, standing in front of the lift-shaft. I too went out on to the landing and, taking him by the arm, said breathlessly: 'Why, what are you doing? Wait a moment, come back inside and let's talk.'

He let himself be dragged quite easily into the flat; but the door remained open. I began again, in a despairing voice: 'For God's sake! I realize I was a bit sharp. But you, on your side, must admit that I was not entirely wrong.'

'D'you want to go on discussing it? Look, I haven't time. Good-bye!'

'But what the hell! Wait, just a minute, just one minute.'

'Good-bye.'

What was I doing? What was happening? Was I going mad? Suddenly there I was on the floor, on my knees in front of Maurizio, I the intellectual, the man of culture, the future film director, on my knees in front of a beardless youth with a milky complexion and golden hair. My eyes were filled with tears and I cried: 'Maurizio, you can't go away like that. Forgive me, I won't say anything more; take the money and forgive me.' As I said this, still on my knees, I tried to slip the bundle of notes into his hand. But his hand did not close upon it; and the notes fell to the ground, scattering themselves over the floor. Crawling on all fours I struggled to collect them, all round Maurizio's feet. My forehead brushed against his shoes and my mouth very nearly did the same.

Then the incredible happened. I bent forward to pick up a note which was lying near his right foot and – whether intentionally or by chance I don't know – I did really touch the toe of his shoe for a moment with my lips. I was 'underneath', more 'underneath' than ever; and this time it was not only metaphorically. I finished collecting the notes, stood up breathless and then joined Maurizio in the study. He was stretched out again in the armchair. I handed him the notes and he put them in his pocket, once again without looking at them. I was troubled at the discovery of the new, unknown aspect of my desublimation; I sought to return at least to the old relationship of inferior and superior, which was humiliating but without any physiological implications. With a pretence of coolness, I exclaimed: 'Now that the business of the five million is settled, perhaps we shall be able to talk about the script.'

My idea still remained the same: to find some way of getting 'on top' with respect to Maurizio. Now that I had taken a calculating look at the ruin into which desublimation might plunge me, I was more than ever conscious of this urgent need. Putting into effect a long premeditated plan, I added: 'I must tell you that I have not got much further with it. In fact, I have come to a stop.'

'Why?'

'Because, in order to continue, I should need some extra information.'

'About what?'

'About you, for example. You have to serve as model for the character of Rodolfo and I know scarcely anything about you.'

'It may be that there's nothing to know.'

'It may be. But I should like, all the same, to ask you a few questions.'

For a moment he was silent. Then he exclaimed: 'Carry on!'

'Let's begin with your father? What does he do?'

'He's a builder.'

'Does he own an important building firm?'

'Yes, I should say so.'

'How old is he?'

'Between forty and fifty.'

'Physically, what's he like?'

'He's a good-looking man, tall and dark, athletic, very active, very enterprising in business.'

'Anything else?'

144

'Anything else? I don't know. He has a passion for football.'

'And your mother – what's she like?'

'She's a beautiful woman, tall and big and blonde, with blue eyes.'

'How old is she?'

'Much about the same age as my father. They're of the same generation.'

'Do your father and mother love one another?'

'Yes, I should say so.'

'D'you think they've ever been unfaithful to each other?'

He remained silent for such a long time that he made me think he did not wish to reply. Indeed, he said finally: 'It's rather a delicate question, isn't it?'

'You're at liberty not to answer it.'

Again he was silent. Then he said: 'As far as I know, I believe they've been faithful to one another. But it's also true that I've never thought about it.'

'For all you know, then, it's a happy marriage?'

'Yes, it probably is.'

'Were they married in church?'

'Yes.'

'Are they religious?'

'Just like everyone else.'

'What d'you mean by that?'

'Oh well, so-so.'

'And are they fond of you?'

'Yes, of course.'

'Very fond?'

'Yes.'

'They've never let you lack anything?'

'No.'

'In fact you had a happy childhood?'

'No doubt about it.'

'Are you on intimate terms with your father and mother?'

'No.'

'Why?'

'It just is so. No particular reason.

'D'you speak to them?'

'Only at table.'

'And what d'you talk about?'

'Things of no significance.'

'For instance?'

'Really I don't know: just ordinary bourgeois conversation.'

'What is bourgeois conversation?'

'Well, we talk about objects that we've bought or would like to buy. We talk about the weather. We talk about friends, relations and acquaintances. Sometimes we talk about the theatrical shows that are going on in the town.'

'And that is bourgeois conversation?'

'Yes.'

'What is the distinction between that and revolutionary conversation?'

'In revolutionary conversation one talks about revolution.'

'Always?'

'Always, directly or indirectly.'

'I see. Are you an only child?'

'No, I have two sisters.'

'What are they called?'

'Patrizia and Fiammetta.'

'How old are they?'

'Eighteen and twenty-two.'

'Are they part of the group?'

'No, they're not part of it; they are bourgeois like my parents.'

'Well now, let's see. What reproach have you against your father and mother and sisters?'

'I? Nothing.'

'So, in a way, you consider them perfect?'

'Perfect, no – why? Nobody's perfect.'

'And yet you have nothing to reproach them with. Per fection consists precisely in the fact that a person or a thing appears to be without defects; in other words, that one has nothing to reproach them with.'

146

'Well, in that sense it might even be possible that I consider them perfect. But only in that sense.'

'Good! You consider them perfect, and yet you would like them to lose everything they possess, to become poor, to go right down in the social scale. In fact you would like them destroyed.'

He replied calmly: 'I consider them perfect, but according to the bourgeois standards of perfection. In the more general picture of revolution, it is clear that they could not, as you say, escape destruction.'

'Your parents and sisters, therefore, are perfect according to bourgeois standards. They are, from the bourgeois point of view, without defects. But will you tell me what "bourgeois" means?'

'The bourgeois are those who retain ownership of the means of production.'

'I presume that this, in the revolutionary sense, is the perfect answer, isn't it?'

'It's the Marxist definition.'

'So that you, in giving expression to it, are also perfect – isn't that so?'

He wrinkled his nose slightly, becoming aware, perhaps, of a trap. But then, obviously, he privately decided that whatever I might say or do counted for nothing, simply because I was 'underneath' and he was 'on top'. 'If perfection,' he replied, 'means adherence to a just and correct political line, then that is so. I am not saying I am perfect, but I am saying that I am trying to be, and that I have that possibility.'

'May I make one remark?'

'What is that?'

'You have given me a description which is drastically simplified and for that reason wholly generic, both of yourself and of your family. D'you know why?'

'Yes.'

'Because you don't take it into consideration that individuals are equipped with qualities and defects which are, in fact, individual; you only consider the bourgeois and the revolutionary. For you the bourgeois, any kind of bourgeois, is perfect, because you wish him to be so, that is, that he should be reduced to the mere question of class. This implies that the bourgeois, for you, is perfect in an absolute sense, precisely because it is thus possible for you to say that he is absolutely imperfect. But let that go. Whatever may be the reason, we thus have, on the one hand, your parents and sisters who are perfect according to bourgeois standards; and on the other, you and your group who are, or try to be, perfect revolutionaries, according to revolutionary standards of perfection. Isn't that so?'

'Let's suppose that it is so. What then?'

So there we were! I wanted to shout at him: 'Therefore it's not ideas, it's not political alignments, it's not interests that count. It's your bourgeois perfection, your perfection as revolutionaries. But these two kinds of perfection have a common origin. Yes, I, the imperfect man *par excellence*, I, the Desublimated Man by antonomasia, find myself confronted by two perfections, the one opposed to the other, the bourgeois and the revolutionary, which, nevertheless, have exactly the same roots: a perfectly sublimated sexual impulse, a perfectly successful sublimation. This explains why I feel myself to be 'underneath' in relation to you, the perfect revolutionary, as also in relation to Protti, the perfect capitalist. For the desublimated man is bound to feel himself inferior, whatever he may do, in relation to the man who is sublimated. That is precisely how it is; whatever may be the political ideas or the class of either the one or the other.'

I should have liked to say these and a great many other things as well; to have given vent to my feelings once and for all. But as usual I felt ashamed of a scientific explanation to which at that moment I was unable to have recourse without an intimation of feeling which Maurizio might have judged to be excessive. In other words, even in the manner in which I clung to the theory of sublimation, I scented the feckless, invidious inferiority of desublimation. So I became confused, and all I could do was to say sarcastically: 'Very well then, nothing. One thing I note, and that's all. I note that, in your family, even though for opposite reasons, you're all perfect.'

'Nothing else?'

'Only that I, on the contrary, am utterly and hopelessly imperfect.'

He said nothing. It might be that he kept silent out of annoyance at my emotional tone. For in point of fact sublimated people abhor everything that is personal, private, intimate. Sublimated people of the bourgeois class tell you this even from the time when you're a child, through the mouths of severe governesses. Sublimated revolutionaries actually make it a rule of Marxist behaviour.

I was thinking of these things, and in the meantime was looking at Maurizio as though expecting an answer from him. But the fact of my imperfection did not seem to interest him in the least. He sat silent, smoking. Then, quite unexpectedly, 'he' intervened. 'You're quite maddening,' he said; 'can't you understand, yes or no, that you would never feel inferior if you would only recognize, once and for all, your own real, genuine, indisputable superiority?'

'And in what is that superiority supposed to consist?'

'Let me say it without modesty: in the exceptional quality of the one who is speaking to you at this moment.'

'I've already heard that sort of talk on other occasions.'

'It's not talk; it's a fact. And you should speak to Maurizio about this fact.'

As usual, 'he' attacked me at a moment of weakness. He was aware of the ambiguity of my relations with Maurizio and brazenly took advantage of it. And so, myself surprised at what I was saying, I began in an embarrassed tone of voice: 'D'you want to know why I am, and why I feel, so imperfect?'

'Why is it?'

'Well, how shall I express it? It is because nature – luckily or unluckily, I don't know – has been exceptionally lavish with me.'

'In what sense?'

'I have been endowed in an exceptional manner from the sexual point of view.'

Maurizio now took off his dark glasses and gazed at me for a long time but without saying anything. I felt the same sensation as when plunging from the highest diving-board at a swimming-pool. I realized that now I had really said it; and that I must pursue the subject at all costs. So, without looking at Maurizio, I resumed: 'It may be that you don't see the connection between psychological imperfection and the large size of a sexual organ. However, there *is* a connection. This consists in the fact that my sexual organ which, if it were of normal proportions and potency, would be merely a part of the body like any other, takes advantage of its own exceptional qualities to tyrannize over me. To express this by a comparison of a political kind, my situation is rather like that of a country in a state of anarchy, where nobody knows who commands and who obeys.'

I had spoken, I had said everything, or nearly so; but the two little magic words that constituted my obsession, 'sublimated' and 'desublimated' – these I had not managed to utter. And the reason for this, as I have already remarked, was that I was too desublimated to admit that I was obsessed with sublimation. Moreover I at once realized that it was not my state of interior anarchy that had most struck Maurizio. After a moment, in fact, in the tone of voice of one who asks a question out of pure curiosity, he inquired: 'And what might be the exceptional proportions of that particular part of your body?'

I looked at Maurizio before answering. Between the two waves of golden hair, cut like that of the youthful pages in certain Renaissance paintings, his face displayed all the characteristics of a beauty which was, to say the least, androgynous. I noted the slightly rosy colour of his nostrils and lips; the transparent, faintly mauve circles under his enormous, mournful, golden-brown eyes; the milky whiteness of his cheeks and throat and neck. At the same time 'he' started whispering in an urgent, insinuating, insistent, insidious, tempting way: 'Why, don't you realize that Maurizio is a young lady? A girl of good family? Revolution – nonsense! Aren't you aware that you yourself, when faced with this little cherub, all roses and lilies and violets, have an undisputed superiority, the superiority of the male, of the truly virile man?

150

What are you waiting for? Why don't you reap the logical consequences of this discovery?'

Listening to 'him', I felt I must be beside myself. 'He' was indeed causing me, in spite of myself, to sink into a murky, ambiguous delirium. Scarcely believing my own ears, I heard myself answering: 'What might be its proportions? Why, I'll tell you at once.'

'What, then?'

I hesitated. Then 'he' intervened, impatient, brutal, saying to me: 'Aren't you going to speak? I'll speak for you.' And indeed there he was, shoving me violently aside and enumerating, in a garrulous, diffuse, shameless sort of way, his own astounding measurements, just as he had done in the car on the day of my meeting with Irene. As he was speaking through my mouth, he was physically breaking loose to such a degree that I hadn't the courage to look down. Nevertheless, even though I could not see him, I could feel, just the same, that he was at the maximum of exaltation. I sought then to take refuge in my customary reflection: I myself don't count in any way; it's all a matter between 'him' and Maurizio. But, strange to say, this time the statement of my own powerlessness and exteriority did not console me at all. Maurizio listened to the detailed description with impassive attention; then, all of a sudden and quite unexpectedly, he gave vent to a childish exclamation: 'Oi!'

'It's true, all the same.'

'Let's see, then; are you able to prove it?'

'In what way?'

'There's only one way: to let me see with my own eyes that nature has really endowed you, as you claim, in this exceptional way.'

Immediately 'he', excited at this suggestion, unconscious of its ambiguity, raged at me to proceed to 'action'. Fortunately a gleam of awareness of what would happen if I followed his advice prevented me from 'acting'. But there occurred, all the same, the accustomed, dreaded identification with 'him', which brought it about that at that moment I was 'he' and 'he' was I. I felt as if I were being lifted from the ground and

151

were flying towards Maurizio. In reality it was not I but 'he' who, rising up from my belly, was mounting upwards and stretching out eagerly towards the object of his desires. I said to Maurizio, or rather 'he' said, speaking through my mouth: 'I have no difficulty in showing that nature has been truly very generous with me. But then you must do the same.'

'Why?'

'Because certain things can only be done by two people at a time.'

Disaster! All of a sudden, like an artillery unit that allows the enemy to approach right under the cannons' mouths so as to exterminate them more surely and completely, Maurizio uncovered his sublimated batteries and fired point blank. Calmly he inquired: 'Now tell me, Rico, aren't you perhaps a bit "queer"?'

Irremediable headlong collapse! All my equilibrium was lost, by allowing 'him' to speak. Now I pushed him aside, trying to regain control, but in vain. I felt I was slipping hopelessly on an insidious, utterly vulgar banana-skin and crashing to the hard ground without finding, as I fell, even the slightest hold to cling to. I shook my big bald head and said, with a hollow laugh: 'What, *me* queer? Really, really . . .'

'And yet . . .'

'And yet what?'

'And yet the suggestion you made me was, to say the least, curious; don't you think so?'

'But it was you who put me, so to speak, upon a point of honour.'

'Yes, but it was you who brought the conversation round to your own anatomy.'

I tried to turn the whole affair into a joke. 'But really! Me queer! My goodness! So I'm not to think about women any more! Really this is just one of those challenges that happen amongst men. "Mine's bigger than yours. No, mine's bigger. Well, let's compare them." When I was a boy it often happened that there were comparisons of that kind between me and friends of my own age.'

No success. It was no use. Maurizio would not let himself

be deflated. Inflexibly, looking me straight in the face, he said: 'Each person has the friends he prefers. I'm not saying that these things don't happen. But I do say that they don't happen, and have never happened, to me.'

I felt I had been finally put back 'underneath' again. This was what came of acting the part of a male with a young lady, with a girl of good family! Desublimated, I had launched myself blindly along the path of homosexual approach and had, instead, plunged up to my eyes in the usual bog of humiliation and shame. Furious, I whispered to 'him': 'Yet another loss of face, you scoundrel, you brigand, you hooligan. But the day of reckoning will come soon.'

Maurizio, in the meantime, had risen to his feet and was making his way towards the door. As he walked into the passage, adjusting his glasses on his nose, he said: 'Thanks for the contribution. I'll report to the group. We'll have a meeting next week and then you can come too and I'll introduce you and there'll be a debate on your version of the script.'

He left the room and I followed him, breathlessly, and rejoined him in the passage. Panting and bewildered, I said: 'How about the direction of the film? Maurizio, if you would put in a kind word with Protti it might be decisive. Flavia's father is the associate producer of the film; and Flavia is your fiancée . . .'

Maurizio opened the door. Then, calmly and seriously, he said: 'I'll speak to Protti about the direction, but on one condition.'

'What's that?'

'That you'll show "him" to me, but without asking me to show you "mine" in return.'

Curiously, as he joked in this way, the accent of his own region became apparent in his voice; he came from a part of Italy famous for its student witticisms. I felt my face burning with shame; mentally I placed this further humiliation to 'his' already weighty account. I said despairingly: 'Maurizio, don't let's have any jokes about it; this is a question of my livelihood.'

There must have been such an intense, such a genuine

153

distress in my tone of voice that Maurizio became serious. 'Very well,' he said, 'no joking. But what I must tell you is that I cannot speak to Protti about the direction until the group has approved your version. That doesn't concern Protti. And you can't ask me to override the group.'

'When will they approve it – when?'

'I've already told you. We'll have a meeting next week.'

'And, once my version is approved, you'll speak to Protti about the direction?'

'We'll see. Good luck to the work. Good-bye.'

The door closed. Immediately I rushed off to the bathroom, tore off my trousers and sweater and went and stood naked in front of the looking-glass. Incredible! 'He' was still in a state of erection – congested, glossy, purplish-coloured, knotty and rigid. An erection, into the bargain, which, against my most determined and violent opposition, had been caused by the heat of my desire being aimed at my work companion.

Then, without touching 'him', I addressed him in this way: 'This time I won't hit you, I won't slap you. Experience has taught me that you transform even blows into pleasure. But I will tell you what I think. You're no longer content with draining away the essence of my creative energy in order to expend it in stupid manifestations of eroticism. You're no longer satisfied with keeping me in the humiliating state of a man who is mediocre, weak-willed and a chronic failure. Now, moreover, you must needs hurl me into the bottomless abyss of homosexuality. And this in the most ridiculous, most grotesque, most humiliating and most shameful manner. In short, what you desire is my final and complete destruction. But it will not be like that. Before you annihilate me, I shall annihilate you.'

Filled with ferocity and uncontrollable rage, I went to the wash-basin and seized hold of a razor-blade on the shelf. I snatched it up with such violence that I cut my finger. I felt the coldness of the edge of the blade in the flesh of my finger-tip; but that did not make me relax my grip. I grasped the blade between two fingers as the blood poured abundantly

154

from the wound and streaked my hand; then I lowered it to my groin.

'Now I'm going to cut you off,' I said, 'with one clean stroke. Like Abélard, like Origen, like so many saints and mystics of the past, I shall be castrated. And you will no longer exist, your arrogance will end up in the rubbish-bin, you vile worm, you disgusting maggot, you filthy piece of gut.'

I threatened, I stormed, I approached the blade close to 'him', but in the end, naturally, I did nothing. The blade fell from my hand to the floor. I doctored my cut finger as best I could, disinfecting it with alcohol; and then I went back into the study. I sat down at the table. I tried to do some typing but could not manage it. My wounded finger prevented me. The only thing left to me was to leave the house and go for a walk, trying somehow or other to work off my anger.

7 Alienated!

It was night. In a dark blue suit, with a white shirt and a striped tie with a dark background, I was sitting on the bed, in Fausta's flat. It had been agreed between Fausta and me that, whenever her presence was required for social occasions, she was to accompany me, but without making any demands, in return, of a sentimental, still less of an erotic, kind. That evening was one of these occasions. Protti, my film producer, had invited us to dinner. Fausta, therefore, was to go with me, as was suitable for a wife. But, when the dinner-party was over, I was to take her back home, say good-night to her in the street and then go and sleep alone, in my own flat.

I was sitting with legs wide apart so as not to crumple the trousers which Fausta, a short time before, had ironed for me. I was smoking, and I was in a very bad humour. Fausta had her back turned to me as she stood in front of the wardrobe looking-glass, putting the last touches to her *toilette*. She was wearing a particular outfit that had once been my favourite: a very short jacket and very low-waisted trousers, so that, between the edge of the jacket and the belt of the trousers, her stomach stood out almost completely bare. Moreover this outfit was a copy of the one she had been wearing when I saw her for the first time at 'Mariú, *modes*'. Then too there had been trousers and a jacket. Or rather, not a jacket but a blouse tied below her breasts.

Once again I noticed, with cruel distaste, that the relationship between the Fausta of those days and the Fausta of the present was the one that can exist between a person and his caricature. In front, her big bare paunch burst forth exuberantly above her belt; at the back, numerous folds of fat overlapped one another like the folds of an accordion. And why was I in such a bad humour? Because I had made up my mind that I would bring up the question of the film direction with Protti that evening; and I was not at all sure that I should find a sympathetic ear. As for Maurizio's promises, I felt instinctively that it was better not to count upon them.

Fausta leant forward to apply eye-shadow to her lids. 'He', of course, with his usual irritating insensitiveness to my states of mind, hastened, with excessively vulgar, waggish gaiety, to bring to my notice the enormous size of the two spheres that widened and split apart below my wife's loins. Mentally I shrugged my shoulders, as much as to say: Don't you realize that I'm not thinking about things like that? In the meantime, however, I felt that my usual psychological mechanism was springing into action. That monumental behind, pointed out by 'him' with his customary indiscriminate concupiscence, aroused in me a desire to be cruel to Fausta, with the object of feeling myself superior to her, of getting 'on top'. I said all at once, in a brutal way: 'Tell me, d'you really think you're the same as you were ten years ago?'

'Why?'

'Ten years ago you were like a reed. Now you're a whale. Don't you realize that certain clothes no longer suit you?'

'It's the fashion to be like this.'

'But a woman with a bottom like yours ought to have the sense not to follow the fashion. Besides, it's not true that you're just following the fashion. You're following something else: the notion you've made for yourself about our relationship.'

'What on earth d'you mean?'

'Come on, get off it! You're hoping to get round me by putting on the same clothes that you were wearing the first time I saw you. Get that idea out of your head; I'm not to be got round like that. Perhaps a get-up of that kind might please the customers at "Mariú, *modes*", but not me.'

'I've never seen Mariú since we got married, and you know it.'

'It's an indecent costume, anyhow. We're going to dine with my producer, at a delicate moment in my career; I don't want people to say that my wife dresses like a call-girl.'

'But what's wrong with this costume? It's a perfectly simple outfit.'

'What's wrong is that it displays that big stomach of yours, as if you were a dancing-girl. All it needs is for you, at the end of dinner, to perform a belly-dance.'

Fausta turned round abruptly and came face to face with me. And then I saw that she was crying, and I hadn't noticed it. Her tears had gathered all round her eyes and had streaked the powder on her cheeks. Leaning her big 'double' face towards me, she stammered: 'But, Rico, why are you so unkind? What harm have I done you? If you like, I'll take off this outfit, even though it's the best one I have; I'll put on a different one; but can't you say things more kindly?'

Alas, alas! More desublimated than me, without any doubt, as regards sexual availability (she was practically always ready to make love), Fausta was, basically, less so than me, when it came to the question of sentimentalism, another typical manifestation of desublimation. She wept easily, but also with astuteness; for she knew perfectly well that I, thoroughly desublimated as I was, was very easily moved. I could not bear to see her cry; it softened me at once. Even now, indeed, I felt a consuming desire to throw myself at her feet, to clasp her legs and ask her forgiveness, plunging my face into that big bare paunch, as into a soft cushion of warm flesh that would bring oblivion.

I controlled myself, however, and resumed: 'Something else is needed besides changing your clothes. What you need is to change yourself. To make the return journey: from the whale to the reed. And, you know, I might apply for an annulment of our marriage with a statement of this precise reason: that the woman I married ten years ago no longer exists; another entirely different woman has taken her place.'

'Well, to come to the point, d'you want me to change or not?'

'No.'

'Then you want me to keep this outfit on?'

'Not that either.'

'But what *do* you want? For me to go naked?'

158

'I don't want anything.'

'Will you please tell me *what* you want?'

'I've already told you: nothing.'

I uttered this 'nothing' with so much fury that Fausta was frightened. She turned back without a word to the looking-glass and in a mad hurry restored her make-up, so that in a moment she was completely ready. We went out into the passage on tiptoe so as not to awaken Cesarino, who sleeps in the adjoining room with the new maid. In the lift I looked at Fausta, saw that she was soothed again and that her big double face already wore the expression of a middle-class lady going off to a party with her husband. Again there came upon me the desire to be cruel to her. This time, however, not merely to put her in her place (that is, 'underneath'), but also because it was essential that she should learn certain things.

The lift stopped and we got out. Fausta walked across the hall in front of me: how majestically did they roll, those imposing, capacious hips of hers, in their fluttering, wide trousers: it was like a great ship in a stormy sea. We went out into the street and got into the car; I started the engine and drove off. Then, as I drove, I said: 'Now look, there's something I must warn you of.'

'What?'

'We're going to Protti's, and there will be his usual court of parasites, hangers-on, flatterers and procurers; and of course there will also be Mafalda.'

'Who is Mafalda?'

'Who is Mafalda? Don't you know – Protti's wife.'

'You mean Leda Lidi?'

'That was her professional name in the thirties. Now she's Protti's wife and she's called Mafalda.'

'I didn't know she was called Mafalda. I knew her under the name of Leda Lidi.'

'You knew her by that name because you've never visited her. But for her husband and her intimates she's called Mafalda.'

'Mafalda. What an ugly name!'

159

Fausta was 'making conversation' just like a middle-class lady going to a party with her husband: I myself did not know why, but this irritated me and revived my feeling of cruelty. I said impatiently: 'Anyhow, it's not a question of Protti's wife's name but of something more important. Now listen to me and please don't interrupt. I was saying that apart from the usual crowd of parasites Mafalda will also be there. Well, I might have said nothing to you. I might have done things secretly. But that's not my habit. So I'm warning you that, in order to face an unfavourable situation, I may perhaps be forced to take certain initiatives.'

'I don't understand. You say things in such a difficult way.'

'You never understand anything. Well then, let us dot the i's. Point number one: I have an ambition to direct the film of which I am now writing the script. Point number two: Protti and his "court" are not too favourable to me. Point number three: Mafalda might be able to influence Protti in my favour. Point number four: the career of Cutica – just to give an example – is due to Mafalda's influence over her husband. Point number five: there is a great probability that I, this evening, may be forced to do what Cutica did. Now do you understand?'

'No. What did Cutica do?'

'Everybody knows what Cutica did.'

'But I don't even know who Cutica is.'

'You don't know because when I speak you don't listen. I must have spoken to you a hundred times about Cutica. He's the person I allude to when I say "The Worm".'

'Ah, the Worm. And so the Worm is Cutica?'

'That's right.'

'I'd never understood that. Besides, you say so many things and I have so much to do that sometimes I don't even hear you.'

'That's in fact what I've just said: you don't listen to me. Now, however, you know. Cutica is the Worm. He's also Protti's secretary. Don't tell me you don't remember what he's like. I've even seen you talking to each other.'

160

'I may have talked to him, but since they never introduce people to me, I don't remember what he's like."

'He looks just like a worm: diminutive, half bald, with a pale face all eyes, or rather all spectacles. He has a mouth which at first sight looks normal; but when he laughs, then it's like an oven being opened. Unfortunately he laughs often. D'you remember him now?'

'Ah, so that's Cutica. Fancy. I'd always thought he was called Mercuri.'

'No, Mercuri's a different person. Let's go back to where we started. You asked me: "What did Cutica do?" and I reply: "He made love with Protti's wife".'

'With Leda Lidi?'

'Yes, with Mafalda. And so, from being a mere errand-boy, he became Protti's secretary. D'you understand now?'

'Yes. But you – how do you come into all this?'

'I come into it because I want to be given the direction of the film on which I'm working at the present moment. And only Mafalda can influence Protti on my behalf, so that the direction may be entrusted to me.'

This time Fausta said nothing. At last she understood.

In the end, after a long and obviously thoughtful silence, she remarked, in her judicious, good-natured voice: 'All this means that, not content with living away from home, you now want also to be unfaithful to me with Protti's wife.'

'You see how you are! It's no good talking to you! In the first place, it's not certain: it will depend on what Protti says to me. If I conclude that he's not favourable to me as director, then I shall have to launch Operation Mafalda. But, in any case, I should not be betraying you. It's a question of work upon which our future depends. I should be doing it not only for myself but also for you and Cesarino.'

'Thanks for the thought.'

'Don't take it like that. On this occasion again you must show that you're an understanding, intelligent wife.'

'Yes, understanding, but not to the point of helping you to betray me.'

'Betray you! With Mafalda! But with Mafalda one's not

betraying anyone. If anything, one's betraying oneself. Why, d'you know how old she is?'

'Yes, yes, you're very clever with your remarks, but this time you're not taking me in. I see merely a shameless husband asking his wife to close her eyes to his relationship with a decrepit old hag, a star of the silent films.'

'What silent films are you talking about? Silent films came to an end in 1933. Mafalda made her first film in 1940.'

'Silent or not silent, she's an old woman and you want to be unfaithful to me with her. You know what you are? A degenerate. Even old women, now. That's the last straw.'

I decided suddenly to take a strong line. The commonplace quality of Fausta's replies showed that we were in fact relapsing – even though this was due to a quarrel – into a perfectly normal type of conjugal, middle-class conversation. Brutally, I said: 'On the contrary, I'm not asking you in any way to keep your eyes closed. I'm asking you in fact to keep them wide open. Take a good look if you like. But don't cross my path. You're my wife and by law you owe me obedience and submission, for better or for worse. Not merely must you not protest, but you must actually help me if required.'

Usually the harsh tone is enough: Fausta swallows her tears and is silent. But this time it seemed that, even for her, what I was asking was too much. She protested: 'Understanding? But have you any understanding for me?'

'I have a right to your understanding. But you have no right to mine. I may have some and I may not. You must behave as I tell you, obey and not breathe a word. Is that understood?'

'Understood – nothing. When I see that you're carrying on with Protti's wife, I shall start a scandal.'

'Kindly repeat what you've just said.'

'I shall start a scandal.'

We were on the Via Flaminia, still in the built-up area. I slowed down and went and stopped close to the ditch. I pulled up the hand-brake, turned off the engine, leant across Fausta's legs and opened the car door. Then I ordered her: 'Get out.'

She did not move. Upon her big double face, swollen, it might have been thought, by some sort of perpetual toothache, I read terror and pain. I knew she was suffering, nevertheless I was not sorry: it was true that we were both of us deeply sunk in the bog of desublimation; but it was she who was 'underneath', whereas I, even though with some difficulty, was keeping myself 'on top'. After a moment I repeated: 'Well then, are you going to get out?'

Again she looked at me, again she did not move. 'Get out,' I insisted. 'Don't compel me to use force.'

At last she spoke. Agonizingly, she asked: 'Rico, why are you so unkind to me?'

Careful, now; I must not allow myself to weaken. Desublimated in any case, it was better to be authoritarian and sadistic than sentimental and masochistic. I said harshly: 'I'm not unkind. But I don't wish to run any risks.'

Two tears slid down her cheeks. Two more were poised on her long false eyelashes. 'I'll do as you like,' she said. 'But don't force me to get out like this, in the road, I beg you.'

'Then will you do what you're told?'

The second couple of tears detached themselves from her eyelashes and made their way down, in the same furrow as the first. 'Yes,' she said.

'Now don't cry. You promise me, then, that you won't make a scandal?'

A further nod of her head, with the consequent appearance of the third couple of tears. 'Yes.'

'That's agreed, then, is it?' The third couple of tears gushed from her eyes and flowed down her face, adding their traces to those of the other two. 'Yes.'

I closed the door, re-started the engine, took off the hand-brake and drove on. I did not feel at all content with myself: generally I laid the blame on 'him' for everything that my conscience did not feel able to approve; but this time I was not successful. 'He', in truth, did not come into it. It was I who had had the idea of making Mafalda intervene with her husband in my favour. It was I who had imposed this cynical programme upon 'him', and it must be admitted that 'he' was

163

disgusted and reluctant. Should I therefore be a 'shameless husband', as Fausta had described me? And a 'sound chap', as, no doubt, I should be described by Protti's 'court', as soon as my relationship with Mafalda became known? In a way, according to common sense, yes. But according to the unwritten law of sublimation, no. For to feel some scruples is characteristic of the desublimated man, who is always undecided, fundamentally, between good and bad, inasmuch as he is incapable of raising himself to a state of sublimation, which is the only true good, the only end which justifies any sort of means, and is superior to all states of vacillation and servility.

These thoughts confirmed me in my decision. As I drove along I heard a loud sniff and the sound of heavy breathing from Fausta. I looked down. Her big bare paunch, shapeless and unrestricted, yet still youthful, overflowed between the jacket that was too short and the trousers that were too low. I put out my hand, following the advice, for once in a way, of 'him' ('Now, give her a little caress, it will please her and it will please me too'), and my fingers landed on the deep circular folds in which the original perimeter of her stomach lay concealed. My forefinger slipped into the hollow of her navel and I probed it a little with my nail. Fausta squirmed. 'You're tickling me, stop it!' she cried.

'D'you love me?'

'Yes, you know I do, very much.'

I took Fausta's hand, moved it to my crotch and pressed it down upon 'him'. 'I love you, too. There's the proof of it.'

I put both my hands to the wheel again. Fausta knew what she had to do now. And indeed I felt her small, short, plump hand releasing my buttons, one after another, from their buttonholes, and delicately feeling its way (the same delicacy with which I had seen her drawing her breast out from her dress at the time when she was feeding Cesarino), until it penetrated to 'him' (already fully prepared), then grasping him with a curious kind of pride, like a general grasping his baton of command.

Her hand remained still for a little, clasping him closely,

164

as though assessing his volume and robustness; then extracting him obliquely, with some difficulty, like someone trying to pass a beam or a ladder through a narrow doorway. But soon, at the sudden glare of two car headlights enveloping us at a bend in the road, she was frightened and made as if to push him back inside again. But I reassured her: 'Don't be afraid, nobody can see anything. In any case the drivers of the cars coming to meet us are dazzled by *my* headlamps. Clasp him tightly, like a nice bunch of flowers.'

'The only thing I don't like about it is that you want to present this bunch of flowers to Protti's wife.'

'Don't worry; at most it will be a loan, not a gift. But now, listen to this little story. There was once a king of the Balkans who had a beautiful wife. During a military parade, as their carriage was proceeding slowly and the troops drawn up in a line were presenting arms and the king was saluting with his hand to the peak of his cap, the queen was meanwhile clasping him underneath the rug that was wrapped round the legs of both of them, exactly as you are doing to me at the present moment. So that in reality the troops were presenting arms not so much to the king as to . . .'

'To the real king.'

'In fact, to the king of kings. Isn't that what you call him?'

'Yes, to the king of kings.'

'And listen to this other story. In the times of the Papal government, a judge promised a pardon to a man condemned to death if he was able to climb right to the top of the Aracoeli steps with a bucket full of water hanging *there*. The condemned man said he would do so if his wife, who was young and beautiful, would walk backwards up the steps in front of him with her skirt hitched up in such a way that he could see her sex. And so the climb began. He, with a bucket full of water hanging on his member; and she, holding up her dress and encouraging him: "Come on, my love, come on, keep it up!" All went well for two-thirds of the way up; and then the man began to lose ground. So d'you know what his wife did? She turned round and pulled her dress up over her bottom. The man rushed up the remainder of the steps and was pardoned.'

At last we reached the gate of Protti's villa. The two leaves of the gate were wide open; three or four very tall pine-trees stood round it. I turned into the drive. Two rows of oleanders with white and red flowers came to meet us in the darkness of the night as we moved forward. I said to Fausta: 'That's enough, now.'

Nimbly, lightly, with the usual delicate, excessive precautions, as though concerned with an object of extreme fragility and exceedingly precious into the bargain, Fausta put 'him' back into his prison and was careful to close the doors.

I warned Fausta: 'Now don't make a fool of me with your clumsy behaviour. Don't speak if you're not sure of what you're going to say. Don't laugh too much. Don't raise your voice. Drink only a very little. Remember you're an ignorant, half-illiterate woman and that, consequently, if there's a discussion that's even slightly difficult, it's better for you to keep your mouth shut. Remember also that you had a very scanty education, that your father's a master builder, and that for a good two years you were a call-girl and must therefore mind your manners on all occasions, by which I mean that you must not only be careful of what you say but of how you say it, and in general of how you move and of what attitudes you take up. And now do up another button of your jacket; your whole bosom can be seen.'

I gave her these warnings, naturally, because I knew from experience that they were necessary. But I could not deny that there was expressed in them, once again, a spirit of retaliation: feeling myself constantly 'underneath' in respect of almost everyone, I was getting my own back with Fausta, the only person in respect of whom I felt myself to be 'on top'.

Fausta protested: 'But you always say that a bosom ought to be seen, that I have a fine one and that it's right that I should show it.'

'You haven't a fine bosom, you have an enormous bosom, like a milch cow. Of course there are men who appreciate a bosom like that: I myself, for instance. But, like that, you're indecent. Remember that you're my wife, and that you must

166

therefore always appear and behave in a decorous manner, like a real lady.'

In the windscreen mirror I could see her buttoning up her jacket and putting on a mortified expression. I concluded: 'And don't rise to your feet when someone greets you or is introduced to you. A married lady should always remain seated and should not rise to her feet except in very rare cases. I saw you last time we were at Protti's: you got up when that boorish American partner of Protti was introduced to you. He's an influential man, that American, he has money; but you are a married lady and you should remain seated. Remember that: you're no longer a little ten-thousand-lire call-girl. You're my wife. D'you see? And when somebody, in a rather old-fashioned way, greets you by kissing your hand, you mustn't lift your hand and bang it against his nose; you must let him raise it himself to his own mouth. D'you see?'

We reached the open space in front of the villa. I went and parked the car a little farther on, in an avenue; then we got out and walked back. The open space was completely circular, and all round it curved the pointed tops of cypresses, against a background of black sky. It was lit dimly by lamps of blue-tinted glass, with an effect of cemetery-like gloom. The table was in the centre, long and narrow; the guests were already seated, facing one another; and the strangely surprised silence that greeted us made me think of a banquet of ghosts. The villa took up the whole of one side of the space. It was in the usual style of the sham Latian farmhouse; rust-red plaster, tiled roof, slanting walls. Lamps shone at the two sides of the door. Waiters in white jackets hurried up and down the steps, carrying dishes.

I said to Fausta, in a low voice: 'We're late. Your fault.'

'No, it was you who arrived late.'

'I didn't arrive late. I arrived punctually.'

Slowly we approached the table. As we walked across the open space, as usual I could not help seeing Fausta and myself as we appeared at that moment. For desublimated people have an inferiority complex and therefore cannot help 'seeing themselves'. Sublimated people, on the other hand, do not 'see' themselves because their superiority complex makes them, so to speak, invisible to themselves. And so there was Fausta, shapeless, flabby, rolling along, with her big double face, her bare stomach overflowing above the top of her trousers, her great bosom (also bare) exploding out of her jacket, and her wide, spreading, swaying hips. And beside her I myself, short, bandy-legged, prominent stomach, big bald head and proud, authoritative face.

This vision, alas, entirely objective and precise as it was, made me exclaim sarcastically to myself: It can't be denied, we're a lovely couple! In vain I sought to react with a redoubling of dignity and self-possession, pulling in my paunch, sticking my chest out and raising my chin; at the same time, my lack of self-confidence was hopelessly revealed by the fact that, without my being aware of it, I had slipped my hand into my pocket in order to take hold of 'him', as though I were trying to reassure myself by means of the only part of my person of which I could be truly proud.

We came up beside the table. And then, with a sudden headlong fall from my artificial haughtiness to the depths of my actual situation, I discovered that the dinner, to which I was convinced I had been invited, was by now coming to its end. The table had the devastated, exhausted look typical of a party at which people have eaten and drunk well. The guests were sitting, some of them sideways, some quite a long way from the table; and on the table itself there was a great disorder of dirty knives and forks, of glasses half full and bottles half empty, of plates with huge slices of water-melon nibbled right down to the rind. It was clear that I had made a mistake. Or rather, more probably, that Protti's secretary had made a mistake when she sent me the invitation. Anyhow it was a symbolic confirmation of my fate as a desublimated person who, after deceiving himself into thinking, for a moment, that he was being treated on equal terms with the sublimated ones, realizes all at once that this was not true.

I whispered to Fausta: 'They've finished eating; the invitation was for after dinner.'

'It doesn't matter to me; I'm not particularly hungry.'

'What has hunger got to do with it, you idiot?'

'Why, what's the matter?'

'Shut your mouth and give me your arm. No, not like that: put your hand on my arm. Yes, that's it.'

We were now close to the table. I waved my hand, in a tentative gesture of collective greeting, and said loudly: 'Good evening, everybody.' In the meantime, however, I had, as it were, taken a quick photograph of the whole lot of them, one by one, just as they were. There was Protti, seated at one end of the table. There was Protti's wife, seated at the other end. And in between them, in a double row, were all, or almost all, the people who composed what for some time, with profound contempt, I had privately called Protti's 'court'. There must have been about a dozen people, a truly select assemblage of hangers-on, flatterers, go-betweens and parasites.

Looking at them, I consoled myself with the idea that there was not a single one of them that was not more desublimated than me. I, even if desublimated, at least know that I am. But not they. They and their worthy consorts were desublimated without being conscious of it. Doubly desublimated, so to speak: both because they were, and because they did not know it. It did not matter that they were costume designers, script-writers, journalists, secretaries, and so on; it did not matter that they all had more success, more money, more prestige than me. What mattered was that, in them, not merely was there not one scrap of sublimation, but there was not even the suspicion that sublimation existed.

I saw them naked, as though I had X-rays in my eyes; I saw them at the two sides of the table, them and their wives, all of them with their legs open, with their sexual organs dangling inert or else gaping half-open, amongst the hair below their ignoble bellies. Yes indeed, the small amount of energy with which avaricious nature had furnished them at birth had by this time seeped away through their lower parts, as water seeps away from a lake without tributaries when dried up by the sun; and nothing remained in their drained, barren heads except the sludge which is commonly called good sense.

Nothing of these thoughts was visible in my face as, pulling Fausta behind me on my arm, I went to greet first Protti's wife and then Protti himself. But at the very moment when, as I said, I addressed a collective wave of the hand to the others present, I could not help noticing, in a special manner, the presence of my arch-enemy Cutica. It was as though, when I took in the table at a glance, I had drawn an imaginary circle round the head of that odious individual, as they do with photographs in newspapers when they indicate a well-known figure in the midst of a nameless crowd. Sitting there was Cutica, just as I had described him shortly before to Fausta: a head not positively bald, but with the bald parts veiled by scanty black hair; huge tortoiseshell-rimmed glasses; a tiny nose; and below his nose that very red mouth, not really large but which, by some unattractive miracle of nature, widens immensely, from ear to ear, when he laughs. Quick-witted, meddlesome, interfering, inquisitive, Cutica had managed, in a short time, to become what I myself ought to have, and could have, become if I had been less conscious of my own desublimation. Because, for practical purposes, it is far more profitable to be desublimated without knowing it than if one does know it. Anyhow he was a worm, Cutica. One of those worms of the tropics which make long tunnels in the human body and then, all of a sudden, when you least expect it, reveal themselves firmly entrenched in some vital organ.

I whispered again to Fausta: 'Cutica was invited to dinner and we were not.'

'Why should that matter to you?'

After their first moment of surprise, the ghosts welcomed us with passable, even if false, cordiality. I heard my name uttered with a characteristic intonation of combined merriment and weariness ('Hello, Rico'; 'How are you, Rico?'; 'Cheers, Rico!'); I saw Protti rise to his feet and, with old-fashioned gallantry, kiss the hand of Fausta who, careful of my warnings, thank goodness, did not raise it and bang it

170

against his nose. Then Fausta sat down beside Protti, and I, in furtherance of my plan, went and sat beside Protti's wife.

Protti seemed cheerful. 'Coffee?' he said. 'Or water-melon? Yes, water-melon.' And then, turning to the waiters and without waiting for our reply: 'Come along, bring some more water-melon; come on, quick! And for me, some more coffee.'

Shortly afterwards I saw a huge slice of water-melon placed in front of me; and, as I pulled off a substantial piece with my fingers and slowly ate it, I observed Protti and his wife as though I were seeing them for the first time. Actually this was true, I was seeing them for the first time. Hitherto I had looked at them as one looks at people with whom one has a person-to-person relationship. That evening, on the contrary, the relationship was between subject and object. I myself was the subject and they were the objects. I had in fact to induce them, whether they knew it or not, to do what I wished.

But can a desublimated man impose his own will upon two sublimated people, as Protti and his wife undoubtedly were? Yes, he can do this, but only on condition that he knows how to fit his own desublimation into the action of their sublimation. In short, I had to wheedle Protti; and I had to seduce Protti's wife.

With these thoughts in mind, I studied them. There was Protti, a handsome man, a decorative figure, an old-style captain of industry concealing his claws in a velvet glove of affable, paternalistic, probably ironical courtesy. He was tall, big, broad, rather massive, dressed always in a dark blue suit with white stripes, a white shirt and a satin tie. The common-place though agreeable face of an American manager, red and glowing beneath thick, well-combed silver hair. Large, black, clear, shining, wide-open eyes. An imperious hooked nose. A showy red mouth, always ready to produce the most seductive smiles. What was Protti to me? A film producer, of course, or rather, 'my' producer, for whom I had been working for ten years, exclusively. But above all, he was simply somebody in face of whom I felt myself fatally 'underneath', rather as I did with Maurizio but in a different way.

Let us now take a look at Mafalda, Protti's wife. I was close to her, touching her with my knees under the table. Have you ever noticed the advertisement for a certain brand of mineral oil in which, incongruously, there is a dinosaur to be seen beside the tin containing the product? Well, Mafalda bore a close resemblance to the great antediluvian beast in that advertisement. The main characteristic of that huge herbivorous animal was that its body, starting from immensely voluminous hindquarters, grew progressively thinner and thinner, terminating finally in a tiny little head perched on the top of a very long serpentine neck. So it was with Mafalda. My eye rested first upon her small head, which was enclosed in a kind of white turban: she had a face like an old cat or an elderly Pekinese dog, with round, watery eyes and a large, dried-up, sulky mouth; then it descended by way of her long, stringy neck to her massive shoulders, less wide, nevertheless, than her hips, which in turn seemed to be far surpassed in amplitude by her monumental thighs. Mafalda, in short, was pyramidal; and I, as I looked at her, could not help remembering the first time I had seen her. She was walking in the garden of the villa, on the far side of a hedge above which emerged her head, her neck and a small part of her shoulders. It did truly look as if, like the dinosaur, she was concealing a huge, massive, sinuous body behind the hedge.

After taking a thorough look at Protti and his wife and confirming myself in the idea that they were both of them sublimated in pursuance of a power that was, indeed, quite different in each case but had been identically achieved, maintained and consolidated, I sought to formulate what I may call a plan of campaign. And so, first of all, it would be advisable to establish a bridgehead in the direction of the Mafalda fortress. Then, having once occupied a position of advantage in the uncertain, marshy Mafalda territory, it would be necessary to launch the frontal attack against the well-camouflaged Protti trench. If the attack failed, I would then have to turn back upon Mafalda and, making use of 'him' as a battering-ram or catapult to break open the unstable doors, to take the strong-point by storm and hoist the flag there. To put it simply, without any military metaphors, to become her lover.

Nevertheless, out of prudence, I consulted 'him' before putting my plan into effect. A strange character, he is: I could have sworn that 'Operation Mafalda' would not arouse much enthusiasm in him; I did not think he was a gerontophile. Instead of which, no sooner had I asked him: 'What d'you say to my plan? D'you agree with it?' than he answered at once, briskly: 'I agree completely. In fact, if you'll allow me, I should like to give you some advice.'

'Advice from you! God help us!'

'You should pay court to Mafalda in a rather old-fashioned way. Why, she's not one of the usual young women of today: she's a film star of the thirties. In those days a certain respect was customary. So don't lay your hands on her. A touch of the sentimental, perhaps even of the spiritual. For instance, eyes looking into eyes. At most, a foot on her slipper, under the table.'

I listened to him and for once admitted that he was right. Certainly Mafalda should be treated with respect, even if later, at the end, the inevitable fall into brutality should turn out all the more precipitate. But then, just at the moment when, convinced of the justness of 'his' theory, I was preparing to proceed to the practical act, I was suddenly disturbed by an argument that had flamed up round the table. Bouncing from one guest to another like an old, shabby ball hit back and forth by tired, listless players, it was the usual discussion I had heard a thousand times: the successful film of the day and why it had been successful and how on earth had it cost so much or so little and who had produced it, and who were the actors, who the director, who the author of the theme, etc., etc.

I said 'disturbed'; but that was a euphemism. I should have said 'indignant', 'nauseated'. For every time I hear artistic matters spoken about in that way I am seized with indescribable rage. Art is the most exalted result of sublimation. In order to obtain this result, I am engaged in an experiment that has turned my life upside down. And this conspiracy

173

of gossips and parasites and go-betweens spoke of art as a 'product'! Truly we were in the full flood of desublimation, unconscious, automatic, ingenuous. Truly, as long as there are people like this, there is no hope for the cinema.

I listened carefully and, of course, after the discussion on profit came the discussion on technique. A logical discussion, moreover: profit in the cinema originates in technique because, according to them, art is no more than a technique like any other technique. Technique! Let's talk about technique! The great excuse of the desublimated! The great alibi! The great revenge! The great consolation!

They are still being led by the nose but they deceive themselves into thinking that they are saved by technique. They are tainted desublimates, but luckily technique is there, all ready to hand, with its cunning devices, so far superior to sublimation! Lustful, but technicians! Promiscuous, but technicians! Pumped dry, but technicians! I had an immediate desire to reach forward over the table and apostrophize them in this way: 'Throw down your masks! Your films are nothing but a kind of tinned amusement, that is to say, pure desublimation. Why not admit once and for all that you're no use? That you are desublimated to the last degree of sterility and impotence!' But, as usual, I hadn't the courage to say what I thought. In reality, only a supersublimated person would be capable of such an intrepid, such a magnanimous intervention, without worrying about what might follow. Whereas I myself am desublimated, as they are; and, like them, I think of the harm and the trouble caused by sincerity. With this difference, however: that desublimation horrifies me, whereas they wallow in it.

Anyhow, I became involved, just the same. I listened and heard the following hair-raising discussion. 'Really the title didn't lead one to expect a success like that. *The Woman without Qualities*: I would not have given a single lira for such a title.'

'And yet the distribution was snapped up at once.'

'You bet it was. With that scene in which she undresses behind a transparent muslin curtain.'

'The woman without qualities. You know what it makes one think of? The lady without camellias.'

'The woman without qualities is a quiet title, but sometimes the devil is hidden behind these quiet titles. The public felt it and . . .'

'I agree. The public is never wrong. It feels infallibly when . . .'

'I *don't* agree. I tell you the woman without qualities is a dull title, which makes no appeal. Besides, what does it mean? Nothing, less than nothing. All women are without qualities, then the usual silly man comes along and finds some qualities in them . . .'

I could not help interrupting at this point, urged on to it by the double impulse of desublimated, self-taught vanity and the indignation of one who was aspiring to sublimation. 'I don't expect,' I said, 'that I'm saying anything new when I recall that the title of the woman without qualities echoes another much more famous one, that of the novel by Musil.' Just imagine! Certainly not one of them had read *The Man without Qualities*; but they had all heard it spoken of. And so, suddenly, I was overwhelmed with sarcastic remarks, as though I had been someone who wanted to parade his own culture; and, furthermore, without any possibility of showing that I was the only one at that table who knew something about Musil's novel. From all sides flew exclamations of this kind: 'Thanks for the information'; or 'Well done, it needed you to tell us that', and similar remarks of the kind. But amongst them all, it was my arch-enemy Cutica who, as usual, was most prominent. Opening his mouth immeasurably wide in one of his customary guffaws, he exclaimed: 'No, no, it's not possible! Here we are back at school! And at our age! And who is it that's responsible? Now we have to hear ourselves being informed that there's a novel called *The Man without Qualities* and that the author of this novel is a certain Musil. What's the use of having one or two university degrees? Of having spent our youth with books? Of having toiled so hard to acquire some culture for ourselves, then to find ourselves treated, on the first opportunity, as illiterates?'

175

These remarks alternated with his usual bursts of laughter, which made him look like an excavating machine whose serrated jaws gobble up an enormous mouthful of earth and then suddenly close and transport it somewhere else. I knew what I ought to do: not merely not react, but also not show any feeling. Instead of which, desublimated and attacked by someone just as desublimated as myself if not more so, I foresaw that I should not manage to remain apathetic as I desperately wished to do. Hatred overwhelmed me, engulfed me, irresistibly. Even though I was lucidly aware that Cutica, in provoking me in such a vulgar manner, expected me to engage him in a grotesque contest; and that this was expected, even more, by Protti, the sublimated petty tyrant of a desublimated court, who indeed incited us against one another by remarking: 'That was below the belt, Cutica. Come on, Rico, defend yourself.' Fortunately, just at the moment when, in spite of myself, I was about to fling myself upon Cutica, 'he' suddenly intervened. 'What are you up to?' he said; 'I'm here, ready and willing, and you leave me in the lurch to talk about this wretched Musil.'

'He' was right. Desublimation for desublimation, 'his' kind was still preferable to the kind that would lead me into a ridiculous cultural duel with Cutica. All I did, therefore, was to exclaim, raising my hands and pretending to be frightened: 'Peace, peace, I give in, I surrender; anything rather than a literary discussion; I prefer my water-melon.' I noticed that the guests round the table, in their disappointment, were gradually shifting their attention away from me and from Cutica. And, after devoting myself seriously to the water-melon for a few minutes, I turned finally towards Mafalda.

She put her elbow on the table, bent her arm upwards and supported her chin in her hand. Her other hand she kept in her lap so that it could not be seen. She was staring in front of her, but it was clear that she was not looking at or seeing anything; she seemed half-asleep, probably she was bored. I asked 'him': 'What ought I to do?'

He answered at once: 'Tell her what you were thinking just now.'

176

'Just now I was thinking that she was bored.'

'Well, tell her that, and then, immediately afterwards, take her hand. But no abruptness, no brutality. Old-fashioned ways are best.'

'He' was right; fundamentally he is always right. With an effort I leant forward and sideways, in such a way that I faced Mafalda and could, so to speak, thread my gaze into her inattentive, dreamy eyes. I saw that she was struck by this manœuvre, if only because of its excessive artificiality. Without leaving her time to recover from her surprise, I asked her: 'Are you bored?'

'Terribly.'

I saw at once that the worst was over. That 'terribly', uttered faintly by the big, dried-up, sulky mouth, was equivalent to an invitation to action. I put out my hand under the table, moved it blindly towards Mafalda, landed it on her knee, moved it up towards her lap and finally was conscious of the back of her hand under my palm. Then I took hold of it and squeezed it.

A surprise! Contrary to my own and 'his' expectations, Mafalda did not accept my advances. She began, instead, to twist her hand inside mine, with unsuspected strength, trying to pull it away. She pulled it towards herself, bent it, contracted it, thrust her fingers against my palm and dug her sharp nails into it. I had the curious sensation that I was clasping a big, lively, rebellious crab. Nevertheless it was clear that Mafalda desired neither a scandal nor an open refusal. All the time she was trying to free her hand she retained the composed, attentive demeanour of a mistress of the house sitting at table with her guests. The struggle between her hand and mine went on for a little. Then, when I least expected it, Mafalda surrendered. She turned her face towards me – her face like that of an old Pekinese dog or an elderly cat – and, looking up at me out of her big, slanting eyes with their wrinkled lids, she inquired of me in a strange, excessively melodious voice: 'And are you enjoying yourself?'

'No.'

At the same time I felt her hand relax entirely and lie

inert and soft in mine. Triumphantly 'he' exclaimed: 'There we are! Now leave it to me.' As 'he' said this, he thrust me brutally aside, self-assured, arrogant, unrestrained. Unwilling though I was, I gave place to him and remained an impotent and passive witness of the erotic duet between him and Mafalda.

What an extraordinary character! He had spoken of 'paying court in the old-fashioned way'. In the old-fashioned way, indeed! Everything happened, on the contrary, not as though we were sitting at table in the garden of Protti's villa, in the presence of twenty people, but as though we were alone, on the ground, amongst the rubbish and the tin cans of a field in the suburbs. And as though Mafalda were not Leda Lidi, the film star of the thirties, but any ordinary unfortunate slut. Mafalda let her hand lie soft and inert; 'he' began pulling it in his direction. Mafalda resisted; 'he' managed forcibly to bring our two clasped hands from Mafalda's knee to mine. Mafalda made a slight movement of opposition; 'he' overcame it by pulling her hand right on top of him. Mafalda obstinately kept her hand open and relaxed; 'he' made her bend it and close her fingers. At this point Mafalda at last decided to grasp 'him'; 'he' then, by now sure of himself, started growing and swelling and stiffening in an embarrassing manner, without any regard for me and for my delicate personal situation. In a truly old-fashioned way, no doubt about it!

At the same moment I noticed a rapid change in both Mafalda's face and body. She looked now at me and now at her guests, swivelling her eyes quickly round as if she were frightened. Her breast rose and fell with a painful rhythm that was visible in her harsh, troubled breathing. From time to time she sighed deeply, as though she were on the point of fainting.

I did not move. This time I really 'left it to "him"'. Partly, also, because I was now faced with a new and different preoccupation. I had a confused sight of Fausta down at the far end of the table, and saw that she was staring at me. I guessed immediately that Mafalda's excitement had not escaped her and a great fear came over me that she would not keep the promise I had managed to extract from her, and that she would really start a scandal, as she had threatened to do. Desublimated people, as one knows, and especially women, do surprising things of this kind. I stared back at Fausta, and then, without making any fuss, I frowned and put my forefinger to my lips, enjoining silence. To my relief, I saw her turn her eyes away from Mafalda and me and, not without a visible effort, lean towards her neighbour.

So everything was now progressing in a more or less smooth and easy way, without any shocks. Mafalda was breathing heavily, sighing, and grasping 'him' tightly as if she were trying to break him. I was smoking with a meditative, indifferent air. The desublimated 'courtiers' were profuse in their fawnings and witticisms and flatteries of every kind. Protti appeared to be enjoying it. My arch-enemy Cutica darted a killing look at me every now and then, but I pretended not to notice. At last Fausta, poor dear, again started brooding over Mafalda and me with anxious eyes; but, frankly, this was to be expected.

Then, all of a sudden, the situation cleared. Protti rose and said to me: 'Rico, you've come to talk to me. Let's go then, come along.' And, without condescending to make certain that I was following him, he went straight across the open space towards the villa.

I rose also, pulling 'him' away from Mafalda's reluctant, disconcerted hand: I ran after Protti and, joining him, walked by his side. We two must have formed a couple that was somehow significant, even if rather ridiculous. Protti tall, vigorous, of commanding presence; I myself much shorter, grotesque, a counterfeit. Protti inattentive, indifferent; I, attentive to his every step, deferential, anxious. Then, all of a sudden, Protti made a gesture which finally ruined me. He placed his arm round my shoulders and said to me in a protective tone of voice (the unsought protectiveness that every sublimated person allows himself to impose upon any desublimated person), and with feigned affection: 'How are you, Rico, how are you?' Linked together in this way, we climbed the steps together, went through the door together and together entered the hall.

Here I stopped, digging in my heels, so to speak, in some sort of fashion, but without daring to release myself from his humiliating embrace. 'I'm all right,' I said. 'But look, Protti, I've got to speak to you, and very, very seriously.'

Protti seemed absent-minded. He removed his arm from my shoulder and looked round him, repeating in an idle sort of way: 'You've got to speak to me seriously, eh, Rico?'

'Yes, not only in my own interest, but above all in yours.'

Well, I was 'underneath', there was no denying it, properly 'underneath'. Protti, after trampling upon me by means of the arm placed round my shoulders, now submerged me once and for all by actually giving me a little tap on the cheek and saying: 'In my interest, eh, Rico? All right then, wait for me here. I'm going to make a brief telephone call and then we'll talk.'

So there I was, left alone, in the middle of the hall. The door, over on the right, had been left open by Protti. If I leant forward to look, I could see him in the distance, at the far end of his study, sitting at a small desk, his healthy pink face bent down in the concentrated light of a green lampshade, as he put the receiver to his ear, dialled a number and then started to speak. It was odd, but he appeared to be speaking in a low voice and to be taking careful precautions not to betray any sort of feeling, as though he not merely wished not to be heard but also feared that he might give himself away by the expression of his face. So it was not true, after all; he did not want to speak to me. He had simply made use of me as a pretext to get away from the table.

Tricks of the sublimated upon the desublimated!

What was I to do? Protti went on talking on the telephone, without raising his eyes. Or he would raise them and perhaps even look in my direction; but, obviously, for him I was not there. And why was I not there? It was clear, evident: Protti, in respect of me, was 'on top' to the degree at which I had become, for him, positively transparent.

180

But then, providentially, Mafalda arrived. I say 'providentially' because it could not be denied that to the, so to speak, impersonal calculations of my plan there had now been added an extremely personal desire to avenge myself on Protti. But how did Mafalda come to be there? Evidently she must have risen from the table soon after us, and, under some transparent pretext or other, had come to join us. I watched her as she came across the hall towards me, a veritable female dinosaur, trailing behind her, below her pear-shaped bust, her massive hips and monumental legs swathed in a very long dress, in the same serpentine manner in which the great prehistoric beast trailed its hindquarters and its long massive tail behind it. Her small head, on its supple neck, was inclined this way and that. Mafalda looked all round: evidently she was seeking Protti.

Finally she saw him, at the far end of his study, telephoning; then she made a disdainful grimace with her big, dried-up, sulky mouth and, coming close to me, whispered: 'Let's leave him to telephone; he'll be there for a long time yet. Let's go in here.'

I followed her, feeling rather worried. For 'him', of course, it was excellent; for me, on the other hand, it might even be the beginning of a disaster: Protti, from the telephone, might see us, might leave the telephone, follow us and catch us; Mafalda would run away; I would be caught in a trap. But there was nothing to be done. Mafalda had seized hold of my hand and was squeezing it in her claws with the same rapacious strength, like that of a carnivorous bird, with which, a short time before, she had squeezed 'him'. She opened a door, pulled me inside and turned on the light. We were in a room with a lot of little green tables, a card-room. It had the usual beamed ceiling, the usual tiled floor, and a big stone chimney-piece. Mafalda closed the door, flung me against the leaves of the door, clung closely to me, put her hand behind the back of my neck and forced me to kiss her.

And what sort of a kiss was it?

An attempt, I might call it, in part successful, to swallow me, beginning with my head, as they say the boa constrictors of Brazil do to absorb a victim often bigger than themselves. Enormously wide, wider and wider as the kiss progressed, her mouth stretched and opened out and expanded over my face, taking in my nose and cheeks and chin. It was like the sucker of a big blood-sucking leech. But this was an elderly leech, flabby and feeble even though extremely greedy, slackened and debilitated by senile lassitude. Meanwhile, from the depths of her throat, her pointed tongue darted into my mouth, swift and penetrating as a snake.

At last we drew apart. Mafalda then made a gesture all of her own, characteristic of the thirties, truly in the old-fashioned manner. She seized my hand and drew it to her breast, over her heart, whispering: 'D'you feel how fast it's beating?'

And indeed the old, anxious heart of the *diva* was beating furiously. Her breath came noisily from her nostrils. From time to time her bosom heaved with a profound and painful sigh. Continuing all the time to crush my hand against her ribs, Mafalda very gently opened the door a few inches, looked out for a moment, then closed it again. 'But Protti . . . ?' I asked.

'Oh, Protti. He's telephoning, he'll be there some time.'

'But he might notice that . . .'

'Don't worry, when he telephones to his family he doesn't notice anything, and, even if he does, he pretends not to.'

I was struck by her sarcastic, grudging tone. I asked in amazement: 'Why, what family?'

'*His* family.'

'D'you mean his parents?'

'Parents, nonsense! His children, and the mother of his children.'

'But you . . .'

She shrugged her shoulders with a bitter, ironical expression. 'I don't come into it. I'm just the wife who hasn't given him any children. Because, you know, my Protti has a vocation as a father. He has a mistress and actually seven children. Seven, I say, no less than seven. Seven children that he'd die for. Four boys and three girls. D'you want to know their names?'

182

'No, it doesn't matter, it's just that I didn't understand . . .'

'He's a good father, my Protti, oh yes, he's a good father. He doesn't have a photograph of me in his wallet, nor even one of his mistress. He has the seven photographs of his seven children. And he likes family life, my goodness he does. He spends his evenings alternately here with me, bored in front of the television, and with them, wallowing in family bliss. And, at least four times a day, he telephones. "How are you? What are you doing? How are things going? What news is there? What's happening? Who has gone out? Who has stayed at home?" A good father, my Protti, an excellent father, a father of the kind that no longer exists.'

She was no longer panting now, she was vibrating. A flood of sarcastic rage shook her from head to foot. She went on whispering, crushing me against the door and speaking into my ear: 'The mother of his children means nothing to him. Absolutely nothing. For him she has always remained the insignificant secretary to whom he dictated contracts. It's exceptional if he ever addresses a word to her. For he's not a libertine, my Protti, oh no, not in the least. Not even a little. The opposite, if anything. D'you know how he begot those seven children?'

The question sounded so strange that I did not know what to say. I looked at her questioningly. Mafalda, in turn, looked at me with a bitter, malicious smile. Then she said: 'With a syringe.'

'With a syringe?'

'That's right: artificial insemination. Because he has a very, very small one, too short to be able to penetrate. Smaller than a child's. And so – the syringe. All seven of them. One good injection for each and that's that. Very modern, isn't he, my Protti?'

Dumbfounded as I was, I could not help saying to myself that this explained everything. Protti was so sublimated, so completely so, that, according to what Mafalda said, he had, positively, 'a very, very small one'. Sublimation, in fact, had

183

been symbolically materialized in him in a sexual organ that had been reduced to a minimum, had atrophied.

There came back to my mind one of the many books I had read as a script-writer, at a time when a film was to be made about Napoleon, which came to nothing for the usual reasons of production. Well, according to Doctor Antonmarchi, the so-called 'great' Corsican also had a 'very, very small one'. '*Sicut puer*', noted the doctor in his memoirs. This constituted a proof. Napoleon, in fact, monster of sublimation as he was, was obviously supersublimated to the point of under-development, to the point of atrophy. I asked in a low voice, just to make sure: 'But what exactly do you mean by "very, very small"?'

She looked at me fixedly with her round, Pekinese eyes, and then indicated half of her little finger. 'Like that,' she said.

'It's not possible!'

'It's perfectly true. If you see him in the ordinary way, sitting or standing, my Protti is so very handsome, so very decorative, so very imposing. But in bed he's like Tom Thumb: you lose it between the sheets. That's when the syringe is needed.'

So spoke Mafalda, behind the half-closed door, in a hurried whisper, and taking a stealthy look every now and then into the hall. Then she said: 'Here's Protti now. D'you remember the fountain near the front gate? I'll go and wait for you there. How soon will you have finished?'

'In a quarter of an hour.'

'Very well, till then.'

She pushed me out into the hall, and she too went out and disappeared, majestically undulating, at the very moment when Protti, in turn, appeared in the doorway of the study. Had Protti seen us? Certainly he had; but clearly it did not matter to him at all. From a distance he said: 'Rico, you wanted to speak to me? Come, let's go in here.'

He led me into the study and I followed; he went and sat down again at the desk and I sat down opposite him; the light from the green-shaded lamp hit me in the face so that I was lit up and he was in shadow. For all his good manners, like those of an old-fashioned nobleman, Protti often made use of such inquisitorial, authoritarian contrivances, like those of a third-degree cross-examination. He was sublimated, as I have said, in pursuance of power; and the man who has power enjoys making it felt by the man who does not have it. Dazzled by the light, conscious of finding myself – I, the desublimate *par excellence*, all sexual organ and no sublimation – face to face with the sublimate *par excellence*, all sublimation and no sexual organ, I fidgeted with embarrassment on my chair; then, in a desublimated manner, I burst out: 'Protti, I've got to speak to you. It's a matter of my career, of my future, of my livelihood.'

I could have hit myself on the head as soon as I had spoken. This was, in fact, the way in which desublimated people speak, or rather yelp, under the illusion that their feelings are not only communicable but also convincing. Whereas sublimated people, for their part, have no need to communicate feelings, for the excellent reason that they haven't any. Through the mysterious metamorphoses of sublimation, feeling, in them, mounts to the brain, cools down as though in a rapid refrigerator and, as it cools, changes its nature and becomes thought, reflection, calculation.

Protti, indeed, received the anxious expression of my passionate state of mind with the same indifference with which a breakwater receives the chaotic surge of a stormy sea, vanishing perhaps for a moment but then, at the backwash, emerging harder and more upright and intact than ever. With a surprise that was too strongly accentuated not to be ironical, he said: 'Why, what's the matter, Rico? I don't understand, explain yourself.'

I wriggled nervously on my chair and then, once more giving way to feeling, since it was not too late to adopt a different tone, I answered: 'You know, Protti, that I am first a man of culture, an intellectual, and only secondly a cinema man. Or rather, I am an intellectual who happened, at a certain moment, to get into the film world. Or, better still, who was predestined to get into the film world.'

Protti said nothing. His face expressed the usual utterly

185

false, urbane affability of a man of the world, with an insincerity so complete that it was even flattering. I continued: 'You have had confidence in me from the very beginning, and I am grateful to you for that. Do you know how many scripts I have done for you so far?'

He smiled and said: 'I should have to have my secretary here to do some research . . .'

'Have a guess at the number.'

'I wouldn't know.'

'Forty-two, in ten years. Counting, of course, the revisions and other extra collaborations. Now I should like to ask you a question. May I do so?'

'Of course.'

'Has it never occurred to you that you're wasting me? In other words, that you might have – I don't say, exploited me, but, in short, made a better use of my qualities?'

'I've always had the impression that the work you were doing suited you, Rico, and that you liked it.'

'Well then, let us say: doesn't it seem to you that the moment has come for me to move on from script-writing to directing?'

At last I had said it. I saw Protti looking at me for a second or two with his big, black, shining eyes, frowning slightly. Then he made me a present of a brilliant smile with his perfect false teeth. 'This is one of those personal things, Rico,' he said, 'upon which other people cannot deliver a judgment. If you feel that it's time for you to move on from script-writing to directing, that's all that is needed.'

'But, Protti, one doesn't move on from script-writing to directing like that, by one's own will, all on one's own. What is needed is the assistance of the production side. What is needed is the producer.'

'Perfectly correct.'

'In my case it's you who are the producer, Protti. It's you and no one but you. You know me, you know how much I'm worth. For my part, I've devoted ten years of my life to you, I've never worked for other producers. Everything, therefore, depends on you.'

186

He did not put up a defence, he did not draw back, he did not lose his composure, oh no; he would not have been the supersublimated man that he was, with a member that was not merely obedient and sublimated but also, actually, 'very, very small', if he had not behaved in this way. With perfect calm, he said: 'Let us admit for a moment that you are right and that everything, as you say, depends on me. But the fact that it depends on me whether you become a director does not necessarily imply that I can entrust you with a director's job.'

'Why not?'

'You gave the reason just now.'

'And what is that?'

'Your culture, Rico. The fact that you're an intellectual. You see, Rico, film directors are not intellectuals. They're ugly brutes who rush head-down into the telling of a story and then tell it from A to Z. A director is available for practically any sort of film. You, on the other hand, as an intellectual and a man of culture, would only be able to make a certain particular type of film.'

'For example?'

'The type of film, to be precise, in which you could demonstrate your culture.'

He was making fun of me, it was clear, in the manner of the great, completely atrophied sublimate who finds himself face to face with a hypertrophied desublimate. He was making fun of me in a gentlemanly, man-of-the-world, sublimated fashion. I protested, with tears in my eyes: 'No, Protti, on the contrary, you don't consider me a man of culture.'

'But what d'you mean, when this is the precise reason why, with all the good will in the world, I don't see what I could get you to do?'

'No, Protti, on the contrary, let me say it again, you're not really convinced that I'm an intellectual, a man of culture, otherwise you would already have put me in charge of a suitable film, seeing that you have it already in hand, that you're actually preparing it.'

I had said it. But he pretended to be dumbfounded. Well, well, it is very, very difficult for one who is desublimated to succeed in entangling one who is sublimated! 'Honestly,' he exclaimed, 'I don't understand you. What film?'

'The film of which I'm at this moment writing the script, together with Maurizio.'

'You mean the film about protest?'

'Exactly, *Expropriation*.'

'But what has culture to do with that film?'

I made up my mind to burst into a derisive guffaw, flattering, exaggerated, in the manner of Cutica. 'That's a good one! I don't agree but I must admit it's a good one. You should say it to those young men: what has culture to do with your protest?'

'Isn't it like that, perhaps?'

I was serious again. 'It's a good one, but, I'm sorry, it's just a quip, and a very witty one too. But if we intend to be serious we must recognize that protest is, above all, a cultural action.'

Strange to say, he at once admitted that I was right. 'Then I will tell you that I see perfectly well how you *could* make that film. I do not see why you *should* make it.'

'I ought to make it because – allow me to say, Protti, that I'm not talking like this out of presumption but because it's true – I'm saying I ought to make it because I'm the only one who *can* make it.'

He said nothing. He looked at me and seemed to be waiting for me to explain further. Encouraged by his silence, I resumed: 'I alone, within the limits of what I may call your stable, I alone – allow me the metaphor – am the horse that can win a race of this kind. What I mean is that I alone, amongst all the available script-writers, have the very special cultural background that is required for the directing of a film like *Expropriation*. There is not only one kind of culture, Protti, there are so many. There is, for instance, the academic, humanistic, formal, conservative culture which for a film like this would be not merely useless but would have a reverse and harmful effect. There is the culture of the traditional Left, an instrument once undoubtedly useful but now outdated, which could only lead to old-fashioned solutions. There is, finally, modern culture, that is, "my" culture. And what sort of a culture is this? I would say that it derives, more or less, from all the most vital currents of modern thought, from Marxism as well as psychoanalysis, from existentialism as well as phenomenology. This modern culture is the inevitable basis, premise and point of departure for a film like *Expropriation*. For this reason, Protti, you should be convinced that this is not an ordinary film to be entrusted to an ordinary director: it is "my" film.'

I had spoken forcibly. No less forcibly, as soon as I fell silent, did I repent of having spoken. For, even with regard to culture, there is one kind of behaviour for the sublimated and one for the desublimated. The sublimated man hides his culture, the desublimated displays it, waves it like a flag. I felt I had given the impression that I was a *parvenu* of culture, that is, to be precise, a self-taught man; and I could not help blushing. But no, not at all. Protti, being genuinely super-sublimated, said the exact opposite of what I, in my de-sublimation, had foreseen. 'There is one thing, Rico – allow me to say so – in which you are particularly lacking.'

'What is that?'

'You're lacking in pride. This is not a film for you. Culture doesn't come into it. It's a cheap film, made in association with Maurizio's fiancée's father, in order to please those young men. It really is not a film that is worthy of you.'

By this time, however, nobody could stop me, I was fairly launched. Distressed, trembling, I cried: 'But, Protti, I know all about protest. I've covered entire memorandum-books with notes. I kept a diary for the whole of 1968. I even rushed off to Paris, though as an observer only, as soon as the May troubles broke out. In my library I have dozens of books on the subject. I've gone into it thoroughly. For me the works of Marcuse, of Horkheimer, of Adorno, Marx, Lenin and Mao hold no mysteries. I'm in a position to prove to you that protest arose contemporaneously in Germany, from the same source that gave us Nietzsche, in France from the revolutionary, anti-social tradition of men like Villon and Rimbaud, in the United States from the hippy and beat movements, as well as from the influences of Oriental philosophies of the Zen and Tao type. Not forgetting such different figures as Ché Guevara, Castro, Dutschke, Cohn-Bendit, Godard, Ho-Chi-Minh, Giap . . .'

I paused. Protti made an ironical gesture, like someone trying to shelter from an imaginary downpour of rain. 'Enough, enough, enough! For goodness' sake! I know that you know a whole lot of things, I've never doubted it. What we must consider, Rico, if anything, is another aspect of the affair.'

'What is that?'

'Your age. You are forty . . .'

'Thirty-five.'

'Thirty-five? You look at least forty, if not more. I was saying, then, you're almost forty now and do you want to get mixed up with a group of worthless little boys? This film about protest – leave it to be made by the people who are, or rather, who think they are, the real protesters. Something different is needed for you.'

'But what?'

'At the present moment, I don't know. Let me think it over. Don't worry. Don't get excited. Let me think. When least you expect it, I'll find a film that suits you.'

He made a very obvious movement, as though to rise from his chair. I realized, with a shudder of cold dismay, that I was going to lose the job of director for good and all. Now directing means art, art means sublimation, and sublimation . . . well, sublimation means my whole life. Another moment and I should be simply the cultural buffoon, the intellectual clown enlivening the guests of his supremely sublimated master with the haphazard culture of a desublimated self-taught person. Another moment and I should be, once and for all, the man who was all member and no power, face to face with the man who was all power and no member. I realized clearly that I was about to perform a base action; but I said to myself, with conscious Machiavellism, that sublimation, in other words artistic creativeness, was an end that justified any sort of means. 'One moment, Protti,' I cried. 'You must

190

see that it is in your own precise interest that it should be I to make this film. I say interest and I mean interest, in the highest sense, that is, not only in the material but also the social, the political and the cultural sense.'

'And what may this interest of mine be, that is, so it seems, threatened?'

Now I was in the mud, so to speak, right up to my knees; and I felt I might as well plunge in up to my neck. 'It is your interest,' I said, 'not only as a producer and industrialist, but also as a man of the upper middle class, a man of distinction, in fact as a capitalist. I hope you won't deny that you're a capitalist.'

'Indeed.'

Indeed what? Who knows? I went on: 'Maurizio and his friends of the group . . .'

'But what group?'

'The revolutionary group.'

'Ah, those boys who meet in Flavia's house, at Fregene.'

'Yes, those so-called boys want to make a film that is paid for by you but is against you. This is the truth. In proof of what I am saying, I will let you have two versions. The first is the one I had done, trying not to do you any harm; the second is the one which Maurizio and the group have imposed upon me. You'll see the difference, and then you'll understand why I myself am the only one who can make this film.'

He did not move, he said nothing, he merely looked at me. The supersublimated figure, towering upon the marble pedestal of power, looked down upon the desublimated one who was sinking gradually into the mud of denunciation and treachery. In desperation, I pursued: 'If you have a minute to spare, I'll explain the whole thing to you. Then tomorrow I'll send you the two versions and you'll see whether I'm right.'

'Cheer up! Yes, I have a minute to spare.'

Without taking breath and now entering completely into my Judas rôle, I gave a hurried account of the two versions of *Expropriation*, stressing particularly the ideological character of my disagreement with Maurizio. I spoke at length, with all the ardour of a traitor seeking to reassure himself by an excess

191

of treachery. Breathlessly I concluded: 'And just so that you may be convinced, do you know who, according to Maurizio, was to serve as model for the expropriated capitalist? You, you yourself. In Maurizio's film you are the cynical, corrupt bourgeois, the exploiter, against whom even his own daughter rebels.'

It was not true. It was I who, one day, in my frenzied desire to please Maurizio, had suggested Protti as model for the character of the capitalist. But Maurizio had pointed out to me judiciously that we ought not to antagonize Protti, otherwise it would be the end of the film. Now, however, I was launched along the path of treachery; and one base action more or less, what did it matter? I saw Protti shake his head, not in the least disconcerted. Then he said: 'If things are really as you say, well, I'm sorry, Rico, but I prefer Maurizio's version to yours.'

Catastrophe! Now even the thirty pieces of silver were being denied to Judas! Now I was being repudiated by Protti himself, whom I had hoped to bring over to my side by treachery. I grew pale and confused, and I stammered: 'But his version is openly anti-bourgeois, anti-capitalist, full of the spirit of destruction.'

He nodded his approval. 'That's what we want. We producers, I mean. Something violent, something destructive, as you say. I'm sorry, Rico; your version would be more lifelike, I don't deny it, but it's sentimental, expressive of intimate feelings, low-toned, weak; it wouldn't make a single lira!'

Almost without meaning to, I said: 'So you're prepared to finance protest, to support destruction. The bourgeois finances the people who wish him dead. The capitalist encourages the people who conspire against capitalism. Perfectly logical, I must say. Certainly, because there is a logic of class suicide, Protti, don't forget that.'

Protti shook his head in a fatherly, indulgent way. 'But in the meantime, above all, let us not trot out big words like destruction, class suicide and so on. These are boys who are enjoying themselves in their own way. We, of my generation, thought only about women. They have put politics in the place of women. Moreover, since you speak to me of the interests of capitalism, I, as a capitalist, can tell you that the precise interest of capitalism is that protesters, instead of carrying out expropriations in a serious manner, should limit themselves to talking about them in films. Yes, even in the most truculent fashion possible. On the one hand it allows these good people to relieve their feelings, but without harming a hair of any-one's head. On the other hand, it's good business, because violent, even destructive, films, for the moment anyhow, bring in the money. And as for myself, as the model of an exploiting, cynical capitalist – well, well, after all it's almost the truth. Perhaps I'm not as cynical as I should be; but capitalist and bourgeois – that I certainly am.'

Protti was escaping me, Protti was slipping through my fingers, Protti was darting away from me like a fish that sniffs the bait and then, with a brisk turn, goes away without swallowing the hook. Distressed, I leant forward: 'But, Protti, in the end this is a question of making a good or a bad film. The film as Maurizio sees it is bad. Bad because false. Protest, as Maurizio and his friends see it, does not exist, Protti. It's a falsification of reality. What good can come out of false-ness?'

Protti smiled. 'The Italian "westerns" are falsifications too, and yet . . .' As he said this, he rose to his feet.

Then I too rose to my feet and, in desperation, barred his way. 'Protti,' I said, 'believe me, I beg of you, for the love of God, you must believe me. I am what is called a born director. I would not make such a fuss if I did not know for certain that I am a born director and that for years you've been doing me a grave injustice.'

'But where's the injustice? You have no economic worries and you aren't short of work . . .'

'The injustice lies in the fact that a great – yes, Protti, I say it loudly and clearly – a great director is condemned for life to do nothing but write scripts.'

'And who may this great director be?'

'The person who is speaking to you at this moment.'

'Come, come, don't complain; your scripts, if I'm not mistaken, are very well paid.'

'Protti, I would do the directing job for nothing. And instead of the four hundred million that the film would finally cost under an ordinary director, I would do it with one hundred.'

Now he patted me on the shoulder. The usual pat of the sublimated hand on the desublimated shoulder. I wanted to seize that humiliating hand and thrust it away violently from me and shout in his face: Yes, *Expropriation* is *my* film, not so much because I'm a man of culture and an intellectual, but because I'm a revolutionary. *I* didn't wait for 1968 to make a protest; I've been making it ever since I was born. I have rebelled above all against your filthy capitalism and exploitation, your filthy, alienated, ignorant bourgeoisie, and against you who are such a typical representative of both the one and the other, you old whoremonger, you pimp, you harlot.

Instead of which, as usual, I kept it all to myself; I did not push his hand away, I did not open my mouth, all I did was to make a movement of impatience with my shoulder, but only a slight one. Protti concluded: 'Get along with you, now you must do that fine script of yours, and do it according to Maurizio's ideas; he's an intelligent, talented boy. As for the job of director, let's leave it for the moment; I'll accept you as a candidate.'

'What does that mean?'

'It means that, when the time comes to choose a director for *Expropriation*, I'll bear you in mind.'

'And when will that time come?'

'Quite soon.'

'And on what criteria do you intend to base your choice?'

'On the basis of the production's interests.'

By now we were in the doorway of the villa. From the top of the steps I could see the big circular space, dimly, lugubriously lit; the cemetery-like pointed tops of the cypresses against the background of the night sky; and, in the centre of the space, the long, narrow table with the whole of Protti's 'court' looking more than ever like an assembly of ghosts, in

194

the faint but staring light from the blue lamps. Chattering, cynical, sceptical, fawning, servile, vulgar ghosts! Desublimated ghosts! I turned abruptly to Protti and said in a decisive, frank manner: 'Thank you, Protti, for having had the courtesy to listen to me. I see you are making for the table. I'm sorry, but I don't intend to follow you. I'm going away, and do you know why?'

'Why?'

'Because you have a "court", Protti. Nothing to find fault with, let that be understood: it's a question of tastes. It so happens that your "court" is composed of individuals that I don't get on with.'

'And what have these individuals done to you?'

'To me, personally, nothing. But I can't endure them, that's all; just as, in any case, they can't endure me. Let's call it incompatibility of character and think no more about it.'

Protti was now laughing in a mild and gentlemanly way, the way of a supersublimated person to whom the passions of the desublimated seem remote, like the frantic wrigglings of a bacillus seen through the lens of a microscope. 'But why?' he asked. 'They're all good fellows. Come on, stay with us a little longer. I'm sure Cutica can't wait to compete with you on some elevated literary subject.'

Making fun of me! He was making fun of me! I drew myself up, stuck out my chest and raised my chin. 'Good-bye, Protti, I really must be going. That'll be for another time. Make my excuses to Signora Mafalda and all those good fellows. Good-bye.'

I waved my hand, turned away from him and went hastily to the table of the ghosts. In a loud voice, I said: 'Let's go, Fausta.'

I saw her rise hurriedly, anxiously, to her feet. Poor Fausta! She must have seen Mafalda run after me into the villa, and goodness knows what she must have thought. Indeed, as we were walking away towards the car, she asked me, with a curious air of compliance – that kind of pained compliance which is characteristic of jealousy: 'What did you do with Leda Lidi?'

After having been 'underneath' for so long, I felt the need to recover the pleasant sensation of being 'on top'. Even with someone like Fausta, so hopelessly desublimated that she was, as it were, reduced to a pulp. Cruelly, I replied: 'Everything, as I had foreseen. She came running after me, we went off together into a big room, and I kissed her. All in order. A fine, long kiss, penetrating into every hole and corner. And then she gave me an assignation.'

'Where?'

'At the fountain near the front gate.'

'But for when?'

'Now.'

'And are you going?'

I was on the point of answering: Yes, of course; when, oddly, 'he' intervened. 'It's useless for you to go,' he said. 'Give her a breathing-space.'

'Don't you like her so much, now? Eh? Is your geronto-philia already over and done with?'

'I'm not saying that. I say, give her a breathing-space.'

I felt that, after all, he was right. For the moment the assault on Fortress Mafalda should be deferred, especially as all the trenches had now been overwhelmed and captured and it was practically as if I had already taken it by storm. However, I said to Fausta: 'I'll see. When we reach the place, I'll decide. This means that, if I keep the appointment, you must wait outside in the road, in the car.'

'But what d'you mean to do with her?'

'Everything.'

She said nothing. She lowered that big double face of hers and appeared to be looking at her big bare paunch as it overflowed above her trousers. I said, perfidiously: 'You drive. Then, when we reach the place of appointment, if I decide to get out we won't have to change places.'

Fausta did not answer. She sat down at the wheel in gloomy silence and I got in too. She started the engine, lowered the hand-brake, and the car moved away.

It moved away, however, with an angry roar, at a high speed. It left the avenue, rushed out into the space in front of the villa and made straight for the table. Another moment, and it would have run full into Protti and his 'court'. I confess that this thought crossed my mind: Yes, let her do it. Let the car squash the whole lot of them, like so many cockroaches. I saw the guests drawing back, frightened and incredulous, as the car approached, as if they were wondering whether this was a joke, or a mistake, or worse; I saw, to my intense satisfaction, that my arch-enemy Cutica actually ended up on the ground, with his legs in the air, and his chair with him; then I woke up and seized the wheel with both hands. The car, with an abrupt swerve, narrowly missed the table and continued straight on, down the drive. We moved along between the oleanders and I said to Fausta: 'My goodness, are you mad?'

'The wheel slipped out of my hands.'

'You might very easily have killed them all.'

'So much the better if I had.'

There was a bend in the drive and then, in the distance, could be seen the gateway with the gates wide open. To the left, amongst the trunks of the pine-trees, I caught sight of a small, dark, circular opening in the centre of which I could just see the round basin of a fountain. A jet of water shone in mid-air, in the indirect light from one of those same blue lamps. A clearly visible figure, unmistakably pear-shaped and dinosaur-like, was seated on a bench in front of the basin. Fausta slowed down and said: 'There she is, over there. D'you want to get out?'

Without hesitation I replied: 'No, let's go on.'

8 Instrumentalized!

Love, true love, as different and remote from eroticism
as it is from affection; the love, in short, that people talk about;
the love that would be the highest outcome of perfect sublimation, higher even than art, perhaps; would this love, in
the absolute, bring it about that the person who loves never
feels, when in the presence of his beloved, either 'on top' or
'underneath', but rather, in a manner as unmistakable as it
is irrational, 'on equal terms', in other words, in a state of
complete identification? I think so. In fact, whereas with
Fausta and with Mafalda – to give two opposing examples –
I felt myself to be either 'on top' or I felt myself 'underneath',
in the presence of Irene – a miracle! – I did not aspire to be
'on top', nor did I suffer from being 'underneath'; but, marvellously and ineffably, I felt 'equal'. In other words, I 'felt'
her, and not myself, only her; in fact I 'was' her.

Could it therefore be that I had penetrated into the
promised land of sublimation? It was too soon to tell. Anyhow,
the identification would seem to prove it. I thought of these
things while sitting at the table in Irene's kitchen, as she, with
a little striped apron tied round her waist and shoulders, was
busy at the stove getting dinner ready for me. I had been
thinking about this visit for a whole week. I had been ashamed
of getting in touch with Irene after the very bad loss of face
that 'he' had caused me during our first meeting. But when I
plucked up courage and telephoned her, she, with (for me)
intoxicating simplicity, had at once spoken to me as to an old
friend and had invited me to dinner.

And now, there I was, filled with profound, quiet joy
from the sole fact of seeing her, of hearing her, of being with
her. The kitchen was all lined with Formica, of the kind that
is an imitation of wood. One of those kitchens in the so-called
'colonial' style, which figure in the catalogues of household

electrical appliances under the comforting name of 'Old America'. Irene, now, was laying the table. On the Formica top she arranged a number of table-mats of green waterproof material; on the mats she placed plates, glasses, knives, forks and spoons of vaguely Scandinavian style. On the shelf beside the stove I could see a heap of cellophane bags through whose transparency I distinguished the green colour of vegetables, the pinkness of meat, the whiteness of cheese and the yellow of the fruit which we should soon be eating. Irene shopped at the supermarket; when she hadn't time even for the super-market, she fell back on tinned stuff. Her huge refrigerator, wide open, appeared indeed to be filled on every shelf with a great variety of cans and bottles.

Irene was standing in front of this refrigerator looking for something. She was wearing her usual very brief miniskirt which, possibly because of her microscopic, coquettish apron, seemed, as it hung above her splendid but fully adult legs, to be more than ever a slightly obscene parody of a little girl's short frock. I wish to emphasize at this point that it is always 'he' who points out the obscenity of Irene's legs to me. In reality I see neither obscenity, nor legs, nor miniskirt, nor any-thing. I see only the complete figure of Irene, diffused with a light of joy. *My* joy at being with her.

Irene took a tin out of the refrigerator and showed it to me: 'Turtle soup, d'you like it?' I answered that I did, and then asked: 'D'you cook every evening?'

'Yes, I have to. I'm alone. The maid comes in the morning and goes off at four.'

'And who looks after your little girl during the day?'

'She's a day pupil at the American St Patrick's College. I take her there in the morning before going to the office. In the evening I go and fetch her after I leave the office.'

'Don't you eat at home?'

'No, I go to a snack bar near the embassy and eat a sandwich or a hamburger. We don't have a long lunch-break.'

'And when you go out in the evening, who looks after the child?'

'I get in a baby-sitter.'

'Snack bar, sandwich, hamburger, supermarket, Old America, colonial style, American College of St Patrick, baby-sitter . . . Would you like to live in America?'

'I've never been there. Why d'you ask me that?'

'Because I feel you're very americanized.'

'Really?'

'Yes, really.'

'If by "americanized" you mean that I like certain things that come from the United States, well, yes, then I am.'

'What do you like best about the United States?'

'I've told you already: I've never been there so I can't exactly say. But if I went there, I think the thing I would like best would be precisely what makes so many people hate that country.'

'And what is that?'

'Capitalism.'

'Capitalism?'

'Yes, does that surprise you so much? Capitalism.'

'You like capitalism?'

'Yes, very much.'

'But why?'

'There's no "why" about it. I like it.'

'But you're not rich, are you?'

'No, I'm not. In fact, I work.'

'Then what does capitalism matter to you?'

'It matters to me inasmuch as I like it.'

'But it's unjust that a few people should have a lot and a lot of people should have very little.'

'I don't love justice, I don't know what to do about it.'

'What do you love, then?'

'I've already told you: injustice, in other words, capitalism.'

She spoke in a sensible, quiet voice, without interrupting her preparations for dinner, going from the refrigerator to the stove, from the stove to the sink, with the calm, precise, measured movements of a mechanical robot in the window of a shop for household electrical appliances; in a kitchen in which everything, even the crusts and the waste paper and the

200

cabbage-stalks, looked clean and functional. I could not help comparing Fausta, a very bad housekeeper, with Irene; and this spotless kitchen with our own, always dirty and untidy; and I said to myself that, in spite of her mistaken sympathy for capitalism, I would wish to have a wife like Irene. But 'he', at this idea, was immediately up in arms. '*I* wouldn't,' he said.

'Why?'

'Because Fausta, when all is said and done, is still desirable. Irene is not.'

'But you're always pointing out her legs to me.'

'Irene is not desirable. She's the kind of woman who is only desirable as a challenge.'

'A challenge to what?'

'Why, to her own undesirableness.'

'I don't understand you.'

'Perhaps I explain myself badly. The challenge comes in reality from Irene, from her complete frigidity and obstinacy. I point out her legs to you because, as I've already told you on another occasion, their hermetic quality constitutes a challenge and arouses one's desire to pull them open. But actually Irene, with this perpetual challenge, encourages not so much desire as violence.'

'Violence?'

'Yes indeed, violence, that is, rape, or even actually murder. She's the kind of woman whom a milkman or a beggar, finding the front door open, assaults and tries in vain to violate and in the end leaves strangled on the bathroom floor.'

'Do you mean by that that you "would like" to murder her?'

'Perhaps so. Perhaps for me it might be the only way of getting into "direct contact" with her.'

'A nice sort of direct contact! And how about love? Ah, but I was forgetting that for you love does not exist.'

'He' was silent for a moment, then, brutally, he stated: 'You don't love Irene, you love the fact that Irene, with her complete obstinacy, does not endanger your experiment in sublimation.'

Again he was silent; then he added: 'D'you know what, if

anything, would induce me to agree to exchange Fausta for Irene?'

'What?'

'Look up and see.'

I looked up. There, in the doorway, had appeared Irene's daughter, Virginia. I looked at her, as, in a curiously insistent way, 'he' had suggested. Thin, long-limbed, her legs white and loose-knit, still without any recognizable shape and going up and up, unvarying in thickness, below her short little dress, she did not, in her figure, show more than her nine years. But her face, curiously, was already that of a woman; and not so much, perhaps, owing to the emergence of a precocious femininity as because of some elusively adult, almost degenerate, quality in her features. Between two waves of smooth, pale gold hair her long, pale face stood out, with its narrow temples, prominent blue eyes, a nose shaped like a drop of water and a full-formed mouth of vivid red. Her curling, open nostrils quivered like those of a rabbit. Her lower lip looked as if it were swollen from the sting of a wasp. There were two purplish marks of fatigue, like scratches, under her eyes.

Cynically, 'he' whispered: 'It's still too soon, now. But in five years' time, at most, she'll be perfectly well fitted to console you for her mother's coldness.'

'Disgusting!'

'Why disgusting? Look at her eyes and at those marks of fatigue under her eyes. She looks like a woman, and perhaps she already is.'

'Stop it, you horrify me. If you wish our dialogue to continue, it's absolutely essential that you should change your tone; I insist upon it. This is not a request, it's an order.'

To tell the truth, I did not feel so much horror as I showed because I was clearly conscious that all 'his' remarks about the mother and daughter were merely a reaction to my own wish to love and be loved by Irene. 'He', of course, was the enemy of love. And, if the notion of sublimation irritated him, of all the effects of sublimation the one that irritated him most was, precisely, love.

Meanwhile, as these thoughts were going through my

202

mind, Irene, like a good, affectionate mother, was introducing me to her daughter. 'Virginia, this is Rico, a friend of mine. Say how d'you do.' Virginia came up to me, gave me her hand and made me a little curtsy, bending her big, bony knee from under her dress. Then she too sat down at the table and immediately opened a magazine of photographs and stories. I inquired of her, in an amiable way: 'What are you reading?'

She did not answer me, nor did she raise her head; all she did was to turn the cover of the magazine slightly so that I could read the title. Irene turned off the gas, took the saucepan from the stove and walked round the table, pouring the turtle soup into the bowls. Then she sat down. For a short time Irene and I ate in silence, looking at one another over the edges of our bowls. At last Irene asked: 'How is your work going?'

'Just as usual.'

'What does that mean?'

'It's going well. In a month, at most, I shall be beginning work on my film.'

'Last time you told me you'd be beginning within a fortnight.'

'There's been a delay. But now, work on the film will start, for certain, in a month's time.'

'Why ever have you waited so long to become a director?'

'I didn't want it; I've refused many offers. I didn't feel sure of myself, not mature enough.'

'What will the film be called?'

'Expropriation.'

'What an odd title. What is it? A film about building sites?'

'Why about building sites?'

'People often say, don't they? – things like this: the Local Government will expropriate the land – or something of the kind.'

'No, it's not a film about building sites.'

'Tell me the story of your film, then.'

I told her the story while she was taking away the soup-bowls and then standing at the stove, turning the beefsteaks on the grill with a fork. The child, as I was speaking, sat motionless, looking at me but without any interest, as she might have looked at any ordinary object, continuously making nervous grimaces, such as twisting her mouth, wrinkling her nostrils, half-closing first one eye then the other, gripping her lower lip with her teeth and then letting it pop out after giving it a good bite. Irene went on carefully turning her steaks without making any comments. By the time I came to the end of the film story, the steaks were ready. Irene placed them on a dish and then served them up at the table. She also put on the table a wooden salad-bowl full of ready-dressed salad. Then she sat down, and only then did she speak: 'I don't much care for the story of your film.'

'Why?'

'I dislike protests, I dislike students, and I dislike everything that has to do with students and protests.'

'What have protests done to you?'

'To me, nothing. But all the same, I can't bear them.'

'But tell me: why d'you dislike students?'

'I don't know. I don't like them, that's all.'

'Perhaps it's because they want to destroy the capitalism that you like so much.'

'To tell the truth, I dislike them for no precise reason. That can happen, can't it? For instance, one enters a room and sees some person for the first time, and one immediately thinks: My God, what an unsympathetic face! One doesn't know anything about that person, one is seeing him for the first time and yet one dislikes him. It's the same with students.'

'Very well, that may be so. But if you had something to reproach them with, what would it be?'

She thought it over for a moment and then said: 'Their ingratitude.'

'Their ingratitude?'

'Yes, they're ungrateful. The capitalism which they want to destroy has given everybody, including them, cars and television, the cinema and the aeroplane, and all sorts of other advantages; they accept all these things and at the same time claim that they want to destroy the thing that has provided them. Isn't that ingratitude?'

204

'In some cases ingratitude is obligatory. I myself, for example, work for capitalism, yet I don't feel any gratitude. It would be a fine state of affairs if one had to be grateful to capitalism. In the last resort even *it* doesn't expect it.'

Irene said nothing. She appeared to be thinking. Then she replied: 'Students are capitalists themselves. It's only those who are sick of the advantages of capitalism who can take it into their heads to refuse them. Working men – they don't really refuse them. Partly because they don't have them and also because they would like to have them. Protesters are like those rich women who eat very little for fear of getting fat. Poor people, on the other hand, go hungry and are not afraid of getting fat. They want to eat and, when they can, they eat as much as they can.'

'In your opinion, then, how ought the story of my film to go?'

'I don't understand, what d'you mean?'

'I mean, how would you show the protesters?'

'As they are.'

'Ungrateful?'

'Yes, ungrateful, and also frightened.'

'Frightened? Where does the fear come in?'

'They're frightened of prosperity because for generations they've been beggars. A car, a refrigerator, a record-player – these frighten them. They see the devil in them. They're frightened of them just as over-pious people are frightened of women.'

Irene spoke with conviction but without becoming impassioned. One could see that she was convinced of the things she was saying to the point of believing that it was a waste of breath to say them. Neither did it matter very much to me, on my side, what Irene was saying. What I liked was being with her, talking to her, listening to her, looking at her. But 'he' did not look upon it in this way. I heard him muttering something or other about stopping 'the chatter' and 'getting to grips'. This meant putting into practice his own fantastic plan of seduction, based, to be precise, upon Irene's sexual habits.

And what did this plan consist of? It had been the story of the relations between Irene and her husband that had caused him to think it up. It was a matter, so it seemed, of suggesting a subject to Irene for one of her 'interior' films in which, somehow or other, I might take part in the capacity of an actor. Irene would introduce me into an imaginary event, as she had once done with her husband. From this, in some way, 'he' maintained that I would be able to move on by degrees to a real, complete relationship.

It was a fantastic plan, as I have already said, because it did not allow one to foresee in any way how I could transform myself from the imaginary interpreter of an imaginary event into a real protagonist in real life. But there it was, just because it was fantastic it attracted me, and I felt that, inevitably, I should soon be trying to put it into effect.

Dinner was over. Irene rose and tipped the plates, one after the other, into the sink, with one hand only while with the other she raised her cigarette to her mouth. The child asked: 'May I get down, Mummy?'

'Yes.'

'May I go to my room?'

'Yes.'

'I'll go, but you must come with me.'

'All right, my treasure.'

Virginia rose, went and stood beside her mother, took her hand. Then, throwing back her head against her mother's lap, pulling back her shoulders and sticking out her stomach, she said in a plaintive voice: 'Send him away.'

'Who, my love?'

'Him. Why don't you send him away?'

'He's a guest, one doesn't send guests away.'

'Send him away, send him away, send him away.'

I felt I ought to make some conciliatory gesture. I put out my hand and took hold of Virginia's, drawing her towards me and saying: 'Why d'you want your mummy to send me away? Don't you like me? But I like you. You see how different we are?'

206

These words were not intended to have any double meaning, they were sincere and they expressed exactly what I felt and thought. But, incredible though it may seem, 'he', in his ignoble, sarcastic fashion, commented: 'I believe it when you say you like her. Just a bit too much.'

Firmly, I commanded him: 'I forbid you to make insinuations of that kind.'

Too late. The little girl, with sure feminine instinct, had without doubt become conscious of 'his' presence. The fact remained that she suddenly let out a piercing scream, tore herself away from my hands and ran to take refuge once more against her mother's legs. Then, stamping her feet, she started again: 'Send him away, send him away, send him away.'

Irene stooped down, put her mouth to her child's ear and spoke to her in a whisper. Then she straightened herself again and said: 'Come, Virginia, say good-bye to Rico and then I'll put you to bed.'

Unexpectedly the child gave me her hand, made her little ceremonious curtsy and said: 'Good-night, Rico.' Then she went off with Irene holding her by the hand.

Left alone, I vented my anger on 'him'. 'You're disgusting,' I said. 'My feelings for Virginia cannot be, and never can be, anything but fatherly. And you must not allow yourself any doubts on that point.'

Strangely enough, this time he did not make fun of me. He replied, in an almost melancholy manner: 'When will you understand, you superficial, frivolous man, that I am desire and that desire desires everything?'

'Even little girls?'

'I said "everything".'

I shrugged my shoulders, left the kitchen and went into the living-room. Feeling restless, I started walking up and down. There was nothing to be done, it always happened like this: 'he' sowed the seed, nothing more than the seed, of an erotic intention; but then, from this seed, wholly against my will, there would develop a robust tree. 'He' had sown no more than the seed of the idea that I might suggest to Irene the subject of an 'interior' film in which I should play an

207

actor's part. And this seed had now developed, as usual, into a tree. But then Irene came in.

She went to the trolley-bar and poured out two glasses of whisky. I asked her: 'What was it you whispered into Virginia's ear?'

'That if she behaved herself with you, you would get her to play a part in your film.'

'What a strange idea! And how ever did such a thing occur to you?'

'It's she who thinks about it. Didn't you see the strip cartoons she was reading? They're not at all strip cartoons for children. They're photo-romances for adults, in which, among other things, there is mention of poor, obscure girls who become film stars. Virginia reads them and hopes, when she grows up, to become a film star too.'

'Or a star of the photo-romances.'

Irene sat down in her usual place, crossed her legs and then, quite unexpectedly, said: 'Tell me about your producer.'

'What does it matter to you about my producer?'

'I've already told you, capitalists interest me. And isn't your producer a capitalist?'

'My goodness, he certainly is.'

'But who is he?'

'D'you mean, what is his name?'

'Yes.'

I was on the point of answering: Protti, when, suddenly, 'he' intervened: 'Tell her his name is Proto.'

'What the devil are you saying? Who is Proto?'

'Proto is the imaginary character who will allow you to get yourself into one of Irene's films as an actor.'

'But why Proto and not Protti?'

'Don't worry about that. Say "Proto" and the name will work.'

'Will work in what way?'

'From the name will come the whole story.'

Mainly out of curiosity, I answered Irene: 'His name is Proto.'

'What a strange name!'

For once in a way 'he' was right: the name worked. Just as though it were some nursery-rhyme learned by heart in childhood, I recited, in a prompt, offhand way: 'It's not really so strange. I would say that, if anything, it's a name that suits the character perfectly. Proto, in Greek, means the first, the principal. It's true that the name of Proteus might perhaps suit him even better.'

'Why Proteus?'

'Proteus was a sea-god in Greek mythology. He was able to change shape, according to occasion, in a thousand ways. The word "protean" is still used today of someone who does a great many things at the same time, who is to be found all over the place.'

'What has this to do with your producer?'

'It has to do with him because Proto, apart from being concerned with films, has also a great many other activities, that is to say, he is protean. Proto is also an industrialist, a financier, a businessman of the highest importance. The cinema, for him, is merely one of the many things that he happens to be engaged in. Proto is really all over the place, he spreads out his tentacles in the most diverse directions. To make a complete list of the products in which Proto is interested is practically impossible. Cement, paper, illustrated magazines, textiles, household electrical equipment – all these and many other things allow him to look upon the cinema as a kind of hobby.'

I myself was now surprised at the evocative power of the name of Proto. In reality it was no longer I who was speaking, but Proto himself, that non-existent character who was speaking for himself through my mouth. Strange to say, however, I felt that this entirely imaginary Proto was pleasing to Irene and aroused her curiosity; whereas the real Protti would probably not interest her at all. Why so?

Briskly and vivaciously 'he' explained the reason to me. 'Irene's interior films are really dreams, and in dreams I find myself in my element. Proto is not an actual person but a dream figure.'

209

I objected: 'It seems to me, really, that Irene's films are just strip cartoons.'

'He' answered in a lively manner: 'What are strip cartoons if not dreams that are drawn and then printed? Keep calm, go on with Proto and you'll see that Irene will introduce him, just as you say he is, into one of her films.'

Crestfallen, I replied: 'That may be. But I've already extracted all that I can from the name of Proto. And now, if you please, Irene wants to know more about him. Unfortunately I don't know what to say to her.'

Unexpectedly, he reproved me. 'I'm surprised,' he said. 'You're a man of culture, or at least you claim to be, and you haven't yet realized that dreams and strip cartoons are made from stale and outdated cultural material.'

'Well, what of that?'

I hadn't time to make him explain. This dialogue with 'him', rapid as it was, was abruptly broken off by the voice of Irene saying to me: 'Describe him.'

'Why, who?'

'Proto.'

I was in the situation of a young cabin-boy thrown brutally into the sea by his unkind shipmates, to teach him to swim. I had to describe Proto or drown. Strangely, all of a sudden, 'his' remark about dreams and strip cartoons consisting of stale and outdated cultural material was revealed in its hidden truth. Yes, I would describe Proto as Georg Grosz, one of my favourite painters, depicted the typical capitalist in far-off 1920. True, genuine and contemporary at the time, the capitalist of his caricatures was today, on the sociological level, 'stale and outdated cultural material'; and consequently an admirable character for a dream or strip cartoon.

Why had I not thought of this before? Like a thread of gold which I held by one end and pulled gradually from my mouth, the description of the imaginary Proto, reproduced from the drawings of Grosz, came from my mouth without effort, as though I were reciting it by heart. 'Proto, then, is short, with long arms, with short legs, a prominent stomach

210

and broad shoulders: a veritable big ape. He has a pear-shaped head, bristling with very short, almost white hair. Indeed Proto is an albino. And his face has one rather unusual characteristic: it is transparent.'

'Transparent?'

'Yes, his glossy, tightly-stretched skin is transparent like cellophane, and through this skin can be seen his other, true skin, pink, an improbable pink, the tender pink of a new-born child. In this uniform pinkness, however, blotches of red can be seen here and there, like coagulated blood, especially on his cheekbones and in his nostrils.'

'What are his eyes like?'

'Glaucous, that is, of a colour somewhere between green and blue and brown. His eyes, too, seem to have a kind of exterior covering. His real eyes are behind this covering, so that the pupils, when seen through it, look glassy and shining and strangely intense, almost delirious. Proto has a minute little nose, shaped exactly like a hook. A hook made of flesh, of a pink scarcely darker than the pink of his face, and with open nostrils, blotched, as I said, with blood. He has a large, but lipless, mouth which is always, for some reason, slightly open in a vaguely threatening grimace, so that you can see his small, close-set, chalk-white teeth.'

For a moment I was silent, surprised at my own glibness. Then, suddenly, I resumed: 'D'you know what his collaborators call him?'

'No.'

'Calf's head.'

'Why?'

'Have you never seen boiled calves' heads displayed on the marble slabs of butchers' shops? They have half-open mouths and white teeth; glassy eyes, lightly iridescent, with diaphanous tones of green and blue and brown – in fact, glaucous. Like Proto.'

'Go on.'

'Go on with what?'

'Go on describing him.'

The name Proto continued to work. From Grosz I moved

211

on to myself, and I decided to endow the imaginary figure with my own main physical characteristic: the exceptional development of the sexual organ.

This was a kind of loan that I was making to Proto, so that Irene might take him on quicker and more easily as an actor in one of her films.

'Proto,' I said, 'is exceptionally well endowed as far as sex is concerned. This is not mere gossip. It is an actual fact. When he is sitting down, you can't help being struck by the size and length of the protuberance which, under the material of his trousers, goes half-way down the inside of his thigh.'

Irene gave a wicked smile. 'Like you,' she said. 'Perhaps he has given it a Latin name, too.'

'Greek, if anything. "Protos."'

'And what sort of voice has he?'

I recalled Protti's voice: urbane, soft, well-bred, ironical, affable.

Here I invented. 'Proto's voice? It's a voice like a guillotine; harsh, cutting. He cuts off his words one after the other, with a sharp stroke, as soon as he has uttered them: decapitates them, in fact.'

'And what sort of a character has he?'

Now I was in for it. At this stage Grosz was no longer of any help. He was a painter, not a novelist. He drew a caricature of a capitalist of the twenties; he did not tell his story. But the name of Proto, luckily, continued to work. After the German painter's caricature, there suddenly rose to the surface of my memory an anecdote which might be true or might be apocryphal, one of those anecdotes that circulate among film people and that I could easily graft upon the figure of my imaginary capitalist, just as a surgeon grafts a missing part upon a mutilated body, borrowing it from another body. Gazing fixedly at Irene, I began: 'He's a sentimentalist. Therefore a sadist.'

'I don't understand; I don't see the connection.'

'Sentimentalism is the most frequent mask for sadism. Why? For the good reason that it inspires confidence as a substitute for feeling and thus causes the victim to abandon

212

himself more easily, in a credulous, defenceless way, to the mercy of the sadist. The latter, at the opportune moment, throws aside his mask and reveals his true nature.'

'Give me an example of Proto's sentimentalism and sadism.'

'He', at this point, like a teacher closely superintending his pupil's task, enjoined me: 'Now be careful. This must be a story which can be, so to speak, transferred just as it is into her masturbatory strip cartoons. So there must be no truth, no psychology, no irony, no reality. Everything must be conventional, false, spurious. It is, in fact, with the false, the conventional, the spurious that I express myself in dreams. As for the true, the real, the genuine – I don't know what to do with them.'

These recommendations from 'him', so subtle and so sophisticated, distracted my attention. Irene noticed this and asked me: 'What's the matter? What are you thinking about?'

'About a story that illustrates Proto's character to perfection.'

'A story that really happened?'

'Of course.'

'Tell me, then.'

'I warn you that it's a little – how shall I say – crude.'

She began to laugh, with that slightly cruel laugh of hers that showed her sharp, white eye-teeth. 'How respectful you've become,' she said. 'What's happened to you?'

I was suddenly moved; and in spite of the infuriated protests which 'he' shouted at me. 'You clown, you buffoon, you comedian!' I stammered: 'A very simple thing has happened to me.'

'And what is that?'

'That I'm falling in love with you, and love, as you know, is respectful.'

I saw that she shrugged her shoulders. 'You think you love me because I rejected you,' she said. 'But it doesn't matter. Now tell me your story.'

'Here is the story,' I said. 'You must know that I am a sort of factotum for Proto. Not only do I write scripts for him, but I also act as his secretary, as his confidant, as his intermediary. Everything passes through my hands, nothing happens without me. I sit in a room next door to Proto's study. He calls me on the intercom, I open the door and I'm in his presence.'

I sat silent for a moment. Actually I had described the situation and the functions of Cutica. And why had I done that? Then I understood. It was because it pleased me to think that Cutica would be capable of doing what I was about to relate. I was avenging myself, in fact, upon Cutica, even if in doing so I was forced to slander myself.

I resumed: 'One day, then, I was in my room as usual, sitting at the desk, when the door opened and in slipped a girl of about twenty, not exactly beautiful but attractive, though inclined to be plump. This girl, with disconcerting impudence, opened the door very slowly, at the same time bidding me to silence with her forefinger to her lips. Then she closed the door again, came over to my desk and said: "The porter didn't want to let Lilla come in. But Lilla is intelligent, she's very cunning. So what did Lilla do? She pretended to go to the lavatory, and now here she is. Ah yes, it's not easy to get the better of Lilla." I asked her: "But Lilla, who is Lilla?" "Who is Lilla?" she said. "There's only one Lilla, and that's me. I'm the one and only Lilla, the real, the unique, the genuine Lilla."

'She was so comic, in spite of her brazenness, that I couldn't help taking a liking to her. I asked her: "And what can one do for Lilla?" Still speaking of herself in the third person, she replied: "For Lilla there is only one thing that can be done." "And what is that?" "Introduce her to Proto." "What does Lilla want with Proto?" "What can Lilla want with Proto? Obviously, a part in a film." "Ah, so that's it? It's clear, anyhow, even if not very original." She failed to notice the irony but, parading up and down the room, she went on: "Lilla knows that she is a born actress. Lilla, in a year, or at most two years, will be the most famous and the highest paid in the Italian cinema. Lilla asks only one thing: to speak to Proto. She'll take care of everything else." "In what way will she take care of it?" "She'll take care of it by means of an infallible argument." "And what is her infallible argument?" You won't believe it, but she took up a position in the middle of the room and, taking hold with both hands of the edge of her skirt, pulled it up, saying: "This is Lilla's infallible argument."

'Just at that moment the door opened and Proto appeared. He looked at me, he looked at Lilla, who remained in the middle of the room with her skirt pulled up, and then he said brusquely: "Why, what's going on here?" "Here's this girl who wants to speak to you," I answered. Proto looked at her again; meanwhile she had pulled down her skirt and was smiling. "But who are you?" he asked. And the girl, immediately, in the same sing-song voice, said: "Who am I? Who could I possibly be but Lilla? The only, the true, the unique Lilla." Her effrontery appeared to arouse Proto's curiosity. "And you wish to speak to me?" he asked. "Yes, Doctor Proto, Lilla wishes to confer with you. Lilla, Doctor Proto, will consider herself the most fortunate woman in the world if you will invite her into your study, for a short business discussion." Proto smiled in his own macabre way, without opening his mouth, merely showing his teeth; then he said: "All right, then. We'll have a business discussion"; and he drew aside to allow her to enter. Lilla entered first, not without throwing me a triumphant glance over her shoulder. Proto followed and shut the door.'

'And then?'

'I waited for a very long time, almost an hour. Then the intercom buzzed: "Rico, come here." I rose at once and opened the door. Proto was sitting at his writing-table, resting his face on his hand. Lilla was sitting opposite him. Lilla was speaking and Proto, believe it or not, was weeping. Yes, his horrible, glassy, delirious eyes were shining with tears, and in his hand his handkerchief was reduced to a little wet ball. Lilla herself appeared to be moved; but not so deeply as to take no heed of the effects of the story she was relating. Naturally it was her own story, and it struck me at once as being hopelessly commonplace, even if painful; so that I, although I have a tender heart, could not help actually smiling at the strip-cartoon expressions that the girl made use of. But with Proto it was different. Proto was moved, he was weeping, and as he wept he kept repeating: "Poor little thing, poor little thing, poor little thing", in a subdued voice, as if talking to himself, the voice of one who was convinced by what he heard.

'I, for my part, stood near the door, waiting for the story to finish. Lilla finally concluded: "And so, Doctor Proto, that is the story of Lilla. Rather sad, isn't it? But Lilla is coura-geous, Lilla is determined, Lilla has never had doubts about herself, even under the worst misfortunes. Lilla knows that, in the end, victory will be hers. And now, Doctor Proto, here is Lilla, sitting in front of you." And Lilla said to him: "Doctor Proto, do what you like with me, you must make the decision, anything you decide will be the right thing for Lilla."

'I now looked at the girl and noticed that her mouth was all smeared with lipstick; I looked at Proto and saw that some of the same lipstick was superimposed, like an impure inflam-mation, upon the pale pink of his lips. Then Proto said: "You know, I was moved by your story. You see, I've been crying. That should please you. I never cry, not even at the cinema." The girl, cocky and self-assured, asked: "Then, Doctor Proto, Lilla can hope?" "Yes, of course. There's never any harm in hoping." "Really?" "Really." You'll never believe it: Lilla bent forward, seized Proto's hand and kissed it. Proto accepted this with a good grace. Then he said: "Now go in there for a little, into Rico's room. I must consult with Rico for a moment."

'Lilla went out. Proto looked at me in silence, for some time, and then finally burst out: "Will you kindly tell me why you brought that boring woman here." I protested: "But, Proto, it was you . . ." He went on: "She came in here and immediately said to me: Lilla's a good girl, a very good girl, and if Doctor Proto likes her, Lilla can prove to him at once what a good girl she is. And then, without more ado, she jumped on my knee and provided me with a practical demon-stration of her 'goodness'. Finally I said to her: "Sit down over there and tell me your story. And now what I'm saying to you is, for heaven's sake get rid of her for me, immediately, and I don't want to see her ever again. D'you see? Never again." I asked Proto, in a logical way: "But what am I to say to her, what am I to do?" And he, carefully articulating his words: "Do what you like with her. I make you a present of her. D'you see? I – make – you – a – present – of – her."'"

That was the end of the story of Lilla. I heard 'him' cry out: 'A splendid story! The idea of making a present of her, especially, was a very happy one. Well done! Making a present of a person is even better than buying and selling her. Well done indeed!' I accepted this praise of my inventive capacity and meanwhile I was looking at Irene to see if the story had had any effect upon her; and I realized that it had. Irene, at the beginning of my tale, had been sitting with legs close together and her bust slightly inclined forward. Now, on the other hand, she was lying almost flat on the cushions and her legs, which shortly before had seemed to be welded to each other, were stretched out from under her skirt, fallen visibly apart. She dug her elbows into the back of the sofa and gazed at me with a disconcerted, defenceless look. Finally she asked: 'What did you do with Lilla, after Proto had made you a present of her?'

I couldn't help thinking of what Cutica would have done in similar circumstances, and replied: 'You can imagine.'

'But what?'

I remained silent for a moment and then explained with obstinate precision: 'She did not want to, of course! But I made her understand that if she did not show her "goodness" to me as well, she would not get a part in the film. So then, even though with many protests in the third person, she showed it to me.'

'You coward!'

All at once, at this insult which I didn't deserve and which did not offend me because it concerned another than me, and which, furthermore, Irene had uttered in a caressing, languishing voice, all at once I realized that the conversation, or rather the relationship, was no longer between Irene and myself but between Irene and 'him'. On the one hand Irene, lying almost flat on the sofa with her legs stretched out and fallen apart; on the other hand 'he', already now at the highest point of exaltation.

As for me, as always happens with me in similar cases, I felt excluded, cut off. But, whereas usually I accept this expulsion and in fact do not dislike watching 'him' in action, observing the goings-on from a corner with no feeling of responsibility; this time, strange to say, his success aroused in me a sudden, unaccustomed feeling, a sort of jealousy. I was, indeed, in love with Irene, and, however incredible this may seem, I was jealous of 'him' and was hurt at the idea that, between 'him' and me, Irene should prefer 'him'. Which was as much as to say that I was hurt because, between love and eroticism, it was the latter that was victorious. I said brusquely: 'Now, pull yourself together.'

The altered tone of my voice astonished Irene. In spite of herself, as it were, slowly, unwillingly, she pulled herself together and regained her composure, all the time staring at me.

I went on: 'And now let me tell you that I invented the whole thing.'

'The whole thing? D'you really mean it, the whole thing?'

'The whole thing. The story of Proto and Proto himself. Proto is not called Proto but Protti. And he's not the monster I described. He's a handsome man, affable, gentle, kindly, urbane. Above all, a very good family man. As for the story of Lilla, that too was entirely invented. Such a person as Lilla never existed, I never introduced her to Proto and Proto never made a present of her to me. I work for Protti, Protti pays me, and that is all; no presents, even at the New Year.'

Irene looked at me and did not appear at all angry. On the contrary she smiled and asked me: 'Why?'

'Why what?'

'Why Proto, Lilla, and the present?'

'Because I wanted to make an experiment.'

'What experiment?'

'I wanted to suggest a story for one of your masturbatory

218

films. In that way you would then put me into your film, and while you were making love with yourself you would, in a way, be making love with me.'

'Very subtle. What made you think that I should adopt your story?'

'There is an invention in that story which, in my opinion, would justify my hope of becoming an actor in one of your films. The invention of a woman who is not bought or sold but actually given as a gift.'

'That's true. It's an effective invention. You can be content: the experiment has been successful.'

'Successful? What does "successful" mean?'

'It means that I shall take into consideration the possible use of the film material you've so kindly provided me with.'

Now, positively, she was making fun of me! I rose in angry revolt: 'Certainly not. I wished to make an experiment, it has been successful and that is enough. But I do not wish – do you understand? – I do not wish to figure as an actor in your films. No films: either in life or nothing. Because I love you, and if, one day – which seems to me highly improbable – I manage to get you to love me, it has got to be in the reality of life and not in the unreality of a masturbatory photo-romance. D'you understand? For all these reasons, I forbid you, absolutely, to make use of my story.'

'What will you do to me if I do make use of it?'

What was happening to me? Or rather, what was happening to 'him'? Suddenly 'he' gave me a most brutal shove, flinging me aside, and answered through my mouth, but with a new kind of voice, never before heard and made unrecognizable by its bloodthirsty rage: 'What would I do to you? That's simple, I'd wring your neck.'

Irene started laughing with that cruel laugh which she reserves for me when she wishes to show me her total contempt: a laugh that is, so to speak, lateral, a laugh that keeps her mouth almost closed in the centre but, at the sides, lays bare her eye-teeth. Then she said slowly: 'You're not going to wring anybody's neck. I shall make use of your story, but not tomorrow morning, nor yet tonight, nor even just after you've gone away, but at once, now, under your eyes. And you will not wring my neck but will stay and watch; that's what you will do.'

Might Irene perhaps be right? I knew for certain that 'he' was a *voyeur*, I knew it, by now, from experience. And when Irene, following words immediately by acts, thrust forward her pelvis, took hold of her skirt, pulled it up over her stomach and spread out her legs in such a way that her black slip was visible between her white, smooth thighs, for a moment I was sure that 'he', even after so many threats, would in the end resign himself to an ignominiously passive and contemplative role.

But no, I was wrong. 'He' desired 'direct contact'; there should be no interior films, no strip cartoons on this occasion. And since Irene not merely rebuffed him but made a mockery of him with her eloquent mimicry, 'he' felt a savage, decisive, immediate desire for her death. This was a matter of a moment. Then, as 'he' whispered, urgently, feverishly: 'Throw yourself on top of her, squeeze her neck, let's finish her off, squeeze, squeeze, squeeze!' suddenly I was already on top of her, I had stretched her out flat on the sofa, I had put my two hands round her lovely white, round, strong neck. But at this point the unexpected happened: Irene suddenly ceased to resist me. I felt that her body had ceased to struggle and lay abandoned beneath me on the sofa, invitingly even though not amorously. She gave me a gentle, reconciled, supplicating look and then said: 'I'm not afraid of dying. You want to kill me? Kill me, then.'

These words were enough to free me from 'him' with the same rapidity and ease with which 'he' had freed himself from me shortly before. I asked: 'You want to die?'

'Yes.'

'But why? Haven't you always told me that you were happy with your little girl, with your work, and with your interior films?'

'Yes, I've told you so, and no doubt I am. But, at the same time, I want to die.'

'You really want to?'

'Yes.'

Now, we were talking. My hands were still round her neck but they were not squeezing it. And it was I who was talking, not 'he'; 'he' was decisively pushed aside and reduced to silence. Irene spoke in a low voice: 'Make me die.'

'A moment ago I was really on the point of killing you.'

'I realized that.'

'But I couldn't do it now. Some things can't be done in cold blood.'

'Why not? Squeeze my neck again, as hard as you can: I promise I'll let you do it and I won't resist.'

'No, that's all done with, luckily.'

'Please!'

'No.'

'Well then, if you don't wish to kill me, let me go because you're crushing me and I'm uncomfortable.'

I let her go. Irene sat up composedly, took up her glass again and was once more the embassy secretary entertaining a friend. I went and sat down on the divan opposite. After a moment I said: 'Very well, then, make use of my invention of the "present", instrumentalize me as much as you like.'

Cruelly and ironically again, she hastened to inquire, with exaggerated solicitude: 'Really? Seriously? You authorize me?'

'Yes, do whatever you like with my invention. And forgive me for laying hands on you. But this idea of being instrumentalized – for a moment it made me lose my head.'

'You didn't lay hands on me; you tried to kill me. It's not the same thing. If you'd just laid hands on me, I would have repulsed you.'

'You don't want a man who is in love with you and is seeking to make love; but you have no objection to a murderer who strangles you. Isn't that so?'

She was taking small sips from her glass, so she merely raised her eyes in my direction and, still sipping, nodded her head.

9   Traumatized!

I awoke with a start and with a feeling that I was not alone. And indeed, when I sat up and looked about me, there 'he' was, I saw him sitting in the armchair at the foot of the bed. He was obviously in a state of exaltation, judging, at least, by his bulk; but at the same time there was nothing exaggerated or unseemly in his attitude. He was sitting upright in the armchair in an urbane, well-bred manner, his head thrown back against the back of the chair, with an air of cheerful satisfaction like someone who has consumed plenty of good food and drink. A big dark vein, encircling him below his head in the manner of a necktie, even gave the impression that he was dressed. In any case, the darkness which filled the room prevented me from distinguishing details. I could divine, in general, the outlines of his figure, which evoked, strangely, the image of a great octopus with a conical hood squatting upon its own tentacles.

'He' said to me immediately, in a casual, informative tone: 'I've come to say good-bye to you. You've done so much in which you've been successful. I'm leaving you. From now on you won't be able to complain of me. For the good reason that I shall no longer be there.'

These words filled me with an unutterable sense of bitterness and even a hint of fear. But I tried not to show it, saying to myself that what mattered most in such a case was to keep calm. Almost jokingly, I said: 'It was your fault if I complained of you. You always behaved so badly. Even now, for instance: apparently you're performing an act of civility, paying a polite visit. Whereas . . does it really seem to you respectable to present yourself in this way? So enormous, so embarrassing, so excited?'

He answered in an almost sad tone of voice: 'I can't help presenting myself like this. If I'm not like this, I'm

222

nothing. Desire – if that's what you're reproaching me with – is in fact my only way of existing. Without desire, no existence.'

'Unfortunately.'

'You would wish desire to present itself in the guise of satiety: an absurdity. I do not know satiety. Satiety, for me, is synonymous with non-existence. If I exist, there is no satiety; if there is satiety, I do not exist.'

There was a moment's silence, and then he resumed, in a less confidential tone: 'Well then, I've come to bid you good-bye. Have you anything special to communicate to me?'

I still had that sense of profound bitterness, that incipient fear. But again I tried to conceal it and said disdainfully: 'But where d'you think you're going? Don't you realize that without me you'd be like a blind kitten? What will you do without me? Nobody will want you, nobody will welcome you.'

'On the contrary. Without you I shall go back, after an unfortunate interval, to being what I really am, freed from the limits and restrictions of your individual case. When I think that, by remaining with you, I have been reduced to casting stealthy, sidelong glances at "men only" magazines! Enough! I'm leaving you. The whole world is awaiting me.'

'The world! Giving yourself airs, as usual! Why not admit the more modest truth? That you're leaving me to go and seek the hospitality of someone who is more disposed than I am to submit to your abuses of power? Some dubious, ignoble individual of the type, for example, of Cutica.'

'Cutica! But will you, or won't you, understand that my choice doesn't lie between you and Cutica or some other person of that kind, but between you and the . . . the cosmos.'

'There we are again, I've already heard this discourse on other occasions.'

'You've heard it on other occasions because it's the truth.'

'What sort of truth is it?'

'That I don't need you, as you appear to believe, but that you need me. That you're not making any concession to me by giving me your hospitality, but that I am doing so to

you by living with you. That, in any case, what we may call
your individuality constitutes, for me, more than anything, a
cage, a bed of Procrustes, a source of annoyances and morti-
fications. Now if my sacrifice were appreciated and recognized,
I might still endure the difficulties to which I am constrained
by my cohabitation with you. But no, not only do you fail to
recognize my sacrifice but you accuse me of arrogance. And
not merely that; you call this supposed arrogance of mine by
a number of strange names. You describe me, continually,
in terms incomprehensible to me but certainly insulting:
lecher, fetishist, exhibitionist, sadist, masochist, onanist,
homosexual, gerontophile and I don't know how many more.
The moment has come when I say: enough. I am going away,
I'm going back to the cosmos, yes, I say, the cosmos; and
I'm not ashamed to say it, the cosmos which is my true and
proper residence.'

'You're not going back to the cosmos, you're going to
Cutica.'

'I understand. You are incorrigible. I tell you: cosmos;
and you answer me: Cutica. How could I stay? Good-bye.'

As he said this, he made a movement as if to rise, or
rather, in view of his strange conformation, to slip down on to
the floor and there, I imagined, to roll, resembling, with his
huge trunk devoid of extremities, one of those disabled beggars
who sit in a box with little wheels and propel themselves
with their hands. Then, all at once, seeing him so determined,
I could no longer contain my bitterness and fear. 'No,' I
cried, 'don't leave me, don't go away. Stay with me. I promise
you that from now on I'll do everything you want. But stay.
Without you, I couldn't go on living. Stay for God's sake,
don't leave me.'

'He' did not at once reply to these words of entreaty.
Motionless, he seemed to be contemplating me with the
disdainful, ironical complacency of a conqueror. At last he said:
'In future, then, will you be really docile and submissive and
obedient?'

'Yes, I swear it.'

'But do you know what it is I want?'

'I know – or rather, I don't know; you tell me.'

'I want you, solemnly and finally, to renounce . . .'

'Sublimation.'

'I don't know what sublimation is. No, I want you to renounce the notion that you are an individual with a distinct, precise identity.'

'Yes, yes, I won't aspire now to be anybody or anything. Yes, I'll give up all attempts to be somebody or something.'

'It is your attempts to exist as an individual, to possess an identity – attempts which in any case are always, regularly, a failure – it is these attempts that automatically transform every sign of life on my part into a transgression. You must renounce, once and for all, any idea that you are that ridiculous, absurd thing that is known as an individual.'

'Yes, I'll do everything you wish. Down with the individual! Down with identity! Down with me myself! Is that all right?'

This time he was silent. It seemed that he had nothing more to say, or rather, that what he had to say could not be expressed in words. He was silent, and I had the impression that he was becoming more and more swollen and congested and dilated, and in a more and more visible way.

In the half-darkness, his head, resting on the back of the chair, had become enormous and was of a dark red that looked almost black, with a gleam of light on its silky, swollen surface which emphasized its tension. He said nothing, staring at me in a silence and stillness which very soon became unbearable. Uneasily, I asked him: "Tell me then, speak to me, I'm prepared for anything; what d'you want of me?'

No, he didn't speak, he would not speak. He stayed quite still, as if overcome by some profound, paralysing malaise. And then, suddenly, a tremor shook him from top to bottom; and, immediately afterwards, a big drop, of a dense, opaque whiteness, gushed forth at the tip, paused, then, drawn by its own weight, slipped down. Another tremor, another drop. Then, at a third and more violent tremor, an abundant stream welled up several times in succession and flowed down, dividing into a number of smaller rivulets. It made me think of the eruption of a volcano, but in a way it was more terrifying, because silent. The white stream continued to gush forth, spread out over the armchair, flowed down in torrents, flooded the floor.

Now the whole room was submerged; and at the same time, astonishingly, strange coloured flowers began to gleam here and there in the compact whiteness. The flowers, first of all, were small, scarcely more than buds; then they opened and became larger and larger and more and more resplendent. Round the flowers were wreaths of green, glossy leaves; then both flowers and leaves rose up from the white flood and grew and became plants and trees; and these plants and trees, in turn, bore myriads of flowers. And then there peeped out here and there amongst the plants and trees little buildings, which were also coloured and shining. There were palaces, churches, towers, houses, all lying along straight roads and round large squares. In short, a whole city arose before my wondering, astonished eyes.

It was a very beautiful city, although, owing to the blinding light that fell upon it and made it glitter, I was not able to observe it in detail. Nevertheless, the beauty of the city was to me a certainty; just as it was a certainty, furthermore, that everything – flowers, leaves, trees, the city – everything came from 'him', he himself now being entirely invisible, hidden as he was behind this marvellous panorama. Then, all of a sudden, I cried out: 'What does all this mean? Is this your answer? What is its significance? What is its message?' And, as I cried out, I awoke.

This time I was really awake and not, as in my dream, imagining myself to be so. The lamp, above the head of my bed, was alight; the book I had been reading when I fell asleep had fallen to the ground. After that dream of luxuriant trees and plants, leaves and flowers, I was struck by the squalid, stupidly austere bareness of the room, with its curtainless windows, its walls without furniture, its ceiling without decoration, its carpetless floor. How much more beautiful had been the room, in my dream, when invaded by tropical forest and the marvellous city half hidden among trees! Of course I had had a wet dream; the sheets were soaked, my stomach all sticky and gummy. I felt disconcerted and irritated, above all because of the obscurity of the message which 'he' had conveyed to me through that strange dream. However it was useless to question him now. I knew for certain that he would not answer me, for the precise reason that, as he had informed me in the dream, for him existence was synonymous with desire, so that, once desire was satisfied, any kind of existence, for him, ceased until a new desire arose.

Stunned and perplexed, I pondered confusedly over these things, sitting on the bed and staring straight in front of me. Then I chanced to look at the clock and discovered that it was barely two o'clock, only one hour from the time when I had gone to bed. So I put out the light, lay down on my side and very soon fell asleep.

Strange to say, next morning 'he' showed that he had by no means vented all his desire in the night's episode; on the contrary, he appeared to be a prey to an uncontrollable frenzy. From the moment I awoke, he pestered me with absurd requests that revealed an almost maniac aggressiveness. He began by suggesting that I should go and see Irene at her Arab embassy. I answered him sensibly that – as in any case 'he' knew perfectly well – Irene did not as a rule leave the embassy until the evening, and anyhow would not be prepared to make an exception for me.

Then he suggested that I should ask Fausta to lunch. I pointed out that this was not possible: I was going to lunch with my mother. Then, in succession, one after another, like the last cards thrown down on the table by a desperate gambler, he gave me the names of various film-extras, stand-ins, air hostesses, secretaries, unoccupied girls with whom, according to 'him', I might have meetings during the afternoon. When, with various excuses and arguments, I turned down all his proposals, he started shouting as though he were beside himself: 'A woman, a woman, for the love of God, a woman! I need to see a woman, to smell the smell of a woman, to hear the voice of a woman, to caress the body of a woman.

Either you give me a woman or I give myself over to despair. The whole cosmos for a woman!'

'He' was so frantic that I stopped working, dressed and went out. As soon as I was out of the house, I understood the reason for his frenzy. It was suffocatingly hot, with a sort of African heat, with a sky completely covered but not exactly cloudy. It was as if the sky had changed colour, from blue to a leaden grey. The sun was nothing but a circular patch of non-luminous brightness in the midst of this diffused, livid expanse. The full summer foliage of the plane-trees hung limp and dejected along the avenue where I was walking, as though afflicted with a sudden withering. A few drops of rain had fallen; the cars moving slowly along in the thick traffic seemed to be speckled all over with a reddish, desert sand which had arrived from goodness knows where. 'He', highly sensitive as he was to changes of weather, had completely lost his head. To calm him down, I said: 'Now we'll go for a short walk, we'll go into a bar and have an aperitif and smoke a cigarette. Then we'll go a little early to my mother's and there we'll find that little fair-haired cook whom you like so much. We'll go into the kitchen under some pretext or other and have a bit of a flirtation with her. Is that all right?'

With the logic of a madman, 'he' replied: 'Let's go to your mother's at once.'

'But it's early. At least an hour too early. My mother will notice that I'm early. And you know how disagreeable my mother is when she notices anything like that.'

'Your mother won't notice anything. And as for the cook, don't pretend to be innocent, especially with me: you came to an arrangement with her three days ago. Have you forgotten that already?'

It was true; but I hoped 'he' had forgotten. And so, in order to satisfy him, I agreed to go to my mother's an hour early. I hadn't my car, which was under repair; so I took the bus. Inside the crowded bus I had to stand, my arm raised to hang on to the strap. The bus went at headlong speed down an avenue on Monte Mario; every now and then, confronted with some obstacle, the driver would jam on the

228

brake, tipping forward the whole crowd that was squeezed inside.

At one of these violent jolts, I finished close up against a woman. The contact forced me to examine her. She was young, with a big head puffed out with exceptionally fine hair which formed a kind of light cloud round her face. Beneath this cloud appeared two huge blue eyes with black lashes and a large mouth of vivid pink, the upper lip shadowed with down of a definitely dark colour. She was small, almost deformed, with a very prominent bosom and buttocks. She did not interest me at all; but at a further application of the brakes and the consequent further collision of our bodies, I realized that 'his' curiosity was already fully aroused. Thus, against my will and in spite of myself, there was created one of the customary intolerable relationships between 'him' and whatever woman might happen to be concerned. Disgusted, irritated, ashamed, helpless, I witnessed this furtive, embarrassing duet, hoping all the time that the bus would arrive at my stop, or that of the girl, as quickly as possible. The bus, however, failed to reach either of the stops and seemed to be doing this on purpose: now a violent jolt would make the woman fall against me, and then another jolt would make me fall against her. Finally, as was to be foreseen, the girl turned round and addressed me, viperishly, in this way: 'Either you stay in your place or I'll call the conductor.'

'He', at once, whispered to me: 'This is a thing that concerns me. Leave it to me.' And I, content, in fact, to remain a mere witness, drew aside. Then 'he', with exemplary impudence, answered through my mouth: 'My dear girl, you're crazy.'

'Don't talk to me in that familiar way; we're not relations. Besides, what do you suppose? That I hadn't noticed?'

'Noticed what? Why, haven't you ever looked at yourself in a mirror? And if you have, why don't you hurry up and have a shave, a good thorough shave with a good razor? D'you really suppose that I'm attracted by women with moustaches?'

Naturally these extremely vulgar, impertinent words made the whole busload of people take sides with 'him'. Many of them started laughing; somebody made a loud comment in a way unfavourable to the girl. She, poor thing, hit in her weak point, did not dare to reply, was silent, and slipped away towards the door. At the next stop, I also got out.

I was furious, indignant, disgusted, sickened. This time, without any consideration, I launched a thorough attack upon him. 'That silly, indecent, vulgar game of the jolts in the bus was a thing you should never have allowed yourself. But let that pass; one loss of face more or less – by now I'm accustomed to it. What I absolutely refuse to tolerate is the words you used to that poor girl. You hurt her, you mortified and humiliated her. You're a blackguard, a worm, a repugnant, disgusting, abject creature.'

'Ha, ha, ha!'

'There's nothing to laugh about. You behaved like a hooligan.'

'Ha, ha, ha!'

'Will you kindly tell me why you're laughing?'

'Because I see a small man with a big bald head walking along the broad, quiet streets of the Prati quarter, gesticulating and talking to himself, so that the few passers-by all turn and gaze at him in astonishment, thinking, no doubt, that he's gone off his head.'

Luckily I had now reached the big ugly block of flats, the colour of yolk of egg, in a composite bureaucratic-baroque style, in which my mother lived. I went through into the immense courtyard, with its scattered, dusty flower-beds and moulting palm-trees; and I made my way by a cement pathway to the staircase marked with the letter 'E'. 'He', meanwhile, continued with his derisive guffaws: 'That girl with the moustache was badly upset; the whole bus was on our side.'

'You mean, on *your* side.'

After the ill humour and frenzy of the morning, 'he' was now relaxed and cheerful, and I knew why, too. He was delighted at the prospect of seeing, very soon, the little peasant cook with the big plait of blonde hair twisted round her head like a piece of new rope round a fine wicker basket. The ancient lift, lurching and noisy, came to a stop; I walked

230

out on to a landing of melancholy, useless spaciousness and went to ring the bell at a modest door of light-coloured wood, highly polished and with brass fittings that glittered with an almost painful brilliance. But, when the door opened, what a disaster! A stiff, hieratic figure, black and wizened, hands in white cotton gloves, severe, clerical face like a half-empty bag, scanty hair gathered into a miserable grey bun on the top of the head, presented itself in front of me with the severe expression of a gendarme and asked me who I was and what I wanted. I replied with dignity that I was the son of the mistress of the house; and then the shadow of a smile lifted the big, purplish lips of the gendarme over a yellow row of horse-like teeth. 'You are Signor Rico?'

'Exactly.'

'I ought to have known. The Signora is not at home, she has gone out. Please come in.'

There was no denying it, this was a servant who took her job very seriously. Tall and black, with the bearing of a high-class major-domo, she ushered me in and led me along the wide, half-empty corridor. I realized she was making her way towards the drawing-room, a gloomy, shut-in place full of furniture which had for years been kept in its summer loose covers, and which my mother did not open except for guests of importance; so I prompted her: 'No, look, not the drawing-room, I'll go into the dining-room. It's simpler.'

The 'gendarme' excused herself with another smile which was, to tell the truth, both kindly and humble, remarking that she was 'new to the place' and did not yet know its usual habits. Then she re-directed her slow, ceremonious march, making for the dining-room. She ushered me in and -- another novelty – went and opened the door of the sideboard and, with her white-cotton-gloved hand, took out a black bottle and inquired whether, in the meantime, I would not care for an aperitif. I declined her offer. The 'gendarme' said she had to go back to the kitchen to prepare the lunch; and I was left alone.

Immediately 'he' demanded: 'What's happened to Sabina?'

231

'I suppose my mother has given her the sack.'

'But why?'

'For the usual reason, I imagine, for which, when I was still living with her, she used regularly to dismiss the younger and more attractive servants.'

'But what reason?'

'Come on, you know perfectly well.'

Now he was silent; and I sat down at the table, which had not yet been laid, and lit a cigarette. I felt nervous, frustrated and very ill-tempered. It always happened like this; he would urge me to ill-considered acts; but, after the usual loss of face, would retire in good order and leave me alone to face the inevitable humiliation. This affair of the young and pretty Sabina being exchanged for an ugly, elderly woman now aroused in me an acute feeling of discomfort. Of all those who were 'on top' of me, my mother was without doubt the one who managed to get herself 'on top' in the way which was, for me, the most mortifying and unendurable.

There was never a decisive clash, never a frontal encounter; rather it was a moralizing 'lesson', indirect, petty, based upon the standards of the bourgeois law of 'things that are not done'. A law that was at the same time devoid of foundation and that, nevertheless, for some unknown reason, infallibly excited, in me at least, odious feelings of guilt. My mother had guessed instinctively that I liked Sabina, or rather that 'he' liked her; but it was not this intuition on her part which infuriated me, rather the method she adopted to impart the above-mentioned 'lesson'.

For at least two months 'he' had been forcing me to pay court to Sabina; but my mother had never remarked upon it to me, nor alluded to it in any way. Methodically she had prepared her 'lesson', which consisted in the replacement of Sabina by a maid who was in herself, by her mere appearance, a 'living reproof'. Then, once she had found the poor 'gendarme' she had summarily dismissed Sabina and had left me to discover the 'living reproof'. As much as to say: You're a sex-maniac. You lay hands on all my maids. So you've compelled me to replace the young, pretty Sabina by this one who is ugly and elderly. How typical of my mother was all this! How characteristic, I mean, of her mentality as a sublimated middle-class woman, moralistic, anti-sex, repressed and, in short, fascist!

Yes indeed, fascist! Having nothing to do, I examined the room in which I found myself, with concentrated aversion. Its furnishings confirmed, in an unmistakable way, the fascist character, as I have said, of my mother's sublimation. I was born in 1935. My mother had been married a few years before. The dining-room was in the style of those disciplined, grievous years: veneered furniture, smooth and dark, in square or cylindrical shapes, with small knobs of white metal in place of handles. Curtains, carpets, materials with patterns of cubes or lozenges shading one into the other. Massive shelves, in a zigzag arrangement, made of the same dark, veneered wood, attached to the walls and supporting horrible majolica-ware ornaments or unpleasant little pots of coarse plants. The so-called 'twentieth-century' style. The dining-room showed its age and revealed the deceitfulness of this apparently strong and essentially feeble style. The deceitfulness of middle-class, fascist sublimation. Here and there, in fact, on pieces of furniture which had entirely lost their original polish, the veneer had come unstuck and in some places was completely lacking, showing the harsh, yellowish plywood streaked with brown tears of coagulated glue. My mother's sublimation was like this dining-room: veneered with a moralism that was inadequately glued to the friable plywood of lower- middle-class conservatism.

Nevertheless, in spite of the contempt which this deceitful world aroused in me, every time I find myself face to face with my mother I cannot help feeling desublimated and consequently 'underneath', hopelessly 'underneath'. Whereas she, even with her wretched, fascist-type sublimation, remains 'on top' of me, unequivocally 'on top'.

As I sat smoking I told myself angrily that my mother was not there, she was not at home, and yet I was already 'underneath' and she was 'on top' because these pieces of furniture 'were' my mother or at any rate represented her vision of the world in an obsessive manner. That vision of the world which allowed her to judge me, to condemn me and, in some way, to humiliate me. All 'his' fault, naturally, since 'he' makes of me a man who is all member and no head – a thing which my mother knows and feels, and of which she makes use with a complete lack of scruple.

I waited for a long time in that silent house, face to face with the twentieth-century furniture, and my anger increased. The sideboard formed of a number of superimposed cubes flanked by two cylinders; the upholstered chairs shaped like hip-baths; the massive table supported on an enormous, short, round stem, reminding one of a mushroom; the lamp hanging from the ceiling, with its black wooden circle studded with a number of white glass globes – all these were there as representatives of my mother. They symbolized the repressive, imbecile moralism of the thirties. Of the fascist bourgeoisie! Nationalist! Militarist! Colonialist! Palaeocapitalist! The moralism of government officials like my father, who went to the ministry in black woollen tail-coats, with gilt eagles on their caps, and gave each other the fascist salute in the over-crowded buses!

I went on smoking and was clearly conscious that my revolt would fail that day as on all other occasions, because, when all was said and done, my mother was sublimated and I was not. She would have been so, moreover, in every case and at all times, with or without fascism. For, as I have already remarked, there are two races of people in the world, that of the sublimated who are sublimated anyhow, in any sort of circumstances, historical or environmental, even with fascism; and that of the desublimated who cannot achieve such a thing even in the most favourable conditions. I myself belong to the latter race, irremediably. And so, in a short time, with my mother, the usual old, smarting humiliations would be repeated, unless, unless . . .

Immediately 'he' rebelled: 'No, you can't do that.'

'Why not? Seeing that it's the only way of getting myself "on top", just for once with her?"'

'No, you musn't do it.'

234

'But tell me why.'

'Because a mother is a mother, when all's said and done.'

'What sort of pulpit does it come from, this exhortation to respect for a parent!'

'A mother is a mother.'

'Aren't we meaning, rather, that a frank explanation between my mother and me, as well as putting her "underneath" in a decisive fashion, would throw the light of reason into the darkness in which you usually cower? And reason, as you know, is what you fear more than anything in the world.'

'A mother is a mother.'

'Stop repeating that refrain of yours, like a parrot: explain yourself.'

At this demand from me he changed tone all of a sudden and said, with strange, concentrated fury: 'Idiot! Your mother might well come every night and bid you good-night in the same way as she did on that March day twenty years ago. But every day, just the same, she would find a way of "putting you in your place", reminding you that, whatever happens, children owe the greatest respect to their parents. You halfwit, don't you know that?'

A voice drew my attention away from my quarrel with 'him'. It was the voice of the 'gendarme'. 'Signor Rico, would you like to look at these magazines and newspapers? They've just arrived.'

I looked up and saw that she was holding out two illustrated magazines and two newspapers. 'Was it my mother,' I asked her, 'who told you to offer me the aperitif and the papers?'

'Yes. She said: Signor Rico will certainly arrive an hour early. Offer him a vermouth and tell him to look at the papers.'

The 'gendarme' went out and I bit my lips hard. So my mother knew that I should come early with the precise purpose of flirting with Sabina. But how had she come to know it? I got up, threw my cigarette angrily on the floor, stamped on it, took a half-turn round the dining-room and,

almost without realizing it, kicked out at one of the upholstered hip-bath chairs. At that precise moment my mother
entered.

She had a big head like me and a mass of curly hair
which at one time had been black but was now threaded with
white. Dressed in black, her figure seemed all dried up and
reduced to a skeleton, from her fragile shoulders right down
to her stick-like legs, from her bosom which had retained an
oddly voluminous character, making one think of a large fruit,
now old and flabby, that had, by some miracle, remained
attached to a dead tree. She came in holding her handkerchief,
as usual, to her nose (which was big like mine) with a fussy
gesture habitual to her. The first thing she did was to stoop
and pick up the cigarette-end I had just thrown on the floor;
then, straightening herself up, with the cigarette-end in the
palm of her hand, she said to me: 'I'm sorry you had to wait.
But that's no reason why you should kick my furniture.
There was no need for you to come an hour early.'

So there we were! Such was the remark, malicious but
kept rigorously within the limits of the bourgeois rules of
good manners, of which my mother made use in order to put
me 'underneath' from the very beginning.

Angrily I replied: 'I beg you, if you wish to amuse me
during long waits of this kind, don't tell your maid to bring
me these magazines and daily papers. I'm not interested in the
deeds of royal and ex-royal families. Nor yet in the political
opinions of industrialists and speculators in building sites.'

As usual, as indeed always, when I touched on certain
subjects, my mother pretended not to have heard. Instead,
she said to the 'gendarme' who had reappeared in the meantime: 'Come on, quickly, Elisa, lay the table.' Then she went
away, without troubling about me any further.

Elisa laid the table; and I followed her with my eyes,
sinking back in my veneered, upholstered hip-bath chair.
First she covered the top of the table with a flannel undercloth.
Then she spread the tablecloth and, as she leant forward, she
raised her leg and displayed an unexpectedly round and
fleshy calf. Incredible! And 'he' commented: 'I agree she's

236

ugly. But, just for fun, and also partly to annoy your mother, I should like to see what would happen if, for instance, you put your arm round her waist.'

'Shut up, you idiot!'

Elisa opened the sideboard, took out plates, glasses, knives and forks and so on with her white-cotton-gloved hands, and laid two places at the table. Out came the old, well-known carafe of second-grade crystal, with its wide belly and long neck, half full of wine. And a bottle of mineral water, half empty too, with a plastic stopper. Here were the forks and knives and spoons with silver handles and the family initials in florid style, the gift of my grandparents who had in turn received them as a wedding present. The salt-container and pepper-pot of yellow majolica in the form of chickens with little holes in their heads. The salad-oil bottle in the same style as the wine carafe.

Elisa, without knowing it, was preparing the place and the instruments of a rite. For my mother was not religious, not in a 'practising' way, except from habit and social duty; her church-going was confined to Sunday mornings. But the rites of the family table, of the social visit, of the theatre, the cinema, the summer holiday and, indeed, of all the things that 'have to be done', constituted, for her, combined and linked together, a kind of bourgeois religion, entirely devoid of any sort of transcendency but not on that account any less carefully observed and 'practised'. A religion, let me say in parenthesis, marvellously adapted to favour the particular type of sublimation that allowed my mother to keep me in a constant, irreversible state of inferiority.

My mother came in again. In silence she sat down, unfolded her table-napkin, corrected the position of the glasses. Then she raised her eyes and looked at me. At that precise moment I myself was also sitting down: innocently, I was holding a lighted cigarette in my fingers. My mother's eyes were directed, eloquently, at my cigarette. I did not take my place but looked round in search of an ashtray, and failed to find one. 'Elisa,' said my mother, 'give Signor Rico an ashtray.' Elisa did as she was told; I stubbed out my cigarette in the ashtray, sat down, and then, naturally, said the one thing that I ought not to have said: 'And Sabina – where is she?'

'I dismissed her.'

'Why? Wasn't she doing well?'

At this moment Elisa came in again, holding a small soup-tureen. My mother helped herself; then I did the same. A small tangle of yellowish spaghetti, shining with butter, lay at the bottom of the tureen. My mother had a delicate stomach; in her house, no sauce with the spaghetti. I put a couple of forkfuls of this anaemic, nursing-home spaghetti into my bowl, sprinkled over it some cheese, also yellowish, taking it from the old-fashioned glass cheese-dish. My mother did not start eating, she was waiting until Elisa had left the room. Then, at last, she replied: 'Sabina – she was doing extremely well. But you wouldn't leave her alone. It was all very well to look at her; but to telephone her, to make appointments! And not outside the house, but here, in my own house, as you did this morning!'

'I never did such a thing. If it was Sabina who told you that, well, Sabina was lying.'

'Sabina was *not* lying and she did *not* tell me.'

'Then how d'you come to be so sure of it?'

'I was present when you telephoned. Sabina handed me the receiver. I listened and heard you say you would come an hour early this morning on purpose to be with her. You thought you were speaking to Sabina, instead of which you were speaking to me. So I dismissed her, apologizing to her, and took on Elisa.'

Bang, crash! Now I was 'underneath', properly 'underneath', and there was nothing to be done. Once again I was assailed by the temptation to put myself 'on top' in relation to my mother, in a sensational, decisive manner, by means of a clear allusion to the episode of twenty years earlier. To say something like: Twenty years ago, what was it that really happened between you and me? Eh, what happened? – but once again I hadn't the courage. 'His' refrain: A mother is a mother, echoed in my ears, tautological, insuperable.

238

For some reason, the taboo comprised in that slogan called up a distant memory to my mind. I was eighteen, I was sitting at a little table, studying, and my mother was bullying me pitilessly with her anti-sex, bourgeois moralisms, taking as her point of departure the fact that I came home too late at night. Then, in sudden exasperation, I got up, took her by the neck and the bottom of the back and thrust her outside the door. Well, I had had a strange sensation as I felt her flesh under my hands. The same sensation, I thought, as one must have from eating human flesh. Yes, striking one's mother (or even merely dreaming of making love with her) was like practising cannibalism. All of them taboo. Theoretically a mother's flesh was like any other. But, psychologically, it was 'sacred' flesh. All these things I thought of, with lowered head, in front of my spaghetti. Then I sighed deeply, shook my head and started to eat in silence.

My mother, however, did not relax her hold and began again, after a moment: 'By the way, guess who telephoned me yesterday, after I'd lost sight of him for years and years? Your friend Vladimiro.'

I could not help being startled: Vladimiro! The last straw would be a collusion between the neurotic, desublimated doctor and my neurotic, sublimated mother. Already angry, I demanded: 'What did he want? And why – what about?'

'About Sabina and what happened between you and Sabina. Vladimiro told me that you had been to see him. We had a long conversation on the telephone. According to him, you're not at all well and what you need is a lengthy treatment.'

'It's Vladimiro who is the neurotic and who needs treatment. He is my age and he hasn't advanced one single step in his career. He lives in a little flat of three rooms and a kitchen, he comes to open the door himself, he hasn't even a nurse or a secretary. Between him and me, it's he who is the hopeless neurotic.'

'I'm sorry, but I can't see what connection there can be between failing in a career and being neurotic.'

I felt uneasy. How, indeed, was I to explain to my mother my idea, or rather my fixation, that success in one's career was in proportion to one's degree of sublimation? I preferred to remark, in a grudging manner: 'What I mean is that he has become neurotic because of his professional failure. He is a doctor without patients and for that reason his judgment is not sound. He says I need treatment because for him I'm a potential patient. A potential milch-cow.'

'It seemed to me that he said very sensible and very just things. I'm very much afraid he might be right.'

'He said things that seemed sensible and just to *you*: Vladimiro is a watch-dog of the bourgeoisie. He notes that I am not adjusted, that I'm not "plugged in", not integrated, and he calls this an illness. No doubt, with his treatment he would cure me, that is, he would transform me into an obliging robot. I know that is what you want. I'm sorry, but I don't wish to be cured. I prefer the illness.'

'I know nothing about robots. Vladimiro didn't speak of robots. In different words, and in a scientific way, he said what I never tire of telling you.'

'And what is that?'

'That women have been, are, and will be your ruin.'

Elisa came in again and my mother, observing the ritual rule of bourgeois respectability which lays down that certain things must not be spoken of 'in front of the servants', broke off the conversation. A great rage came over me and I decided on the spot, privately, not to collaborate in the rite. Elisa offered me an oblong dish in which, half-submerged in whitish water, lay a long, boiled fish, falling to pieces and with its eye staved in and its mouth open. I helped myself and, as I did so, I said ironically: 'Why don't you speak? Evidently, according to you, Vladimiro said that women have been and will be my ruin. My answer is that Vladimiro cannot have expressed himself in that way. Now what do you say? Why are you silent? Perhaps you don't speak because Elisa is here and it's not right to say certain things in front of the maid? But Elisa is a woman like you, she's a person like you and me. I have no secrets from Elisa. Come on, then. Say it in the presence of Elisa, say that Vladimiro confided to you that I am a sex-maniac; say it, then, so that Elisa will know it too and I shall be content that she should know it.'

My provocation did not seem to have any effect on my mother. She went on eating, her eyes lowered, as if she had not heard. Elisa, infected in turn by this impassiveness on the part of her mistress, also acted as though she had not heard me. She handed me the bread-basket, poured me out some wine with her cotton-gloved hand, and then went away. My mother, after waiting unyieldingly until Elisa had closed the door, said: 'And yet, Rico, that was precisely what Vladimiro gave me to understand.'

'Precisely what?'

'That women, for you, have now become a real, positive mania.'

'Vladimiro, more than anything, behaved extremely badly by giving away a professional secret in telephoning to you.'

'On the contrary, he behaved extremely well. I am the only person to whom he could speak. What would you have preferred – that he should telephone your wife?'

'I beg you to leave Fausta out of our conversation.'

'I only wish I could. But then she would have to be outside your life too.'

'She is inside my life and there she will remain.'

'Anyhow, Vladimiro told the truth. You're intelligent, you're cultivated, you're exceptionally gifted in everything that has to do with art and culture. Notwithstanding, you've been left behind by all your university friends because of your passion for women. There's not one of them that hasn't got ahead of you in his career.'

'Certainly Vladimiro hasn't.'

'Leave Vladimiro out of it; he's a scholar rather than a real doctor. Besides, don't bother about the others; just take a look at yourself. Have you ever seen yourself in a looking-glass? You're a young man, yet you're completely bald, your face has already gone to pieces and you have bags under your eyes, like an old man. And you have a paunch.'

241

'I haven't a paunch, I've a stomach.'

'Paunch or stomach, what does it matter? Again I say to you: women have been and will be your ruin. Vladimiro is right: you're slipping into a state of mania. The day will come when no one will visit you and no one will invite you. They will all be afraid for their wives, their sisters, their maids, their cooks.'

My mother was 'on top', oh yes, she was 'on top' all right! And she was dancing on my head, so to speak, without scruple and without consideration. Again I felt the temptation to lay her flat with a single blow by explicitly alluding to the episode of twenty years before; and again I gave up the idea. But it was not for that reason that my anger died down. Like a torrent whose bed has been diverted, it rushed off in a different direction. 'Now look,' I snarled, 'once and for all: these are my own affairs; and I beg you not to stick your nose into them. Otherwise I shall talk to you about your political blunders.'

'Blunders? What blunders?'

'I shall talk to you about Mussolini who was your god, and for that reason you made me wear a black shirt at five years old – for that was all I was – and made me add his name alongside those of Jesus and the Madonna in my evening prayers.'

'Mussolini was a great man. It was the people of Italy who didn't deserve him. We need another Mussolini today.'

What was happening to me? In my rage I brought out the secret of secrets, my psychoanalytical obsession which hitherto I had confessed to no one, not even Vladimiro. 'Mussolini was *not* a great man,' I said. 'He was a typical desublimated man, worthy dictator of a people who were also to a great extent desublimated. His cult, however, brought it about that the small degree of sublimation of which the Italian people was still capable was put to the service of his desublimation. Mussolini was the living symbol of an erroneous inversion of the scale of values; sublimation submissive to desublimation. And you, you prostrated yourself, with your sublimation,

242

before his obscene desublimation. With the faith that is owed to a god, you worshipped a sackful of filth.'

'I don't know what you mean by all this jargon. I suppose Vladimiro would understand you, and of course he would prove you were in the wrong. I know only one thing: that Italy, in Mussolini's time, was strong and respected. In any case it's always better to prostrate oneself before a great man than before a prostitute.'

'And who, pray, might the prostitute be?'

'It's the truth, it's not a calumny. You met her when she was plying that trade. Or isn't it true that Fausta was a call-girl?'

So here we were again, and I was on the point of crying out: Was it in fact a dream, or was it reality, the thing that happened twenty years ago? – but for the last time I got the better of myself. But the effort of control was turned into violence. I seized my plate in both hands and smashed it down on the table, so that it was broken in the middle into two equal parts. 'Fausta is my wife,' I shouted, 'the companion of my life, the mother of my son. And I forbid you to speak of her.'

My shouting had no effect on my mother, first of all because she was accustomed to it; and also because she had privately made up her mind, a long time ago, that it must not have any effect upon her. Moreover she knew perfectly well, as also did I, what the conclusion of the scene would be. Again it was a matter of another familiar rite which had been observed for years. My mother would allude to Fausta in a highly disrespectful way; I would shout at her, perhaps even break a plate or a glass and then leave the dining-room. But I would not leave the flat. I would go out into the corridor and thence into my mother's bedroom. Almost automatically I would sit down at her dressing-table, in front of the mirror and, still automatically, start examining my face, looking for and finding a pimple which I would then squeeze. This almost unconscious occupation would soothe me. So that, when my mother came and joined me, I would by that time be almost calm. My mother, too, would seem to have calmed down. Our altercation would not be resumed, my mother and I would start a conventional mother-and-son conversation. Finally I would kiss my mother on the forehead and go off home.

And so it happened on that day. After smashing the plate, I got up from the table and left the dining-room, banging the door. In the passage I avoided the front door and went straight into my mother's bedroom. This, too, was in the 'twentieth-century' style. I walked round the bed, went and sat down in front of the dressing-table, put my face close to the glass and examined myself with an attention which was at the same time both relentless and absent-minded. I looked at my big bald head outlined with ruffled locks of hair, at my eyes with the bags underneath them, at my dictatorial nose and my large, proud mouth. I found a pimple on my left cheek, close to my ear. I squeezed it hard; a little blood came out, which I wiped away with my handkerchief. Then my mother entered.

Our conversation developed in the following way. 'How is the little boy?'

'He's well, just a bit fretful because he hasn't had a summer holiday this year.'

'Children need to go to the sea. Why doesn't Fausta take him to Ostia or Fregene in the car?'

'Unfortunately it is I who need the car. And we have only one.'

'There are very good buses. There's one that stops not far from where you live. Anyhow, why have you all stayed in town?'

'I'm waiting to take on the direction of a film.'

'That shouldn't have stopped you from sending Fausta and the boy to the seaside. You still have time, there are still August and September.'

'Fausta doesn't want to go to the seaside without me. She says she gets bored because she doesn't know anyone.'

'But it doesn't take long to make acquaintances. I'm sure Fausta would find company. There are so many young married women at the seaside with small children who don't have to go to school.' Etc., etc., etc. The rite continued, one of the many by means of which my mother supports her

244

middle-class universe. The rite of mother and son, of mother-in-law and daughter-in-law, of grandmother and grandchild. We went on for quite a long time, then I sighed and looked at the clock. I announced that I must go.

The last phase of the rite: the leave-taking. Today, possibly because our encounter had been harsher than usual and there had therefore been a greater temptation to overcome my state of inferiority by alluding to the episode of twenty years earlier, instead of giving my mother the usual kiss on the brow I suddenly threw myself on the floor at her feet. I pressed my forehead against her thin legs with the same gesture that I had made with Irene, but with a different feeling and intention. I thrust my head towards my mother's lap because I wanted to go back into it, to disappear there, to cease to suffer, to cease to exist, to return whence I had come, to return to nothingness.

It may be that my mother understood this longing for annihilation. Partly because it did not contradict her own particular, funereal type of sublimation. I felt her stroking my bald head with her cold, wrinkled palm.

I gave two or three groans that were sincere enough. Then I rose and kissed her on the brow. 'Good-bye, Mamma.'

'Good-bye, Rico.'

I left the room thinking: Thank God, from today, for at least a week, we shan't talk about it again. Ugh!

10 Challenged!

Nothing to be done: no integration for the one who wanted it! After my unsuccessful attempt to get Protti to entrust me with the direction of the film and while waiting for my relationship with Mafalda to mature, I took up work again on the version of *Expropriation* in accordance with the interpretation that Maurizio had imposed upon me. I was in fact convinced that, if I wished to get the job of director, I must in any case throw overboard the 'Spoilt children playing at Revolution' version which had been duly worked out by me; and adopt, instead, the other version, as supported by Maurizio: 'Technicians of Revolution who have made a mistake and are striving to find a just and correct course of action.' But very soon I ran into a difficulty of what I may call a poetical kind. Obviously I could work in a mannered way, like the good craftsman I was; that is to say, not 'inventing' the story but 'fabricating' it. But here I was brought to a halt by this problem of poetry, that is, of that special kind of truth which is truer than the truth and which distinguishes what is 'created' from what is 'produced'.

This time it was not, indeed, a matter of some ordinary film which could later be shot by some ordinary director. It was a matter – until it was proved to the contrary – of 'my' film, of a film, that is, of which I myself should be the director. And so I felt that recourse to mere technique was not enough. I knew these things from experience. If one starts with a faulty subject, one will inevitably have a faulty film. If one produces a subject instead of creating it, then, in turn, the film itself will be, not a creation, but a product. So I came to find myself in a distressingly contradictory position: basically it depended to a great extent on Maurizio whether the direction of the film was entrusted to me; but, if I accepted Maurizio's version, I was almost sure that I should make a bad film. If, on the other hand, I did not accept it, the end of the matter would be that the direction, without any doubt, would be entrusted to somebody else. The first consequence of these reflections was that, when Maurizio came to see me that day, my embarrassment expressed itself in an imprudent, evasive, stupid question: 'Have you handed over the five million?'

'Yes, of course.'

'Who to?'

'To the comrade who looks after the administration.'

'Did you tell him it was I who gave it?'

'Of course.'

'And what did he say?'

'Who?'

'The . . . the comrade administrator.'

'He said: "Certainly Rico is a great revolutionary, to be counted with Mao, with Ho-Chi-Minh, with Lenin and Marx."'

I blushed. There I was, from the very beginning, 'underneath', as usual. Though mortified, I said reasonably: 'There's nothing to joke about. You should realize, Maurizio, that five million is, for me, a huge sum. It's understandable that I should want to know whether my contribution has been appreciated.'

Maurizio sat silent and still, his face turned away from me in profile, looking, as always, like some figure in a painting which, however much one walks round and changes the visual angle, remains always the same. Finally he said: 'Really I don't know why you gave us that sum which seems to you so huge. In your place I wouldn't have given anything.'

'Why?'

'Because you're not a revolutionary and you don't believe in revolution. In fact, fundamentally, you're a counter-revolutionary.'

'Yes, a counter-revolutionary who makes a contribution of five million.'

I thought I had caught him there. The five million would at least have served the purpose of shutting his mouth each time he tried to overwhelm me with his political argument.

Once again I was wrong, however, understanding nothing, in my habitual desublimated condition, of those who are sublimated. Slowly, apathetically, he replied: 'The five million is no proof whatever that you're a revolutionary. Especially since things have occurred recently which prove the contrary.'

'What things?'

'You went to Protti and tried to put the comrades of the group and myself in a bad light. You told Protti that we were making a film against capitalism and against himself.'

Another catastrophe! Disconcerted, I stammered: 'Who said so?'

'Protti told me so himself.'

'Protti didn't understand at all. I gave him an account of the two versions, yours and mine, so that he should have an idea of the difficulty of our work. That was all.'

I waited hopefully for Maurizio to engage in a discussion. On careful consideration, an argument between equals, in which Maurizio would throw my betrayal in my face and I would defend myself and even perhaps go over to the counter-offensive, would lessen my sense of inferiority. But Maurizio was 'on top' and intended to remain there. He gazed intently at me as I warmed up to defend myself, but he did not interrupt me. Finally he said: 'It doesn't matter, in any case. I wanted to say that, to make you see that five million, or even five hundred million, don't suffice to make a revolutionary. But now there's another question.'

I felt uneasy. Maurizio was avoiding an encounter and thus thrusting me even farther 'underneath'. Irritated, I asked him: 'What more is there?'

'I've come to fetch you. There's a meeting of the group today at Fregene, at Flavia's. As agreed, I'll introduce you, announce your contribution and then a discussion on the treatment of the script will follow.'

I did not hide my satisfaction. My introduction to the group, announced and postponed again and again, had hitherto been one of the means made use of by Maurizio to keep me 'underneath'. I was pleased, and inquired: 'Are we going there at once?'

'Yes, at once.'

'Excellent. What will the debate consist of?'

'I'll introduce you and then the discussion on the script will follow.'

I was truly pleased. First of all the introduction: I present to you Comrade Rico, my talented collaborator on the script of our film. Then the announcement of my remarkable contribution: Comrade Rico has made a contribution of five million lire; applause for Comrade Rico! Finally the discussion: Allow me to open the debate on the script of *Expropriation* which Rico and I have worked out together. In short something dignified, serious, committed, progressive, elevated, cultural. Something friendly, encouraging, cordial. The meeting of two generations, theirs and mine. The point of departure for a secure, long-lasting, profitable relationship between them and me. I would exclaim enthusiastically: I'm pleased. I'm very pleased. We belong to two different generations, you and I. But why shouldn't we work together? Actually, that is how scripts ought to be made; not by one person alone, nor by two, but by a group. This might be the beginning of a new and truly revolutionary experiment.

Maurizio was already walking in front of me along the passage. We went out of the flat together. In the lift, as it carried us down to the ground floor, I asked: 'Why Fregene?'

'Flavia's parents' villa is there, and it's empty. It has a very big living-room, well suited for meetings.'

'But how about the headquarters in Rome, for which I gave the five million?'

'It's not ready.'

'What's missing?'

'The portraits. We've ordered them from Milan, but they haven't arrived yet.'

'What portraits?'

'Portraits of Marx, of Lenin, of Mao and Stalin.'

'Stalin, too?'

'Of course.'

I said nothing. I looked at him. He was driving, with his pretty, feminine head, like that of a Renaissance page, in profile. The milky whiteness of his face stood out against the whiteness – less white by comparison – of the white cotton of his suit. The rosiness of his nostrils, of his lips and his ears, the faint violet marks of fatigue under his eyes, made me think, all of a sudden, of the classical madrigals in which there is mention of 'roses and violets' in respect of women's complexions. All at once I asked: 'Flavia thinks like you, doesn't she?'

'About what?'

'I mean, she shares your political ideas?'

'Yes.'

I was silent for a moment, then I resumed: 'I suppose Flavia's parents are perfect, like yours, aren't they?'

'I don't understand.'

'Don't you remember? Some time ago we agreed that your parents, to you, were perfect, inasmuch as you couldn't find any fault with them apart from being bourgeois.'

'Ah yes, I remember.'

'I repeat, then: are Flavia's parents like yours? That is to say, perfect inasmuch as Flavia has no fault to find with them except that they are bourgeois?'

'I suppose that's so.'

'This would mean, then, that both as parents and as social figures they are unobjectionable: a good father, a good mother; she, a respectable married lady, he, a distinguished professional man.'

'He's not a professional man: he's a civil engineer.'

'Even better. A civil engineer. Words that are positive in themselves: civil engineer. Let us come now to Flavia. How do her parents take it, that she should be a member of the group?'

'Badly.'

'Like yours, as regards yourself?'

'More or less.'

'But, apart from the fact that you're protesters, what fault have your parents to find with you? That you're a bad son and daughter, that you behave badly, that Flavia is a nymphomaniac, that you are a whoremonger, that you're both drug addicts, or what?'

Without turning towards me, and almost without moving his lips, he said: 'Flavia a nymphomaniac, I myself a whore-monger, the two of us drug addicts? What on earth are you thinking of?'

'It was only a manner of speaking. Your parents, in fact, apart from the protests, don't have any fault to find with you?'

'I think we may say so.'

'So your parents, to you, are perfect, and you, to them, are the same. Except that you find fault with your parents for being bourgeois; and they find fault with you for being protesters. Isn't that so?'

'Very well, then. But what are you getting at?'

What I should have liked to say was: I'm trying to get at this. Even if it's for opposite reasons, you and Flavia on one side and your parents on the other all have something of the same abominable perfection that goes with sublimation. Little does it matter whether you are sublimated in favour of revolution and your parents in favour of conservatism. The important thing is that you're all tarred with the same brush and that the difference between you, not to say the opposition, is merely apparent. You are all people with power, the whole lot of you, and your true opposite, your real opponent, is *me,* desublimated, weak-willed, a poor wretch well endowed by nature but incapable of transferring his natural gifts to the social level. But, as usual, I bit my lips: it was impossible for me to speak to anyone, least of all to Maurizio, about my obsession. I answered vaguely: 'I am not trying to get at anything. I've already said that we belong to different generations. I'm trying to understand you: that's all. Now, if you'll allow me, I'll ask you one more question, a rather – how shall I say? – delicate one.'

'Come on, then.'

'Are you and Flavia lovers?'

'You want to know whether we go to bed? Yes, certainly.'

'How long have you been doing that?'

'Ever since we met. Two years.'

'But d'you do it often?'

251

I saw his golden eyebrows frowning above his black glasses. 'What a question!'

'I'm sorry, but I really would like to know.'

'But why?'

'Again, to understand you better. D'you do it often, then?'

He was silent for a moment. Finally he replied: 'No, rarely.'

'What d'you mean, rarely?'

'Not so very often. Sometimes we go as long as a month without doing it.'

'But why? You're young, you love one another . . .'

'What d'you mean? Anyhow we're very busy. And then it very rarely happens that we're alone: for the most part we're with the group. And after all, Flavia lives with her parents and I with mine.'

'If one wants to make love, it's easy to find the means and the place.'

Now he remained silent for quite a long time. Then he affirmed: 'The fact is that neither I myself nor Flavia is much interested in love.'

'You're not interested. And why is that?'

'There's no "why" about it. It just is so.'

'What form does this lack of interest take?'

'Really I don't know. Anyhow we don't think about it. When we do it, we don't enjoy it very much.'

'But let me see. You love Flavia and you don't like making love with her?'

'It's perfectly possible to love and at the same time not to take pleasure in making love.'

'Perhaps, for physical love, you might prefer some other woman?'

'No, Flavia suits me in every sense. But we don't like making love so very much. In the first place it's tiring, then one sweats and gets dirty. And finally, after doing it, one loses all desire to do anything. I don't know why, but it seems to me that it's – how shall I say? – a rather ridiculous occupation.'

252

'Does Flavia think like you about it?'

'I believe so. But we've never really talked about it.'

'Then how d'you come to know that she thinks like you?'

'Because I see that it doesn't interest her.'

'But you're going to get married, aren't you?'

'Yes, certainly.'

'Perhaps you'll even have children.'

'I suppose we shall.'

'Am I wrong in thinking that you're not interested in starting a family, either?'

'It's not that. It's a question of freedom of action. We're so absorbed in the activities of the group that, in a way, we don't feel any need to start a family.'

'I myself, on the other hand, have a wife and a son – a family, in fact. And I like making love with my wife.'

He said nothing. It was clear that I didn't interest him. I could not help adding: 'But I should much like to know what you mean when you state that something doesn't interest you?'

'What do I mean? Exactly what I say.'

'That is equivalent to saying that a thing can actually be important, but, since it doesn't interest you, it doesn't exist?'

'That may be so.'

And so, for him, I didn't exist! Like love! Like everything that was not revolution! Nevertheless I was content, all the same, because I had demonstrated to myself the true foundation of my hypothesis. This triumph of mine, modest as it was, was not agreeable to 'him'; 'he' observed maliciously: 'What d'you think you've proved by your questioning? The advantages of sublimation?'

'Let us put it like that.'

'On the contrary, no. All you've proved is that Maurizio and Flavia and their parents are simply wanting in temperament; they're just like boiled fish, or seaweed, sexually underdeveloped. That's all.'

'What does it matter to you? Why are you so bitterly opposed to sublimation?'

'Because it doesn't exist and can't exist. But above all because you don't decide to accept the knowledge of your superiority over all these people.'

'A superiority which would consist in your exceptional size, length, thickness, etc. Isn't that so?'

'Yes, that's so.'

I shrugged my shoulders; here was nothing new, just the usual vanity. But now we had reached Fregene. In the summer night the pinewood, with its tree-trunks leaning this way and that, looked, in the light of the occasional headlamps, as if it had been disturbed by a recent storm. We turned and drove along a straight avenue bordered by gardens. Through the gates there were glimpses of the façades of villas. Some were lit up; and beneath the porches could be seen people sitting in deck-chairs, conversing, while menservants in white jackets went round with trays of drinks. On the gravel paths children, at this hour already in bed, had left big balls with coloured segments, tricycles painted red and yellow. At the far end of the avenue were two rows of cars parked against the pavements. Maurizio slowed down and stopped. I inquired, as I got out: 'It's here?'

'Yes, it's here.'

Maurizio led me in through the gate, advanced slowly, hands in pockets, along a path at the far end of which I saw the villa, a low building of red brick, on one floor. We walked along the clean gravel between borders of brilliant green, harshly lit by lamps hidden in the box hedges. Under the portico was sitting someone who, as we entered the garden, rose and came to meet us. It was Flavia, Maurizio's fiancée.

As she walked towards us, I had time to look at her. Her face was long, white and equine, beneath a bulging mass of red hair. I was struck by her eyes, which were large and pale, of a dull blue that stood out against the ghost-like whiteness of her face. She walked listlessly, moving her long legs with what was perhaps an intentionally frivolous awkwardness. Her ungainly dress, from the opening of which rose a straight neck, swelled out into a kind of big bundle a little above her waist. Another protuberance, also like a voluminous bundle,

254

lifted her dress at the bottom of her back. There she was, then, in, so to speak, close-up: with the eyes and the pallor of a ghost and, on her cheeks, her neck, her chest, on her arms and legs, a hail of red freckles. Her voice too, like her movements, was affected and full of smart-society emphasis, as she said: 'You are terribly late. The group have all been assembled for some time. They're pawing the ground and protesting. What on earth have you been doing?'

'The traffic,' said Maurizio. 'This is Rico.'

'How are you?'

Flavia shook my hand in a curious way: softly, sensually, but just when it seemed that her clasp was on the point of turning into a caress, her fingers opened and my hand was left hanging. I said to her: 'I'm very pleased to meet your group. I'm sure the debate will be very interesting. It will be an encounter between two generations. And these encounters are very useful, they should happen more often. It's only a pity I didn't know about it before. I would have jotted down some notes.' Flavia gave a little well-bred laugh which she stifled beneath her white, freckled hand. She said ambiguously: 'I'm sure the debate will go very well even without notes.'

She walked beside me, listless, affable and at the same time somewhat haughtily, as if from an unconscious habit of the snobbery she had repudiated. In the meantime 'he', evidently impressed by Flavia's attractiveness, began whispering the usual absurdities: 'Pretend to stumble on the gravel and knock against her hip, slightly sideways so that she may become conscious of my existence, of my admiration, of my desire.'

The intolerable creature! To make such remarks to me just at that moment when I was at last about to be introduced to the group! With the risk of giving Flavia a wrong idea of me and of ruining everything! Of course I took good care not to listen to these suggestions. Instead, I said gaily to Maurizio: 'I'm grateful to you for this meeting with the group. I've contributed five million but I don't in the least regret it. There are experiences that can never be paid for sufficiently.'

'You're right,' replied Maurizio.

Flavia led us into the house. Passing through the porch, we went through a french window into the living-room and immediately found ourselves behind a table, facing three rows of chairs occupied by about thirty boys and girls: the group. The room was long and narrow, with a low ceiling; the furniture had been removed to make way for the chairs; the only furnishings that remained were the marine-type decorations customary in such seaside dwellings – harpoons, life-buoys, rudders, nets, lobster-pots, figureheads, tortoise-shells, which were hanging here and there on the walls. On the table, which was covered with a red cloth, were a microphone, a bottle of water and two glasses. To the left of the table, hanging in the air, I saw something that surprised me – a real, proper set of traffic lights, with the three lights, red, yellow and green, exactly like the ones at crossroads even though smaller. With my eyes I followed the flex leading from these lights. It went along the wall on the left and then came down at the opposite end of the room to a small table on which stood a black box with a dial covered with knobs. At the table, in front of the box, sat a young man.

In a low voice I asked Flavia: 'What are the traffic lights for?'

'To time the speeches.'

I looked round the room. They were all young men and girls of, as they say, good family, even if not all, necessarily, of families as rich as those of Maurizio and Flavia. Pullovers, scarves, cardigans, capes and trousers of linen, velvet or wool, in vivid colours; sandals and shoes of unusual shape; several beards and a good deal of long hair; but, in contrast with so much liveliness in clothes and hairstyles, a singular, unexpected, surly composure in their behaviour.

I felt myself being stared at, examined, assessed, weighed up, judged. Then, suddenly, while I was still wondering what sort of a welcome this was, I heard the click of the lights above my head. I looked up and saw that the yellow light had been turned on. At the same time, in an evident relation of cause and effect, all the young people rose to their feet and applauded. Their applause, however, did not appear spontaneous.

They clapped their hands with a unanimity and a rhythm too regular not to be deliberate. And how long did the applause last? Possibly for a minute. In any case I had the impression that it lasted a long time, too long to be sincere and due to feeling alone. As I imagined that they were applauding me, I felt embarrassed and strove to hide my embarrassment by joining in the applause myself. But then, strange to say, as though to indicate to me that I ought not to be applauding, another click of the lights brought the hand-clapping in the room to an immediate stop. I looked up. The light was now green. Maurizio advanced to the table and raised his arm as if to announce that he wished to speak. Then, in the silence that followed, he said: 'Let me introduce Rico to whom, as you know, Protti the producer has given the task of collaborating with me on the script of *Expropriation*.'

Click. I looked up at the lights and saw that this time the red light was on. I thought quickly: yellow light means applause; green light means a speech; and red light? I learnt immediately. The young people, remaining seated and dragging their feet on the floor, began to repeat in chorus: 'Ché yes, Protti no.'

The red light, therefore, signified the opposite of the yellow light; that is to say, the opposite of applause; that is, disapproval, hostility. I did not feel, now, like joining in the chorus against Protti. Furthermore, if Protti came to know about it, he might easily take his revenge by giving me no more work. I was aware that this was a not very revolutionary reflection: but how can one avoid thinking certain thoughts? So I assumed a vaguely understanding smile and waited for the chorus to finish. Unexpectedly, at this point, 'he' whispered: 'Please take a look at Flavia.' I looked.

Flavia was standing beside me and, in order to look at her, I drew slightly back. 'He' immediately became excited and went on: 'Look how tall she is, how thin and cadaverous and loose-knit and lanky! And nevertheless how laden and burdened she is in her bosom and the lower part of her back! And with what a disturbing casualness she has thrown herself sideways across those books, so that the thin stuff of her scrappy dress sticks to the more convex parts of her body. She's a regular maypole. But what a lot of lovely, appetizing things hanging from it, like on a Christmas tree!'

'And I, in order to please you, am to climb up this pole?'

'Yes, precisely.'

Click. I raised my eyes: the green light. The cry of 'Ché yes, Protti no' stopped at once. Maurizio stepped forward, arranged the microphone on the table and said: 'During our last meeting I explained the changes that Rico had introduced into the script. I also told you that I had opposed these changes, that I had forced him to recognize that our version was the only proper and correct one and that he had promised to respect it. At this point it is my duty to inform you that, as a proof of his change of heart and of his goodwill, Rico has given up all ideas of compensation and has handed over the sum of five million to our administration.'

Click. I was so sure that the light would be yellow that I did not even look up to make certain of it. Instead, I assumed an air of demure, discreet modesty in expectation of the imminent, undoubted applause. But I was like someone standing naked under a shower who turns on the wrong tap and lets loose a jet of cold, instead of hot, water. The applause did not come. Instead, there burst forth an extremely hostile chorus of 'Ché yes, Rico no', accompanied by the same dragging of feet on the floor. Then I made up my mind to look up at the light; it was red, unmistakably red. At this sight I felt my face changing its expression and even its shape, changing in spite of myself from its feigned, proud modesty to sincere, distorted dismay. I listened incredulously, hoping, almost, that I had heard wrong. But no, I had heard perfectly well and it was perfectly true, the young people were shouting in chorus: 'Ché yes, Rico no.' And how about the five million?

Click. The green light. At once the chorus ceased. Maurizio resumed, just as if he had guessed my thought and intended to answer me: 'You did not applaud the news of the gift of five million and you acted rightly. The five million handed over to our administrator in no way proves that Rico is a revolu-

258

tionary. And now something new has come about which proves that our mistrust of him was more than justified.'

Maurizio was silent for a moment, looking round the room, and then, inexplicably, he looked at me. I say 'inexplicably' because I did not understand the reason for this expressionless, colourless, inert, apathetic look. It was the look of a painted figure in a picture, in a museum. I was furious, dismayed, confused; but Maurizio did not seem to be aware of it, for he was not 'alive' but 'painted'. After a moment's silence, he went on: 'This is the new thing that has happened. A few days ago Rico went to see Protti and told him that our intention was to make a film against him and against the system. The aim of what I can only call this counter-revolutionary denunciation was clear: to alarm Protti, to get him to prefer Rico's own version to ours, to sabotage the film. Luckily Protti, for his own reasons, did not agree. In fact, it was he himself who advised me of Rico's move.'

Click. I was sure that the light could only be red and this time I was not mistaken. Still remaining in their seats, the young people started repeating again in chorus: 'Ché yes, Rico no', rubbing their feet on the floor. I felt utterly crushed. And, into the bargain, with the burning consciousness that, owing to my good faith as a good-natured, warm-hearted, desublimated person, I had fallen into a trap which had been carefully prepared by an unrestrained pack of immature, supersublimated youths.

For indeed the whole crowd of those assembled there were more or less like Maurizio, sublimated by birth, by family tradition, by social environment. All of them were, in fact, of good family; and 'good family' in this case meant families whose members had been sublimated for at least five generations. What matter if in the past they had been civil servants, bankers, generals, judges, doctors, lawyers and were now, on the contrary, or at any rate thought themselves to be, revolutionaries! Sublimation was always the same thing, whether clothed, as then, in double-breasted grey flannel suits in the English style, or, as now, in pullovers. And I, typically desublimated as I was, had allowed myself to be drawn,

259

lured on by vanity, into the trap of a so-called debate which in reality was taking the shape, more and more, of a veritable lynching.

These thoughts reassured me a little. They at least displayed a clear grasp, on my part, of the desperate situation in which I had placed myself. And now I must confess that, in my agony, 'his' voice was welcome to me when, quite unexpectedly, he whispered to me: 'Maurizio has lured you into an ambush.'

'He has indeed.'

'You must take your revenge.'

'And in what way?'

'Steal his fiancée.'

'Are you crazy?'

'No, I'm not crazy. Didn't you notice how she looked at me when we met in the garden? Trust yourself to me, for once: it'll be all right. Take your revenge, then.'

'But this isn't the moment. I'm faced with a kind of revolutionary tribunal, I'm accused of counter-revolutionary plotting and I must defend myself. And you come and tell me that Flavia took a look at you; what are you thinking of?'

'Rubbish. The group, the film, the director's job, the traffic lights, Ché, revolution, counter-revolution, the bourgeoisie, the proletariat – they're all nonsense. For you there's only one thing that should count.'

'Yes, I know – you.'

'Don't put it like that. Avenge yourself, that's the point, by making use of me.'

Click. The green light. The hostile chorus ceased abruptly. Maurizio adjusted the microphone again. 'We are not here, however, to condemn Rico, but to give him the means to recognize his own errors, to make an adequate self-criticism and to declare his change of heart. And so, if you agree, I will invite Rico to speak.'

Click. The yellow light. The young people applauded Maurizio all together and with a special kind of rhythm: a short hand-clap and then a long one, a short one and a long one. They were applauding Maurizio for having 'unmasked' me; and indeed I felt myself truly 'unmasked', in other words, with a naked and defenceless face as though hitherto I had concealed and protected it with a mask.

Another click; the red light. Now for the third time they shouted in chorus: 'Ché yes, Rico no.' I noticed that they repeated the refrain and rustled their feet in a hesitant sort of way which showed complete indifference even though it was disciplined, looking idly from side to side and with faces empty of any kind of expression. There was, in short, a plan that had been studied and pre-established in detail; and they were carrying it out without any real hostility towards me, just as though I were a faceless, anonymous, interchangeable enemy. They were lynching me thoroughly; but, if there had been somebody else in my place, the lynching would have come about just the same.

In the meantime, however, even while the hostile chorus was interminably prolonged, I realized that in a short time I should have to speak and asked myself miserably how I ought to reply to Maurizio's accusations. I had three alternatives. Firstly, to face the accusations with firmness, with dignity, with intelligence, denying everything, exculpating myself, declaring myself innocent. Secondly, to go over to the attack, to denounce the ambush, to insult them, to go away, slamming the door behind me. Thirdly, to do what I was asked to do, that is, to admit my guilt, to submit to self-criticism, to declare myself penitent.

Of the three courses of action, the first was the one I preferred on what I may call the intellectual level. To the second I was attracted by sheer indignation. But the third, strangely enough, was the one that attracted me most, though in an obscure, inexplicable, confused sort of way. I felt intuitively that it was an inferior, masochistic way of behaving, the way of the desublimated when faced with the sublimated, of the man who is 'underneath' when faced with the man who is 'on top'. But it was also a way of understanding myself, of explaining myself to myself. Why, in truth, had I gone to denounce the group to Protti? Simply to obtain the job of director? Or from some other, deeper motive?

Click. The green light. It was up to me to speak. Suddenly I made up my mind and chose the third alternative. I took a step forward to the table, and this movement in itself sufficed to release my feeling of guilt. I discovered to my surprise that my eyes were filled with tears and that my breast was swelling with some kind of emotion. 'In the first place,' I said, 'I admit that Maurizio has told the truth.'

Click. The red light. Once again, with an idle but disciplined air, hesitant and indifferent, the young people took up the refrain: 'Ché yes, Rico no.' Click. The yellow light. Maurizio came forward and was greeted for the second time by that special uneven applause, like the Morse code. Then another click announced the green light. Maurizio approached his mouth to the microphone. 'Well then, Rico, you admit that you have been guilty of delation, of betrayal, of sabotage and other counter-revolutionary courses of action?'

'Yes.'

'Explain to us why you acted like this.'

'From an irresistible backwash of bourgeois spirit.'

'What do you mean by that?'

'This is what I mean. I am a professional script-writer who for ten years has been linked with commercial-type production. Your film constitutes a challenge to all that has hitherto been my means of livelihood. An ideological, political, moral, social challenge. Integrated as I am into the system, I felt immediately that your film threatened the system and therefore myself as well, in my earnings, in my ambition, in my ideas, in the society of which I form a part. I felt an envious rage, a confused, helpless resentment. I felt that you were all of you 'positive' and I myself 'negative'; and that my negativeness must, yes indeed, *must* strive to destroy your positiveness. And so, while on the one hand I pretended to agree with your ideas and carried my pretence to the point of handing over a contribution of five million, on the other hand I exerted myself in every way to damage you, to hurt you, to do you all the harm I could. In the first place I sought to sabotage the film by composing a version that was low-toned,

262

expressive of intimate feelings, sentimental, in a word, bourgeois. Then, when Maurizio became aware of my manoeuvre and frustrated it by forcing me to accept his own just and correct version, I decided to attack you on the production side. I went to Protti, I went with him to his room and explained that the film as you had conceived it was anti-bourgeois and anti-capitalist. Finally, with the object of setting him even further against you, I invented the completely new idea that you had taken him as model for the character of the expropriated capitalist.'

So that was that. Luckily I had succeeded in keeping back my tears. I had spoken calmly, in a clear, orderly fashion. Had I spoken the truth? In the context of the relationship between the group and myself, perhaps I had; in the absolute sense, obviously I had not. On the other hand there had been a point in my speech when falsehood and truth had become confused and interchangeable, and that had been when I asserted that I had felt, with helpless rage, that they were positive and I was negative.

While I was actually saying this, I had become lucidly aware that this antithesis might very well be reversed. And that the same justification that I had allowed myself for betraying them and denouncing them to Protti – that is, my desperate longing to become a director – might even be merely the unconscious mask of that positiveness and negativeness of which, every time, I was both the wearer and the expression. But what sort of negativeness, what sort of positiveness? Not certainly, a negativeness and positiveness of a political and social, of a bourgeois and proletarian kind, or of right and left. No, it was something more profound, more original, more obscure: the negativeness and positiveness which I was in the habit of attributing, respectively, to desublimation and sublimation, and which on this occasion, on the contrary, showed themselves inexplicably confused and ambivalent.

These thoughts occupied my mind, and then I became aware that Maurizio on one side and Flavia on the other were now looking at me as though expecting a supplementary, conclusive affirmation from me. So I pulled myself together and declared: 'Yes, I admit that I acted as a counter-revolutionary, an informer, a traitor.'

Strange to say, now, after accusing and insulting myself, I felt, physically at least, much better. Certainly I had lied; but evidently my lies were, in a way, health-giving. I added: 'In short, I admit to being a worm.'

Click. The red light. The audience took up the last word of my declaration. They repeated in chorus: 'Worm, worm, worm,' shuffling their feet on the floor. This time again, however, they still retained the same disciplined but sluggish air as before: obviously the fact that I was a worm was, as far as they were concerned, discounted. I folded my arms across my chest and waited, coolly enough, until they had finished. I saw Flavia looking at me sideways, a curious, slightly treacherous smile at the corner of her mouth. Maurizio, on the other hand, had his profile turned towards me and once again looked like a Renaissance page in a little picture in a museum. Since the young people still continued to shout that I was a worm, Flavia, as though urged by an irresistible impulse, moved suddenly towards the microphone and, before I had time to draw back, passed between me and the table. But it was a narrow space, and so Flavia, as she passed, could not help rubbing her behind against my belly.

This, it appeared, was what 'he' had been waiting for for some time. Immediately I felt his proportions changing (this was his way of expressing himself; and there was nothing to be done) and there he was, whispering to me feverishly: 'Hey, what did I tell you? What about it? Who was right? What d'you think? She did it on purpose. In the garden she had "looked" at me. Now she wanted to "feel" me.'

'It's not true.'

'What isn't true?'

'That she wanted to "feel" you.'

'But I'm telling you that – '

'Don't tell me anything. Just as, a short time ago, she didn't look at you, so now she didn't feel you. You're an incorrigible liar.'

'Supposing I provide you with a proof that – '

264

'You won't be able to provide any "real" proof. It will simply be a matter of one of those illusions, those mirages which are your own speciality.'

'Well, give me a free hand and I will – '

'For goodness' sake! Supposing the proof fails? And Flavia shames me in front of this species of tribunal? I can already hear her saying: "Not content with having betrayed us, the worm, at this very moment, has played another of his tricks: he has been disrespectful to me," etc., etc. For goodness' sake!'

Meanwhile Flavia, stooping over the microphone, was saying: 'Rico has made his self-criticism. Now you must say whether you accept it and whether you agree that he should continue to work with Maurizio. Or whether you would prefer Maurizio to choose another collaborator.'

Click. The yellow light. They applauded Flavia in the same uneven manner, like a Morse code, with which they had clapped their hands for Maurizio shortly before. The applause, however, lasted longer, in homage, perhaps, to the mistress of the house. Thus I had the means of turning my attention to 'him'.

Careless of my warning, there was every sign that 'he' was now seeking to provide the proof of Flavia's complicity; she, after she had spoken, had remained leaning forward with the palms of her hands resting on the table. In this waiting, listening position her body almost formed a right angle and her behind was sticking out. And so, what did 'he' do? Although perfectly conscious that Flavia's attitude was not intentional, suddenly, with unexpected impetus, he dragged me forward towards her. And certainly he would have succeeded, according to his usual famous expression, in 'establishing direct contact', if I, recovering from my first moment of surprise, had not checked his bold, unseemly thrust with an energetic counter-thrust backwards.

Angrily, sorrowfully, 'he' protested: 'But why? She's asking for nothing better. Don't you see that she's placed herself in that position deliberately for my benefit? Why do you always have to be so timid and so cowardly?'

'I'm not timid and I'm not cowardly. But I don't want you to provide me with any proof, at any rate not here.'

'Why not here?'

'Because it doesn't do to mix the sacred with the profane. Everything in its own time and place. They hate me, they've laid a trap for me, that may be so. But we are still concerned with a meeting that has a particular aim and, whether you like it or not, a character – what shall I say? – of a certain respectability. You, on the other hand, in your sadistic way, wish to commit a kind of profanation, to cause a kind of contamination.'

'What are you talking about?'

'Get on with you, I know you. Your desire isn't frank and simple and crude, as on other occasions. It arises, instead, from a confused, twisted impulse of revenge: "Ah, so you repress me, you sublimate me! And I avenge myself, under your very eyes, by making an assault on Flavia's buttocks." You must admit, if you're honest, that that's how things stand.'

'I admit nothing. And as for sacred and profane, will you or won't you realize that the sacred is on my side and the profane on theirs?'

During this squabble, quick as lightning as usual, the lights moved from yellow to green. The applause stopped. Flavia stood up straight and said: 'Livio.'

Livio got up from the second row, came up to the table, took possession of the microphone. He was a short young man, minute and slim, narrow in the shoulders and hips, with a small, snake-like head, snub-nosed, blunt features and a dark complexion. He wore a yellow sleeveless pullover and green trousers. Without looking at me, he said hurriedly: 'I'm of the opinion that Maurizio should change his collaborator. Rico has confessed that he's a worm. What I say is: where's the sense of working with a worm?'

Sublimated! Completely sublimated! I felt this instinctively from the cutting, angular, dry, methodical quality that emanated from his whole person. The lights gave a click, and the yellow light started a lengthy, rhythmical applause;

266

Livio threw me a curious, challenging glance, shrugged his shoulders and went away. The lights changed again. 'Ernesto!' said Flavia.

It was Ernesto's turn. Fair-haired, with a red face and blue eyes. Not so very tall, but broad-shouldered, in a white sleeveless vest and trousers with broad stripes, like a planter from the Antilles. His bare arms, bulging and strong, were reddened by the summer sun. There was a look of wildness and of fatuousness about his eyes and mouth. He, of course, like Livio, was sublimated; but with a different kind of sublimation, less cerebral, more muscular. In a harsh, virile voice, like a he-goat's, he pronounced: 'There are mercenaries fighting for capitalism in the Congo. And there are those who are fighting for the same capitalism in quieter areas, for instance in the Italian cinema. The places are different, but all the rest remains the same. I share Livio's opinion: let us send the mercenary back home.'

Click. The yellow light. Ernesto went away, to a rhythmic applause like that which had greeted Livio but of greater warmth. Obviously the metaphor of the mercenary had pleased them. The green light came on and Flavia said: 'Bruno!'

A veritable bear came forward. Fat, tired-looking, listless, massive, in a thin black sweater that stuck to his chest and paunch. Linen trousers, also black. Open sandals. There was a band of white skin between his sweater and his trousers. His feet, too, were very white. His fat, bulging neck towered above his sweater, supporting, from the chin upwards, a face that was also bear-like, with a snub nose, a low forehead, hair *en brosse*. Bruno considered me for a moment in silence, and I had time to work out, in his case too, the hypothesis of a sublimation which was perhaps analogous to Protti's and was due to physical insufficiency or positive atrophy. Then Bruno, verbally sluggish but eloquent and as if to imply that it was not worth while to waste breath on a worm like me, held out his thick white arm with his fist closed and his thumb turned down. No doubt this was a souvenir of some historical film with a Roman subject; or possibly of an illustration in a school history book. He remained for a moment with his 'thumbs down' gesture well in view so that they could all interpret his gesture correctly, then he lowered his arm, shook his head, just like a bear which has devoured a small fish, turned heavily round and went off. Seen from behind, one was struck by his almost complete lack of buttocks and by the wide separation of his monumental legs, of the type commonly called bandy-legs. The usual obligatory applause broke out. The yellow light was replaced by the green. 'Patrizia,' said Flavia.

Patrizia, who was sitting in the front row, reached the table in one step. Sublimated? Certainly. In the obtuse, constipated manner of girls brought up by conventional parents with the sole object of making a successful marriage. She was dark, with a pretty, regular-featured, pink-enamelled face, like a china doll or a wax madonna; her eyes large and black and gentle; her nose tiny and blunt-tipped; her mouth heart-shaped. Her soft bosom swelled tenderly under her pale blue and green striped sweater. Very narrow white trousers tightly enclosed legs that might have been machine-turned. Visibly troubled, slightly breathless in fact, she stared at me with childish hatred. Or possibly she was hating her own hand which was stuck into one of the two front pockets of her trousers and which, as she looked at me, she was trying, without success, to extract. Then, all of a sudden, the hand came flying out abruptly. The fist was closed, as though Patrizia had grasped something at the bottom of her pocket. Hastily, clipping her words, she cried: 'This is my answer!' At the same time she raised her arm and threw a handful of little ten-lire coins into my face.

What happened to me then? All at once something inside me was let loose, dissolved, released. And then it rose up and up to my brain. It was like a snake, a living snake of creative energy which, from the bottom of my back, climbed rapidly up my spine to the back of my neck, up to the exalted place where thought is formed. Could this be sublimation? In any case, I felt myself transported into a new dimension, lighter, freer, wider. Driven on by a superlative, unpremeditated

268

force, I leant forward and spat in the face of the pretty girl who had thrown the coins.

The spittle caught her on the cheek, under her right eye. I saw her put her hand to her pocket, pull out a handkerchief and slowly wipe her face. Then the delicious creature came up so close to me that her nose was almost touching the tip of mine and hissed into my face: 'Bourgeois!'

I was too well pleased, too proud of my unexpected, triumphal entry into the club of the sublimated to be offended by Patrizia's insult. In fact, as she walked back to her place with a pronounced but still elegant swaying of her curving hips, I followed her with a look that was full of gratitude. I owed her no small debt, no less, indeed, than my advancement from a state of abject desublimation to one of (I hoped) decisive sublimation. I heard, as in a dream, the click of the lights announcing a change of colour; then the usual applause broke out. First there was a long handclap, then three short ones, then a long one again. The young people were all on their feet. They were clapping their hands and repeating: 'Fla – via, Fla – via, Fla – via!'

Flavia came forward again, right in front of me as I stood, now, a little back. The audience continued the carefully articulated chorus of her name; several times she raised her thin arm and her long, white freckled hand, as though begging them to be silent. But they persisted with their applause; and then Flavia bent forward with her hands resting on the tablecloth, as she had done earlier, her body forming a right angle and her backside sticking out. My joy at having achieved, all at once and without effort, the progress from desublimation to sublimation that I had so longed for, had distracted my attention. But 'his' attention, alas, had not been distracted. For 'him', the sight of Flavia bending over the table, and his own excitement, were one and the same thing.

At the same moment, with real, genuine horror and unspeakable, helpless dismay, I felt that the snake of creative energy which shortly before, when I had spat in Patrizia's face, had climbed right up into my brain and was comfortably coiled there without seeming to feel any wish to move; I felt, I

269

say, that the snake was now uncoiling, was leaving my head and making its way, head downwards, along my spinal column, in a return journey. I wanted to halt it, I wanted to shout at it to turn back, I wanted, so to speak, to seize it by the tail: but it was all useless. It came down more and more rapidly, more and more determinedly, head downwards; and as fast as it came down, 'he', revived and, as it were, nourished by the sight of Flavia's buttocks, grew and rose up and became hard and huge.

Meanwhile the refrain had ceased. Without altering her stooping position, Flavia put her mouth close to the microphone and started to speak in a 'smart society' tone of voice, snobbish and slightly haughty, yet proving that she was flattered and moved: 'Thank you, thank you, thank you from my heart for the confidence in me which you show. I haven't much to say. I feel, however, that I ought to speak, if you will allow it, from the personal point of view, if I may put it like that? Well, as you probably know already, when we composed the theme of the film, Maurizio and I, we took your humble servant as model for the character of Isabella. And who am I? Or rather, who do I think I am, who do I hope to be? Well, I would like to say: all that you wish me to be, but not one of the usual dolls of the bourgeoisie. That, if you will excuse my presumption, I am not, really I am not. And in fact the character of Isabella, in our script, was not a doll, quite the contrary.

'Who was Isabella? Isabella was a comrade who, after the failure of the attempted expropriation, was instructed by the group to write a critical report to be read at a debate on the causes of the said failure. The reading of the report, to be done by the off-screen voice of Isabella, was to be a running commentary on the film which, finally, was to take the shape of a simple flash-back, recalling the facts, of course, but also, above all, self-critical. When the reading of the report came to an end, the film came to an end too. The group then recognized that the attempt at expropriation had failed and, after thanking Isabella for her report, decided unanimously to set up a research committee to work out and prepare a new operation of expropriation. This was the Isabella of our script, inspired – allow me to say this, comrades, without false modesty – by what I am and what I really feel I am.

'Now what did Rico do? To begin with, Isabella did not read any report, nor was there any revolutionary group to listen to it. Isabella was a young, rich, bourgeois lady, mother of two children and married to Rodolfo, who had now come to his senses, was integrated, and had become a university professor in a provincial town. In spite of her fine house full of books and furnished with every convenience, in spite of her money, her children and her husband, Isabella was bored. Then she began to recall, in an off-screen voice full of nostalgia, a now far-distant episode of her youth. Evidently that had been a very lovely period in Isabella's life. In fact, to make use of Rico's own words, the "heroic period" of life, during which even people who are predestined for a vegetable life, such as Isabella, believe in a whole lot of stupid, senseless things, as, for instance, that the world can be changed for the better; and do a whole lot of foolish, imprudent things, such as, for instance, forming a revolutionary group. At the end of her recollections of the heroic period of her life, her husband arrives, tired and happy, from the university, where he has given a fine lecture on some classic or other of Italian literature. Isabella and Rodolfo embrace and the whole thing concludes with a beautiful conjugal kiss, as in the films of the thirties.

'I said I was speaking from a personal point of view. And that is the absolute truth. I ask you all, in fact: can you really believe that in a few years' time I shall be married to Maurizio – a Maurizio who has come to his senses and is integrated – and that I shall be living in the provinces and shall have a swarm of children and shall consider these years that we are now going through as the heroic period of my life, etc., etc.? Tell me whether I ought not to consider it an insult – such an interpretation of my modest character, which, I don't deny, may be full of defects but is certainly not as Rico has described it in his version.

'Thank you for having had the patience to listen to my

271

personal point of view. Thank you, thank you, my heartfelt thanks to you all.'

Click. Flavia was silent, still bending forward, and so she remained while the green light changed to yellow and a well-disciplined rhythmic chorus of handclapping broke out.

She was stooping over the table; then, as though to stretch her tired knees, she suddenly altered the position of her legs. Her right leg was bent forward, her left extended backward. Flavia now bent her left leg forward and extended her right leg backward.

And then, against my will, the detested 'direct contact' took place, about which 'he', evidently, in spite of my prohibition, had never ceased to think the whole time.

At the very moment when Flavia, in changing her attitude, gave two abrupt jerks with her pelvis, one to the right and one to the left, 'he' shoved me forward, impetuously, taking me by surprise. Caught by the movement of her buttocks, 'he' was struck first from the right and then from the left, like one of those oval balls hanging from gymnasium ceilings to be hit by boxers in training, with alternate blows from each of their gloves.

This pushing back and forth lasted no more than a second, for Flavia, clearly, was conscious of the inopportune, ill-bred approach and straightened herself up in a great hurry, as if she had been scalded.

Deeply irritated by his disobedience, I exclaimed: 'Serves you right: you wanted to gain the upper hand and now you're punished. Unfortunately, however, the one who will now be involved will be me, as usual. And how indeed can I possibly justify your indecent behaviour to Flavia?'

'He' did not answer me. For a moment, in a simple-minded way, I attributed his silence to an understandable mortification.

Alas, how wrong I was! All of a sudden, to my unspeakable confusion, treacherously, and with the ease and spontaneity and insensibility of resin trickling from a tree-trunk, 'he' discharged himself, or rather, 'he' poured himself down between my legs. And with such effortless, uninteresting

272

facility that I would scarcely have noticed it unless I had become aware of the warm, thick flow of the ejaculation on my skin, on the inside of my thigh.

It is difficult to describe my feelings when confronted with that abominable creature's indecent treachery. I was, alas, in company with Flavia and Maurizio behind a table at a debate, in full view of the meeting of a revolutionary group. But I believe that, if I had been alone, I should have screamed with rage, bitten my hands, torn my hair, beaten my head against a wall, scratched my face and rolled on the ground. Perhaps I might even have been capable of putting into effect that old threat of mine, grasping a razor and cutting 'him' off at the base with a single blow.

I thought of all these things and at the same time had a furious feeling of remorse such as, I imagine, must have assailed the hermits of the Thebaid when, in the solitude of their caves, they had failed to resist the subtle, surprising temptations of the most imaginative of the devils. My groin wet and sticky, my whole body turned to stone, my mind overcome by an enormous confusion, I stood quite still and was scarcely aware of what was happening around me.

Luckily the situation was abruptly relieved and brought hurriedly to an unexpected conclusion, thanks to an apparently commonplace but in reality significant incident.

The handclapping for Flavia went on for as long as the yellow light which had started continued to shine. Things went on like this for quite a long time: the young people clapped their hands; Flavia, no longer stooping forward but erect, as though at attention, her arms at her sides, politely acknowledged the applause; Maurizio, for his part, was more than ever immovable and expressionless; and I myself, standing behind them, was struggling against the discomfort and anger that consumed me.

Then it became strangely evident that the handclapping was being prolonged beyond the estimated limits. The yellow light continued to shine; but a certain tiredness, a kind of disorder appeared to creep into the rhythm of the applause which by this time was no longer so strict.

Finally, when the yellow light persisted, the applause broke down. Some of the young people went on clapping with the same rhythm; others clapped without any rhythm; others again were no longer clapping at all. Suddenly a voice emerged, isolated, from this confusion, and protested jokingly: 'Hi there, when are you going to stop? Our hands are beginning to hurt.' Immediately they all stopped applauding. Flavia drew herself up and, in the silence, inquired: 'What's the matter, Paolo?'

I watched the young man in charge of the black box at the far end of the room as he angrily pressed the knobs, one after the other. Then Paolo, in a voice of exasperation, replied: 'The matter is that thing is no longer working.'

'Try again.'

'It's no use trying: it's stuck with the applause.'

'You mean the yellow light?'

'Exactly.'

Flavia did not lose heart; she turned serenely to Maurizio and said: 'The lights are no longer working. I should think we might bring the session to an end for today.'

Maurizio nodded his head, went to the microphone and said: 'Owing to a technical hitch, we find ourselves compelled to bring the session to an end. I propose therefore that we should accept Rico's self-criticism provisionally and postpone the conclusion of the debate to a date in the near future. In the meantime Rico and I will go on with the script, keeping to the proper, correct original version formerly worked out by Flavia and myself and unanimously approved by the group.'

He stopped speaking and drew back. At once Flavia went forward and announced: 'And now some long, sincere, warm applause for our beloved president.'

The young people all jumped to their feet and clapped their hands. Since there were no lights, it was applause of the traditional type, spontaneous and disordered. In spite of my confusion, I could not resist quietly asking Flavia: 'Who is the president?'

'It's Maurizio.'

The applause lasted a minute and a half; I timed it

furtively by my wrist-watch. After the applause, the young people got to their feet and, amid a noise of chairs being moved, went off, a few at a time, by a door at the far end of the room. I watched them, in a stupefied sort of way. And then, suddenly, 'his' voice – no, I was not mistaken, it was really 'his' voice – whispering to me: 'Come on, now, confess: wasn't it wonderful?'

Dazed as I was, I did not know how to answer him. 'He' persisted: 'Why are you so furious? Don't you realize that Flavia, at the very moment when the boys of the group were yelling "Worm" at you, was wanting you as her king? Don't you realize that, at the moment when they were all raging against you, with their real, pre-arranged lynching, it was just as if she had cried out: "Yes, this is my king and I am his queen"?'

I had no wish to answer him. If I had answered, I should have had to say: I persist in believing that Flavia was not concerned. But, even supposing that you are right, the matter does not concern *me*. For that reason, I beg you not to bring me into it. I know nothing about it. The whole business was between you and Flavia.

Answering him would have meant, actually, taking him seriously. And taking him seriously would have meant forgiving him. And I, at that moment, was angry with him, I detested and hated him. So I clenched my teeth, frowned and followed Maurizio and Flavia out of the room in silence. Some object or other was worrying me, between my neck and my vest. I put my hand to it, took hold of it and looked. It was one of the small ten-lire coins that my attractive challenger, Patrizia, had thrown in my face, shortly before, as a sign of contempt.

11 Fooled!

A double visit, that day, first Flavia and then Maurizio. Let us begin with Flavia.

The doorbell rang at an unusual time: three o'clock in the afternoon, and it was a Sunday, at the end of July. Envisaging the only two reasonable hypotheses – a telegram or a mistake – I got down from the bed on which I was resting, hastily donned a dressing-gown, went to open the door and almost bumped my nose against the voluminous bulge created by Flavia's bosom under her usual crooked little dress. I looked so astonished that she made it into a pretext for bursting out laughing, with a kind of laughter, however, that was forced and frivolous and that seemed to me to conceal some embarrassment.

'Why, aren't you ashamed?' she exclaimed. 'When you come to open the door you should at least close the front of your dressing-gown.'

It was true; in my haste, I had left my dressing-gown hanging open over my bare, hairy legs and even a little higher up. Feeling confused, I closed it, and followed Flavia as she now walked in front of me, making her way with a strange deliberateness (for she had never been there before) in the direction of my bedroom. I hurried after her. 'No, not that way,' I said; 'let's go into my study.'

'Why? Where does this lead to?'

'Into my bedroom.'

'Well, let's go into your bedroom.'

'It's all untidy; I was resting.'

'I don't mind about the untidiness.'

There was an ingenuous note of challenge in her voice, which, naturally, did not escape 'him'. 'He' whispered to me, indeed, with his usual insufferable vanity: 'She's come for me.'

Flavia opened the door. In the room the window was shut

and the light was on. Since it was Sunday, it had not been cleaned and tidied since Saturday morning. The bed was unmade, the air was tainted and full of a mingled smell of sleep and stuffiness and cigarette smoke. Flavia looked round and again burst out laughing. 'What a bare room!' she exclaimed. 'Nothing but a bed and a chair. I'll sit on the bed and you on the chair. Or vice versa.'

I said nothing. I went to the window and pulled first the cord of the curtain, then that of the roller blind. The room, facing north, was filled with a strong but indirect light. I explained: 'I don't like furniture. Besides, this place is only temporary.'

'Why temporary?'

'I'm going to live here for a year. Then I shall go back and live with my wife.'

'You have a wife?'

'I have a wife and a son.'

'And why don't you live with them?'

'We decided, my wife and I, in full agreement, to live apart for some time. I needed to be alone, to concentrate, to take my life in hand.'

'To concentrate or to live like a pig?'

Her question, uttered in a tone of candid and almost flattering provocativeness, exploded in the air like a harmless soap-bubble. She went over and stood at the corner of the window and in a playful sort of way took hold of the curtain-cord and twirled the leaden counterweight. I also went over to the window and stood at the opposite side. I replied calmly: 'To concentrate.'

It was I myself, of course, who was calm. 'He', on the other hand, was by now in a state of such agitation that, almost mechanically, I put my hand into the pocket of my dressing-gown, took hold of 'him' through the silken material and twisted him half round, crushing him against my stomach so that he should be seen as little as possible. But my manœuvre did not escape Flavia, who swung the counterweight of the curtain-cord straight in the direction of my pocket, saying: 'Concentrate, eh? No, you're just a pig. Take that hand out!'

She spoke in a shrill, aggressive voice, clear and silvery in tone. I protested: 'But I . . . '

'Take it out, pig! Can't you see you're just a pig?'

Resigned, I pulled out my hand; while 'he', insufferable creature, whispered: 'Well done, Flavia! Quite right! Why hide me? Why hide the beauty of the world?' My dressing-gown was now no longer in very good order; but, after all, what could I do about it if an understanding had suddenly been arrived at between 'him' and Flavia, overriding me, depriving me of authority, and from which I felt myself excluded?

Flavia leant her head back against the wall and stuck out her stomach. Underneath her dress the sharp bones of her pelvis stood out; her crotch was a convex, oval swelling. She was gazing at me, smiling slightly with her thin lips, looking more ghost-like, more equine than ever, with her long, white, freckled face surrounded by its great mane of red hair. Meanwhile her hand was shaking and twirling the counter-weight of the curtain-cord. Then she asked: 'Are you a great friend of Maurizio?'

'We're friends, certainly.'

'Are you sure you're a friend of his?'

Bump! The counterweight, swung forward by that long, thin, white hand, came and struck 'him', with remarkable precision, on the back. A hard blow which, of course, made him cockier than ever. I answered Flavia: 'Yes, I'm sure of it.'

'I myself, on the contrary, don't think you are.'

Bump! Another blow from the counterweight. 'He', jubilantly, kept count: 'That makes two.' 'What makes you think that?' I inquired.

'The fact that you're a pig.'

'That's no answer.'

'What d'you mean, it's no answer? A pig can't help betraying his friends, that is, he can't help behaving like a pig.'

'And who says so?'

'That you're a pig? *I* say so.'

'I've never betrayed anybody.'

Bump! 'That makes three,' 'he' exclaimed, in an ecstasy

of joy. Flavia smiled benignly, treacherously. 'Oh really?' she said. 'And what did you do the other day during the debate? You behaved like a pig, as always.'

'What d'you mean?'

'What? So that's it, is it? The pig denies having behaved like a pig.'

Bump! 'He' was counting again: 'That makes four.' In exasperation I exclaimed: 'Stop calling me a pig! And stop playing with that counterweight!'

Flavia smiled in a strange way, with a wise, indulgent smile, as though my protest seemed to her a just one. '*You* stop, first. Don't you realize that you're indecent? I'm a woman, and you owe me respect. Where's your respect, pig that you are?'

Bump! 'He', in his delight, actually counted wrong. 'That makes seven,' he said. Angrily, I mentally corrected him: It's not seven, or even six, but only five. Then I asked Flavia:

'Will you kindly tell me, then, what you want of me?'

'To admit that you're a pig.'

Bump, bump! Now it was not a single blow but two at the same time. 'He', meanwhile, was storming at me: 'Let me go free, let me come out. I want her to see me, I want her to admire me, I want her to acknowledge, in me, the beauty of the world.' I asked Flavia: 'What must I do, in your opinion, to admit that I'm a pig?'

This time, strangely enough, she did not speak, nor did she swing the counterweight. Instead, she made a curious gesture with her hand, at the same time both impatient and imperious, towards my dressing-gown, the sort of gesture, I could not help thinking, that might be made by someone who, when officially unveiling a monument, gives a sign for the covering sheet to be removed.

I did not move, although 'he', driven nearly mad, was shouting: 'Come on, set me free, display me, exhibit me!' Then Flavia took a step forward, put out her hand, pulled the end of the dressing-gown cord, the knot of which at once came undone, took hold of the edge of my dressing-gown and pulled it open. So there I was naked, a whole vertical strip of me from my feet up to my chin; but Flavia, still not content, stretched out her arm again and enlarged the opening. Then she took a step back and said, between clenched teeth: 'There's the proof now that you're the greatest pig in the world.'

What a lot of pleasure she derived from calling me a pig! And with what hypnotized eagerness did she fix her big, pale eyes upon 'him' as 'he' now, at the peak of exaltation, rose up and formed an acute angle with my stomach! I kept still, and once again had the disconcerting impression that it was not I, but only 'he', that had been laid bare by Flavia. 'He', exclusively. I myself, enveloped in my modesty, was somewhere else, somewhere or other, and had nothing to do with it, did not share in it, did not count. As usual, the relationship was between 'him' and Flavia, solely between those two.

Flavia, in the meantime, was twirling the counterweight in the air, like a top; then, all of a sudden and perhaps without intending to, she swung it in 'his' direction, in such a way that it struck him right on the tip. I could not suppress a cry of pain. Flavia immediately exclaimed, in a sorrowful voice: 'I'm sorry, I didn't mean to do it, I'm sorry.' Then she took a step forward, put out her hand and rapidly stroked 'him' with the tips of her long, thin fingers, inquiring apprehensively, solicitously, affectionately: 'Does it hurt?'

I shook my head. At the same time I could not help noting that Flavia's remark confirmed the exclusive relationship between herself and 'him'. She had said, in fact: 'Does it hurt?' and not, for example, 'Do you feel any pain?' She now let her hand fall to her side but did not take her eyes off 'him', repeating, as though talking to herself: 'What a pig you are! You can't deny, now, that you're a pig. There can't be many pigs like you, in fact there can't be any. You're the greatest pig I've ever met in my life.'

She spoke as if she were alone. In reality she was speaking to 'him'. It was about 'him' that she was thinking, not me. Again I had the feeling, fundamentally reassuring, of a relationship between 'him' and Flavia which excluded me and relieved me of all responsibility. It was a mysterious relationship, for 'he', usually so loquacious, was now dumb; and Flavia,

280

for her part, did nothing but repeat mechanically that 'pig' insult, as though it were the ritual epithet of some magic formula.

All of a sudden I remembered the god Fascinus whom 'he' was accustomed to claim as his ancestor, in the grotesque learned discussions between us. That was how things were, it was true, that was exactly how things were: 'he' was Fascinus, the god who fascinates; and Flavia was the person fascinated. I now understood why neither 'he' nor Flavia spoke; and once again, and with greater reason, I felt excluded. Unfortunately, however, my feeling of exclusion expressed itself in this incautious remark: 'I've already told you not to call me a pig. The pig is not me but "him". And stop exciting him!'

I was forgetting, when I spoke like this, that the split in my personality between 'him' and me was an entirely private and jealously kept secret of mine which hitherto I had revealed to no one.

Unexpectedly, Flavia at once grasped the true meaning of my words. She stepped back, returning to her same corner, and gave a mischievous laugh. 'But who is "he"?' she asked.

Embarrassed, I kept silent. At the same moment, I don't know how, my dressing-gown slipped off my shoulders and there I was completely naked and, with my stocky, robust body and 'him' sticking out, gigantically, from it, resembling a big, twisted tree-trunk with a single large, sinewy, leafless stump rising from it. Flavia again gave her clear, silvery laugh, like that of a hysterical schoolgirl. '"He" . . . so that's "he"? And you speak of him as if he were a person independent of you? Perfectly correct. And I bet that this person has a name, isn't that so?'

Disconcerted by her acuteness, I murmured: 'Federicus Rex.'

'Federicus Rex? Quite right, you're called Federico and he's called Federicus. But why Rex? There must be a reason, I imagine. Possibly because he's . . . so regal? In any case, according to you, it's not you who is the pig, but "he". That's right, too. But also convenient. I, for instance, don't make any difference between myself and "her". If I were a sow, so would "she" be, and vice versa. It goes without saying that I don't give "her" any kind of name. In any case my name is the same in Italian as in Latin: Flavia.'

'Regina.'

'What d'you mean, regina?'

'Flavia Regina, Queen Flavia.'

'Ha, ha, that's true, I hadn't thought of it: Federicus Rex and Flavia Regina. Two monarchs, two crowned personages, two potentates: king and queen. The last king and the last queen: Federicus Rex and Flavia Regina. Once upon a time there was a king, once upon a time there was a queen. Ha, ha, ha, what a pretty story!'

She laughed till she cried, bent double, her hand to her stomach. What happened to me then? Suddenly, the thing that I had feared came to pass. My feeling of exclusion and neutrality in face of the relationship between 'him' and Flavia was reduced all at once to a willing and disastrous identification. I left it to 'him'; I gave him his head; I let him take the initiative. And 'he' took it, did he take it indeed! Stark naked, I rushed suddenly upon Flavia, with 'him' oscillating stiffly in the air in front of me, like the antenna of a tram that has come unhooked from the cable. I seized hold of Flavia. not by her arms or hands, but directly at the spot where, under her dress, was hidden the thing which I had just baptized by the name of Flavia Regina. And so, for a moment, through the thin stuff of her dress, I gripped the thing that had been the real partner in the conversation with 'him'. But it was only for a moment. Immediately I was caught by a slap hard enough to make my head reel. I tried to catch hold of the hand that had hit me: another slap. Then Flavia fled across the room, a white, freckled, long-limbed nymph pursued by a lusty-membered imitation of a satyr. I tried to grasp her, but Flavia was extremely agile and eluded me every time I was on the point of catching her. Meanwhile, in a voice which was not in the least troubled but, on the contrary, disagreeably reasonable, she ordered: 'Leave me alone, you're mad, I tell you, leave me alone!'

Yes indeed, I was mad. My madness consisted in my having by this time completely surrendered myself, without restraint, to my inveterate desublimation. Flavia and I were now face to face, with the bed between us, breathless – a situation from a light comedy film of the thirties, to which 'he', however, still in a state of exaltation, added a detail of a somewhat unexpected kind. Flavia kept her eye on me, watching my movements closely. Then, suddenly, she leant forward and cried: 'D'you know why I came to see you today?'

'Why?'

'To tell you that we have no intention of entrusting you with the job of directing our film. And you know why? Because my father and Protti have decided to give the job to Maurizio.'

I was so dismayed that I became suddenly rational. 'Then why,' I stammered, 'why not have let me know this before the debate?'

'What has the debate got to do with it? The debate was not concerned with the directing of the film but with the script. You won't be the director but you'll still be the script-writer.'

'You ought to have told me, all the same.'

'We didn't know. It was decided only yesterday.'

'And you came to tell me this today?'

'Precisely. Since I shall be assistant director and Maurizio felt a little embarrassed, I told him that I would see about informing you. But now let me go. If you touch me, I'll scream.'

I had no intention of touching her. I had now got the upper hand of 'him'; and furthermore he himself, in a moment, had adjusted himself to the new situation and had weakened and drooped and languished. I now saw myself as I really was, naked and ridiculous and despairing. I heard Flavia say good-bye, but I did not raise my head. After a little the front door closed with a minimum of noise, politely. Alas! I lowered my eyes and looked at 'him'. He was small, shrunken, creased, shrivelled, decrepit: a little circle of wrinkled tripe. I said to him, then, with a sigh: 'Now I'm left with only one card to play: Mafalda. Everything depends on you, entirely on you.' At the same moment the front doorbell rang.

12 Fascinated!

I went to open the door. I almost jumped backwards in surprise: it was Maurizio. With his black glasses and his black shoes, his white shirt and his white suit. He behaved in his usual way, passing by me without saying a word, walking in front of me towards my study, keeping his hands in his pockets. I followed, disconcerted: possibly he had been down in the street waiting for Flavia; possibly he knew that I, or rather 'he', had assaulted Flavia. I was seized with an abrupt, distressing feeling of guilt. Frightened, I foresaw that Maurizio would say something to me, just one sentence but of the scorching kind that only the sublimated are capable of uttering, which would fill me with shame and crush me completely. But no, I was wrong. Maurizio merely inquired, in a careless manner: 'Is it long since Flavia left?'

Obviously he was lying. He was pretending that he had not been waiting for Flavia downstairs; that he did not know that 'he' had caused me to assault Flavia. Why should he be lying? Probably in order to lure me into one of the customary traps. I decided to find out the lie of the land by denying, positively, that Flavia had come to see me. Pretending to be surprised, I replied: 'Was Flavia supposed to be coming here? I haven't seen her.'

He said nothing, he showed no feeling; as usual he was refusing to give me satisfaction. He threw himself into the armchair and lit a cigarette. In the meantime, as I said before, I was studying the lie of the land. My untruthfulness was all at once revealed to me as being both useful and fertile. In fact by denying that Flavia had come, I had also denied, implicitly, that I knew I could no longer count on the director's job; and thus I was in a position to reverse the situation between Maurizio and myself. A poor consolation, but a consolation nevertheless; I could behave like the fox with the grapes in the fable, that is, I could make a sensational renunciation of something that had already been refused me. I would show myself indignant at the treatment that had been inflicted upon me at Fregene; I would shout that I had had enough of him and of Flavia and of the whole lot of them; I would declare that I no longer had any wish to go on working with him on the script. A good idea!

All this, of course, would take place as if in a play, in which my own pretence would compel Maurizio also to pretend. For Maurizio knew that Flavia had been to see me, since he himself had sent her; and he knew that Flavia had told me not to go on counting upon the job of director, since he himself had charged her to tell me. Never mind: he would be bound, even for a few minutes, to play the game and accept the fact that I was refusing what he had already, previously, denied me. Sitting down at the table and turning slightly towards Maurizio, I said: 'You ought to have telephoned before coming.'

'Why?'

'Because I might not have been here. Or I might have had somebody with me.'

'In that case all you had to do was not to open the door.'

'Excuse me: suppose I hadn't wanted to see you, after what happened at Fregene?'

'D'you want me to go away?'

'No. Now that you've come, I prefer it so. I'll take advantage of it to speak to you with complete frankness.'

He said nothing. I rose and started walking up and down the room. As I walked, I launched out into the following Philippic: 'Let us put our cards on the table, let us both throw away our masks, let us talk as man to man. Well then, I must tell you that your conduct the other day at the meeting of the group was indescribable. In what way? I had asked you to introduce me to the group for no ulterior motive, out of pure ideological enthusiasm. As a proof of the genuineness of my revolutionary sentiments, I handed over to you five million lire, no contemptible sum in any case and, in relation to my own means, positively enormous. And you, by way of thanks, lured me into a trap, caught me in an ambush. In order not to arouse my suspicions, you assured me, in mellifluous tones, that there would be a debate on a high cultural level; that they were all expecting me with sympathy and curiosity; that my contribution of five million had been duly appreciated. Confidently and calmly, convinced that I was about to participate in a frank, fertile, useful exchange of ideas, in an honest and illuminating encounter between two generations, I went with you to Fregene, to Flavia's villa. But, be that as it may, as soon as I entered the room in which the meeting was being held, I found myself faced with a ridiculous trial, or rather, a grotesque attempt at a moral lynching. With the group forming the tribunal; with yourself acting as public prosecutor; with Flavia as clerk of the court; with a whole absurd judicial ritual staged and organized to the smallest detail, on a basis of traffic lights, of green, red and yellow lights and prefabricated applause, as though an ideological debate could be regulated by the same standards as are valid for street traffic.

'So there I was, defenceless, unprepared, unarmed and unsuspecting, faced with thirty persons – but why should I call them persons – with thirty wolves, thirty hyenas in fact, coldly resolved to tear me in pieces. As for yourself, not content with having treacherously deceived me by luring me into the ambush, you then placed yourself at the head of the brilliant and courageous operation. Throwing off the kindly mask of a friend, you showed your true face as an enemy. You denounced me publicly as a traitor, an informer, a counter-revolutionary influence and I don't know what else; that was not enough: you derided my contribution of five million. After your indictment, the trial began. Trial? I should say, rather, summary execution. Any intervention on my part was greeted by hostile choruses; yours, and those of Flavia and of the group, by unconditioned applause; the whole thing regulated by the grotesque workings of the ridiculous, police-like traffic lights. I was insulted, attacked and condemned by youths who only yesterday were wearing shorts; handfuls of coins were thrown in my face by dolls from a seaside beauty

286

competition, as if to signify that I was a Judas, a man who had sold himself. Yes, indeed, a man who had sold himself; it would be laughable if it didn't make one weep. A man who had sold himself by giving five million, taking them away from his own family. Five million which, anyhow, I should never have dreamed of earning with a film like *Expropriation*. But we'll let that pass.

'The lynching found its crowning glory in the self-inflicted wounds of the declarations that were extorted from me by the old, tried method of systematic intimidation. At that point, as though it were a matter of no importance, you closed the meeting under the pretext of a breakdown of the lights, thus showing, implicitly, that without the discipline of what we may call street-lighting the group was incapable of carrying on the so-called debate by itself. A fine debate, in truth! With me forced to act the part of an ideological pedestrian, imprudent and absent-minded, predestined to be crushed at the cross-roads of political conformism by you of the group, transformed into so many dogmatic motor-cars impatient to run me over.

'But that was not all. By closing the session you made sure, with enviable brazenness, that all had gone well, both for you of the group and also for me; and that thenceforth there would no longer be any problem. You and I would start work again, good friends as before. Oh no, oh no, oh no! No more of that impertinence! Enough! You don't lynch a man and then come and tell him that all has gone well. That there are no more problems. It's true, in any case: a man who has been lynched *has* no more problems, because he has been liquidated, destroyed, and his problems, logically, have ceased to exist with him. But that's enough!'

I shrugged my shoulders angrily and stopped in front of Maurizio. He remained quiet and still. He did not even raise his eyes: a Renaissance page smoking a filter-tip cigarette. Finally he asked: 'What, in short, do you intend to do?'

'To leave all this.'

'What d'you mean by that?'

'To finish with the script. To stop seeing either you or

Flavia or the group. Never again to hear the *Expropriation* film mentioned.'

'And how about the five million? D'you want the five million given back to you?'

I scented danger. So far, somehow or other, I had kept myself 'on top'; now, craftily, Maurizio was trying to push me back 'underneath'. Shrugging my shoulders, I replied: 'The five million – keep it. I wouldn't know what to do with it.'

'D'you mean that seriously? Why, you've always asserted that those five million represented a great sacrifice for you.'

It was true, he was right; as he always was, in any case. I ought to get those five million given back to me – that at least. But my usual cursed desublimation prevented my admitting that I was burning with the desire to have my money back. As always, if a man is desublimated he will admit anything except that he is so. I answered with another shrug of the shoulders: 'Yes, it certainly was a sacrifice. But now I've stopped thinking about it. I repeat again: I wouldn't know what to do with them. Buy a whole lot of Mao's little red books, to the value of five million!'

'And the directing of the film? Don't you realize that in this way you're finally giving up the job?'

So there we were! I was caught! My back to the wall! In a trap! At the bottom of the pitfall! Maurizio had sent Flavia to announce that I must not count on getting the job of director; but at the same time, as I had foreseen, he was accepting my pretence and asking me whether I intended to give up the idea of that same job which, shortly before, through the mouth of Flavia, he had informed me would not be entrusted to me in any case. And so, if I answered him that I knew everything and was not giving up anything for the good reason that I had already been obliged to give it up, I should be bringing about the collapse of my pretence and admitting that I had lied.

If, on the other hand, I took up a disdainful attitude with regard to the director's job as I had already done about the five million, I should risk compromising, for good and all, the very slight possibility that still *perhaps* remained to me of becoming a director. For it was impossible to know whether Maurizio's question was merely a new example of one of his usual traps, or whether it might conceal a tardy recognition of error. Fundamentally, that would be the only explanation of his precipitate arrival immediately after Flavia's departure. In short, if my supposition were correct, Maurizio must have come to restore the hope that Flavia had taken away from me.

I decided in the end not to compromise myself; and with an air of hesitant, petulant ill-humour, I remarked: 'I would be ready to take up the work again if I could trust you and Flavia and the group.'

'And why don't you trust us?'

'Who could, after the lynching you subjected me to?'

'We didn't lynch you.'

'Oh, really? Let's say then that you prepared an ambush for me and I fell into it.'

'It was a normal meeting of the group to which, in any case, you yourself forced us, inasmuch as we had realized that *we* couldn't trust *you*. As you can see, the two sides during the meeting were exactly the opposite of the way in which *you* look at them. We had every reason to find fault with you; you had no reason to find fault with us.'

'Really, really!'

'You can't deny that you went to Protti and that you tried, by every possible means, to injure us, Rico.'

'Yes, I went to Protti. All the same, things are not like that.'

'How are things, then?'

Again I saw myself thwarted. At the meeting I had admitted that I had gone to see Protti from a 'backwash of bourgeois spirit'; but I had not admitted that I had gone to him to extract a promise concerning the directing of the film, which was, after all, the truth. To admit it now would mean removing all credibility from my self-criticism; and putting my own vulgar, personal profit in place of the 'backwash', which after all was anyhow a psychological motivation of a certain complexity; and this would mean putting myself even more 'underneath' in relation to Maurizio. So I avoided a head-on encounter, and said irritably: 'Things stand in such a way that, instead of the criticism and self-criticism about which you had spoken to me, I found myself faced with real, positive aggressiveness. And don't come and tell me it was a normal meeting. For instance, I'm sure that you and Flavia and the members of the group have never undergone such treatment.'

'How d'you know?'

There was a moment's silence. Then I went on: 'Don't tell me that you and Flavia have had to go through the ritual of the traffic lights, of the prefabricated hostile choruses, of the public confession of crimes you never committed and of coins thrown in your faces.'

'The details were different, but the important thing is that we have been criticized and have criticized ourselves.'

'For having done what?'

'For not having done anything; for being what we are, or rather, what we were.'

'And what is that?'

'Bourgeois, born and brought up in bourgeois families.'

I looked at him and saw that not merely was he serious but also – which was what struck me – he was not *too* serious. Just enough to mention something which, by now, he and the rest of the group considered to be expiated and undisputed. Feeling myself, once again, to be on the point of going 'underneath', I stammered: 'But no one is to be blamed for being what he is. One can be blamed only for doing what one does.'

'Who told you that? There are different kinds of guilt. One can even be guilty for being what one is. All that is needed is to feel acutely guilty about it.'

'If one hasn't done anything bad it's impossible to feel guilty. It doesn't make sense.'

He was not listening to me; he seemed to be following the thread of his own thoughts. At last he said: 'It seems not to mean anything to be born bourgeois. On the other hand, when you dig down all sorts of things come to light.'

'What sort of things?'

'One thinks, in all good faith, that one is a revolutionary. But then one discovers that one has remained bourgeois.'

'One discovers? But how?'

'By what you call a lynching: by criticism and self-criticism.'

'But Flavia, for instance, has she submitted to criticism?'

'Certainly.'

'Has she made a self-criticism?'

'Of course.'

'And what did she say?'

'Plenty of things.'

'Plenty of things?'

'Yes, plenty. More than she foresaw she was going to say.'

'And was she attacked like me?'

'Even worse.'

'Worse?'

'Flavia, in a way, exposed herself to criticism more than you. She is a girl who was born into a certain kind of family, received a certain kind of education, lived for some time in a certain kind of way, has a certain manner of presenting herself and of expressing herself. She was an easy target. And indeed they truly didn't spare her. They said what they thought.'

'Everything?'

'Yes, without any consideration.'

'Did you throw coins in her face?'

'Coins, no. After all, she wasn't working for the system, like you. All she did was to be born in it.'

'And in the end Flavia was humiliated, like me?'

'Much more than you.'

'Why?'

'Between you and Flavia there's this difference, that in your case it was a question of a detail, that is, the film; whereas in Flavia's case it was her whole life that was under accusation.'

'And what did Flavia say about her life?'

'She said that hitherto it had been completely wrong, from top to bottom.'

'How did she say that?'

'Sincerely.'

'What does sincerely mean?'

'It means, for example, with tears.'

'Did Flavia cry?'

'Yes.'

'But why?'

'Because she had repented of having been what she was.'

'And did you do the same as Flavia?'

'Yes.'

'You mean you declared yourself guilty of having been born into a bourgeois family?'

'Yes.'

'With what result?'

'The result, you can see.'

'I don't see anything.'

'You're right, these are not things that one can see. But Flavia and I have transformed ourselves.'

'From what into what?'

'From bourgeois into revolutionaries.'

I now remained silent, seeking to collect my ideas. Evidently Maurizio was telling me the truth, or rather, what he considered to be the truth. As to the transformation of which he spoke, either it had really taken place or else – which came to the same thing – he was genuinely convinced that it had taken place. Except that that was not the point. In reality Flavia and Maurizio had transformed themselves merely by becoming, in an even more emphatic manner, what they had been before. Birds of prey, predestined to fly 'on top'; the revolutionary transformation had simply reversed the direction of their flight, that was all.

I myself, on the other hand, the ground-level worm, had been crawling along 'underneath' before the meeting of the group; and I was continuing to crawl along 'underneath' now, after the meeting. Flavia and Maurizio had simply moved over from bourgeois sublimation to revolutionary sublimation. I, on the contrary, was desublimated, and desublimated had remained.

I looked at Maurizio, and once again I felt myself to be almost a racist, telling myself as before that there were two races of people in the world, the race of those who are sublimated always on all occasions, on the right as on the left; and the race of those who remain desublimated, whether they are reactionary or revolutionary. The world was split in two. I was on one side of the split; Maurizio, Flavia, Protti and plenty of others, on the other side. All the rest was mere idle talk.

At the end of my lengthy reflections, and with a sudden burst of impatience, I said: 'You two have certainly been transformed: if you say so, I have no reason to doubt it. On me, however, the meeting of the group has had no effect at all, even though I was criticized and made an abundant criticism of myself. I have remained exactly as I was. If I was bourgeois, well, I have remained bourgeois.'

'You can't tell. Probably you're on the way to a radical transformation, but you don't realize it.'

'I realize the opposite. That I'm not on the way to any transformation. I have proof of it.'

'What proof?'

'A short time ago I denied that Flavia had been here. I had my reasons. Now I admit it: she did come.'

'Yes, I knew. I waited downstairs the whole time she was with you.'

'Well, I have been so little transformed by criticism and self-criticism that I assaulted her.'

'I knew that too. It was the first thing Flavia told me when she came down.'

'Isn't assaulting a friend's fiancée perhaps a bourgeois way of behaving?'

'It is.'

So there I was, thrust down decisively 'underneath'. Down to the bottom! Without mercy! For ever! I could not resist the desire to make a last effort to come up to the surface again. 'Nevertheless,' I said, 'as regards the bourgeois way of behaving, you've done worse yourself. I tried to rob you of your fiancée. But you have robbed me of the film director's job.'

Maurizio was silent for a few seconds. A silence which I interpreted as a sign of embarrassment, or even of shame. But no, I was wrong as usual. With absolute calm, perfectly sublimated as he was, he replied: 'But, Rico, try and be reasonable. This film has got to be of use to the working class. Now you yourself admit that you have remained the bourgeois intellectual you were and have always been. How then can you suppose that we should entrust you with the directing of a film that we want to be animated with genuine revolutionary spirit?'

Sunk again! There was nothing to be said! The argument was irrefutable. But its irrefutability much resembled a blow with an oar such as, in a naval battle, one of the victorious sailors might bring down upon the head of an enemy who had fallen into the sea, to ensure that he should be irretrievably drowned. Nevertheless, I objected: 'Well then, if it's like that, if I'm a bourgeois intellectual beyond remedy, why do you want me to go on working on the script?'

'First of all, because you're a professional at the job and from that angle you can make yourself very useful; and then also because, let me repeat, one never knows, it may be that you're being transformed without realizing it.'

'D'you really believe that one day I shall be able to consider myself a revolutionary intellectual?'

So that was that! There I was, lying at Maurizio's feet, subdued, crawling, subjugated, fascinated! And he had his heel on the back of my neck. I had given up the idea of directing the film, and was almost pleased to have done so. And now I was actually begging to be allowed to keep, at least, my inferior position as script-writer. Maurizio, meanwhile, had risen to his feet. Adjusting his dark glasses on his nose, he said quietly: 'It will depend on you.'

'Or on you of the group?'

'No, on you, entirely on you.'

I too had risen. Maurizio placed a hand on my shoulder and added: 'What am I to tell the group then? That you want your five million back? That you don't want to go on collaborating on the script?'

'Tell them that I don't want the five million and that I shall go on collaborating.'

We looked at one another. It was like a still taken from the middle of a film: I myself looking into Maurizio's eyes; Maurizio looking into my eyes; Maurizio's hand on my shoulder. The picture which had caught the moment of my downfall, or perhaps – if I was to attach importance to the incipient levitation caused in 'him' by the contact of that hand – of my final seduction. Then the stillness was broken, the picture moved, the film began running again. Maurizio said: 'Well then, when would you like us to meet to start work again?'

'Tomorrow?'

'Very well, tomorrow.'

I was so bewildered, so lost, so distracted that I scarcely noticed I was walking with Maurizio into the entrance-hall, and when the door closed I was surprised to find myself alone. Mechanically I went to the telephone which had started ringing at the far end of the passage. I took off the receiver and placed it to my ear. It was Fausta. She immediately asked me: 'Are we going to Protti's party this evening?'

'I'm going, but not you.'

'Why not me?'

'It's better you should stay at home. Your presence might have an unfortunate effect.'

'You want to be left alone with Signora Protti?'

'Exactly.'

A long silence. At last I heard her voice imploring: 'After the party, you'll come on to me?'

I was 'on top'; and I confess that, at the end of a day during which I had been all the time, invariably, 'underneath', first with Flavia and then with Maurizio, I felt a considerable relief. 'What should I come to see you for?' I said. 'Not that thing, no, seeing that I shall be doing it with Mafalda. So what?'

'Why are you so unkind, so perverse? There's such a thing as affection, isn't there? I'm not asking anything of you. Just that you should love me a little.'

Desublimated, I sagged and was moved. Nevertheless I answered, unkindly: 'Come on, go to bed and don't bore me any more. We'll talk tomorrow.'

'Good-bye.'

'Good-bye.'

Poor Fausta!

13 Castrated!

That same evening, as I was driving towards Protti's villa, I said to 'him': 'D'you see? That's what sublimation is. Flavia excited and provoked me; that was all very well. But when, in the end, I decided to give you free play, bang, bang! I got a couple of slaps enough to take my breath away.'

'He' did not reply. 'He' was in an extremely bad temper, as I knew. After the fiasco with Flavia, Mafalda now added a further reason for his displeasure. For I had confirmed to him, officially, so to speak, as we came out: 'The great moment has come. This evening I shall defer, provisionally, my experiment in sublimation. I shall allow you, in accordance with your own favourite expression, to come into direct contact with Mafalda. Yes, you can have free play, you can do what you like, without any limitations whatever.'

This solemn announcement, upon which I had forced myself to bestow a flattering, promising air, like that of a father saying to his son: 'You're now of an age to have the front-door keys; there they are; enjoy yourself' – this announcement did not impress him at all, to judge from the complete silence with which he greeted it. Evidently, though he had many times repeated to me that for him age did not count, the prospect of coming into 'direct contact' with Mafalda did not please him so much. In order to see what lay behind his silence, I insisted: 'In short, to sum up, Flavia's visit was a real, proper lesson in the matter of sublimation.'

Caught at his most sensitive point, he finally reacted and inquired ungraciously: 'And in what did the lesson consist, please?'

'In the fact that Flavia preferred the sublimated pleasure which she derived from the renunciation of pleasure, to what we may call the desublimated pleasure which you offered her.'

'But what pleasure can anyone find in renouncing pleasure?'

'The pleasure of power.'

'But where does the power come in?'

'First of all, there's the power over you. Then, as a very close consequence, the power over others. Let's be clear about it; power, not potency. The first is a characteristic of sublimation, the second, of desublimation. You have potency; but, just because you have potency, I do not have power. Let's come now to the lesson afforded by Flavia's visit. Flavia renounced her own potency; in compensation, she had power over me. I, on the other hand, did not renounce potency, at least you contrived that I should not renounce it; therefore, logically, I had no power over Flavia. But then, seeing that that's how things stand, I might as well make use of my potency in a utilitarian way, or, to put it plainly, make use of you to obtain, in exchange for your services, certain purely material advantages. That's the end of the lesson.'

'He' remarked acidly: 'To put it simply, the material advantage, in this case, would be the job of directing the film.'

'Put simply, yes. But things should never be put simply.'

'Why?'

'Because power begins precisely from the moment when things are no longer put simply.'

'What does it matter to me? I know only one thing.'

'What's that?'

'That, after six months of privation, you're offering me an old woman.'

'Come on, she's not old, she's simply mature.'

'Mature for the grave.'

I started laughing, and then said: 'And even if it was like that? Isn't it true that you've always maintained that age doesn't count and that bodily decay in a mature woman can be just as exciting as the immaturity of the same body, in the same woman, thirty or forty years earlier? Have you said this or have you not?'

'Yes, I have said it, but . . .'

'You've said it, and when I replied: gerontophile – d'you remember? you retorted: "Gerontophile, and why not?"'

'Yes, I agree. It's quite true. But a great deal depends on circumstances. For instance, the evening you took Mafalda's hand under the table, I was ready. Circumstances had made Mafalda desirable to me. But now . . .'

'Now?'

'Well, now the whole thing is so cut and dried, so organized, so pre-arranged; and at the same time it's all so desperately utilitarian.'

'But even on that evening usefulness was, fundamentally, the chief object I was aiming at.'

'Yes, but it was at least something new. Novelty, as you know perfectly well, always appears disinterested and spontaneous.'

'Come on, stop grumbling. I know you'll distinguish yourself again this time, won't you?'

'He' did not answer; he had a grudge against me; I felt I must let him relieve his feelings and, for the rest, must have confidence in his irresistible and almost automatic readiness. I drove on in silence. In the darkness on the motorway headlights were turned on, dazzling, blinding me for a moment, then turned off, turned on again, and disappearing as they passed close to me. All of a sudden, at the tenth kilometre, my own headlights revealed, in staring, lugubrious perspective, a straight stretch of black asphalt with railings dividing the carriageways and red reflectors and, beyond, half-way along the straight stretch, where a side road joined the main road, a woman sitting on the fence. A prostitute. She had one leg stretched out; the other was bent, with the foot resting on the bar. In that moment of intense light I could see that she was wearing a very short skirt: my glance went straight as a sword, up and up between her legs to a dark shadow which perhaps was not a shadow. I noted these things with coolness and precision; then I flicked down the switch of the headlights so that everything vanished – motorway, reflectors, asphalt, fence and woman – in the darkness of the night.

In a flash 'he' protested, with an inhuman yell: 'Back,

back, go back!' To tell the truth, I feared at first that I had run over a pedestrian or lost a part of the car. Then I understood: it was merely the girl sitting on the fence that I was about to lose. At any rate I reversed, thinking that it would not be wise to disappoint him, especially in view of the services that I should require of him in a short time during the evening at Protti's. However I remarked: 'What's come over you? Just a tart like a thousand others.'

'No, no, she's different from the others. Didn't you see the way she was sitting on that fence?'

There she was again. She was young, about twenty. I stopped the car and leant out of the window to have a better look at her. She had a brown face and black, slightly slanting eyes with lids so close together that they looked like two slits. Her cheekbones were prominent, her mouth protruding but lipless, her face sharp-featured and hook-nosed. She looked like an Inca, an Aztec, an American Indian. On her head she wore a beret white as milk, beneath which her black, glossy hair stood out conspicuously. By now I had stopped for too long to drive off without doing anything. I thought of indulging in a purely theoretical bargaining, just so as not to keep too tight a rein on 'him'. But I was not in time to start a conversation: 'he' ordered me, brutally: 'Not too much talk. Get her into the car and we'll go back home at once.'

'Tell me, are you going crazy?'

'I said: not too much talk. If you want me to help you in your muddle with Mafalda, you must give me this girl, and at once. Otherwise – nothing!'

'What d'you mean, nothing?'

'Nothing with Mafalda.'

'What, d'you mean you might . . . ?'

'Be good-for-nothing with Mafalda? Yes, precisely that.'

'But be reasonable: if I give in to you now and we go home with this girl, what shall I manage with Mafalda later? Damn all!'

'Don't worry; leave it to me.'

I have already remarked upon 'his' incurable megalomania. I said to myself that we were in trouble again: 'he' was promising more than he could fulfil. I answered in a decisive manner: 'Not another word about it.'

'No Mafalda, then.'

'But be reasonable.'

'Ha, ha, ha! Be reasonable! But I'm not born to be reasonable. That's your concern, it's your speciality.'

I could not say he was wrong: it was my concern to be reasonable; and I did in fact try to make use of reason. I said firmly: 'Protti is expecting me. Besides, even your potency has a limit. If you lose face with Mafalda, it's a disaster, for me at least; if you lose face with this girl it's not a disaster for any-one, neither for you nor for me. I don't wish to run any risks. For that reason I'll make you a suggestion: I'll make an interim payment to this kind of Roman Aztec and fix an appointment with her for later, after Mafalda.'

'I answer you in my turn: not another word on the subject.'

'But why?'

'Because I want the Aztec, at once.'

'At once, no.'

'Yes, at once.'

'Then there's nothing to be done and I'll drive on. It means that I'll do without you this evening with Mafalda.'

'But in what way?'

'You know there are plenty of ways.'

The threat of doing without 'him' produced its effect. 'He' protested: 'No, no, no. Very well, give her an appoint-ment for later on. But supposing she takes the money and then doesn't come?'

'I'll give her the halves of two ten-thousand lire notes on the understanding that she'll get the other halves at my flat.'

'And supposing we're late at Protti's and she finds the door locked and nobody at home?'

'Quite right. Apart from the two pieces of the banknotes, I'll give her the front-door keys. It's madness, I know, but I want to show you that I'm capable even of madness in order to please you.'

This discussion took place in the twinkling of an eye;

time, between us two, is entirely a matter of convention and has nothing to do with time by the clock. Thus, when I leant out to make my suggestion to the girl, in reality it must have been barely a few seconds after I had stopped near her.

She listened to me without showing any surprise: she was evidently accustomed to having all sorts of peculiar things said to her. She listened as peasant women listen in the market behind their baskets of eggs or fruit: attentively but without looking at me, turning her eyes far away in the direction of the cars passing along the motorway. She kept one hand on her knee, the other one resting on the fence behind her: her hand was small, red, slightly swollen, her oval nails, painted dark red, were sunk into the flesh. In the end, she said: 'I say, d'you know how strange you are?' – in a harsh, warm voice in which I detected more indifference than wonder.

I insisted: 'Strange or not, tell me if you agree. Well, then?'

'Well, then, yes, I agree.'

Hurriedly I took out my wallet and from my wallet two ten-thousand lire notes, which I tore in half; then I pulled out a page from my notebook and hurriedly wrote down my name and address and telephone number. I wrapped the keys of my flat in the paper and handed them to the girl together with the two halves of the banknotes. She took the whole lot, slipped it into the pocket of her coat and then asked: 'Is there anyone in the flat?'

'No, there's no one. Go in, go to the bedroom, get into bed and wait for me. When you hear the bell ring, come and open the door.'

'All right, as far as I'm concerned. But I shouldn't like there to be anything underneath all this.'

'There's nothing at all. I have an urgent appointment and I haven't time. But I want to see you, all the same.'

'Till later, then,' she said in a conclusive manner; and, without taking any further notice of me, she got down off the fence and went and put her head in at the door of a car which had just stopped close to mine. I drove on.

As if talking to myself but in reality addressing 'him', I

302

commented: 'If I told anyone what I had done with this girl, I should give them the impression that I was mad.'

'And what would life be without madness?'

I came to the gates, wide open as usual. But here there was a novelty: on the gate-posts, at each side of the entrance, two torches blazed with flickering flames – the indication of a party. I turned in and started up the drive, preceded and followed by other cars. More torches were blazing at intervals amongst the oleanders. In the darkness beyond the oleanders could be seen the glitter of numbers of cars parked higgledy-piggledy on the lawns. I reached the open space in front of the villa. Like a flagship at anchor in a foreign port, the villa seemed dressed overall with burning torches; their red flames outlined its contours against a background of black sky. The open space was full of cars. I went and parked farther on, on the grass; then I got out and walked towards the villa. The entrance was ablaze with light. The guests were packed in a dense crowd in the hall, their backs towards me, looking at I knew not what. I cast my eye all round, feeling lost. Those backs were ignoring me, excluding me; and that was enough to re-awaken in me a social inferiority complex that had never been entirely allayed. But then, luckily, Cutica arrived. I say 'luckily' because, in some circumstances, even an enemy like Cutica is better than nobody. While, in order to give myself some semblance of dignity, I was feigning a curiosity that I did not feel, standing on tiptoe and trying to see, he came up behind me and gave me a great slap on the back, making me jump. Then, with one of his usual embarrassing guffaws, he cried: 'Halt! Who goes there? Caught red-handed in spasmodic curiosity!'

'Spasmodic, indeed . . . but after all what's going on in there?'

'Why, don't you know?'

'I'm sorry, but I'm not up to date with the latest novelties of the Casa Protti.'

Another guffaw, another slap on the back. 'You've come to the right person for information. It's I who have looked after the organization of the party.'

'Congratulations. A new aspect of your multiform activity.'

'Well, what's going on in there is what once upon a time was called "tableaux vivants" but which now, more appropriately, I should describe as a "happening". A series of happenings on a single theme.'

'On what theme?'

'Slave-girls.'

I could not help recalling that one of Irene's masturbatory films also had this theme. 'A magnificent theme,' I said. 'And how do these so-called happenings take place?'

Again Cutica almost dislocated his jaw in one of his overboisterous bursts of laughter. 'This party,' he said, 'is all that's left over of a film about the treatment of slave-girls in Africa, which Protti wanted to make and then didn't make. Many of the women that you see round about will shortly be walking past across a platform. Fittingly naked and loaded with chains, like the slave-girls of the good old times, they will be put up to auction. A slave-driver, his face painted with lamp-black, will see that the most recalcitrant of them will be caressed with a whip. As they are exhibited on the platform, the pitiless slave-driver will point out in detail the physical excellences of the unfortunate girls exposed for sale. Then somebody in the audience will make an offer. But not in our little native lire – what fun would there be in that? Rather, in the money of those times, of the days of slavery – Maria Theresa thalers, sequins, Spanish doubloons, ducats, louis d'or, etc., etc. The offers, of course, will be made seriously; and the amounts will be paid later in lire. And these lire – guess who they're going to benefit. They're in aid of African refugees. It seems there are a great number of these in concentration camps here and there in Africa. In fact it's a typically African party in aid of the Africans.'

For the third time he gave a guffaw and slapped me on the back. I felt an irresistible necessity, now that I had recovered from my social inferiority complex, to get Cutica 'underneath'; to put myself 'on top' in relation to him. A struggle between the desublimated, as I knew; but, basically, I had never been, and I hoped, never would be, desublimated to the same point as Cutica. I said, dryly: 'An idea in extremely bad taste.'

I saw with particular pleasure that his laughter died on his lips; however his mouth remained half open, rather like the toothed jaws of an excavating machine when work is interrupted. 'And why?' he asked.

'I respect women too much to be pleased by a spectacle in which woman is debased and degraded and humiliated.'

Bang! I had trampled on his head so as to make him sink at least up to his neck. Disconcerted, disorientated, he tried to gain time, and exclaimed: 'Ha, ha, ha, that's a good one!'

'Why is it *good*? What good is there in what I said?'

By now he had already recovered. And, with the greatest brazenness, he acted the part of a man who is astonished. 'Rico, are you talking seriously, or what?'

'I'm not joking at all. I said what I thought and I thought what I said.'

He assumed the air of a doctor, surprised yet scientific, examining an unexpected patient. He looked at me, assessed me, scrutinized me: 'Rico, are you feeling ill, by any chance?'

'I feel extremely well, I've never felt better.'

'But what you said makes one think that you . . .'

'I should feel ill if I watched a show in which the pornography-lover that lies at the bottom of every man's heart was exploited. For that reason I'm afraid you won't see me among the spectators at your happenings.'

'But, Rico, is it really you who are saying this to me? Or did you by any chance sleep with your bottom uncovered?'

'I slept very well, without any part of my body being uncovered. At this point I wish to inform you that I hate flatterers and boot-lickers and toadies.'

He was an actor, or rather a mime, of the *commedia dell'arte* of the Atellana farces, servile and always ready to change his mask. After acting a kind of caricature of the rôle of friend meeting friend at a party and then of a surprised man who can't make head or tail of what is happening, he now, with his usual exaggerations, pretended to be indignant.

305

'Enough of that, sir. Who d'you think you're talking to at this moment?'

'I hate pimps.'

'Who might the pimps be?'

'And racketeers.'

'And where are the racketeers?'

'And hangman's assistants.'

'Be careful what you say.'

'The hangman's assistant, or *tirapiedi*, in case you don't know, derived his name from his function, which was, to be precise, pulling, literally, at the feet of those who were hanged.'

This little historical–philological explanation finally put him 'underneath'. He opened his eyes wide behind his thick lenses, opened his mouth like a fish out of water. He was choking and gesticulating wildly. How splendid it was to be 'on top'! With what voluptuous delight I held him 'underneath'! But Cutica's recovery was rapid. Inexhaustible, he had recourse to the acting of a new role, this of course again a gross caricature: that of a man who, for love of peace, not merely admits he is conquered but goes over spontaneously to the other side. 'Listen, Rico,' he said, 'are you angry with me? Perhaps I've offended or hurt you in some way, without meaning to?'

I myself, in turn, was disconcerted by this amazing change of tack, and for a moment I was left speechless. What effrontery! To transform oneself, on the spot, from the offended to the offender! Turning the omelette under my nose and without burning it, into the bargain! In an ill-tempered fashion I admitted: 'No, as far as I know you haven't offended me.'

'I'm sorry, you know, but perhaps I reacted too strongly against your negative opinion on the subject of the slave-girl happening. Please forgive me. And we'll remain friends as before, won't we?'

He was 'underneath'; but so much 'underneath' that I had a suspicion that the whole thing was a pretence and that actually, somehow or other, he had succeeded in putting himself 'on top'. Then he held out his hand to me. In astonishment, I could not help shaking it. But what was I to do now to make sure which of us two was the superior? Quite simple: he had been Mafalda's lover; I must force him to act as a go-between, in other words, ask him to bring me in touch with Protti's wife. That would be to place him seriously in a state of inferiority, not by words but deeds. Lowering my voice, I asked: 'Where's Protti?'

'Protti's not here.'

'Oh, that's fine! He's giving a party and he's not here!'

'Protti often does that. He left this morning for Paris.'

'And Signora Protti – where is she?'

'Mafalda? She's here, but she never comes down to these parties before one or two.'

'But where is she now?'

'I imagine she's upstairs in her bedroom, getting ready.'

'D'you think I could go up and knock at her door?'

'But what d'you want with Mafalda?'

'A film-producing firm has begged me to approach her. They would like her to take a part as a middle-aged woman.'

'Mafalda, as you know, hasn't worked for thirty years and has no intention of starting again. You must find someone else.'

'From you one can't conceal anything. I am – how shall I say? – attracted by Mafalda.'

'Attracted by Mafalda?'

'Yes, what is there strange about that? I like Mafalda.'

'And does she like you?'

'I have some reason to believe she does.'

'I'm sorry, but how do I come into all this?'

'You have a certain ascendancy over her.'

'What on earth d'you mean?'

'Come on, everybody knows you've been through it.'

'She's Protti's wife. To me she is sacred.'

'Sacred?'

'But, to put it briefly, what d'you want of me?'

'I want you to act – excuse the term, but it's the truth and between friends the truth can be told – to act to some extent as pimp for me.'

307

I had said it, at last! Then I looked at him to see how he would behave in face of so explicit and so offensive a request. He had just one moment's hesitation, one single moment. Then his histrionic instinct prevailed: he would not only act as pimp for me; he would act the part of a pimp in an exaggerated, excessive, caricature-like manner. And so indeed, already entering into the character, lowering his voice, half-seriously he said: 'You want me to act as pimp for you? With pleasure. But I still don't see how. You certainly won't expect me to push you physically into Mafalda's arms?'

'Let's begin by going upstairs, shall we? There are too many people here. Once we're upstairs, I'll explain the whole thing to you.'

Promptly and eagerly, as was suitable to the part he was playing, he went off up the stairs. After reaching the gallery, I followed him through a long, narrow, dimly-lit passage, like a passage in a hotel. Here too the style was rustic, vaguely Iberian: terracotta floors, doors with carved bosses, a ceiling with small beams. We stopped and looked one another in the eyes. We were of the same height, Cutica and I; and to anyone seeing us at that moment in the darkness of the passage, close together, furtively plotting together, without doubt we must have looked like two characters from classic comedy, at the same time both comic and sinister, apparently different but fundamentally identical. 'Well,' said Cutica, 'no one can see us here. What did you want to speak to me about, then?'

I had a moment of regret before I replied. I could not in fact help realizing clearly that Cutica's assistance was in no way necessary to me. I could go and see Mafalda by myself, with the certain knowledge of being welcomed immediately and kindly. But I needed, I needed absolutely to put Cutica 'underneath' and myself 'on top'. In the end, feigning perplexity, I said: 'In spite of everything, I don't feel at all sure. It's true that a little time ago Mafalda gave me some hope. But with women one never knows.'

He looked up at me, ironically: 'You're telling me! What are we going to do, then?'

'Now look: you must put in a good word for me.'

'A good word? But in what sense, good?'

'I'm sorry, I haven't explained properly. What you must do is to reveal to Mafalda . . . the truth about me.'

'And what is that truth?'

There we were, the moment had come. I leant forward a little and whispered in his ear: 'The truth about me is that I've been exceptionally well endowed by nature.'

He stared at me, opening his eyes wide behind his glasses. Then he opened his mouth and, next moment, broke into one of his embarrassing guffaws. 'Endowed?' he said. 'What does *endowed* mean?'

'It means furnished, provided, from the sexual point of view.'

'Is that really the truth?'

'Yes.'

'And you wish me to tell this to Mafalda?'

'Yes.'

Another guffaw. He took hold of my arm and, just like the classic type of pimp whose role he was playing, asked me in a low voice: 'Endowed, very good. Exceptionally, very good. But in what measure?'

'Immeasurably.'

'Ha, ha, ha, immeasurably! What are you, then? A Rubirosa type?'

'It's nothing to make fun of.'

At once he was serious again. 'I'm not making fun of you. I was asking because I shall have to give Mafalda some sort of precise information. That's the least I must do, don't you think?'

'Then you're prepared to do me this favour?'

'Certainly. If this is all you want.'

'You don't mind? I realize, as I said, that I'm asking you to act as pimp for me. But with a friend like you . . .'

'One can even ask him to act as pimp. Why not? Of course. What are friends for, otherwise? Look, wait here a moment for me.'

Without giving me time to say anything more, he walked away, went and knocked at one of the doors, waited a moment and then disappeared. And I then felt disappointed and reflected that, in actual fact, I had not succeeded in putting myself 'on top' in relation to him. Shrewd and intuitive, he had been aware of my desire to humiliate him and had parried the blow by acting, as I have already remarked, a caricature of the role of comedy pimp, instead of truly serving as a pimp for me. Thus he had managed not to fall into the trap I had set for him, pretending to be what he was not and did not wish to be, as though for his own private amusement.

But soon he was back again: he came hurriedly towards me and whispered: 'Come along, you're expected'; then he led me to Mafalda's door.

We went in. It was a dressing-room with a number of wall cupboards of the same sort of carved wood in the Spanish manner. Mafalda was sitting at the far end of the room in front of the dressing-table, her back turned towards us. Her hair was enclosed in a kind of white turban. Her head was small, her neck looked wider than her head, her shoulders were wider than her neck and her hips wider than her shoulders. I could see her face in the mirror of the dressing-table, the face of an old Pekinese dog or an elderly cat: wide-open, childish eyes set in large, bruised-looking sockets; a little nose with slits for nostrils; a huge mouth with big, sinuous, pouting lips. She was wearing a kind of Oriental robe with wide sleeves and a deeply-cut low neck, so transparent that it was possible to see, at the bottom of her back, the dark cleft dividing the whiteness of her massive buttocks.

Cutica moved resolutely across and stood with his back against the window, so that he was in front of Mafalda. I myself kept discreetly at a little distance, pretending to be embarrassed.

Cutica, still waggishly playing the part of go-between, began in this way: 'Mafalda, here is our Rico who wants to speak to you.'

In the looking-glass I could see the big Pekinese eyes staring at me curiously. Cutica continued coolly: 'And now I can withdraw. I have acted, so to speak, as outrider for Rico, and it only remains for me to go away. But Rico asked me expressly to do him a special favour. And I agreed. What would one not do for a friend?'

The big eyes considered me afresh, with interest; then they turned towards Cutica. 'The favour, Mafalda,' said the latter, 'which Rico asked me to do him was, to put it briefly, to be introduced to you. But first of all we must understand what "to be introduced" means. In the usual way, when one introduces somebody, one praises his moral and intellectual qualities. Well, in Rico's case, there is nothing of that. Rico is a natural sort of man who prefers to be introduced for what we may call his "natural" qualities. In this preference one must, in my opinion, recognize Rico's gratitude to nature. You will ask me at this point: why is Rico grateful to nature? And I reply: Rico is grateful to nature because nature has been generous with him. What do I mean by these words? Do I perhaps wish to allude to those intellectual and moral qualities which I mentioned a moment ago? No, those qualities, too, certainly come from nature, but not directly: in order to be developed they have to be cultivated. In Rico's case, nature's generosity must be seen, instead, as a gift which does not demand any special attention or, if you prefer it, maintenance, on the part of the one who receives it. For that selfsame reason one can call it generosity. In short, Mafalda, our friend Rico, to put it briefly, is a virile, a very virile, an excessively virile man.'

A smile that was almost malevolent in its sulky joylessness crept across Mafalda's big, chapped lips, over there in the looking-glass. Then the lips moved and there issued a voice which struck me as curiously melodious: 'Thank you for the introduction. But there was no need of it. I have known Rico for a long time.'

'But not under the aspect of which I have just been speaking, Mafalda. At least, I don't think so.'

'I have still to get dressed. Will you sit down in the meantime?'

At this invitation Cutica immediately made a quick movement towards the door. 'No, no, I won't, I must go down as soon as possible to see that everything goes as it should. So

I'll go, I'll go in *more* than a hurry. But I'll leave Rico. So long, Rico, so long!' He bowed several times, faithful to the last to his caricatured, exaggerated role, then, just like an actor who has finished his performance, he almost ran out of the door. And I was left alone with Mafalda.

During Cutica's little speech the big Pekinese eyes had never for one moment ceased staring at me from the mirror. As soon as the door closed Mafalda, still continuing to look at me, asked: 'Is it true, what Cutica said?'

'I should say, yes.'

'Very interesting. I had rather thought as much on that other occasion. But I didn't know it was actually a question of a phenomenon of nature.'

'And yet that's just what it is.'

'Why are you standing behind me? Won't you give me a kiss, to begin with?'

Docilely I approached and leant forward from behind her back. Mafalda twisted her neck round, like a snake or a swan or some other animal with a long, supple neck, and managed to place her head in such a position that her mouth met mine. Her big, dry, thirsty lips rested upon mine, opened, widened, overran my face as though they wished to swallow it. At the same time her tongue, abrasive and of unusual thickness like that of a calf or some other bovine creature, penetrated into my mouth and lay inert upon my own tongue, as if resting on a couch. I pretended to groan from pleasure at such a kiss: but actually I was groaning with pain because Mafalda, pulling me from behind and keeping me still with her hand pressed against the back of my neck, was forcing my cervical vertebrae into a distressingly twisted position. The kiss went on for a long time, my vertebrae were racked with pain, I felt myself suffocating. At last, to my enormous relief, Mafalda loosened her grip and let me free. 'A kiss does one good every now and then, doesn't it?' she said. 'Now go over there.'

I obeyed and went over to where Cutica, shortly before, had placed himself for the delivery of his pimping cajolery. I sat down on a stool, crouching with my legs bent and my hands on my knees. I watched Mafalda take, from among the many bottles and boxes and flasks on the dressing-table, a tube of lipstick, then lean her face towards the looking-glass. She turned her lip inside out like a glove, wetted it with saliva with the tip of her tongue, then stuck it out and passed the point of the lipstick vigorously over it several times. All this was done with her right hand. Then, suddenly, she took the lipstick in her left hand and stretched out towards me her right arm which, in an unexpected way, turned out to be strangely long, in fact indefinitely extensible, like an articulated garden pump. She stretched out this round, muscular arm towards me from its wide sleeve and, still looking at herself in the mirror and touching up the red of her lips, directed her hand blindly towards my belly. Meanwhile she asked me: 'Why haven't you been to see me before?'

'I was busy.'

The hand landed on my trouser-belt, slipped in under the buckle, took hold of the catch of the zip fastener and started pulling it down, but unhurriedly, as though trying, in fact, not to go too fast. Then, all of a sudden, 'his' voice – but how changed! – protested, plaintively, querulously: 'No, no, no, tell her to leave off at once, stop her, push her hand away!'

'Why, what's happened to you?'

'What's happened is that I don't want to, I absolutely don't want to. D'you understand? I don't want to.'

'You're not going to tell me that now, at just this moment, you want to draw back?'

'Yes, that's just how it is. Don't expect any help from me, any support, any assistance.'

'But what is it, are you crazy?'

'No, I'm not crazy. You did very wrong to ask Cutica to proclaim my exceptional qualities. Because this is an occasion when I just can't manage it.'

'But you had promised me . . .'

'I promised nothing. I let you talk. You said you were sure I would do myself ample justice. Instead of which – no, I shall not do myself justice.'

I bit my lip. I had been convinced that at the right

moment 'he' would function automatically; and yet now, unexpectedly and for no reason, he was being difficult. Meanwhile Mafalda's arm was like a big snake issuing gradually from its lair, and her hand was thrust into the opening of the zip. Her fingers pushed aside the edges of my shirt and crept between those of my drawers, and were on the point of reaching 'him'. All at once 'he' screamed, as though terrified: 'My God! Draw back, move, get up, anyhow do something so that she can't touch me! My God, if she touches me, I shall die!'

'But why?'

'There's no "why" about it. I don't want it, I don't want it, I don't want it.'

'I can't draw back any farther. There's the window-sill. Kindly tell me what's the matter with you.'

'The matter is that this hand, fumbling about blindly, frightens me and repels me.'

Mafalda was now putting eyeshade on her lids with her left hand, bending her face towards the looking-glass, as though what her right hand was doing did not concern her. I hoped that 'he', at the moment of 'direct contact', would, as I had said to him previously, do himself justice; but I no longer felt so sure: I was conscious, now, of something new and hostile in 'him', something resembling a rebellion, which alarmed and frightened me. And indeed, when Mafalda's hand, after meandering for a long time, slowly and cautiously, like a snake among the lettuces in a vegetable-garden, finally reached 'him', the disguised threat in his exasperated 'I don't want it' proved true. Brought out skilfully and delicately into the air, in spite of his protests (amongst which, several times repeated: 'If only her hand was warm, but it's as cold as death'), and lying in Mafalda's palm, 'he' was nothing more than a little circle of shrivelled, wrinkled skin. Meanwhile I heard him shouting: 'I am small, I have never been so small and I wish to remain small. You can depend on that. I'll actually disappear.'

At these words I was filled with panic. 'And how about the director's job?' I asked.

314

'I don't care a damn about that.'

'But for me it's a question of life or death.'

'Not for me. I am by nature disinterested. Career, fame, success – all these are things that don't concern me.'

'Then tell me what I'm to do.'

'Do the best you can.'

Mafalda, in the meantime, was bouncing the bundle of my genitals up and down in the palm of her hand as though it were a false coin. Everything that usually was heavy had now become light; everything that usually was full now seemed empty. What was I to do? That rude suggestion of his: 'Do the best you can', gave me the idea of stimulating him by bringing up the recollection of other women. I closed my eyes and recalled to memory, in turn, Fausta's big bare paunch, the dark shadow between the legs of the Roman Aztec sitting on the fence, the involuntary blows from Flavia's buttocks, the burning blushes of the American tourist in the church, and a great many other details which, in the more recent past, had given 'him' the opportunity of revealing himself in all his potency. But all my efforts proved useless. In spite of the mental images improvised with such expertise by my docile, complaisant imagination, 'he' did not produce so much as a tremor or a shudder or any hint of even the smallest levitation. To such a degree that I actually had the impression of an empty space in my groin, as if there were nothing there. I opened my eyes in a fright. But no, there 'he' was, lying lost in Mafalda's palm; she had now finished making up her face and was looking alternately at 'him' and at me, with a doubtful expression, as much as to say: Is that all?

Despairingly I murmured: 'It's no use; I'm too much afraid that Protti may come in suddenly.'

'Protti's not here. He's in Paris.'

'The maid might come in.'

'Wait here for me a moment.'

She put 'him' back in a great hurry, as best she could, just as a surgeon puts back the entrails extracted during an unsuccessful operation into the body of a patient who is now dead. Then she rose, in all her pyramidal, dinosaur-like majesty,

315

went to a side door, opened it and directed me: 'Wait for me. When I call you, come in.'

Left alone, I immediately attacked 'him' furiously: 'Will you kindly tell me, what does all this mean?'.

His retort was to suggest urgently: 'It's a good moment. Let's run away.'

'I wouldn't dream of it.'

'But what d'you mean to do?'

'Now look: we're going to join Mafalda in the next room, and once we're there you'll do your duty? Understood?'

Now he was silent. I mistook his silence for consent, and added: 'Now come on, keep calm, don't get nervous, don't worry, let yourself go. It's a matter of five or ten minutes at most. Then we'll leave, we'll drive home and there we'll find the Aztec waiting for us.'

In the meantime I had undressed. Without giving him time to breathe I went to the door through which Mafalda had just disappeared and opened it. More melodiously than ever, the film star's voice warbled: 'No, don't come in, I've got nothing on.'

'Nor have I,' I answered, and I went in. In the reddish half-light I surveyed a bedroom in the same Spanish style. A bed with a canopy and pillars; a beamed ceiling; damask on the walls; even a *prie-dieu* with a sacred image. The wardrobe door was wide open and concealed Mafalda who was looking at herself in the mirror, and of whom all I could see was her bare feet on the floor. I walked round the door and went and stood behind her. Mafalda was in a slip and brassière. I set to work to undo the latter; her two breasts, no longer supported, plopped into the palms of my hands, hastily held out below, like a couple of soft, heavy bags full of flour or sugar. She twisted her head round towards me and asked: 'D'you like me?'

I wanted to reply: It's not I who should like you, it's 'he'; but, as usual, I hadn't the courage. I answered with a barely audible 'Yes.' Mafalda had a strange posterior, not exactly prominent but, it might be said, octagonal in shape, and of a curious flatness which did not exclude bulk. And now she started moving it against my belly, with a complicated yet scarcely perceptible swaying of her hips. Then she turned her head towards her shoulder and asked me: 'Do you like that?'

'Yes.'

It was a lie. Of course I did not like it; but, unfortunately, nor did 'he'; and he persisted, to my dismay, in taking no notice of it. Mafalda's continued rubbing, instead of making him increase in size, merely caused him to move round and round, like a little wad of rag. With the idea of arousing him, I put out my hands and ventured upon an exploratory caress. Alas! I felt as if I were handling a number of soft, half-empty cushions of unequal size, attached, more or less, to the structure of her skeleton. Two of these cushions were swaying over the cavity of the thorax; a third, stuck on to the corners of the pelvis, shifted and dropped from either side; two others, oblong in form, seemed to be 'revolving' round the thigh-bones. Mafalda's whole body, in fact, moved upon its bones as though on the point of becoming detached from them. Throwing back her head, she asked me: 'You're not frightened any more now?'

'No.'

We went off together towards the bed. Then, abruptly, Mafalda broke away from my arm, threw herself flat on her back on the bed, opened her legs as wide as she could and pulled me down on top of her, by my arms, much as one pulls a blanket over one before going to sleep. So there I was, firmly settled between her wide-apart thighs, groin against groin, my chest on her chest, my face buried in the pillow amongst her hair. Once again, in this embrace, I felt Mafalda's body moving and turning round her bones, and then the thought occurred to me that perhaps, some day, her flesh would slip off her, like the flesh of an animal that has been subjected to long boiling, and nothing of her would be left on the bed but a clean, dry skeleton.

Unavoidable thoughts, it may be; but not exactly exciting. 'He', in fact, pointed out to me acidly: 'Necrophily, I warn you, cannot be learned at a moment's notice; it requires long psychological preparation.'

317

This time it was I who did not answer. I was frightened, humiliated, desperate; I felt 'him' to be an enemy, decisively and mysteriously, and I no longer knew what to say to him. Meanwhile Mafalda was moving underneath me, as though looking for 'him'; but all she found was a little wad of skin, nerveless and without substance. Then, in a rush, she threw me on my back and fell on top of me. I now had the impression – exceedingly disconcerting, since I was accustomed to 'his' exceptional services – that, of Mafalda and myself, it was Mafalda who was the male, if for no other reason than that it was she who moved, she who was, in her way, penetrating. I was indeed aware, at each of these powerful movements of her pelvis, of a violent pressure and, as it were, an advance which alas, on 'his' side, corresponded symmetrically to a yielding and an equally noticeable retreat. To such a degree that I suddenly had the strange, disturbing sensation that I was no longer a man but a woman and that, in the place where once 'he' had been, with all his cumbersome presence, there was now an emptiness, an absence, positively a cavity.

At this point Mafalda, evidently still cherishing false hopes, changed her method. She thrust me aside on the bed, sat up and leant across my belly, turning her back to me, bending her head and supporting her cheek on her hand. I did my best to comply with her, lying out flat, relaxing, abandoning myself to her. At the same time I concentrated my mental effort upon 'him', desperately exhorting him in this way: 'For the last time I beseech you: help me, save me.'

'He' did not reply; he still did not exist. I placed my hand on Mafalda's bent back: it was damp with sweat. Above her massive shoulders her small head, enclosed in its white cloth turban, was now going up and down with stubborn, feverish violence. I stretched and arched my body, I concentrated; nothing. I let my eyes wander over Mafalda's body, seeking a cause for excitement in its strange conformation, like that of an enormous pear made of flesh; again nothing. Finally I tried to arouse the missing excitement by sighing and groaning, in the way that nurses do with babies, when they imitate the rustling sound of urination: still nothing.

Mafalda now gradually relaxed her zeal; a few more dives with her head, brief as the peck of a bird; then I saw her stay motionless, her head still bent, as though unable to believe her misfortune. I was aware, to my dismay, that as soon as she raised herself up I should find myself face to face with an extremely disagreeable situation. I felt myself incapable of dealing with it. And immediately I took my decision.

Mafalda was still stooping and her back was still turned to me, when I put my hand to my side and fell back groaning on the bed. It was the old trick of a sudden illness to which I had occasionally had recourse when, carried away by 'him' into a mercenary adventure in the darkness of a suburban avenue I had then found myself faced, in a fully lit room, with some decrepit harpy. I groaned and stammered: 'I'm ill, I'm feeling ill. Quickly, something strong, some brandy . . . It's come, I felt it, it's come, I felt it coming . . . Quickly, I'm ill.'

Mafalda, in spite of these lamentations and these urgent requests, did not appear to be in any hurry. She rose slowly, turned and, laying her hands on the two sides of my body, bent over me and stared fixedly at me with an obviously malevolent expression. 'You'll find the brandy on the ground floor, as much as you like,' she said. 'But, Rico, d'you think I'm taken in?'

Her voice had changed: it was no longer melodious, but dry and ironical. I protested: 'Don't you believe me?'

'Certainly I don't.'

'D'you imagine I'm impotent?'

'What d'you want me to imagine?'

I said nothing. Mafalda went on, sarcastically: 'We're like Don Juan, like Casanova, we stretch out hands under the table, we kiss behind the door. But when the moment comes, we feel ill – bad heart, eh, Rico?'

'But on that other occasion you *felt* that I wasn't impotent.'

'What are we to call it? Not impotence – what, then? Inhibition?'

'You're right, and yet I swear to you . . .'

'I'm fed up with having to do with men who are in theory

extremely potent and in practice impotent. Very well then, you all of you have your reasons: Protti's is too small, you actually haven't got one. But why d'you get married, then? Why d'you make advances? Why don't you leave me in peace?'

'Forgive me, I had a moment – as you quite rightly say – of inhibition; it happens to everyone, but we could try again . . .'

'Go away, go away, get out, go away, go away, go away!'

I was suddenly assailed by a bewildering variety of blows and slaps, of punches and clouts and scratches. Mafalda, on top of me, continued to scream: 'Go away!' – but at the same time she prevented me from going, crushing me under her body. At last I gave her a violent shove and pushed her away; I freed myself, jumped off the bed and ran out of the room, pursued by her final invectives which, all at once, turned into broken, angry sobbing. I came into the dressing-room and locked the door; I dressed in furious haste and rushed out into the corridor. But as soon as I was outside – like a guest who, to satisfy the needs of nature, has made an incursion to the upper floors of the house where he has been invited – I started walking in a calm and dignified manner between the two rows of doors. 'He', at present, was silent. I myself merely said, with profound, genuine despair: 'Now I shall not only not get the director's job, but Mafalda will be my enemy: you've ruined me.'

Then, suddenly, something unforeseen and terrible occurred. 'His' voice, unrecognizable, funereal, evil, sinister, declared slowly, pronouncing the syllables carefully: 'Don't you understand that I did not help you because I do not wish you to become a director?'

'But why?'

'Because your energy, your vitality, that force, in fact, which your idiotic Freud calls sexual impulse, must be devoted to me, to me exclusively.'

14 Projected!

And so there had been, finally, a frank and explicit declaration of war between me and 'him'. Everything was now clear. 'He' did not wish me to become a creator, an artist, a director; that is, he did not wish me to pass on from desublimation to sublimation. He wished, instead, that I should remain desublimated all my life, in other words a ridiculous buffoon, a hangman's assistant, a sycophant, a jester, a pimp of Cutica's sort, with an enormous member and a cowardly mind. He wished likewise that I, a buffoon in my, so to speak, public life, should be, in my private life, a good husband, a good father, a good patron, a good citizen and, above all, a good sex maniac.

All these things do not contradict each other. Rigoletto who, being a hunchback, was supposed also to be, according to popular rumour, exceptionally endowed like me, was at the same time, as is well known, an excellent father and an excellent citizen. 'He' wished, in short, that I should only be capable of producing offspring, because, while artistic creation cannot but be destructive, children, for their part, with adequate brain-washing on the basis of the mass media, can be made into anything one likes, that is, can be made just as, or even more, desublimated than their parents. For a work of art is, indeed, a living thing; but a child may be born dead, even if it seems alive. Now a living being is always revolutionary; whereas a dead person, obviously, cannot but be conservative. Therefore, long live eroticism, which desublimates man and makes him into a good citizen! Long live mass sex, the better to keep the masses 'underneath'!

All these things and many others whirled through my head as I walked with a slow and dignified step along the corridor of the first floor of the villa.

When I reached the gallery I went to the balustrade and

321

looked down. The crowd still thronged the doors of the reception-room with backs turned towards the hall; no one was speaking; in the complete silence they were all craning their necks and rising on tiptoe in order to see better. As for me, I could see nothing, for the gallery hid the reception-room doors. I could hear, however, and so form a fairly precise idea of what was going on. A male voice, shrill, farcical, amplified by a loud-speaker, was mimicking the cheapjacks of the public auctions. 'Look, gentlemen, take a good look at her. She was born in Rome, a city famous for the beauty of its women; she's perfect, she might have been turned on a lathe. Now turn round. What, you don't want to turn round? Come on, slave-driver, touch up her legs with the whip, but not too hard, otherwise you'll spoil my wares. You don't want to be whipped? You'd rather turn round? Very well then, turn round and show us the other side of the moon. There she is, gentlemen, the little Roman slave-girl, the little pocket Venus. Take a look at her and tell me where you'll find another one like that. Yet she's not too expensive. We're putting her up for sale for the price of thirty thousand Maria Theresa thalers.'

'A hundred thousand Venetian sequins.'

'A hundred and twenty thousand Milanese ducats.'

'A hundred and fifty thousand French louis d'or.'

'A hundred and sixty thousand Spanish doubloons.'

'A hundred and seventy thousand Papal scudi.'

The auction was in progress. At that precise moment, one of the many 'walkers-on' or 'stand-ins' present at the party was allowing herself to be bought and sold, exhibiting her appropriately stripped and chained body on the platform. I started walking slowly down the stairs, resting my hand on the banisters. No one saw me, no one took any notice of me. I slipped away, behind all those backs, out into the open.

On the open space in front of the villa the cars were standing all round, pointing towards the house; in the middle of the space the chauffeurs were gathered in a group. I walked along the cement pathway beside the wall of the villa, until I came to the corner. Then I would have to cross the drive and make my way to the field where I had parked my car. But a mysterious impulse caused me to turn and follow the pathway along the villa wall. I acted as though in a delirium; but I felt that this delirium had a logic of its own. On that side the villa had no doors, only windows. They were all open, but in darkness; they all looked, probably, into inhabited rooms which were, at the moment, uninhabited. I quickened my step as though I had a perfectly clear plan in mind and had not much time left in which to carry it into effect. Actually my mind was empty of intentions, but oddly, at the same time, I knew for certain that in a short time I should do something important and decisive. I reached the corner of the villa. I turned again and found myself on a narrow path between the wall of the villa and a laurel hedge. On this side were the kitchens; farther on, in fact, a bright light came from two open doors and illuminated a slight widening of the path full of dustbins and packing-cases. But I did not go as far as the kitchens. Suddenly I came to a halt under one of these ground-floor windows. And why did I stop? Because, all of a sudden, I had discovered the reason why, instead of getting back into my car, I had walked along the path round the wall of the villa. Now I went into action. I took a packing-case from among the many that were lying about, placed it under the window, climbed on to it and seized a plate with a lighted candle on it from the window-sill; then for a moment I hesitated. The window was wide open, but a curtain made it impossible to look into the room. It was probably a minor sitting-room, with armchairs and sofas and mats, all inflammable stuff. I calculated that, if I dropped the candle between the wall and the curtain, the latter would catch fire and the fire, in turn, would spread to the rest of the furniture. The fire would smoulder slowly enough; so that nobody would perish even if Protti's villa, the symbol of my defeat, was reduced to ashes. I made up my mind, stretched out my hand and dropped the candle into the room.

I climbed down from the packing-case and waited in a careless sort of attitude, leaning back against the wall of the villa. I wanted at least to smell the smell of burning, at least to see the first smoke, or even, perhaps, the first darting flame.

But no, there was nothing, absolutely nothing happened. The window remained dark and quiet, without smoke, without flames. In the darkness and quietness of the window there was, indeed, something malevolent, hostile, perhaps even mocking. In the end I grew impatient; I climbed back on to the packing-case and again looked over the window-sill.

I saw nothing. The curtain was between me and the room. I drew it aside with my hand, but I still saw nothing, for the room was in darkness. So I took my cigarette-lighter from my pocket, snapped it alight and explored the dark space, introducing my hand between the open sides of the curtain. In the flickering light of the little flame the room was finally revealed as a bathroom. The floor was of flower-patterned tiles; a white porcelain wash-basin glimmered faintly in the shadows. But where could the candle be? I looked down. Right underneath me was the lavatory-bowl. The lid was raised. I stretched out my hand, holding the lighter, as far down as possible. The little flame, feeble as it was, allowed me to distinguish something dark at the bottom of the bowl. Something that had fallen into the water and now lay submerged at the bottom: the candle which I had dropped shortly before, thinking to set the curtain alight.

Strange to say, this vulgar, mean symbolism of real life did not distress me, in fact it left me completely indifferent. Calmly I put my lighter back in my pocket and climbed down from the packing-case. The fire, it was true, had failed to light, the candle had ended up in the water, but, in compensation, a hypothesis as luminous as a flame had fastened upon my mind and I felt that it would soon flare up.

I crossed the drive and went into the field towards my car. Opening the door, I got in, started the engine and went off. As the car bumped and slid over the soft grass of the field, I became aware that the tiny fire which has just come alight in my mind was truly flaring up. It was not the real fire with which I had intended to reduce Protti's villa to ashes. It was – how shall I describe it? – a psychological fire. But, of the two fires. I very much preferred the second. Which, in fact, is more important, things or man? Protti's villa or the solution of the greatest problem of my life? In brief: the gesture or the salvage of consciousness?

In reality I had understood what had happened inside me at the very moment when I had thrown the candle into the room. It was a very simple thing that had happened: all at once I had passed from desublimation to sublimation. Magically I had, as Maurizio said, transformed myself.

Yes, indeed, it had been sublimation, it had truly been sublimation in its most exact, its most assimilated, its most inspired form. And little did it matter if my vital energy had been diverted to an act of destruction, instead of turned towards an artistic activity such as the directing of a film might have been. Little did it matter. There are times when to sublimate means to construct; and times when to sublimate means to destroy. Construction and destruction are two social activities that are equally necessary, important and useful. Evidently we are living in a time of destruction.

But had I not perhaps had the same sense of sublimation when I spat in Patrizia's face, after that silly little thing had thrown a handful of coins at me? Yes, in all probability, that too was sublimation. But what does this mean? That there is a contradiction between the first and the second sublimation? Not at all. It means that I am more revolutionary than the revolutionaries; that the real revolution is that of the desublimated against the sublimated; and that, in reality, in every sublimated man there is hidden a man of power, just as in every desublimated man, a rebel.

Meanwhile I drove down the avenue, reached the gateway, came into the Via Cassia and started off into the night. In the darkness the headlights of cars came to meet me, passed close to me, vanished. Other headlights appeared behind me. For an instant the black sky would be lit up and reddened as though by an aurora borealis of a new kind, then the car would appear and the lights would change. As I drove along I felt that, in my head, that first idea had blown away the skull-cap of obtuseness that had enclosed it; and that now, one after another, like the tremors of a volcanic eruption, other ideas, other intuitions were exploding. A torrent of thoughts, at a

325

very high temperature, poured out of my mind, abundant, uninterrupted.

Sublimated! Never again desublimated! Never again 'underneath'! But not sublimated by birth, by social origins, by longing for power like Maurizio, like Flavia, like Protti, like Mafalda, like the bourgeois youths of the group. No, sublimated because I had rebelled seriously! Because I was a revolutionary without fixed intentions, without background! A revolutionary in the pure state, without any conditioning, truly subversive, truly destructive! Sublimated to deny everything, to overthrow everything, to destroy everything!

In the light of these reflections, the candle I had thrown into the room at the villa appeared to me as a symbol rich in significance. The candle was revolution; the lavatory-bowl into which it had fallen, capitalism; the water in which it had been extinguished, the corruption with which capitalism studies to extinguish revolution and deceives itself into thinking it is doing so. For the moment things had gone badly. The candle had fallen into the bowl and been extinguished in the water. But it would not always be like that. Next time I would throw the candle where it ought to be thrown and the fire would flare up, would blaze, would destroy everything. In vain would all the latrines of capitalism open to swallow my candle! In vain would that same capitalism press an anxious and trembling hand upon the levers of its lavatory-cisterns! The flame would rise like a giant, would not be extinguished until the destruction was complete. Sublimated because rebellious! A whole era of my life had been brought to a conclusion. A new era was beginning. Rebellious because sublimated!

In this state of exaltation, proper to what I may call a sublimated neophyte, it is easy to imagine the effect upon me of 'his' voice, low-spirited, feeble, timid, asking me: 'Are you angry with me?'

'With you? No, on the contrary. By your just refusal to consent to a vile compromise, you have, without meaning it, finally diverted my vital energy towards worthier aims. No, I'm not angry with you. In fact, I ought to thank you.'

326

'But where are we going now?'

'What does it matter where we go? We're going towards the future, towards revolution?'

'Yes, but *where* are we going?'

'He' was right, however. Where was I going? In my flat there was the Aztec from off the fence, to whom, as I suddenly remembered in an acute crisis of desublimation, I had given the keys of the house. To go and see Fausta was not to be thought of; almost, then the Aztec would be best. Where was I going?

Suddenly, like a brush-stroke in an almost complete picture, came the memory of Irene. Once again all became clear, all was settled. Yes, indeed, sublimation, *my* sublimation as a rebel had made me spit in Patrizia's face, she who was a false revolutionary and a real woman of power; had made me throw the candle into the room of the capitalist Protti; but above all, for some time now, had made me love, with an impossible love, Irene.

Yes, I would be the rebel, the destroyer who loved an ideal, unattainable woman! The fearless cavalier of the subversive sublimation dedicating his exploits to an inaccessible lady!

To 'him', at the end of these reflections, I announced: 'We're going to see Irene.'

15 Diverted!

I was in front of Irene's house. The buzzer on the gate sounded and I entered the little garden and walked in the darkness, along the gravel path, past the strange shadowy forms, cones and spheres and cubes, of the pruned trees in the flower-beds. I went into the villa, walked up one flight of stairs and then another, turned, and there were Irene and Virginia standing in the doorway of the flat watching my arrival. I looked up at them as I finished climbing the stairs. Both mother and daughter were wearing extremely short skirts; but whereas Virginia's was as it should be, the little short dress of a child, Irene's dress gave one a feeling that it was a parody. And a parody of what? Of innocence, of childish ambiguity. In the case of the little girl, the skirt showed long, pale, bony legs which had nothing feminine about them. With Irene, on the other hand, whose skirt came little farther down than her crotch, it made one think of a woman at a fancy dress party who had, with doubtful taste, dressed up as a little girl.

As I came up, I asked: 'How is it that the child hasn't gone to bed?'

'The television. Besides, when I stay at home, there's no way of making her go to bed.'

Virginia greeted me by bending her big, bony knee in her customary little curtsy, that of a well-brought-up child. She looked as if she had grown in too much of a hurry. Two purplish marks underlined the watery blue of her eyes. The somehow excessive redness of her full lips made her cheeks appear, by contrast, even leaner and whiter. 'I'll put her to bed now,' said Irene, 'and then we'll talk.'

She closed the front door and went off, holding Virginia by the hand. I followed. Irene opened a door, turned on the light and went into a room. I stayed on the threshold.

It was a long, narrow room. The furniture was painted a

light pistachio green. The bed was green, the wardrobe was green, the little table in front of the window was green, the chair in front of the table was green, the wall-paper was green, the carpet was green. On the green bed-cover was sitting, with legs stretched wide, a headless doll dressed in pink. I looked for the head and saw it on the floor, under the table. The head had its eyes open and seemed to be watching.

Just for something to say, I asked: 'Why did you take the head off your doll?'

'She always had her eyes open and so I thought she wouldn't be able to sleep and Mummy says that if you don't sleep you may get ill and even die and I didn't want my doll to get ill and die and so I took off her head to put her eyes back in place so that she would go to sleep but it was no use and her eyes stayed open and so she never sleeps and she'll get ill and perhaps she'll die. I could take her eyes out but then she'd be blind and perhaps she'd die just the same.'

She was abundantly talkative, but her talk was strangely halting and embarrassed and continually interrupted by the search for a new phrase to hook on to the preceding one. It proceeded, in fact, by means of 'ands' and 'thens' and 'sos'. 'That doll,' said Irene, 'is simply broken. Tomorrow we'll take it to the man who mends dolls. But only if you go to bed now without any fuss. Otherwise, no mending; you'll have to keep it as it is.'

As she said this, she took the child under the arms and made her stand up on the bed. The child made all the movements that were necessary for allowing herself to be undressed, and meanwhile continued chattering, with difficulty hooking brief phrases one upon another, phrases which she seemed to find at the last moment, just when one might think she was going to stop talking for good. Irene pulled off her dress over her head and the child obediently raised her arms, still continuing to talk from inside the dress. Now the child was in her panties. Irene took off these too, slipping them away from under her feet, and then Virginia stood in front of me naked. She was extremely white, with a whiteness that seemed tinged with green, possibly from a reflection of the green paper on the wall against which she was leaning. Her thinness showed the ribs under her skin, and the bones of her pelvis; and it brought into relief, below the hollow stomach, the oblong swelling of her crotch. Her sex looked like the mark of a finger-nail in soft wax; or like a vertical mouth, in line with her navel; but a white mouth whose closed, full lips were fixed in silence. Irene held out pyjama trousers to the child, and they too, curiously, were green like the furniture of the room. But Virginia this time broke off her overworked chatter and refused them with decision. 'No, no pyjamas,' she said.

'Why?'

'I'm hot, I'm hot, I'm hot.'

'Come on, put on your pyjamas; you can sleep with only the sheet, or on top of the sheet. But you must put on your pyjamas. Poor children sleep naked because their parents haven't the money to buy pyjamas. But you're not a poor child.'

'No, no, no, I'm hot, I'm hot, I'm hot.'

She remained leaning against the wall, waving her arms as she pushed away the pyjama trousers which her mother held out to her, ready open. In these gestures of refusal she curved her stomach outwards and stamped her feet. I noticed that Irene threw me a strange glance. Then she dropped the trousers and said hurriedly: 'Very well, then at least get under the sheet.'

The child immediately, volubly, obeyed. She stooped and squatted down, pulled back the sheet and with one jump was in bed. Then she covered herself with the sheet right up to her chin, opening her eyes wide and making grimaces with her mouth and nose. Irene sat down on the edge of the bed and said: 'Now say your prayers with me: "Our Father which art in Heaven . . ."'

Docilely Virginia repeated, staring with absent-minded, restless eyes: 'Our Father which art in Heaven . . .'

It occurred to me suddenly that, from the time I entered the house, 'he' had given no further sign of life. Not even the sight of Irene's parody-like legs, which generally aroused him in an almost automatic manner, not even had this sight worked on this occasion. Was this proof that the process of sublimation had now reached the 'angelic' degree when one no longer struggles against 'him' but simply ignores him? Or was it that 'he' was being silent and peaceful because, as usual, he was preparing some dirty trick for me?

Vaguely uneasy and worried, I left the doorway and went into the living-room. It was hot. The two windows were wide open but the curtains were not moving: there was not a breath of wind. A big bunch of flowers on the table attracted me with its brilliant colours. I touched one flower, then another: it was a bunch of artificial flowers. At that moment Irene came in. Without saying anything she prepared two whiskies, handed me one of the glasses and went and sat down on the sofa. After a moment she said dryly: 'I didn't like the way you looked at Virginia while I was putting her to bed.'

Now, for once in my life, I felt completely innocent, because 'he', as I have just noted, had, so to speak, disappeared, from the very moment when I entered Irene's house. Irene's unjust, disagreeable accusation aroused a sudden anger in me. In a forceful tone, I retorted: 'D'you know what I was thinking as I looked at Virginia?'

'Something sexual, I imagine.'

'Yes, but not in the sense that you evidently believe. I was comparing her sex, white and pure and as though made of light, with what yours must now be: darkened and hardened and made almost callous from thousands of masturbations.'

'Thank you, you're very kind.'

'Wait. And I was saying to myself that innocence is now no longer enough. You yourself, as a little girl, were as innocent as Virginia. Nevertheless one day, without any sort of trauma, from a stimulus that came, as it were, from the very air you breathed, you began masturbating, imagining you were being bought and sold. In fact, precisely because you were innocent and naïve and open to suggestions that came to you from the world in which you happened to have been born, you masturbated with those particular dreams and not with others. I have just come from a party where, for charity, they gave a show which consisted in putting up naked, chained

331

women for auction. It seems to me logical that, in a world in which parties of that kind are given, you were not able to get excited except by imagining that you were being bought and sold.'

Oddly enough, at these words, uttered in a resentful tone, Irene calmed down. 'However, I don't understand,' she remarked, 'how Virginia comes into all this.'

'In point of fact I was wondering, as I looked at her, whether some day she would be masturbating like you and with the same dreams, in spite of the admirable education you're giving her.'

She started laughing, in a cruel way: 'Aren't you, by the way, a man of the Left? Don't you perhaps want to destroy capitalism? Have a revolution and Virginia won't masturbate. After the revolution nothing and no one will be bought and sold any more – isn't that so?'

'Yes, that's so.'

She laughed again, showing her sharp, white eye-teeth. 'But perhaps she will masturbate just the same, dreaming that she is being forced to make love with a commissar of the people, or, more simply, with her own immediate superior in an office or a factory. Because, when there is no money, there is power. Am I right?'

I remained silent: I did not desire to become involved in a political discussion with Irene. After a moment she resumed: 'By the way, d'you know I've introduced you into one of my films, so for some days I've been making love actually thinking of you?'

'How d'you mean?'

'I made use of your story about the girl Lilla, whom your imaginary Proto gave you as a gift. I put myself in Lilla's place; but all the rest remains the same.'

'Do you dream, then, that after making love with Proto you do it with me?'

'No, that doesn't interest me. It's the idea of the gift that interests me.'

'At what point does the film finish?'

'It finishes at the precise moment when Proto gives me to

you. I follow you into the next room: orgasm, and end of the film.'

'If you dreamt of making love with me, that would mean that you love me.'

'But I don't love you.'

Sadly I said: 'We were speaking of revolution just now. I'm sure that if revolution came, real revolution, there would no longer be either money or power. And you would no longer masturbate.'

'What would I do?'

'You would love me and I would love you and we would embrace and be one body with, as they used to say, two souls. Or, if you prefer, two bodies with a single soul.'

She looked at me, for some reason, with affectionate and melancholy compassion. 'My poor Rico,' she said, 'perhaps it would be like that, but where is the revolution?'

I said nothing. Calmly, cruelly, she went on: 'If revolution came, I can already see myself masturbating early in the morning with a little film about my own deportation, imprisonment, or perhaps even being shot. The important thing for me is not capitalism or revolution. The important thing is to be a *thing* and to know that one is so, and to take great pleasure in imagining that one is so.'

'In that case the revolution would not have been a real revolution.'

'But how is one to know when a revolution is a real revolution?'

Again I was silent. Harshly, she insisted: 'In short, aren't you content with my making love and thinking of you?'

Suddenly I realized that I truly loved her, and it was with the disinterested love, free and completely exempt from 'his' influence, that could only be the effect of successful sublimation. In fact, suddenly the sublimation 'worked'; without knowing what I was doing (in the same way that I had recently thrown the lighted candle into the room at Protti's villa) I flew to her feet, embraced her knees and stammered: 'I love you, Irene, with a real love, but I don't wish now to become your lover because I've seen that it's not possible. I came this evening to make you a proposal.'

'What proposal?'

'I came to ask you to let me live with you. Don't say no. I'll never again try to make love with you. We'll be like a married couple who have lived together for a long time and who have ceased for some time to have physical relations, though they continue to love one another with a true, deep love. I'll be a husband to you; I'll be a father to Virginia. I earn a respectable amount from scripts for commercial films. Even though I'll go on supporting my wife and son, I shall have enough left to contribute generously to your home expenses. I shall be content if I can have a room with a bed to sleep on and a table for work. I'll go out with you whenever you ask me to, to the cinema, to the theatre, to restaurants. We'll spend our Sundays together. We'll travel together. I'll help Virginia with her homework, take her out for walks, go and fetch her back from school. I shall always be fond of you and all I ask is that you should be fond of me in the same way, affectionately and intellectually.'

I was on the point of saying 'in a sublimated way', but I bit my lip. All the time I was in floods of tears and the tears were trickling down my nose and dripping on to the floor. Finally I heard her voice saying in a reasonable manner: 'But we scarcely know one another. Yes, you love me and I believe you. I can even admit that I feel a certain affection for you. But from that, to living together . . .'

'If you like, we'll draw up a contract. I'll put it in writing.'

'You have a wife and son. With your wife, it seems, you still make love. The boy is yours. Why do you wish to take up with a woman who doesn't love you and who has a daughter that isn't yours?'

'Because the love that I feel for you is the only thing in my life that can take the place of artistic expression.'

'But why d'you want anything to take the place of artistic expression?'

'Because I now know for certain that I'm not an artist.'

'You will be: aren't you going to make a film?'

'No, I'm not going to do that now.'

'You'll do it.'

'No, I shan't. I shall live with you, like a monk, like a medieval mystic. To me you will be the ideal, unattainable woman to whom I shall dedicate my finest thoughts. If I return to my wife, I shall fall back, on the other hand, into the most ignoble, satisfied mediocrity. The abject mediocrity of desublimation.'

'Desublimation? What a funny word; what does it mean?'

'There's no need for you to know. One day, if we live together, I'll explain it to you. I'll tell you what sublimation is and what desublimation is. I'll teach you all sorts of things. I'm a ridiculous man, with short legs, a prominent stomach, a big bald head, and perpetually embarrassed by the presence and the arrogance of a member that's out of all proportion. I look like a buffoon, a clown, a pimp, a Thersites, and probably I am. But I'm also a cultivated man, I've read thousands of books, I know what is a fine line of poetry, a fine page of prose, a strictly expressed thought. But culture serves no purpose, with me; worse, the only use I make of it is for writing commercial scripts; but to you it will be useful, because you're intelligent but ignorant and with the aid of culture you'll be able to bring richness and variety into your life and to understand all sorts of things which you don't understand at present. I'll teach you, I'll open new horizons to you. I'll be useful to you, really useful, and in exchange I won't even ask you for a kiss. All I ask of you is to live with you under the same roof.'

I talked and talked and talked, all the time in floods of tears. Irene said: 'I really don't know why you have this passion for me. I feel I don't deserve it. I'm an ordinary sort of woman, no longer very young, not so very intelligent, extremely ignorant as you yourself make me see, not very brilliant, physically barely passable. And, into the bargain, I have a sexual habit that excludes any kind of relationship which isn't merely friendly. I should like to know what it is that you find in me?'

At these words, reasonable as they were, I stopped crying

335

and, sniffing and wiping my eyes, I asked in a plaintive voice:
'So you don't want to?'
    'I really don't think so.'
    'But do at least put me to the test.'
    'What d'you mean?'
    'Allow me to sleep with you tonight, in the same bed.'
    'What a strange idea; and what for?'
    'In order to prove to you that I can be close to you without
making love.'
    She said nothing. She appeared to be reflecting. Then, to
my surprise, she answered: 'Very well, provided you promise
me you won't try to do anything, anything at all, not even to
caress me.'
    'I swear it; look, I swear it on your own head.'
    'My poor head! Very well. Let's go, then.'
    She seemed to be in a hurry. Furtively I looked at my
watch and saw that it was one o'clock, and I recalled that
Irene rose early to go to the embassy. I followed her as she
went from the living-room into the passage, turning out, as she
went, the lights which were still burning. When we reached
her bedroom I looked round with curiosity. It might have been
a room in a hotel and not even an expensive hotel; it was
convenient but rather bare and impersonal. But, as I realized
at once, the anonymous character of this room was not that of
the mercenary hospitality of hotels, but rather of the sexual
rite, like all rites, anonymous, which Irene celebrated there
every morning.
    And there were the instruments of the rite: a wide, but
not a double, bed, too narrow for two people but wide enough
for a single person to move about in it with complete freedom;
an armchair at the foot of the bed, placed in such a way that
Irene, undressing and putting down her clothes upon it, as she
was doing at that moment, could, at the same time, contem-
plate herself in the mirror; the triple mirror or cheval-glass,
like those that are to be seen in dressmakers' shops; and
finally – very revealing – a three-legged stool placed in front
of the cheval-glass.
    Irene finished undressing. She was naked and it was the

336

first time I had seen her naked. But, even more than by her nudity, I was struck, in a rather disagreeable manner, by the indifference with which she showed herself naked to me. Evidently I did not exist for her; what I mean is that 'he' did not exist; but at the moment it seemed to me that I and 'he', for once, were the same thing. I watched Irene as she unhooked her brassière, freeing her very beautiful breasts which were spherical, white, luminous, firm; then she took off her girdle and, bending down, slipped her panties over her feet. Then with her hands she rubbed her stomach and hips, reddened by the elastic; and then scratched among the blonde hairs of her crotch as though to restore life to their compressed, inanimate curls. Finally, walking on tiptoe, she went to the far end of the room and opened the doors of a wall cupboard, turning her back on me.

I looked with intense affection at her rather broad and massive back, at her buttocks, like her breasts perfectly white and spherical, and, particularly, at the shape of her legs, no longer obscene as when she was dressed and keeping them bent and close together; but innocent and childish, rather like those of some young, plump girl. Without turning, she said to me: 'Get undressed. I'm sleepy. I'm tired and I want to get to bed at once.'

I undressed in turn, depositing my garments one by one on the arm of the chair. Irene turned and came towards me, still on tiptoe. She threw something on to the bed. 'There are some men's pyjamas,' she said. 'I think they belonged to my husband.' She had her own nightdress over her arm; she went off again towards the far end of the room, saying: 'I'm going into the bathroom. When I've finished, you can go there too.'

Left alone, I put on the pyjamas. But they were too long, the trousers and the sleeves dangled from my feet and hands. I took them off again and, quite naked, started walking about the room. 'His' silence now began to worry me. What lay hidden behind this obstinate taciturnity? Could it possibly be sublimation? A sublimation so drastic as to make 'him' lose his voice altogether?

Suddenly I put the question to him: 'Why are you silent?'

'. . . . . .'

'Is it perhaps because you fear that, from now on, sublimation will induce me to terminate my dialogue with you?'

'. . . . . .'

'Don't be afraid, it won't happen. What next! Between you and me there will always be a dialogue. I wish that to be so. But as a dialogue between servant and master ought to be. No use telling you which of us will be master and which servant. Our dialogue, anyhow, must be quite different from our quarrels of recent times. It will be a well-bred, correct, rational dialogue, contained within the limits of a well-understood subjection on your side and an equally well-understood authority on my side. Something, in short, civilized, urbane, decorous...'

'. . . . . .'

'It goes without saying that I am not in any way denying what I may call your exceptional qualities. For me you will always be the king of kings. Even though now you will no longer be anything but a part of my body.'

'. . . . . .'

'Come on, why don't you speak?'

'. . . . . .'

'Speak, I order you to speak, d'you understand?'

'. . . . . .'

I thought all of a sudden that perhaps this was love, real, genuine love: the silence of the sex. Indeed, I loved Irene, but I was certain that I could never be loved by her. In such a situation, 'his' silence probably implied a sublimation so complete as to render any dialogue superfluous. Having abandoned the idea of communicating with Irene by means of 'him', I had nothing more to say to 'him' and 'he' had nothing more to say to me. The dialogue between 'him' and me was, fundamentally, a dialogue between lust and love. 'He' was reduced to silence because love had conquered.

Irene came in again. Her long transparent nightdress reached down to her feet. She went straight to the bed and got in under the covers with the remark, just like a wife talking to her husband: 'Hurry up, if you've got to go to the bathroom. I'm dying to go to sleep.' Without delay I went into the bathroom and closed the door.

'His' silence, in spite of my conviction that I was now finally and completely sublimated, continued to worry me. And so, while I was urinating with legs apart, standing in front of the lavatory-bowl and holding 'him' delicately between two fingers, I gave him the following talking-to: 'After all, you've nothing to complain of. You would be wrong to bear a grudge against me. I have dethroned you from only half of my life, the half that I live in a state of wakefulness. But the other half, the half that I spend sleeping, will be yours, wholly yours. I shall allow you to be the undisputed master of my dreams. In my dreams you will be able to do everything that you wish to do: love, in the first place, with anyone you like, and then all the so-called perversions, from bestiality to flagellation, from homosexuality to incest, from sadism to masochism, from fetishism to necrophilia. Everything. Yours will be an immense field and I impose no limits upon you: you can dream of anything, whether symbolically or realistically. Is that all right?'

'He' said nothing. Then I resumed: 'There is more than that. You won't even be forbidden to daydream, as it's commonly called. With daydreaming, the territory over which you will have undisputed sway will be even further extended. You'll dream by night and daydream by day. What more do you want?'

The silence persisted. I concluded: 'Don't you intend to speak? So much the worse for you. You're sulking, eh? But all the same it can't be said that your new situation is gloomy. Hitherto I have called you Federicus Rex. Henceforth I shall also call you The Dreamer. Don't you like that?'

Still 'he' did not answer. I shrugged my shoulders and, leaving the bathroom, went back into the bedroom. Irene's blonde head was sunk into her pillow; her eyes were closed and the sheet was drawn up to her chin. Without opening her eyes, she said to me: 'Get into bed on the side of the wall and don't speak to me because I'm already half asleep. Good night.' As she said this she put out her hand and pressed the switch of the lamp. The room was plunged in darkness.

Feeling my way, I slipped into the narrow space between the bed and the wall. Lifting the bedclothes, I wormed my way in and lay flat on my back. It was hot, and the bedclothes had been reduced to a sheet and a light cotton coverlet. I placed my arm behind the back of my neck and listened. Irene was already asleep: I guessed this from her steady but quiet breathing which was now and then oddly interrupted by sighs and changes of rhythm. After sighing, Irene always moved a little, as if to settle herself more comfortably in the narrow space that she occupied in the bed.

Now I, in turn, moved, because, from lying still, one of my legs had become numbed. Then I noticed that, in unconscious accord with me, Irene also moved. I turned on to my right side and she, after a little, also turned on to her right side. I waited a short time and then turned on to my left side. Irene, after a moment, also turned, sighing, on to her left side. Finally I lay flat on my back; Irene sighed again and lay on her back. After this I did not move any more; I started thinking.

And so, I said to myself, Irene moves when I move, she turns when I turn, she lies on her back when I lie on my back: and all this in her sleep. What does it mean? It means that there was a mutual understanding, an obscure tie, between us two. Of this mutual understanding, of this tie, Irene was not conscious and I was. I loved Irene and I knew it; Irene perhaps loved me and did not know it. But she revealed her own love by obediently conforming to my movements with the movements of her own body. 'In her sleep', however. Therefore I had to bring it about that in future this understanding, this tie should be transferred gradually from the unconscious to the conscious, from sleeping to waking. In spite of her masturbatory rites, Irene was a woman like all other women and, in favourable circumstances, would not suffice to herself but would have need of a man in order to feel herself complete. I would therefore have, in future, to create these circumstances.

I thought about these things and suddenly I felt happy. I would be Irene's chaste companion until the day when she felt the need to have me as her lover. But I must not force the situation; everything would come about of its own accord.

With these thoughts in my head I fell asleep; I slept without dreaming for a long time and then I had the following dream. I was walking with Irene and the little girl in the direction of the church in the E.U.R. quarter. It was night, with the moon at the full, but the moon could not be seen. Our black shadows lay across the paved street which was lit with a cold lunar light; our faces looked livid and strongly marked. We went up slowly towards the church, and up the flight of steps. The leaves of the great door were closed; the dome stood out clearly against a background of black sky. We came up to the door and, marvellously, the two leaves opened slowly as if of their own accord; in front of us yawned the darkness of the central nave. No lights were burning inside the church except for one small lamp, far, far away, in the apse.

This lamp cast a feeble glimmer in which there was the vague outline of a gigantic black shadow, much as the shadows of mountains are outlined against a lighter sky in Alpine valleys on moonless nights. It was a towering shadow, cylindrical in form, and pointed. It looked like an enormous projectile, a colossal missile placed upright. Irene murmured: 'Now I'll get Virginia to say her prayers and then I'll put her to bed.' Then, all of a sudden, following the uncertain contours of this sombre presence, I recognized 'him'. Yes, there was no doubt about it, this cone of darkness, of a blackness so thick and so compact, was 'him', truly 'him', grown beyond measure, this time, and attaining the proportions and the aspect of a monstrous fetish. I said in a low voice to Irene: 'But surely you don't want to get Virginia to say her prayers in front of "that thing"?' Irene replied dryly: 'Certainly I shall.' 'But there's some misunderstanding.' 'What misunderstanding?' 'Something is where it ought not to be. Something has been substituted for somebody.' But before Irene had time to answer me, the child let out a shrill cry, broke away from our hands and ran away towards the apse. I saw her little white dress getting smaller and smaller and more and more vague as she ran off, and finally it disappeared. At that point I awoke.

I was lying on my left side; before my eyes was the wall of the room, with the light falling on it. Slowly I lifted my arm from below the sheet and, without turning round, looked at my wrist-watch and saw that it was eight o'clock. I put my arm back under the sheet and, still without turning, stretched it out behind me to explore the bed beside me. But, however far I thrust my fingers, I found nothing but emptiness. Finally I twisted round, being careful to make no noise, and then I saw Irene.

She was sitting on the stool in front of the mirror, and she was naked. Her small blonde head was inclined towards her right shoulder. Her bust, with its broad shoulders and scarcely defined waist, seemed also to be inclined towards the right. She supported herself with her left hand on the edge of the stool. She was reaching forward with her right arm so as to allow her hand, I guessed, to be plunged in between her legs. Her left leg was bent back at an almost acute angle, with the foot against the feet of the stool. Her right leg was stretched stiffly out sideways. Her foot was almost touching the metal support of the cheval-glass.

I raised myself on my elbow so as to see better. The masturbation could only just have started. Over Irene's shoulder, if I leant forward, I could see her face reflected in the mirror, her eyes closed, her lips half-open, and an ecstatic expression as though of inner contemplation. She kept her eyes closed because she was following her 'film', picture by picture, slowly, emphasizing, according to all appearances, each picture with a pressure of her hand between her legs. Every now and then she would possibly be stopping the film, at some especially interesting picture; possibly, every now and then, she was turning it back in order to look again at a picture which she felt she had not looked at enough.

What film was it that Irene was following at that moment? She had told me, herself, the evening before: the film she had drawn from my story of the imaginary Proto and the imaginary Lilla. The story of the film producer who gives a girl as a gift to his secretary. No doubt Irene would take a long time to exhaust the masochistic content of the idea of the 'gift'. What point had she now reached in her viewing of the film? There was no knowing; perhaps she was seeing herself in the act of offering herself to the sadistic Proto. Or possibly the sequence of the 'gift' was already imminent.

These thoughts ran through my mind as I looked at Irene's face in the mirror and saw that it was very beautiful, with a transfigured, spiritual beauty. Jealously I said to myself that probably no man would be capable, by means of his own love, of making that eager, ecstatic, smiling face as beautiful as it now was. Then I looked at Irene's back. The stillness of her body contrasted with the light, rhythmical movement, backwards and forwards, of her elbow. Her small, motionless head, inclined towards her shoulder, continued to give a feeling of contemplative concentration of great intensity. Everything took place in a profound silence, the silence, I could not help thinking, of masturbation, which is mute precisely because it is solitary.

How long did this stillness, this silence, last? It seemed to me an eternity. The eternity of a rite which seems brief to those who are celebrating it and sharing in it and long to those who are present at it without sharing in it. Then suddenly the right leg which was stretched out sideways appeared to go rigid. A shudder spread down from the hip to the knee, throwing the muscles into relief. The toes tightened and bent outwards as if to snatch at the air. At the same time the small blonde head started slowly rotating on the strong, white neck; the hips moved to the left; the shoulders leant in the opposite direction to that of the hips; and a slow rolling movement, in time with that of the head, twisted the buttocks now to the right and now to the left, in such a way that the cleft dividing them curved now to one side and now to the other.

Then suddenly, after the stillness, the silence, too, was broken. A warm, hoarse, urgent, subdued, passionate voice, quite different from Irene's usual voice, began repeating, with melting sweetness, the monosyllable of amorous consent:

'Yes . . . yes . . . yes . . . yes . . .' Irene was saying yes to herself; yes to the life that she led with herself; yes to the mental image of herself which her own imagination gradually placed before her. More especially, she was saying yes to the character of Proto, to herself as she tempted Proto, to Proto as he gave her to me, to myself as I accepted the gift. She was saying yes to everything that I hated and that I had introduced into my story precisely because I hated it.

Her 'yes's' now became more and more frequent, more urgent, more breathless, more submissive. Until finally they became fused, amalgamated, into a single subhuman, almost terrified lament. I looked into the mirror. Irene threw back her head and very slowly opened her mouth. At the same time her lament became more and more subdued and was transmuted into a strange howling sound, a silent howl, so to speak, perceptible only in the movement of her mouth which opened wide as though to howl and yet uttered no sound at all. Then, all of a sudden, her body was contorted in a brief, violent convulsion; her legs leapt up, stiffened, and were abruptly bent again; her head rolled, was thrown back and then fell forward and downward, her chin fixed on her breast. She remained motionless, looking down. She had had the orgasm and was now intent upon its final tremors, like someone who has witnessed a grandiose sunset and is intent upon the last rays, on the horizon, of a now vanished sun. Seen from behind, Irene's motionless body looked like that of a condemned man who has suffered execution by the Spanish method of the garrotte: hands folded in her lap, head bowed, eyes downcast. Then a last convulsion, starting from her loins, for a moment straightened her back and her head, in a violent movement, like a horse rearing, which came to an end almost at once. Her head sank again on to her breast; again she was motionless; this time the orgasm was truly finished. But then, after a long pause, suddenly her right elbow started moving again, at first imperceptibly, then in a more and more visible way, backwards and forwards. Her right leg was stretched out again, sideways, rigid. Her left hand gripped the edge of the stool. Irene was beginning again.

I don't know what happened to me. I don't know how I got dressed. I crept out on tiptoe, without making any noise, behind the back of Irene, who did not see me because she had her eyes shut. I reached the door and went out into the passage. The next door, as I knew, was that of Virginia's room. I opened it and went in.

For a moment, having closed the door, I stopped still, close to it. I was conscious that I was on the point of doing something terrible; but at the same time I felt I should do it. 'He' was commanding me to do it; and was commanding me in a new manner, without words, silently, causing me to act like a sleep-walker, like an automaton. I put out my hand to press the light-switch. The room was lit up as though it were still night. I looked at the bed and saw Virginia wrapped only in a sheet, asleep. She was lying on her side, her red, full lips standing out against her thin white face. Her fair hair lay scattered over the pillow. Still moving like a sleep-walker, I went close to the sleeping child. I knew well what 'he' wanted of me; his congested, furious hugeness led me to foresee it; but I did not rebel. Our shared silence revealed my defeat. Once upon a time the arguments that divided us went to indicate my own independence, my ability to choose. But this dull, stifled, sinister silence was a clear sign of 'his' victory. Then I put out my hand to take hold of the sheet.

All of a sudden 'he' spoke. Sure of his own mastery and of my obedience, he said: 'The first thing you must do is to press your hand over her mouth to prevent her from crying out. If she struggles, put your other hand on her throat and squeeze without hesitating.'

'Then what you want is her death?' I asked.

'I don't *want* her death. *I am* her death.'

This pitiless remark aroused me from my automatism. No longer was I a sleep-walker, a robot completely in 'his' power. Imprudently 'he' had spoken, and I had found the strength to answer. Now we were no longer one, but two: 'him' and me. Making no sound, I put out the light, turned towards the door and went out of the room on tiptoe.

16 Devoured!

Immediately, as soon as I was out of Irene's house, I spoke to 'him' in the following way, more frightened, perhaps, than angry: 'So that was why you didn't answer me, that was why you persisted in keeping silent. Because you were setting that horrifying trap for me. But my guardian angel was watching over me. Luckily for me, your complacency betrayed you. You spoke and I answered. Words saved me. Now I shall make use of words to tell you that you're a monster.'

'. . . . . .'

'How can I ever trust you again? How can I free myself from the terror you inspire in me? Above all, how can I forget? You will always fill me with horror and fear and disgust.'

'. . . . . .'

'In spite of all this I shall have to go on speaking to you, unfortunately. And that is because I now know very well what your silence means. Alas, not only shall I have to abandon the idea of sublimation; but henceforth I shall have to be careful that you don't plunge me into an abyss of ignominy and misfortune.'

'. . . . . .'

'So this is my terrible fate: to live with a monster; to be unable to ignore him; to be forced, for fear of the worst, to carry on a continual dialogue with him. Has there ever been a man more unfortunate than me?'

'. . . . . .'

'You've destroyed everything, sullied everything. How shall I ever be able to face Irene again? Can I again suggest going to live with her? To be a husband to her and a father to Virginia? Yes, indeed, a fine husband, a splendid father! And all this is your fault, you miserable wretch!'

'. . . . . .'

'Now look, you fill me with horror, with such horror that the horror contaminates me and I feel a horror of myself, if only because I allowed myself, though only for a single moment, to be completely dominated by you. But what fills me with more horror than anything is the intolerable, yet inevitable, fact of having to live with you. I can't ignore you, I can't make use of you, I can't dominate you; I see myself condemned to an eternal quarrel, as utterly sterile as it is exhausting. I think it would be best to put an end to all this. The shame and despair aroused in me by your last betrayal make this decision easier. It's true that I didn't even touch Irene's daughter. But tomorrow you might try the same trick again, and you might succeed in getting the better of me in one of my moments of weakness; and then, truly, there would be nothing left for me but to kill myself. I might as well not wait for tomorrow and kill myself now. I prefer to kill myself now, when I haven't yet done any harm, rather than tomorrow after having done it. My suicide would therefore be at the same time both an act of despair and of altruism. By killing myself, I should prevent you from causing the death of Virginia in the future.'

All these and many other such things I said, while 'he' went on pretending to be deaf and dumb; then I stopped the car and opened the dashboard locker: in it I kept a pistol. For, like all desublimated people, who know or fear that they are cowards, I had a passion for firearms. I possessed two more pistols: one I kept in my new flat, and one in Fausta's flat. This one I always kept within reach in my car, for so-called 'self-defence'. Defence against whom? Until today I had never asked myself that. Now, suddenly, I understood: against 'him'. My defence would consist, quite logically, in suicide. I should kill myself so as to be no longer forced to live with 'him'. 'He' had not wished, and still did not wish, to leave me; it would be I myself who left 'him'.

Calmly I took off the safety-catch of the pistol, slipped a bullet into the chamber and then placed the weapon on my knees. I was half-way along a wide asphalted avenue: I could not kill myself in a place like that; it might happen that, at the very moment when I pressed the barrel to my temple, a policeman would appear at the window, ask for my documents and impose a fine upon me – a fitting parody-like conclusion to a life which had been nothing but parody. Still keeping the pistol on my knee, I started the engine again and drove on. At the first side-road I turned, went on for about a hundred metres and stopped.

I was desperate; but at the same time I was perfectly clear in the head. It was true that it was 'he' who was the cause of my suicide. But the fact remained that I myself ought to have stopped in the passage instead of opening the door and going in to look at the sleeping child; and this I had not done. Fundamentally 'he' had done, so to speak, his duty; I, on the other hand, had not done mine. Therefore it was just that I should punish myself. Furthermore, I was tired of life. That phrase, which usually sounds like a commonplace, suddenly acquired an undeniable accent of authenticity. Yes, I was tired of my desublimated life. Like a foolish and obstinate ant that had fallen into the funnel of an ant-hill, I had tried again and again to climb the sandy slope as it caved in, but in vain. Now I should let myself slide down, once and for all.

I grasped the pistol in my fist, placed my forefinger on the trigger. Then I sat still for a moment, without lifting my hand: a cyclist was going past with a slight rustling sound of rubber tyres. He might see me pointing the pistol at my temple; and he might intervene. I would wait until he had passed. He was a fair-haired young man in a red sweater on which something was written in black letters; he was perhaps training by himself for some cycling competition. I followed him with my eyes, thinking: When he turns, I'll shoot. Then, just at the moment when I could already see him turning at the end of the road, suddenly 'his' voice rang out, at last: 'Stop, you idiot!'

I replied logically: 'I'm not an idiot. What I'm about to do is, on the contrary, intelligent. And why is it intelligent? Because I've thoroughly understood the situation in which I find myself and I see that there's no solution except death. Idiots don't understand a problem and find a solution. Only intelligent people do that.'

'This would be true if you had really understood your situation. But you haven't understood it, either thoroughly or superficially. That's why I call you an idiot.'

'Let's hear, then, what the truth of the situation is, according to you.'

As I said this, I put the safety-catch back again, opened the dashboard locker and replaced the pistol. I was curious to hear what 'he' had to say to me. There would then still be time to take the pistol out again and shoot myself. 'He' was silent for a moment, then he replied: 'It would take too long to explain things to you thoroughly. All I will do is to make my own thoughts clear by means of an example which, incidentally, you yourself provided me with, involuntarily.'

'And what is this example?'

'At a certain point you decided to desert your wife and child, to leave home and live alone, in complete chastity, in order to achieve – compulsorily, so to speak – your so-called sublimation. You looked for a flat, found one and moved. But, let me stress the fact and I beg you to take note of it yourself, you did not furnish it. You put in merely such furniture as was strictly necessary: a bed, a table, an armchair, a couple of ordinary chairs. The flat is bare; and, without you yourself being aware of it, it is the very image of your life as you have decided to live it now: bare of all ornament, all satisfaction and pleasure, wholly concentrated upon an idea which is not so much positive as negative: the complete suppression of every activity on my part. But what happened then? In the bareness of your life, so well symbolized by the bareness of your flat, just because you don't wish me to exist I actually exist more than ever, in fact I'm the only thing that exists. My existence, which has become more and more obsessive, is nourished by your desire to suppress me. So, whereas when we still lived happily together I was, so to speak, everywhere in your life and therefore not merely your "member", now that you have denuded your life, I am always and only your "member". This very drastic reduction of my multiform nature to the organ which is its symbol, but certainly not its only manifestation, causes me to concentrate myself in this organ and to make it my sole means of expression. This explains your sex mania, which was once endurable; but which, from the moment you left home, has become obsessive. This also explains your sudden desire for Virginia. I am like a big tree, extremely rich in branches and leaves; but you have pruned me brutally, have cut off my leaves and reduced me to a single stump, and then you wonder that the stump becomes gigantic, threatening, immoderate. Yes, you are right to fear that the thing may be repeated and that next time I shall succeed in overcoming you. But in reality it will be you who, because of your repressive fixation, will be overcome of your own accord. You who, clouded by your obsessive desire to achieve your so-called sublimation, do not realize that at the end of the road towards sublimation there can be nothing but death.'

'He' finished speaking and, strangely, after a moment burst into sarcastic laughter. Disconcerted, I asked: 'And now, why are you laughing?'

'I'm laughing because I've made you such a didactic, such an instructive, such a moral little speech, absolutely at variance with what I really am. I did it to stop you killing yourself, knowing well that these were the only words that could convince you. Otherwise, my speech would have been entirely different.'

'What would it have been like?'

'He' was silent for a moment, then he said: 'In a town in the south of India there is a temple excavated in the rock. One goes down a dark spiral staircase and finds oneself in a subterranean cave. There, as far as the eye can reach, one sees a gallery, dimly lit by a few feeble lamps, the roof of which is supported, not by pillars and arches, but by two rows of fantastic monsters. There are animals with human heads and the bodies of beasts; or with the heads of beasts and human bodies. One walks for a long way beneath this vault that swarms with menacing figures and, at the end, one reaches a small circular room, almost dark. In the middle of the room, surrounded by an iron railing, there am I, or rather my image. I am carved in stone, in a state of erection, at the highest point of congestion and potency. In front of me there is a continual crowd of men, women and children, kneeling and praying. They scatter garlands of flowers on the ground, they rain handfuls of petals upon me, they pour over me votive oils which shine in the half-darkness so that I appear to be having a continuous, uninterrupted ejaculation. Why am I telling you this? Because, after having stopped your suicidal hand, I consider that the moment has now come to advise you that you must no longer regard me, as you have always tried to do, as a mere part of your body, not so different, after all, from your hand or your ear or your nose, but as a god, in fact as "your" god. What happened a short time ago in Virginia's room has, essentially, a usefulness of its own. It creates, finally, a just and correct relationship between us. Yes, I am your god and henceforth you must worship me. And remember, there exist neither children, nor women, nor men, nor old people, nor young people. There are no animals, there are no plants, there is nothing. There is only my universal presence. A little while ago, in Irene's daughter's room, I was, at the same time, both you who were about to rape Virginia and Virginia who was about to be raped by you.'

I reacted with extreme violence: 'Ah yes, a god, you would be a god? Get along with you! It would be laughable if it wasn't something to cry about. But then, if you're a god, I am a super-god. For, if I wish, I can control you, dominate you, and even, perhaps, destroy you.'

Strangely, 'he' made no answer to these words. He was silent, in a decisive sort of way, as though he had nothing more to say. Then, in a quieter and more reasonable tone, I went on: 'But I want, for once, to have some advice from you. You are right: the empty place in which I live, away from my family, is my life; and in that life, bare as it is, it is impossible that you should not become magnified, become an obsession. So, in the first pace, I shall return to Fausta and my son. Furthermore, it will be well to give a new shape to our conflict. You are not a god and I am not a super-god. I am a poor wretch afflicted with too much temperament; you are the instrument of that affliction. I shall try to take up my former life again.'

'He' did not speak, but seemed to be awaiting the 'true' conclusion. I continued: 'And as for your *bête noire*, sublimation, I prefer to think that I am a failure, a man of weak will, a professional film man without any talent, rather than admit, even for one single moment, that such a thing is not possible.'

Again silence. I said nothing for a moment, then I concluded: 'So I shall continue to be the poor desublimated creature who has hopes of sublimation and who, comforted by that hope, does not cease for a moment to struggle against you, even if he is then, on most occasions, forced to yield to you.'

By this time I had reached Fausta's street. And then, as I was parking my car in the usual place in which I had put it for so many years, all of a sudden the omnipresent, omnipotent god whom, according to 'him', I ought to worship, was transformed in a most disconcerting manner into the usual frivolous individual, impudent, intemperate, reckless, giddy, lacking in judgment. It was just as though nothing had happened; as though I had not been only a millimetre from final catastrophe; as though the temptation to crime and the consequent temptation to suicide had not even touched me – there 'he' was, sprightly as anything, exclaiming: 'Lower your eyes and look at me. What d'you say to that? And all for Fausta! I can't wait to see her again. I'm really delighted to come back home.'

'He' was so enormous that I was compelled to place myself askew in the tiny lift because, with 'him' in this unprecedented state, it was impossible for me to stand straight. The lift started going up. And then 'he' started bawling: 'Set me free, pull me out, let me breathe.'

'Here in the lift? You're crazy.'

'No, I'm not crazy. I want us to give Fausta a surprise and I want her to understand that it was I who wished you to come back home and to be reconciled with her.'

'Very well, as soon as we're in the flat I'll set you free.'

'No, here! You must do it here and at once.'

'The lift has a glass door and somebody might see you.'

'I want them to see me. That's what I want. I want everyone to see the beauty of the world.'

352

So there was nothing to be done. I satisfied 'him'. Unfortunately, at that very moment we were passing the second-floor landing. The face of an old woman, a respectable lady with an emaciated countenance framed in white hair, was for a moment visible to me beyond the glass door, as she opened her eyes very wide at the sight of 'him'. Dismayed, I said: 'I know her, she recognized me; she's a fellow-tenant. How can I ever dare even to look her in the face again? Tell me that.'

'She has seen the beauty of the world, perhaps for the first time in her life. Don't worry.'

Tac, tac, tac, tac, third, fourth, fifth, sixth floor. The lift stopped and I got out, preceded by 'him'. I closed the doors of the lift; I put my key into the door of the flat. But Fausta had put up the chain and the door did not open. So I pressed the bell and waited. Meanwhile 'he' was raging: 'What an idiot she is! Barricading herself in the flat. And I'm dying of impatience. Ring, come on, ring the bell again!'

To satisfy him. I pressed the bell once more. Standing stiffly in the air, 'he' seemed now to be rising up, in short, successive jerks, as if to bring himself to the level of the keyhole and look into the flat. At last I heard a slight bustling sound. Then Fausta's voice asking: 'Who is it?'

'It's me, Rico.'

Fausta's hand undid the chain, the door opened, and she appeared on the threshold in her dressing-gown. She looked at me, looked down, saw 'him' and then, without saying a word, put out her hand to take hold of 'him', as one might take hold of a donkey's halter to make it move. Then she turned her back to me, pulling 'him' in behind her, and, with 'him', me. She went into the flat; 'he' went behind her; I followed them both.